ALSO BY MELISSA GOOD

Dar and Kerry Series
Tropical Storm
Hurricane Watch
Eye of the Storm
Red Sky At Morning
Thicker Than Water
Terrors of the High Seas
Tropical Convergence
Stormy Waters
Storm Surge: Book One
Storm Surge: Book Two

Other Titles
Partners: Book One

Partners

Book Two

Melissa Good

Silver Dragon Books
by Regal Crest

Texas

ISBN 978-1-61929-190-4

First Printing 2014

9 8 7 6 5 4 3 2 1

Cover design by Acorn Graphics

Published by:

Regal Crest Enterprises, LLC
229 Sheridan Loop
Belton, TX 76513

Find us on the World Wide Web at
http://www.regalcrest.biz

Printed in the United States of America

Author's Notes

A lot of people asked me—why sci-fi? And the truth is I have been a fan and reader of science fiction and fantasy since I was old enough to go to the library and bookstore on my own. Science fiction opens the mind to unlimited possibilities. All of that reading led me to science fiction conventions, which was where I was first exposed to the power of community. So gratifying to learn that if you were a nerdy person, who loved science and the stars, and reading, that there were so many others who were just like you.

They say our young girls in this country are sadly lacking in "STEM"—Science, Technology, Engineering and Math. (I think) I got my introduction to three of the four from those books with the little rocket ships on the spine and I took that introduction and it shaped how I thought and what I did to this very day.

~Melissa Good

This book is dedicated to the North Miami Beach public library, which had to deal with my checking out and occasionally returning most of their collection of science fiction books.

Chapter One

A ROLL OF thunder echoed over a dark sea, as a single hulled fishing boat plunged through swells heading in the relative direction of home.

The ice pack loomed in the darkness, its incessant crackling and popping sounding over the waves. Jess pulled herself back inside to study the comp, peering at the rearward facing scan intently. "Did we lose them?"

Dev was finishing up some data. She turned and studied the scanner, her shoulder coming to rest against Jess's. "We haven't gotten ping backs on anything in about two hours," she said. "Since we saw that cone."

"Sometimes I hate weather, sometimes I love it," Jess said. "Okay let's run along the ice. At least we've got some cover if something comes at us." She let her gaze slide to Dev's outline. "I like that suit."

Dev glanced down at herself, her body encased in her new lined jumper. It was warm and comfortable, and she was really happy with it herself. "Me too. Maybe we can go back and get you one sometime?"

Jess sighed. "Not for a good long while, Devvie." She sat on the stool next to the captain's chair and leaned her elbow on the arm of it. "I have no idea if they popped lava on that one. Might have taken out the whole place. Charles could be flash fried by now if he didn't get out in time. Happens." She shrugged. "They know the risk."

Dev didn't speak for a moment, then looked at Jess. "Do you mean all those people might be dead?"

"Might be."

Wow. Dev felt a chill down her back. All those people, even the girl who'd cut their hair. She watched Jess's face, seeing nothing other than vague interest there. "You knew what was going on."

"Sure," Jess said. "I've been near one of 'em a couple times. I caught the bumps. They did too, set the alarms off. People would have rushed for the boats, that's why I wanted to get ours off first."

"Should we have helped the others?" Dev asked, hesitantly.

"No. That's not our gig."

"I see." Dev said. "Interesting."

"Anyway." Jess gently blew in her ear. "Enjoy your duds."

"Thank you, Jess. It's very comfortable. I feel a lot better now wearing it."

A relaxed and happy smile appeared on Jess's face. "You're welcome. I never had a tech I wanted to buy stuff for before. It's a kick. Besides, I can't wait to see you wear that thing in the citadel. There are a ton of us who never made it out to the market, much less on their first month."

"And now they might not get a chance," Dev said softly. "Isn't that what you said before?"

"Oh, Charles'll survive. He's an old salt." Jess got up and stretched. "He'll dig out and start over. I don't think for a minute he didn't get out. Probably had a tunnel dug down to the water with a boat waiting." She turned to the hammock. "Mind if I sack out for a while?"

"Absolutely not," Dev said. "If anything unusual happens, I'll wake you up."

Jess rolled into the swinging bed and exhaled, allowing her body to relax for the first time in a day. She was disappointed that the mission was cut short—and yet—based on her near ass kicking, she now had to wonder if she'd really been ready for it.

Was this just fate's way of covering her? Maybe she could figure out another plan after they got back to the citadel. She could talk Bain into letting her take another team with her. It wouldn't be as status as if she'd done it herself, but she had a legit med marker after all.

Wasn't her fault the mission got called. She wondered what the emergency was. She wondered if it wasn't a status call on her part for Bain to recall her specifically for it. Could even be a better chance with less risk for advancement.

Good opportunity for her. For them, she corrected herself in her mind. She glanced over to where Dev was seated, busy checking controls. The pale light from the console outlined her body, and Jess wished briefly that they could tuck into a safe spot in the ice so she could take the time to peel Dev out of that sexy number.

Jess closed her eyes, folding her hands over her stomach and letting her body accept the rhythm of the waves. She was almost asleep when she sensed motion close by, then the added warmth of a blanket being tucked around her and the gentle touch of Dev's fingers closing on hers.

It made her feel happy. She returned the squeeze and opened one eye, to find Dev gazing down at her with what could only be a look of affection, something Jess only barely remembered from her childhood.

Then Dev tucked the blanket in a bit more and smiled, moving past her to refill her cup from the dispenser.

Jess smiled back, letting her eyes close and her mind release itself into sleep. Fate. Her last conscious thoughts mused. It had to be fate.

DEV WAS GLAD to see dawn light appearing in the sky, giving outline to the ice pack to her right, and the choppy ruffled waters beneath them. It had been a long dark night, and she was tired, both from struggling to keep the boat on course, and the strain of picking her way through the stormy weather.

Jess remained peacefully asleep this time, and Dev was going to give it a little while before she woke her up. She was looking forward to it, imagining how good it would feel to curl up in the hammock herself and close her eyes. She peered along the ice outside.

It was white in all the grayness, the clouds overhead roiling and moving, though the rain had stopped for now. White, with glimpses of beautiful blue in the cracks, the edge of the flow here high above the boat's level.

It was interesting, and it gave her tired eyes something to look at while they rolled along. She'd gotten used to the motion, and it was starting to feel natural to her.

Suddenly, motion caught her eye and she looked to the left, seeing something in the water. Surprised, she stood a little taller, reaching over to code the scanner and direct it forward. As the boat got closer, she could resolve the movement and realized it was an animal swimming.

The animal turned its head toward her and she let out a tiny gasp of surprise. "Oh!" She hopped a time or two. "I think that's a bear!" Its fur was white, though plastered from the water, and it had dark eyes and a big dark nose. Dev cut the engines and felt the boat slow, not wanting to risk hitting the animal.

The motion change woke Jess. "Whoa." She said, groggily. "Don't tell me I slept all the way back. Devvie you didn't let me do that didja?"

"No, no..." Dev raptly watched as the animal got to the wall of ice, then stopped swimming and stuck a paw out of the water, scraping at the surface. "Oh, Jess. Look. It's a bear, isn't it?"

Jess obligingly rolled out of the hammock and joined her, leaning on the console. After a minute of study, she grunted. "Yeah, it is." She patted Dev on the back. "Congrats! Ya found one."

"What's it doing?" Dev put the engines in idle, watching the animal.

Jess studied the bear. It was clawing at the ice, its head tipped up looking at the ridge high above its head. "I think it's screwed," she said. "Musta fallen off the top there, and can't get back out of the water." She pointed at the high edge of the flow, where there was a visible chunk taken out.

"Oh." Dev felt her elation fade. "What will happen to it?" She looked up at Jess.

Jess shrugged. "Eventually it'll get tired and drown. Nowhere for it to go."

"Oh." Dev said, softly. "That's terrible."

"It's just a bear."

Dev turned to regard her seriously. "Wasn't it just a seal, that time?"

Jess remained quiet for a long minute, her eyes blinking gently as she watched the bear. Then she turned her and looked at Dev. "Why do you always want to go around helping people and things?" she asked. "People and things you don't even know?"

Dev accepted the question at face value. "Because that's how I was made," she said. "I'm supposed to help people if I can. Take care of people. Like people. You're supposed to expect that of me."

Jess nodded slowly. "Techs aren't like that," she said. "Agents aren't. We all sort of hate on each other most of the time." She straightened. "But you're different, huh?"

"Yes." Dev seemed sad about that.

"Maybe I am too sometimes." Jess scrubbed her hands through her hair. "Let me throw my jacket on and see what the hell I can do for that damned bear. Keep the boat steady." She went to the door, grabbing her coat on the way as she shook her head. "Please come save me if the damn thing starts to eat my head."

Dev put her hands back on the controls and trimmed the engines, waiting for Jess to appear on the bow. She kept Jess in view, watching her go to the front of the ship and peer over the side as the boat edged toward the animal.

She was glad Jess was going to help it, even though it had seemed that the idea put her into some discomfort. The thought of that sent a surge of energy through her that pushed back the exhaustion.

If for no other reason than she had to figure out what to do about the bear if it started eating Jess's head.

JESS PUT HER hands on the rail and peered at the bear, who was paddling in circles next to the ice flow. The animal was beginning to tire, and it eyed her warily as it tried to pull itself up onto the wall.

"Why am I doing this?" She wondered aloud. "Hey, bear! C'mere."

The bear continued paddling.

She watched it try to climb up again, and then an idea occurred. With a grunt, she went around the side of the boat, down the channels on either side of the control chamber and through the tunnel to the rear deck.

Emerging onto it, she went to the very back of the fishing area, to the rear where the big wheel was that pulled the nets on board. Behind it was a hatch. She remembered the hatch being open when the nets were being reeled and the water pouring onto the deck.

"Hmm." Jess went to the elevated section where the controls were and climbed up, still a bit foggy from sleep. She sat down on the seat and studied the knobs and switches. She pressed the one for comms and leaned closer. "Hey, Dev?"

Silence for a moment, then the comms crackled back at her. "Yes, I'm here."

"Turn the boat around so the back's facing the ice." Jess said. "I'm gonna try something."

She felt the shift under her immediately, and as she explored the knobs, the view around her changed from gray mist and open sea to the white of the ice flow. She could hear the bear splashing and as the boat stopped moving, she found the controls for the back hatch and triggered them.

A large section of the back deck folded down, and the water flowed across the deck toward her. "Dev." She triggered comms. "Back up." She felt the engines shift into reverse as her partner realized what she'd done. A faint smiled appeared as they started to move slowly in reverse, heading for the paddling animal.

Jess leaned on the console and waited, as the engines cut out and they drifted toward the ice. After a moment she could see the bear through the gap, and as she watched, she saw the animal's head turn toward her and then its body changed direction and headed for the half sunken deck.

Instinct? Jess observed in fascination as the bear reached the boat, and half climbed, half sprawled onto the open deck, panting hard. "Hey, bear." She waved at it, hoping like hell it wouldn't decide to attack her.

But the animal just lay there breathing hard, staring at her.

Jess closed the back of the boat up and leaned on the comms key. "Get moving, Devvie. Let's find someplace to let this thing off before it recovers and decides to have us for lunch." She tapped her fingers on the console as the engines re-engaged, noting the movement was not really much to the bear's liking. "Take it easy, buddy."

The bear pushed itself up into a sitting position, its tongue hanging out. It was a startling pink color, vivid against the yellowish white fur and the black nose. As the speed picked up, it looked around in some alarm, shaking itself and sending a shower of water over the deck.

It was bigger than she'd imagined. Its body was twice the length of hers, and its feet were gigantic. As it turned its head toward her and opened its mouth, she spotted fangs as wide as her hand.

"And I brought your fuzzy white ass up on the boat with us," Jess mused. "Damn I'm an idiot."

Despite that, it seemed sort of cute to her, and she noted its small, cupped ears and appealing expression. "You got lucky, buddy." She informed the bear. "If the owner of this thing were here you'd be a rug already."

The bear regarded her, then lay back down on the deck, apparently not quite recovered from its swim. It seemed content to accept its ride, at least for the moment, so Jess decided she'd leave it there and go back upstairs and get herself properly woken up.

She suspected Dev was hopping up and down waiting for her turn to look at the bear anyway. Jess smiled as she climbed down from the control stand and ducked into the tunnel, heading back to the control center.

"OH MY GOODNESS" Dev's eyes widened, the chill hitting the sides of her eyeballs as she climbed up onto the control platform and peeked over the console. There, sitting in the middle of the deck was the bear, looking huge and furry and more amazing than anything she'd ever seen.

"Don't go near it." Jess's voice warned in her ear cup. "You'd make one mouthful for it."

"I won't." Dev leaned her arms on the surface, avidly watching the animal. It was looking around, blinking its eyes as the wind blew over the deck and ruffled its drying fur.

It was gigantic. It hadn't looked so big when it was in the water, but now on the deck it sure did. "Hey, there," she called out, holding her breath as its head swung around and it looked at her. Hesitantly, she waved at it. "Don't worry. Jess is going to find a nice iceberg for you to climb up on. Okay?"

She wasn't sure if the bear understood language. Doctor Dan had once told her about something called a dog, which understood some words, and another called a monkey that could use symbols to communicate, but she wasn't sure where the bear fell on that bell curve.

Its head was roundish, and she wished it would get closer so she could see it better—and just as she thought that, it did.

It got up, and walked around in a circle. Its front legs were a little shorter than its back ones, so it looked sort of funny when it walked. Dev got back behind the console when it reached the wall and stood up, stretching its front feet up over its head.

"Wow! You're tall!" She peeked cautiously out at it. Its feet had big, black nails on the ends of its toes, and as she watched, it scratched long, dark grooves into the metal of the ship. "Oh no! Don't do that. The fisherman won't like it."

The bear looked at her, and now she could see that its eyes were a deep brown, not black as she'd first thought. They were deep set, and watched her with what she thought surely was some intelligence. After a moment, it dropped back down to all four legs and sauntered over to where she was, sitting down on the deck and opening its mouth.

The teeth were equally gigantic. Dev wondered what the bear ate. "Hey, Jess?"

"Yes? He's not doing anything is he? I can't see him." Jess's voice answered, sharp and intense.

"No, just sitting here." Dev said. "Should we give him some food?"

"Like what, your leg?"

"I was thinking more like the bait, like what we gave the dolphins." Dev said, grinning a little at Jess's dark humor. "Can we give it a name?"

"No." Jess's tone lightened. "Please don't give it a name."

Well, that wasn't a no to the fish. Dev climbed down from the control room and went to the locker, opening it and peering inside. There were buckets of half frozen fish bait inside, and she picked one up, taking it with her to the control console.

She climbed back up and peered out, finding the bear now rolling on its back on the deck, waving its legs in the air. "Hey, Jess? I think it's a girl."

"Really?"

"I think so." Dev removed a chunk of frozen fish from the pail and tossed it onto the deck, waiting to see what the bear was going to do about it.

Hearing the thunk, the bear turned its head and then turned over, sliding across the wet surface and sniffing at the chunk. It opened its mouth and sank its teeth into it, then shook its head and ripped off a piece, chewing it with evident enthusiasm.

"I guess it eats fish," Dev said, tossing the animal another chunk from the pail. "Cool." She pronounced the word carefully. "That's cool, right?"

The bear sat down on the deck and grasped the second fish between its feet, holding it so that it could chew at it. The act was so people like, it made Dev grin. "Can you see it, Jess?" She called into the comms. "It's sitting here eating fish."

"Stop making me hungry." Jess said "Aren't you for that matter?"

"Yes." Dev tossed another fish out to the bear. "Sorry about that. Would you like some of this frozen fish?"

A low snicker sounded in the comms. "Not unless you're changing your name to frozen fish."

Dev cocked her head in puzzlement, as she threw more chunks out. "Why would I do that?" She finally asked. "Do you not like my name?" She watched the bear get up and fetch the last piece she'd tossed, then without warning, it came over and stood up, putting its feet against the outside of the control platform and peering in at her. "Oh!"

"What?" Jess answered instantly. "Dev?"

Dev stared at the bear, now only an arm's length from her. She could smell the fish on its fur, and the musky pungency of the fur itself, the nostrils on the big, black nose flaring. Without really thinking about it, she held out a piece of fish to the bear.

It sniffed it then opened its mouth and very gently took it from her, before it sat down again to finish its meal.

"Dev!"

Dev nearly jumped out of her skin. "Yes!" She blurted. "Yes, I'm fine. Sorry." She leaned against the console and stared at the bear, her heart beating fast. "I was just giving her the last part of the fish." She watched the bear lick her lips with satisfaction and yawn, exposing those huge teeth.

It was so amazing.

The animal got up and walked back over, jumping up to put her paws against the metal of the console. She poked her head inside and snuffled at Dev and before she could think better of it, Dev extended her palm out to the moist looking nostrils.

The bear sniffed her fingers, then the pink tongue appeared and licked them, feeling warm and rough in an explosion of sensation that made Dev's eyes open up wide. "Oh, wow," she whispered, extending her hand just a little and touching the fur under the bear's jaw.

It was soft, and oily feeling. For a moment, the bear regarded her, then she pushed off the console and went back to the middle of the deck, sitting down and yawning.

Dev bounced silently in place, then she scrambled down from the platform and bolted for the steps to the control center, eager to tell Jess about the bear, and its cold, wiggly nose, and its fur.

"YOU TOUCHED IT?"

"Yes." Dev nodded. "Just a little. It licked my fingers." She held up her hand, displaying all five digits. "Then I touched it here." She reached over and touched Jess under her chin. "It was amazing!"

"It's amazing you still have your arm," Jess said wryly. "You're a nut, you know that?" She gazed at Dev with what actually seemed like a touch of envy. "I've seen one of those things rip a man apart."

"I think she was glad I gave her the fish," Dev said. Then she grinned. "I'm glad I got a chance to do that."

"Crazy." Jess ruffled her hair.

Dev came over and threw her arms around Jess, hugging her fiercely. "Thank you for saving her, Jess. That was so awesome."

That had been so terribly pointless and stupid. Jess enjoyed the hug anyway, and the enthusiasm that came along with it. "Anything for you, Devvie." She replied simply. "You make me want to be a complete idiot. Good thing for both of us for some reason I'm really liking that."

"Um. I don't mean to," Dev muttered. "At least, I don't think I mean to."

Jess took her hands off the controls of the ship and put her arms around Dev, savoring the tingle as their bodies pressed against each other. She took a deep breath, feeling an ache in her chest that shortened her breathing and nearly made her lightheaded.

"Wow." Dev reluctantly released her. "Should I get some of the rations? And I'll make hot tea, okay?" She felt Jess's arms tighten, and the pressure of her lips against the top of her head, before she was released in return, to let the chill of the steel chamber once again brush her skin.

That was somewhat uncomfortable. Hugging Jess was definitely nicer. She lifted her eyes and met Jess's, as her partner took back hold of the controls, and exhaled.

"It would be nice to find an ice cave at this time, wouldn't it?" Dev asked in a serious tone.

Jess smiled, her blue eyes twinkling. "If we weren't under recall, we'd already be in one." she said. "I already broke the rules messing around with that bear. If they find out at base I'll be under discipline, so do me a favor, huh? Don't tell anyone."

Dev went over and started preparing the tea. "What does that mean?" she said, after a pause, glancing over her shoulder. "Helping the bear was incorrect?"

Jess settled herself in the command chair and pushed the hair off her forehead with one hand. "When you get a recall like that, you're supposed to do an immediate return to base. No stopping, no side tracking, nothing."

"It didn't take very long," Dev said.

"It's the idea of it." Jess said. "I'd get about...probably six zaps for it." She flexed her hands, her body twitching a little. "Most I ever had before now was four."

Dev brought over some hot tea and honey, and set it down in the little swinging holder that kept it steady with the motion of the boat. She leaned on the chair arm. "I don't think I understand," she said. "I don't have any programming for that."

"No, you wouldn't," Jess said. "Techs don't get zapped. They don't make the decisions. That's my job."

"Ah." Dev touched Jess's wrist, running her thumb over the prominent bone on the edge of it. "It's a bad thing, then."

"It hurts. A lot," Jess replied. "Doesn't leave any marks, but it's like touching a power port. You ever do that? Makes your whole body go stiff, and then it hurts." She picked up the tea and sipped it. "That's what being zapped is like. They do it up in the assembly hall, where we had the induction ceremony."

"I see," Dev said, though she really didn't.

"They don't want us to break the rules." Jess flexed her hand again, with a small grimace. "You get zapped enough times, you stop wanting to."

Dev considered that for a while. "But you helped the bear."

"Yeah, I did. Because you wanted me to." Jess sighed. "I don't know what's wrong with me. I know better."

"Jess, I would feel a lot of discomfort if you got in trouble and got hurt because you did that," Dev said. "Just for helping a bear."

Jess leaned back and studied her, dark lashes fluttering a little over her pale eyes. "I didn't do it for the bear." She smiled briefly. "Don't worry about it, Devvie. They won't know unless we tell 'em. No recorder on this thing." She reached over and traced the fine, pale brow over Dev's right eye. "You got nice lines."

Dev felt a slight sense of confusion, caught in that intense gaze. Then she nodded and smiled, reasoning that her partner must know what she was doing, after all. She squeezed Jess's wrist, and then went back to the preparation area and investigated their supplies.

Now that the excitement was mostly over, she could feel tired again, and she did. "Jess?"

"Hmm?"

"Will you wake me up when you let the bear go?"

Jess chuckled softly. "Sure." She looked up as Dev brought over two portions of fish, poached in some kind of spicy liquid. "Feel like sacking out? You look tanked."

Sacks. Tanks. Dev put a piece of the fish in her mouth while puzzling this out and then her eyes popped open wide. She spit the fish out and stared at it. "Ouch!" She went over and got her tea, sucking down a mouthful. "What is that?"

"Fish." Jess snickered. "Not used to those spices, huh?" She broke off a piece of her own and chewed it. "I like it. Reminds me of mudbug boils we sometimes did back home."

Dev stared doubtfully at the chunk of regurgitated fish in her hand, then sighed, and closing her eyes, popped it back in her mouth. She chewed, then swallowed with an obvious effort, chasing it down with another long swallow of tea. The fish burned her mouth, and the scent of it got back up into her nose and made her sneeze violently.

Very discomforting. Dev looked unhappily at her meal. "I don't think I can eat this. Would you like the rest?"

"Give it here. Go get something else." Jess held a hand out. "At least I found one thing I can do that you can't." She took possession of the offending food. "What a relief."

Dev handed it over without delay. "I think I'll just get some rest." She said "I can have something later, after we let the bear go," she added. "And you know, Jess, there are lots and lots of things you can do that I can't. All I can do is drive the carrier and make tea."

"And you're modest too," Jess said. "I think that's what I like the most about you, Devvie." She shifted in her chair and studied their course, as the boat plowed stolidly through the waves. "You don't talk about how good you are, you just do it."

Dev climbed into the hammock, curling up with a soft ball of fabric for a pillow, and a piece of the same to cover her that still carried Jess's scent on it. She lay there quietly with Jess's words turning over and over in her head, feeling the impact of them as they thrummed deeper and deeper into her consciousness.

They touched something inside her. Something she realized went deeper than programming. "Hey, Jess?"

"You talking in your sleep?"

"No." Dev smiled, a little. "You know what I like the most about you?"

"Uh, oh." Jess chuckled. "What?"

"You."

JESS WATCHED THE wall of ice go by, her thoughts a million miles away.

Or more precisely, about arm's length away focused on the

soundly sleeping figure in the hammock just behind her.

She didn't begrudge her the rest. After all, Dev had piloted the boat through the night, letting Jess get a whole shift worth of sleep herself. But she wished Dev was awake so she could talk to her and hear her voice.

There was something odd and weird about that. Jess swung sideways in the chair so she could study Dev's quiet breathing. She knew it was out of the ordinary for her to be so fixated on something other than her job. She knew it wasn't right that it was impossible for her to focus her attention on the mission, or even the operation of the boat when her thoughts kept drifting back to Dev's smile.

Jess lifted one hand and pinched the bridge of her nose, aware of how unsettled her body felt, and how her breathing was uneven. Was she sick, maybe? Maybe she'd picked up a case of coastal flu. There was a sense of dislocation in her head that she remembered from the last time she'd gotten it.

Or she thought she remembered it. Certainly it hadn't been accompanied by the almost irresistible urge she had to get up and join Dev in the hammock, craving the feel of her body and the warmth of the skin-on-skin contact though, now had it?

With an unhappy sigh, she forced her attention back to the water, feeling a sense of intense aggravation at the never-ending white ruffled surface, and the glacial slowness of their progress. Though even getting to the carrier wouldn't do much, because they'd have to go right back to the citadel.

Right back to the citadel, to whatever problem was waiting for them. No time to relax, and tumble into that nice, soft bed together, able to focus on the pleasure of being together and not having to worry about some damn wave turning them turtle.

Her breathing shortened, as she thought about what that moment would feel like, finding her eyes closing, and her heart starting to pound.

"Shit." Jess shifted and stood up, picking up her now cold tea and taking a swallow. "Drive the fucking boat." She muttered, glancing at the vid and knowing a moment of deep envy as she spotted the bear curled up fast asleep on the deck of the damn thing, the wind coming over the railing ruffling its fur.

But a moment later, she half turned again, leaning against the console as she watched Dev sleep, curled up on her side, the faintest of smiles visible on her face.

"So, what is it about you, huh, Devvie?" Jess whispered. "Are you making me crazy?"

She thought about that for a few minutes, and grinned wryly. "More crazy?" She sighed and sat back down, resting her head on her fist as she adjusted the throttles, her eyes tracking out over the water, searching for the slightest sign of a berg. The first one, she decided, she'd head for so she could get rid of the bear.

The fact that Dev had asked her to wake her up when she did really didn't factor into it at all. She was content to let her get what rest she could before that, wasn't she?

Sure.

Her thoughts circled back around, and she carefully let those last words Dev had spoken sound in her head again. "So." She muttered. "The thing she likes most about me is me." She gazed soberly through the big glass windows "What in the hell does that mean?"

A low rumble of thunder attracted her attention, and she immediately turned to the scan, checking the radar and peering past it out the window. Along the horizon, she spotted a dark, almost black cloud and knew the exactly opposing emotions of exasperation at the weather and elation at the knowledge she'd need to find shelter from it. "Hot damn!"

"What?" Dev was half out of the hammock before she was properly awake, blinking her eyes. "Is something wrong? Are you all right?" She put her hands on the back of the chair as Jess muffled a laugh. "Is the bear okay?"

Jess resisted the urge to turn around and hug her. "Yeah, sorry about that," she said. "Storm's up ahead. I'll need to find some shelter in a while. Didn't mean to wake you up. G'wan back to sleep."

Dev was peeking beyond her cat scan, watching the bear stretch out on the deck, flexing its feet in contentment. "Okay." She rubbed her eyes. "Does that mean we'll have to stop?" She asked, after a pause

"Yep"

"I see. Won't that break the rule?" she asked. "I don't want you to get in trouble, Jess."

"Can't control the weather and they know it." Jess said. "Don't worry about it. Just get some rest. It might even bypass us," she said. "I'll try to keep my yap shut now."

Dev gently put her hands on Jess's shoulders and briefly leaned against her. Then she climbed back into the hammock and curled back up, closing her eyes as she waited for her heart to settle back down

AS SHELTERS WENT, it wasn't going to be much. Jess leaned forward and peered through the worsening weather, the gale force wind shoving the bow of the boat to one side as she searched for the inlet.

Hours had passed, long ones in which she'd crouched in the command chair and worked to keep the boat from turning turtle in the waves. A glance at the monitor screens showed her the back deck, where her somewhat unwelcome passenger was now huddled against the inner wall to escape the wash of surf rolling across the rear of the boat.

Trip from hell. Jess sighed, then nearly catapulted out of the chair when she felt a touch against her back. "Yeoop!" She jerked her head around to find Dev standing behind her, a bemused expression on her face. "Oh, it's you."

Dev looked around her then back at Jess. "Were you expecting someone else?" she asked, in a serious tone. "I'm sorry. I didn't mean to alarm you." She peered out the window. "Wow."

Jess felt her heart start to settle, and she unlocked her muscles, returning her attention to the storm. "Yeah, piece of shit weather," she said. "I'm trying to make for an archipelago we can hide in—see?" She squinted and pointed through a break in the squall at a smudge of slightly darker gray against the gray of the sky and the gray of the water. "We get in there, we can let our friend out, back off and tie up."

Dev studied the nav comp. "Oh. This is not so far from where we got on this boat." She pointed out. "Wouldn't it be better to try to get there? It seemed like good shelter."

"Sure, if you want them to shoot your buddy on the back." Jess said. "Not to mention, shoot us. We made better time back then. I thought we had another day of this to get back that far."

"Oh." Dev frowned "So then how are we going to get back to the carrier?"

"Let me get back to you on that. One potential life threatening disaster at a time." Jess fought the controls, as the seas rose suddenly and rocked the boat.

"Want me to take this now?" Dev asked, diffidently. "You look cold."

Jess wasn't going to argue. She slipped out of the chair and let Dev take her place, noting Dev seemed freshly scrubbed and had a fresh jumpsuit on, with her lined one over it with the top part draped down behind her unfastened "Wait a minute. How long have you been awake?"

"About a half hour." Dev got herself settled and adjusted the throttles. "I didn't want to bother you when you were concentrating."

Holy crap. Jess stared at Dev's slim back in shock. Had she really been that oblivious? "Well," she grunted. "Least you got some rest."

"I did." Dev said in a cheerful tone. "It was nice. I liked how the motion felt."

Jess went to the back of the control center where they'd brought their things and got herself sorted out. She could see where Dev had changed and repacked her carry sack neatly, and the carefully folded packet that had contained some fish she'd apparently consumed.

Jess regarded the station. She saw her own meal had been set out for her, with a covered cup of tea next to it. She touched the cup with her fingertips and smiled. "Thanks," she called up to the front.

"You're welcome." Dev answered, as she turned the bow a little and headed closer in to the ice.

Jess undid the catches on her suit and stripped out of it, ignoring the chill of the air as it hit her now bare body, though it made her start shivering. She took a sanitary kit out and wiped her skin down, giving her shoulder a cursory glance before she changed. The injury was almost healed as she'd expected, and she pulled the sleeves up over her arms and fastened the suit over her.

It brought immediate warmth and she exhaled in relief as the mild shivers abated. Braced where she was between the console and the wall, the motion of the ship was no more than annoying, and it felt good to be standing after all the hours crouched over in the chair.

She was stiff and a little achy though.

Cautiously, she flexed her arms and twisted to either side, relieved to only feel mild discomfort from her back. Maybe that one, too, was finally healing. "About fucking time," she muttered under her breath.

Med had told her, matter-of-factly, that the toxins on the knife had almost killed her far more surely than the six inch cut it made, but even knowing all that didn't ease the frustration of dealing with how long it was taking her usually robust body to recover from it.

Ah well. Jess uncapped the tea and sipped it while she opened the food packet with her other hand, bracing her body against the wall. "You're so nice to me, Devvie." She said. "I notice you left me the spicy one though."

Dev smiled, visible in the reflection from the windows. "I'm sorry. I just can't eat that," she admitted. "I've never encountered anything like that before."

Jess chewed the fish with a sense of melancholy appreciation. "My mother used to cook with these kind of spices," she said. "Reminds me of her fish gumbo. Most of the time the citadel doesn't use anything more exciting than sea salt. Wonder where these bastards got this from? I didn't see any at the market."

"I don't know," Dev said. "We didn't have anything like that in the creche. I am sure they would have tried that on us if there had been, they tried everything else."

"Don't feel bad. Same for us when we were in school. I ate seaweed so many ways I thought for sure I took on a green skin tone there for a while. My favorite thing back then was pizza."

"Pizza?" Dev carefully piloted the boat through a pair of back-to-back waves. "I don't think I've ever heard of that."

"It's kind of a flat bread thing, with soy cheese and little sardines. They used to get rid of the crap from the nets that way, but I liked it." Jess finished one packet and started on a second, aware of being really hungry. "Wish I had one now. There's just so much of this cold crap I can handle at one time."

"That sounds interesting," Dev said. "They don't have that at the base?"

"No. They consider it junk. Don't want to give it to us. We're supposed to put stuff in our bodies that makes them work better. That's the theory anyway." She swallowed the last of the second packet and started rooting around for more. "That's why those parties are so damn popular. We get stuff we don't usually get."

"Like those brown things."

"Exactly."

"Those were really good."

Jess chuckled. "I knew we were two of a kind when I saw you scarfing those." She drained her tea and put the cup in one of the holders, then went over and joined Dev at the controls. She studied the cloud pattern, and put her hand on Dev's back. "Can we go any faster?"

The slightly darker lump on the horizon was now visible as a gray, craggy outline, rising from the surging sea. She could hear the surf roaring as it broke against the stone, and around the edges a thick roiling fog was drifting. "See if you can get between those shoals."

Obediently, Dev pushed the throttles forward, and aimed the boat for the looming rocks, as the storm rolled over them with increasing fury. The rocks looked dangerous. "I don't remember seeing those before," Dev said. "We were farther to the south going the other direction."

"We were," Jess agreed. "We're up into the Greenland Archipelago. Should be safe though, never had much population." She draped her arm over Dev's shoulders as they eased between two tall, jagged spires and as they did, the winds dropped, and the seas got calmer.

"Wow," Dev said. "That's much better."

It was still raining almost sideways, but the boat now made better headway as they threaded their way through half hidden rocks outlined in white and green froth as the stone walls rose up on either side of them. Past the rocks there were further gray lumps, and over all a mist was rising.

"Yeah, that is much better." Jess studied the landscape. "Haven't been here in years. There's just this small southern bit that's not under ice. See, the glacier picks up there." She pointed. "Mostly seals live here."

Dev brightened. "Really?"

"Mm." Jess pointed at a rock escarpment. "That's where I killed my instructor. We use this as a training base."

"Oh." Dev watched the water calm as they moved farther inside the waterway, where bare stone rose on either side of them. They were protected from the wind and the waves, and as she throttled down the engines, they both heard a loud sound from behind them.

Jess responded instantly, bounding over and grabbing her blaster from its holster, getting to the door and through it before Dev could even open her mouth.

The hatch slammed.

"I think that was the bear," she said to the empty room.

A moment later, the hatch slammed open and Jess popped inside. "Bear," she explained briefly. "I think it wants to go home." She closed the hatch and rejoined Dev, dripping rainwater all over the deck. "See that inlet there?"

"Yes." Dev turned the bow toward it. "Is this where the bear lives? How did you know that?" She peered at Jess in bewilderment.

"Bears live here," Jess said. "I don't know if this one does, but we can let it off there." She pointed at an outcropping of rock that overhung the water just barely. "It can figure out what to do after that."

They heard the loud noise again, a rough, barking roaring sound that made the metal vibrate under Dev's fingertips. "Is the bear mad?"

"Bored. Sounds like me when I'm stuck inside too long," Jess replied.

Dev didn't really think the bear was bored, but she merely nodded and continued to edge toward the sheltered area, seeing a rock overhang just past it where they could probably let the boat sit while the storm passed. She watched through the window intently, looking for evidence of the seals Jess had mentioned, highly entertained with the idea of seeing both animals here on one trip.

"You know what it sounds like?" she said, after the bear made the noise again. "It sounds like she's calling out to someone."

Jess regarded her with a tolerant grin.

"Maybe there's another bear here." Dev didn't catch the look. "Maybe she has a friend." She put the engines into idle as they neared the rocks, and drew in a quick breath as she saw something moving "Oh! Look!"

Jess thumped lightly against the console and peered out the window, blinking a little as she saw two fast moving off-white forms galloping toward the boat. "What in the hell?"

Dev's eyes lit up. "They're little bears!" She bounced in place. "Oh! Look at them!" She grabbed the scanner and flicked through its programming, selecting the record function and focusing it on the animals. Then she set the scanner down and swung the boat sideways a bit, putting the back of it up against the rocks. "Jess, look. She knows them!"

Jess sighed. "She does," she admitted, watching the bear scramble up onto the side of the boat and then jump to the rocks, where the two smaller bears met her. "Gimme those controls. Go look at it. Chances are you'll never get to see this again."

Dev didn't hesitate for an instant. She grabbed the scanner and went to the door, working the hatch and popping through it. She scrambled down the steps and forward onto the bow, going around to the side against the rocks where she could get a good look at the bears.

The big bear was greeting the little ones with every evidence of happiness, licking them as they stood up on their back legs and patted her with their front ones, making small, cawing sounds.

Dev got it on the scanner, bouncing up and down on the balls of her feet. The little bears didn't seem to mind either the rain or the noisy boat idling next to the rocks, and she got a good shot of them as they raced around the bigger bear in circles.

The bear sat down and let them climb over her, and then rolled on her back and patted them with her front feet.

It was amazing. How had Jess known to bring her exactly here? Dev felt a sense of awe at her partner's intuition. She had known! Of all the places in the whole wide ocean, to bring the boat here, right where the two little bears were waiting for her?

Amazing! She turned and looked up into the control center, seeing Jess leaning on the console and watching the bears with a big grin on her face.

Even if she pretended not to care, she did. Dev nodded a little to herself. Sometimes the proctors were like that. Sometimes, even Doctor Dan was. But the truth of them would shine out at times, like it was with Jess right now. She could see her face, and see the unguarded happiness in it and she knew.

She knew there was a good and big heart in her partner. No matter what she said about her conscience.

Then the rain started to come down harder, and Dev felt the boat move away from the rocks toward the overhang. She walked along the rail, keeping the bears in sight as long as she could, then waved at them as they pulled past.

The big bear looked up at the motion, and opened her mouth, letting out one of the roars.

Amazing. Dev grinned, shutting the scanner down as she shook the icy rain from her eyes and headed back for shelter. It didn't even matter that she was now wet through and cold, not if it meant she'd gotten to see that. She trotted back up the steps as the boat pulled under the overhang, then she paused as it became evident that the overhang was much more than that.

There was a cave there, and the engines sounded suddenly much louder as Jess steered into it, and then they were out of the storm entirely and in a big, dark space.

Jess turned the boat's lights on as Dev entered the control room, and she looked out in surprise as the cave became visible. There was a very rudimentary dock there, and weather worn equipment lockers, and she recalled Jess saying they trained in this place. "That was amazing, wasn't it?"

Jess smiled. "That was pretty cool," she admitted. "You don't get to see cubs very often."

"Is that what they were? They were really beautiful." Dev observed the scanner, bringing up a shot of the two smaller animals and showing it to Jess. "See?" It was a close-up of the two, their appealing faces turned toward the scanner, small pink tongues showing along with the dark eyes, and the small curved ears.

"Mm." Jess idled the engines. "That one," she put a fingertip on the screen, "is almost...almost as cute as you are." She watched Dev blush a little, then she looked up and her expression changed completely. "Now that, on the other hand, isn't cute at all."

The lights had swept to the deeper part of the cave, and now outlined a large, hulking form that was all too familiar to both of their eyes.

"It's a carrier," Dev said, after a long shocked moment.

"Bet I know which one it is too," Jess replied grimly.

"The one that attacked this boat? The one with the pirates?" Dev shifted the scanner and started a routine. "Is this where they are?" She paused and looked up. "Are they here?"

Jess's eyes were flicking everywhere, her hands tense on the controls. "All very good questions, Devvie," she muttered. "Let me park this thing and let's find out. At the very least we found us a faster ride."

"I see." Dev ran her fingers through her damp hair. "That's very interesting."

"Could be getting way too interesting."

Chapter Two

JESS FINISHED TYING up the boat, her ears cocked to pick up anyone approaching. So far, the cavern had been silent and was apparently empty, but she was old timer enough not to trust that.

Dev stood on the dock, scanning the interior of the cavern with her hand held comp. She had her tech jumpsuit on, and her jacket over it, the gusty wind puffing the pale hair on her head in various directions. Jess watched her for a moment, and then she went over to join her, peering over her shoulder. "Anything?"

Dev studied the screen. "Nothing alive," she said. "Just the carrier and some frozen dead animals." She shifted the pack on her back, twin to the one Jess was wearing that contained all their gear.

They had left all the stuff they'd bought for the scientists on the boat, also a few of the black diamonds. The rest were tucked into Jess's pack, along with the few things they'd picked up for themselves.

Jess relaxed a little. "Let's scope the place out. See what we can find before we steal that carrier." She started across the ice, pausing for a moment to lean a gloved hand against the ice, lifting her boots up one after the other and slapping her steel spikes into place. "Slippery."

Dev nodded, having already extended her own boot appliances. She dug her feet into the surface a little as she followed Jess, conscious of the steady stream of vapor coming from her lips in the cold.

The carrier crouching balefully at the end of the cavern stirred in her a very mixed emotion. Certainly that would get them home faster, but Dev felt a sense of profound disappointment that they weren't going to have just a little while to be still and practice that sex thing. Dev sighed and squared her shoulders, putting thoughts of that aside as she climbed up the slanted ice path that led away from the water.

The cavern didn't look lived in. Aside from the few old crates, and some rusted ladders half buried in the ice, there was no sign of human habitation, and as they moved up the slope her scanner confirmed that. There were no residual bio markers, save a few traces she tracked to the carrier itself.

That, she reasoned, was likely the one that had attacked them. It had the same silhouette, and the markings on it matched the pictures she'd taken during the battle. She slowed as Jess did, the agent pulling her blaster from its holster and holding it ready in her hand.

A motion of her thumb, and the safety was off. Dev heard the faint sound of the internal power pack spooling up and glanced down again at the comp, sweeping the area past the carrier to see if anyone was going to try and stop them. "No bio returns," she commented, in a low utterance.

"Good." Jess swept the pad the craft was parked on incessantly, her peripheral vision hunting for any motion past the edges of the iced shelf. Even if Dev's comp didn't pick up anything, she was never really sure until her own senses confirmed it.

Quirk of the brain. She knew Dev could be trusted, and she knew in fact this particular tech could be trusted, but still. There was a place for human instinct in their business and few knew that better than she did. So she cautiously moved forward onto the platform, feeling the bite of her crampons against the ice. "Carrier giving off heat?"

"No," Dev said. "Exterior temperature is ambient."

"Good news." Jess approached the craft and paused, then knelt to pick up a small piece of ice. She stood and considered, then she tossed the ice at the carrier, both of them twitching a little when it hit the hull and dropped with a faint thunking clang.

Dev studied the comp readout, seeing no reaction in any of the electrical spectrums to the intrusion. "No scans," she said, as Jess moved very carefully over to where the entrance door was. "I'm not getting any indication that systems are active on board."

She slid the comp into its holder and walked closer to the vehicle, studying the external engine housings that seemed old and misshapen to her eyes. She ran a cautious hand over the edge of the surface, feeling it flex under her touch. Her eyes lifted to watch Jess, who was studying the entry pad. "Do you think you can open it?"

"I'm sure I can open it. Question is, can I open it and still have it be operational or anything more than a scattering of burned metal bits coated with my blood?" Jess mused "Ah, hell. Life's short." She pulled her glove off and reached up to put her hand on the pad.

Dev blinked in surprise, her breath catching as she waited for a response from the carrier, knowing what the systems were programmed to do when unauthorized persons tried to enter them. For a second, she thought she sensed a power surge, then the hatch opened with an anticlimactic click and swung outward.

It smelled old inside. Musty air and the scent of burned electronics wafted out, and Dev's nose wrinkled. "Reminds me of some of the old storage chambers in the creche," she said.

Jess regarded the inside and shrugged. "G'wan in there and see if we can get airborne in this thing. I'm going to hunt around, see if the pirates left anything." She watched Dev climb cautiously inside and then she picked up a big chunk of dirty ice and put it in the entryway, so the hatch couldn't close all the way if it developed a mind to. "Be back."

Dev eased inside the carrier and wrinkled her nose. The inside was dirty, the floor caked with mud and boot prints, all of the surfaces scuffed and worn. There was even adhesive tape holding things together, and Dev spent a moment just looking at everything and wondering if it wasn't safer for them to just stay with the boat.

With a sigh, she edged her way up to the pilot's chair and brushed some caked mud off it, then sat down and put her pack down by her boots. She reviewed the controls for a minute or so, then nodded to herself as programming kicked in and she touched the comp and systems boards, mildly surprised when they responded.

On batts, of course, and they were nearly drained. Dev damped the comp and focused on bringing the engines online, hoping the dirty looking pods outside didn't either blow up or fall off.

She triggered the startup sequence, drawing enough power to bring the propulsion systems online with a slow, tired whining sound that set her teeth on edge. She watched the readouts anxiously, trimming the power leads when they spiked erratically.

For a moment everything went out, then came back up and engines started generating power, sending a light shudder through the frame of the carrier.

Not normal or good. Dev frowned at the console and scooted up a little closer, concentrating on coaxing the old components into service. It was all mostly off-balance at the leads, and it was obvious to her that no one had done maintenance on the carrier for a very long time.

Senseless, if they had to fly on it. She clucked her tongue a little and started making adjustments, tweaking the batteries as they started to take on charge. Every few seconds she glanced up through the mud and ice encrusted windows, seeing nothing but crashing waves at the entrance, and a solid wall of rain outside.

The boat was rocking at its dock, and very briefly, she wondered if the bear and her little cubs had gotten under cover before the storm hit.

She hoped so. She was glad she'd gotten to see them, in any case.

At last the consoles started to come online and graphs were settling, as she balanced the incoming power from the engines and gave the batteries enough juice to power up everything else. She regarded the comp as it flickered into focus, unsure of whether to even trust anything it was telling her.

The carrier was totally compromised. She could see tape and cables with ports snaking out of places they didn't belong, and she assumed the systems had been hacked to allow anyone to drive it. In their carrier, the controls were keyed to the chips and the bio scans of herself and Jess. Even the techs who serviced it couldn't actually start it up and fly it.

Hence, why she had to perform the commissioning flight when the carrier was put back together. This craft, on the other hand, didn't even check her identity. She hadn't felt the twitch in the chips at all, and the hatch had opened at just a touch, there was nothing in comp that indicated it knew who had opened the door.

Dev glanced outside, then peered around to the side, where Jess had disappeared. There was no sign of her partner and that was making her very unhappy. It took a lot of effort to drag her attention away from that thought, and back to the carrier.

With another sigh, she started a preflight routine, her hands a little hesitant on the much older controls. Once that had begun, she got up and examined the interior, checking to see what was inside it that might be useful to them. There was no expendable storage anywhere. Everything seemed to have been stripped out to make room for people to ride inside it and it was mostly bare frame and strapping.

The weapons console was so battered, there were no legends on anything anymore. Just a couple of knobs and the grips that would fire the guns. The chair was a bare frame too, and Dev wrinkled her nose as she thought about the contrast between this, and the new chair Jess had been so happy with.

She hadn't regarded their craft as either luxurious or comfortable, but compared to this one, it certainly was. Dev checked the water supply and found it empty, then peered into the extremely basic sanitary facility and wished she hadn't. "Hmm." She hoped they wouldn't be in this thing long, just long enough to fly it to the other cavern and pick up their own.

Unless Jess would want to bring it back to the citadel for them to study, of course, or... Dev paused, wondering if her partner might not just want to destroy it, so that no one could use it again.

That seemed likely. Her peripheral vision caught motion, and she turned and peered out of the hatch, hoping to see Jess's familiar form heading her way. Instead, she saw a sleek looking animal jump out of the water onto the ice, making a loud noise that startled the life out of her.

It was far away, on the pier next to the boat, and she watched it in fascination as it galumphed along the ice. It had a small head and was gray, and as it got closer she could see its face. She wondered suddenly if it was a seal.

Wow. She bounded back and got her comp and brought it back over to scan the animal, hoping it was, since she really wanted to see the creature that had so appealed to Jess.

Dev smiled as it came closer.

THE CAVERN WAS crude and basic, and always had been. Jess made her way along a hand chopped passageway, listening carefully for either cracking ice or pirates. She had her blaster in one hand and her knife in the other, and she was moving with as much grace as she could on ice with crampons on.

She was glad they'd found the old carrier. It meant she could get back to the citadel a lot faster, find out what the recall was about, and, as a bonus, get props for finding the old thing and a pirate hideout.

Pure dumb luck, of course, but she'd take it.

Now she just had to check the back cavern to make sure she wasn't leaving any of the bastards at her back, and she could take off with Dev, go pick up their carrier, and get back home.

As she neared the end of the passageway she slowed, cocking her head forward and listening hard ahead of her. There was nothing but the crackling of ice, but she stopped anyway, opening her mouth and drawing in the air, trying to taste any hint of anything out of place on it.

A puff of air hit her, and she twitched as the smell of death got into her nose. She started forward with more caution, her breathing starting to slow as her focus tightened. After a few moments, she stopped and triggered her comms on shortwave. "Dev, Dev."

After a pause, the earpiece rustled. "Here."

"Secure," Jess uttered. "Tac."

"Ack," Dev responded at once.

With a nod, Jess released the comms and continued forward. As she came around a bend in the passage, she got a lungful of stench, and grimaced. "Ah, this ain't gonna be pretty." Another bend, and she could see the back cavern ahead of her, a large space she remembered them using for tactical storage and the ice class.

Now as she entered, she stopped and quickly scanned the space, finding both death, and the source of the stench, which wasn't it. Sprawled over the ice were large, heavy looking animals she recognized, and that was what smelled, but scattered among them were black forms frozen in the ice splayed out in patches of red stain.

One of the animals spotted her, and barked.

Jess held her ground, hoping the sea lions weren't in the mood to rush her, and edged closer to the first of the bodies.

Frozen solid, its face was stretched into a rictus of pain, one arm and part of its shoulder blown away by what looked like a blaster. It might have been one of the attackers from the other night. The body was encased in a jumpsuit just like hers, but the face wasn't familiar to her.

It made sense if they were the same. Jess walked over to the second body, which had been cut completely in half. She studied it, then pointed her own blaster at the ice and set it to heat, directing the beam at the frozen form until it separated from the ground.

She turned it over and found herself looking at someone she did know. "Damn."

A strong prickling tweaked her shoulder blades, and she looked around, seeing the sea lions start to shift around and move. She took a step back and turned slowly in a circle, searching for the source of their disturbance. Across the cavern she spotted a half buried box, and she moved around the open water in the center to examine it.

The sea lions shifted, and one dove in the water, disappearing underneath the surface. Jess remembered there was an undersea entrance to the place, and she was careful where she put her boots as she felt the ice under her shifting. A brief grin touched her lips, remembering the dare she'd won over that narrow, icy cold gap.

Counting the bodies, she nodded as the tally seemed to match the party that attacked them. She got over to the box and kicked it open, surprised when she recognized the contents as Interforce tactical gear.

New. She picked up a kit and looked at it. Brand new, with the current quarter's dates on it.

"Huh." She saw another passage behind the box that she didn't remember. She triggered comms. "Dev, Dev." She was reasonably sure the most dangerous thing around her was that bull sea lion, who'd been eying her, but something inside her tickled her to contact her partner anyway. "You there?"

"Here. Is everything all right?" Dev responded.

"Yeah. The bus up?"

"Yes," Dev answered. "There is a...I think there is a seal near me."

Jess grinned briefly. "Sea lion. Found a lot of 'em back here. Going to check out a hall. Be back over there in two minutes."

"Excellent."

Jess clicked off and stepped around the box, ducking past the embedded glow lamp in the ceiling and moving down the passage. As she half suspected, it revealed a crude living space, full of sleeping bags and furs, and the remnants of human garbage.

If nothing else, it confirmed these pirates had stolen the Interforce name, nothing else. She'd expected to find at least one chamber kept in their style, but even the least grungy was still unbearably messy. She walked inside it though, and studied the interior.

Very basic. Just a hole chopped out of the ice, with a single lamp giving a very dim light inside. There was a hammock with both ends pinned into the walls, a plastic box for storage, and in the corner, a round metal pipe with a cover that was sunk down into the ice.

Jess grimaced in pure human reflex at the thought of using that very primitive sanitary facility. She shook her head and went to the box, opening the top and looking inside. Her jaw tightened and she reached inside, picking up a set of creds, and a small plastic case that she could see the glitter of chips through the top of. She tucked them into a pocket and sorted through the rest, mostly cans of stale looking biscuits and tea.

"And you gave us up for this?" she muttered. "Shithead." She left the detritus where it was and moved on, going to the end of the chopped corridor and poking her head into what was apparently their main living chamber.

It contained nothing but a mixture of hacked together chairs and a surface frozen into the ice that was probably a table. Everything was strewn everywhere, and it occurred to her that whoever had killed the pirates had probably also taken whatever valuable items they found.

She pulled the case from her pocket and regarded it. Then she put it back and stood still, letting her head swing from left to right, committing the scene to memory. She turned and walked slowly back up the corridor, stopping to look inside all the chambers and duplicating the scan.

Techs had comp. Agents had eidetic memory that was inbred but also trained, to make record of things when comp wasn't available or practical. Jess knew she could have asked Dev to come back here with her scanner, but this would work as well, once she let them put the leads on and replayed her memories.

Not exactly as reliable, when you were up against discipline since there was always a chance you could forcefully misremember something, but in this case, it would do.

Jess left the chambers and went to a small rise of ice, jumping up onto it and repeating her slow review of the bigger cavern. The sea lions watched her curiously, but didn't seem inclined to do anything else and she hopped down after a minute and started toward the back tunnel.

So. Someone had found the pirates, and obliterated them. If that was the case, why not also destroy the carrier? That was a valuable transport, despite its age, and leaving it seemed off kilter to her. On the other hand, the carrier had been left intact, and so had the Interforce credentials. Maybe it was a message to them?

To her? But how in the hell would they expect her to happen by here?

The precise blaster fire pretty much fingerprinted the other side. The question foremost in her mind though was, why? The pirates were doing their best to trash Interforce's reputation, so why would the other side object? Why weren't they, in fact, behind the whole scheme?

Wasn't really adding up. Jess picked her way among the bodies and edged around the sea lions, most of whom were sprawled asleep, strangely uncaring of her human presence among them. Motion caught her eye and she turned her head to see one of the big animals ripping at one of the dead pirates, chewing a chunk of frozen flesh and blinking amiably at her.

Jess shrugged wryly. "Bon appétit." She got up onto the ledge that led to the boat dock cavern, glad to leave the stench behind as she entered the narrow passageway and thought about how to phrase her report to base.

Training camp compromised. Jess wondered when the last class was held there? Probably not anytime in the recent past, based on what she'd found. Jess emerged into the cavern and paused, spotting the carrier, now obviously powered, the engine cowling emitting steam into the air. Seated across from it was a big sea lion, watching with intelligent interest as the various control planes moved as Dev tested them. "Hey, bubba." She waved at the sea lion.

It barked at her.

Jess saw Dev's head turn in the window and spot her, and a moment later the hatch creaked open. With a sense of surreal normality she boarded the carrier, glancing around at the decrepit interior with a grimace. "Hey, Devvie."

"I'm glad you returned," Dev said. "There are others approaching this area."

"Uh oh." Jess stripped out of her coat as she sealed the hatch, moving forward to look at the scan. "Maybe they're just looking for shelter. Storms about to come over the top of us." She studied the readout. "Ident?"

"Not Interforce," Dev said. "Preliminary comp indicates two RS25007 medium long range transports."

"Bad guys." Jess sighed. "Well let's stay put and quiet. See if they pass us by. There are a ton of caves in the area." She leaned on the back of the chair Dev was sitting in. "They're heavily armed. We could take them out in our rig, but from the looks of this one it'll be enough for us just to fly."

Dev nodded emphatic agreement. "The power packs are at only 10 percent effective. I don't know how much we can send to the weapons systems."

"Definitely stay put." Jess gently blew in her ear. "Maybe we can find out what they're doing and earn us a bonus."

Dev regarded the comp, then turned her head slightly and looked up at Jess's profile. "Right now?"

Jess kissed her. "Not exactly right this minute."

"Excellent."

THE STORM FINALLY subsided, and as far as Jess was concerned, that kinda sucked. Her body was all warm and sensually stimulated and she really wanted nothing more than to keep sharing that big, and rickety bare shelf she and Dev were perched on, and to hell with the bastards outside.

Jess sighed, convinced she was likely losing her mind.

"Comp shows them moving," Dev said.

"Yeah, I know. Guess we better get our asses going, huh?"

Dev considered that. "Well, do you want to chase after them, or let them get away without seeing us?"

Jess made a deeply thoughtful noise in her throat. Then she surrendered to duty and got up, running her hands through her hair as she pondered the idea that coincidentally it seemed her bio alt companion was also losing her mind in the same kind of way.

Weird and odd and exciting and completely absorbing to the point she had to wonder if they weren't going to fly themselves right into an iceberg because of it and not even care.

Dev had gotten up and gone to the pilot's seat, perching on it as her hands started their disciplined dance over the controls, pausing only to hitch her jumpsuit back up onto her shoulders and fasten the catches Jess had so recently undone for her. She ignored the comms from the carrier, settling the buds connected to her own portable comp instead.

Jess went over and sat down on the raw rack provided for the weapons station. It poked her in the back with extreme discomfort and she seriously hoped Dev would not be doing any of her more extreme aerobatics before they could get back to their own carrier and her comfortable new bucket. "This thing going to lift?"

"I think so." Dev looked back over her shoulder. "Should we try?"

"Go for it. Might as well find out inside the damn cave. If we crash land at least I can swim."

"I can sort of swim." Dev settled her hands and feet on the controls and triggered the lifting jets. With a drunken stagger, the craft lifted up off the ice, skewing sideways before she got enough thruster control to steady their flight. "Hmm." She made some adjustments. "I don't remember this device looking so unstable when it attacked us."

Jess was holding on tight to her seat, peering up at her partner. "That didn't sound good."

"I was only halfway joking about the whole swimming thing. If this is going to take a dive, put it back down."

"I find it very hard to understand how someone would keep a carrier in this type of condition when they expect it to fly." Dev's voice took on as much of a disapproving tone as she was capable of. "It's just not correct." She made another adjustment and the carrier leveled out, the engines producing a more normal rumble. "Hmph."

"Wrencher." Jess chuckled softly. "Bet you can't wait to get back to our bus."

"Absolutely," Dev said, working hard to keep the carrier going in a correct direction. "Very much looking forward to it." She aimed the vehicle at the entrance to the docking cavern, watching the scan closely as they emerged into the free air, the rain still coming down and coating the bay in a deep gray mist.

The gray masked them, and against the rough water, the carrier was almost invisible. Dev hovered a moment, getting a feel for the directional jets before she moved cautiously out over the ruffled surface, glancing in the rear scan to find nothing but ice behind them, half obscured with rain.

She took a deep breath and settled into her seat, keeping low to the water as the scan picked up the two transports rising on the far side of the bay.

"Jess." A touch on her back made her twitch a little, but then Jess was leaning on the console next to her. "There they are."

"There they are," Jess repeated. "And what they are, is the bad guy's stock transports. What in the hell are they doing up here?" She studied the profiles. Both were about as wide as the old carrier they were in, and twice as long, designed to hold cargo or people on long haul voyages.

Lightly armed. Jess searched the sides of them for mods, and found only the standard guns forward, no unusual profile that might hide the kind of heavy weaponry they had on their own rig.

She checked the nav, pondering the possibility the damn things were just lost. They were in the no man's land, after all, just the wrong side of the continental shelf that marked the start of her side's territory.

Dev eased the carrier forward, using the craggy islands in the middle of the bay and the mist to hide their presence. She suspected the enemy had scan too, but why they hadn't reacted to it by now was a mystery to her. She could see them lifting up cautiously, and then she realized why they hadn't seen them as the side of the forward one cleared the edge of the island and they could fully see them. "Jess, look."

Jess was busy looking. "Took a hit." She studied the hole in the side of the transport. "From one of ours. That's a sigma twelve land based." She tapped something into the portable comp, and then leaned on the console again. "Wonder which base they came close enough to for that." She drummed her fingers on the console. "They stray too close to Sidney?"

Dev slid closer, as the two transports hovered, the one that was damaged moved around as though testing stabilizers. Given the gaping hole in the side, she understood that. And now that she was looking for it, the other transport was missing a directional tail fin. "They are both damaged."

"Sure are," Jess said. "Now I know why they didn't look for us. They were hiding to save their skins."

They were both looking at the hole when a flutter of motion turned the gap from black to white to black again, and then they saw bodies struggling.

"What in the hell?" Jess leaned further. "Get that on comp."

Dev held the carrier steady and directed the portable scanner at the action, as the fight continued for a brief moment, before the transport abruptly heeled over and then pitched skyward, its engines revving as it sped off. The second craft bolted after it, leaving them in their old, stolen rig behind.

Jess bit down the urge to chase them. "Let's get our bus," she said. "Something's going on." She pushed off the boards and headed back to her seat.

Dev nodded. "Yes," she agreed. "Let me recalibrate this for nav and..." She paused, blinking at the screen. Then she made an adjustment and peered at the readout. "Jess."

Hearing the tension, Jess swerved back toward her and peered over her shoulder, as Dev manipulated the image on the screen and set it to maximum zoom.

The hole in the transport abruptly resolved, and the faint, far off struggling figures sharpened into recognizable forms. Two of the bad guys, one that she knew, and a third that made Dev suck in her breath in shock. "Doctor Dan!"

Then all three disappeared and the transport started moving, the image ending in the comp.

Jess straightened up, for a long moment completely still and silent. "Bet I know what that recall's about," she said, grimly. "They must have gotten to Base Ten."

Dev was stunned. "They've got Doctor Dan!" she said. "They were hitting him!"

Jess picked up the scan and replayed it. "He was hitting them back," she said dryly. "C'mon, Dev. Let's get our rig and get back to base. See what they want to do about it."

Dev put her hands on the controls again, but slowly. "We're not going to go help him?" she asked, in a soft, distressed voice. "Jess!"

"Not in this thing." Jess nudged her. "Get moving. We need to get an encrypt and decent guns." She went back and took her seat as she felt the carrier lift and start to speed up. "Son of a bitch. Did they grab him from Base Ten, or was it an inside job?"

Incredible. The first attempt had seemed audacious, but they'd turned it back and she figured they put a bigger guard on.

Or did they? Could it be part of the leak? Jess glanced up at the window and saw Dev's expression, a mixture of anxiety and fear that surprised her a little. "They took him for a reason, Dev. They won't hurt him at least until they get him back."

"We should help him," Dev said, quietly. "He's a good person."

"We might end up doing that when we get back to base. Bain will tell us what he wants us to do," Jess said. "We might have been recalled specifically for that."

Dev's eyes met hers in the reflection of the curved window. "Why do we have to wait, though, if they want us to do that? Won't that take a lot of time, going back there?" she asked. "Won't they get away? What if they hurt him?"

"Dev, we have to go back because they recalled us," Jess said. "It's a rule. We don't obey it they'll send someone out to take us down. That won't help him either."

Dev was silent for a long moment. "I see." She nodded faintly. "I understand what that means. I just wish we could talk to them and see if they would let us go." She paused, then cleared her throat. "Or not ask them and go anyway."

Jess was dumbfounded. The last thing she expected her live-by-the-law partner to suggest was a deliberate breaking of the rules. "Um." She sorted through her options. "I said maybe we could get an encrypt session back on our bus, and maybe...hey maybe when we call in they'll send us back for him."

That seemed to cheer Dev up a little. "You think they would do that?" She pushed the throttles forward a little, getting the lumbering craft to speed up. "I'm sure they'd want us to go help Doctor Dan."

Would they? Jess fastened the bare straps of the seat around her. She'd gotten a sense that Bain and he were friends, but in the corps friends were negotiable currency. Would Bain use him if he had to? Jess guessed that yes, he would. That was one of their skills, after all.

No sentimentality. You just achieved your goals, there was nothing personal involved. Jess glanced up to find Dev still watching her in the reflection, a look of worried trust on her face.

Yeah. Nothing personal. Jess sighed and rubbed her temples.

HARD TO SAY which one of them was more relieved when they came around the last bend of ice in the middle of a sleet storm and saw the iceberg that housed the fisherman's main docking facility. The place was deserted, according to the scanner, which picked up only the residual markers of their carrier itself.

Dev set the old carrier down outside on top of the ice sheet, and shut it down as quickly as she could. The engine pods had almost stopped generating power, and though she hadn't wanted to bother Jess with it, since her partner seemed to be thinking hard, their environmental systems had shut down a short time before.

She released her restraints and put on her jacket, fastening the catches as Jess opened the hatch and ducked a face-full of stinging sleet.

"Put your hood up." Jess seated her blaster and extended her crampons, turning her back to the wind as she got out of the decrepit vessel and fastened the chest straps on her pack. "Hurry up, Dev. Storm's getting worse."

Freaking storms. Dev was developing a true dislike for them, since they seemed to always be preventing them from getting somewhere they needed to be. She got her pack on and followed Jess, sucking in a shocked breath as the icy wind blasted her.

She grabbed the hatchway and held on. She was buffeted hard, then felt a grip on her arm and then Jess was pressed up against her. "Wow."

"Yeah." Jess locked arms with her and they moved cautiously along the ice, bending over to keep a lower profile against the wind. "Stay down. If it shifts and blows us into the water, we're screwed."

Dev didn't even bother wondering what that meant. "Okay." She took a firm hold on her partner and concentrated on keeping on her feet as they inched their way down the ice wall toward the water.

"Easy." Jess ducked, as a wave crashed against the wall and doused them both. "Oh crap."

Brr. Dev found words driven right out of her by the chill. She blinked hard to remove the seawater from her eyes and then grabbed for Jess as another wave caught her and almost pulled her off the wall. She gripped a crack in the ice with one hand, and hauled Jess back with the other, feeling the sting of the sleet against her skin.

Highly discomforting.

"Thanks." Jess got her grip on the ice back and glanced at her. "Let's get our asses down from here." She moved faster, hopping over some icicles and starting downward with Dev right behind her. They reached the base of the iceberg just as a rumbling peal of thunder vibrated through them and shivered loose a chunk of the ice wall.

"Jess!" Dev caught it out of the corner of her eye and bolted forward, thumping into Jess and sending her hopping forward as the ice crashed down behind them and dusted them with sharp, cold particles. "Oh!"

Jess went with the motion, hurdling the last chunks of ice and bolting into the ice cavern hidden by the curve of the burg. "Dev!" She twisted around, trying to catch sight of her. "Hey!"

"Right here." Dev skidded in after her, crashing into the wall as they were abruptly protected from the vicious weather. "Wow."

Jess pressed back against the wall and cautiously peered past the curve of it, wary even though the scan had marked it empty. You never could tell, after all. Sometimes the ice made comp crazy, and you could find yourself on the wrong end of a blaster that way.

But there were no boats in the dock, and the inside of the big cavern was, in fact, empty. Jess relaxed a little and moved in farther, running her eyes over the carrier parked on the rear deck. "Glad to see that thing."

"Me too," Dev said, quietly.

They walked quickly across the frozen floor and up the ramp to the back area, Jess striding ahead and touching the hatch pad on the side of their rig.

The hatch opened and the ramp extended, welcoming them with a scent of fresh new components and silicone. Jess waited for Dev to slip past her and then closed the hatch, sealing them into a small bit of peace and quiet and safety. She went over and stowed her pack, then went to her seat and dropped into it. "Ugh."

Dev got her own pack into its holding position and stripped out of her heavy outside jacket. She hung it on the back of her chair then sat down, very glad to feel the seat conform to her and swivel into position. It felt very good to be back in this space, and she took a moment to savor it before she faced the consoles and contemplated starting everything up. "Should we call the base?"

She looked in the mirror when Jess didn't answer, finding her peering up at the ceiling with her hands clasped over her stomach. "Jess? Maybe they'll tell us to go help Doctor Dan."

Jess got up and walked over, taking a seat on the ground next to Dev's chair. "They won't tell us that," she said, quietly. "They would already have sent us." She clasped her hands together, her long fingers twisting slightly. "Dev, we have to go back to base."

Dev exhaled. "What if they hurt him?" She asked, in a soft voice. "You said he was a friend, that he was part of Interforce, didn't you?

Wouldn't they want you to help?" She leaned forward and put her hand on Jess's wrist. "Why wouldn't they tell us to go help him?"

Jess sighed. "It's not that simple, Dev. They recalled us. That means they need us there. It might have something to do with them getting him out. They could have really damaged the citadel. People there could need help, too."

Dev fell silent. "I see," she finally murmured.

"So soon as it stops sleeting, and the winds drop, we'll get going. I'll blow up that old piece of junk on the way out so no one else can use it." Jess said. "Maybe...maybe when we get back there, I can talk to Bain. See if he'll let me take a squad out." She watched Dev's face, seeing the sadness of understanding there. She knew she wasn't fooling her. "Or maybe he won't, but we need to go back."

Dev knew if they waited even another little while, there would be no tracking the transports and she would never see Doctor Dan again. She knew it, and looking into Jess's pale eyes, she knew her partner knew it too. She also knew Jess didn't owe her any explanation and that her insistence was giving her a lot of discomfort.

It made her very unhappy.

Jess put a hand on her knee. Dev looked up to find an unexpected compassion in Jess's eyes, and that made her feel even more unhappy. "I'm sorry."

"S'okay." Jess rubbed her knee with the side of her thumb. "He's a friend. It's tough."

"Yes."

"I know," Jess said, looking away. "After my father retired, he kept low key as hell, but one day," she exhaled, "they got him. They took him. My mother called me and I went to ops and..." She stopped talking. "I argued with them and that's what got me four zaps."

Dev covered Jess's hand with her own, feeling a lot of discomfort both at her own upset and now at her partners. "Oh, Jess."

"They sent his body back in pieces," Jess said. "So it didn't help either of us."

Dev felt extreme discomfort, unsure of what to say.

"So I get it, Dev." Jess raised her eyes. "But if we break this rule, I'll get a lot more than four, and you'll end up going back topside."

Dev felt her heart give a double thump. "What?"

"They'll wash you out," Jess said. "They won't deal with a tech who breaks ranks—breaks rules." She saw Dev's eyes grow round and wide with horror. "They'll cancel your contract."

Back to the creche? Dev's mouth went dry and she knew a fear of a totally different kind. Back to the creche, and have to leave Jess?

Go back to being just one of the many?

Dev found out right at that moment just how human she actually was as she was flooded with an intense wash of utter self-interest that nearly made her faint. "I see." She took a breath and released it. "Okay.

I understand." Her eyes lifted to Jess's. "I don't want that to happen."

"No."

"I don't want to leave you," Dev added, in a very small voice.

"No," Jess repeated softly. "I don't want that either."

They both looked at each other, and at the same time, sighed. Dev licked her lips and swallowed. "I don't like thinking about this."

Jess grimaced a little. "Me, either." She got up and went to the dispenser, glancing outside. The sleet was still coming down and she could see huge rollers crashing against the iceberg's entrance. "Let's get something hot into us."

Dev swiveled around back to the controls, and started doing her preflight checks. The first thing she checked was the recorder, scanning it quickly to determine if anyone had approached the carrier.

They hadn't. She was glad. The systems were all as she'd left them, power levels were normal, everything seemed fine. Except for her. Dev spared a hand off the console to rub the bridge of her nose, hoping her stomach upset would go away before it overwhelmed her.

She checked comms, but other than the forwarded recall, there was nothing in storage. Still feeling a lot of discomfort, she started turning up systems, bringing the consoles online and spooling up the engines. Jess's words kept echoing in her head, though, and she felt her breathing tighten every time she thought about going topside.

It felt even worse than thinking about Doctor Dan.

Something in her knew that was selfish, but she was helpless against the chill in her guts even thinking about going back to her sterile little pod, and seeing the looks from everyone up there. Back to being a dev unit. Just another failed idea.

Oh. Ugh. And maybe—without Doctor Dan?

A shiver worked down her back. Dev forced herself to set aside her worry and focus on her work. Her work was important, and she knew Jess was counting on her to get them home.

Home. Dev swallowed hard and got everything online, slipping her ear cups on and tuning comms to listen. The external sensors of the carrier brought her the sound of the storm, and the crackling of ice and she nearly jumped when Jess very gently curled her hand around a warm cup. "Oh!"

"Take it easy." Jess patted her on the back. "Don't freak out on me, okay?"

Dev took a sip of the hot liquid. "I won't," she said. "I don't even know what a freak is, much less how to get one out." She exhaled slowly. "I hope the storm stops soon. I don't want us to get in trouble."

"It's gonna be fine, Dev. We'll work it all out when we get back. We don't...I don't think we have enough information to know what's going on anyway."

"Okay."

Jess let her hands drop onto Dev's shoulders, but she remained quiet. She watched the ruffled water as she started up an absent, gentle massage, listening to Dev swallow. As she felt her own breathing come under control, the tension under her fingertips relaxed.

Dev glanced at the comp. "I think met is showing a break," she said. "Should we go?"

"Go," Jess said, releasing her and returning to her console, dropping into her seat and fastening the body restraints. She felt the rumble of the engines as the power to them increased. She reached over and picked up her own tea cup, leaning back as the landing jets fired and they started to move.

She had a little time, now. Time for them to fly to the base, a long flight since they wouldn't be stopping at Quebec to break it.

Time for her to think, and to consider things. Review all the comp. "Want a snack, Dev? I'll fire something up once we get clear of the ice."

There was a long moment's silence, then Dev cleared her throat. "I'm not really hungry, thank you."

Jess sighed and closed her eyes. Plenty of time to deal with her freaking out tech. "Yeah, me either."

Maybe too much time.

IT WAS DARK and there was another storm. Dev rubbed her eyes, focusing hard on the forward scan that filled in details of their path she couldn't see through the window. Her shoulders were tense, and she was tired, but she'd kept quite the last few hours while Jess worked over the comp in her station.

A glance in the mirror showed her partner leaning forward, staring at the comp pad with her elbows resting on her knees and her chin braced on her fists, a perceptible furrow creasing her forehead.

Dev went back to her controls, flexing her hands a little as she checked the course. She had the carrier on autonav, but the weather was shoving them around a lot, and she didn't want to stray too far from the throttles.

Deciding they were on safe course for the moment, she triggered the release on her strapping and stood up, stretching her body out as she walked quietly over to the drink dispenser.

"How's met?" Jess asked, after a moment.

"We are going around the edge of a storm," Dev answered. She selected a beverage and watched as it was assembled. "I think once we get past it our flight will be smoother."

"Anything on comms?"

"No." Dev took her cup and turned, leaning against the console and regarding Jess. "Just two nav beacons on autonomous."

Jess leaned back in her chair and put her hands behind her head. "That's strange," she said. "Should be some chatter." She regarded Dev's slim form, encased in its lined jumpsuit. "Do an all scan and see if you pick anything up. At the least, Northern should be checking in. We're not far from there."

Dev nodded. "I will," she said. "Do you think someone saw or heard the other machine blowing up?"

Jess's lips tensed into a smile. "You'd think, huh? That old training cave is inside Northern's scan range. I should get them on comms and tell them I took care of their pirate problem for them."

"I think they will be surprised."

"I think you're right." Jess pulled a pad over and synced comms to her station. She put her headset on and tapped out a code, setting the comms channel to scan the local bandwidths. "Let's see if they have a beacon out."

Dev went back to her seat, but didn't take it. She stood by her chair watching the consoles, giving her back a chance to straighten and lose its stiffness. She felt the rumble of the carrier's engines through the soles of her boots, and she resisted the urge to close her eyes.

She was still upset, and still worried about Doctor Dan. But she was also tired, and looking forward to getting back to the citadel. Maybe Jess was right, and they had more information about what had happened, and then they could figure out what to do about it.

Maybe they were already doing something about it. Maybe Bain might have sent someone out already to try and help, or at least find out where they were taking him.

She hoped so. Maybe by the time they got back to the citadel, it would be over and Doctor Dan would be safe. Dev leaned against the front console and looked out into the darkness. It would be nice to get just some time to rest and sleep, she reasoned, in the comfortable bed in her quarters.

"Huh."

Dev turned, and saw the frown on Jess's face. "What's wrong?"

"Not getting anything on scan," Jess muttered. "Not even a listening beacon."

"What does that mean?"

Jess folded her arms over her chest. "I'm not sure. It could just be met interference. Happens sometimes. Or maybe the rig at Northern got knocked off line. That happens sometimes too." Her eyes flicked over the pad. "I don't want to send a squirt out, it'll ident us."

Dev set her cup into its holder and walked back over to where Jess was sitting, coming round the side of the weapons console and looking at the comms display Jess had up. The spectrum was empty, that she could see herself, without even the background scatter she was used to flickering once in a while. "That is quiet."

"Too quiet," Jess said. Then she exhaled and pulled the pad over, bringing up the control surface and keying in an encrypted data channel. "I didn't really want to do this."

Dev just watched quietly, one hand on the back of Jess's seat, as she finished setting up the call request and initiated it. She pressed her ear cup a little more firmly and concentrated, as they waited for a response.

For a very long moment there was nothing. Then a soft burble sounded and the comms link went from pulsing to green. "Ten, ten," Jess said.

"Ack," the response came back.

"Inbound, passed North. No sig," Jess reported.

"Ack," the response repeated. "Standby."

Jess settled back in her seat. "Least we got a response," she said. "I wonder if they heard something."

"Drake."

The voice coming back startled both of them, and made Jess lean forward. "Here, sir." She started moving her knee in a nervous motion.

"Don't bother with North," Bain said. "Where the hell have you been?"

"As far as Market Island, sir. Had to transfer back via boat, steal a pirate's old carrier, blow that up, get my bus back, and now we're inbound," Jess said, succinctly. "Situation?"

"Just get here as soon as you can, Drake," Bain said. "We've got trouble."

Jess felt a mixture of excitement and pleasure, along with a tinge of apprehension. "Ack." She fell back into battle speech.

"Tell him about Doctor Dan?" Dev whispered, anxiously watching her face.

Jess hesitated, then triggered the comms again. "Sir."

"Drake?"

"We spotted two black trans outbound with battle damage."

Now the silence was on the other end. "Ah," Bain finally said. "Interesting coincidence."

Jess and Dev exchanged looks. "I'll squirt the comp," Jess said, when the silence continued. "We saw activity."

"Do not bother, Drake. Just get here," Bain said. "Out."

Jess studied the closed channel for a moment, then reached up and canceled the sub carrier. "So."

Dev went back to her area and sat down in her chair, triggering the restraints. She leaned forward into flight position, and ran her eyes over the controls, trying hard not to throw up her recently drunk tea. "So I guess you were correct," she said, after a minute. "They wouldn't send us."

"No, I figured they wouldn't," Jess answered quietly. "They knew what my vector was. They'd have rerouted us when they sent the recall."

"I see."

"Sorry, Dev."

"It's all right," Dev said, after a bit.

Jess got up and came over, sitting down on the carrier deck next to her chair and leaning back against the console. She extended her long legs out and sighed. "Let's wait until we get back and find out what happened," she said. "I know I keep saying that, but I don't know what else to tell you."

Dev glanced down at her. "It really is okay," she said. "I just remembered something that Doctor Dan once told me. He said it was so important to get all the facts first, before you do something because, for example, if you're thinking of walking out a door, it would be very helpful to know first if there was vacuum outside."

Jess chuckled softly. "Yeah. It's a hoary old saying in the corps. Know what teeth are in the mouth you're sticking your hand into." She reached over and put her hand on Dev's calf. "Glad you get that."

Dev did get it. She wasn't entirely sure she agreed with it, but she understood that she had very few options to do anything else. One of the other things she'd learned from Doctor Dan was patience, and now she knew she had to be patient and wait to see what would happen.

"Want some rations?" Jess asked. "We've got another twelve to the base."

"Yes," Dev said. "But maybe we could get some rest. My eyes are bothering me. We're past the storm now and met's clear the rest of the way."

Jess smiled more easily. "In that case, let me get the bunks set up. Chances are we don't get any downtime when we get back, so we'll take advantage of some good weather now." She got up and patted Dev's shoulder, heading back to the rear of the carrier to put the sleep platform in place.

She wasn't sure if she should feel anxious or not. The fact they'd gotten Bain on the wire as soon as she called in seemed like it was a good thing, but he'd sounded pissed off about her taking so much time to get back. She pulled the shelf down into place, and popped the doors on the sleep bag storage, tugging the two plush bags out and sliding them into place.

Well, she'd been halfway across the planet on a mission. Jess patted the two bags and turned to rummage in the ration case when she stopped, staring into it as her mind registered what she was doing. She looked over at Dev, who was taking readings and adjusting knobs, pretty much what a tech was supposed to do, but here she was not only catering to her partner, but enjoying doing so.

What the hell?

"Thank you." Dev had joined her. "Should I get you some tea?"

"Um." Jess pulled out two ration kits and handed her one. "Yeah, sure. Thanks." She sat down on one of the fold out stools and opened her meal. It was fish rolls and mushroom cakes, and just looking at it felt like being back in the citadel. "That stuff on the boat was better than most of this."

Dev was seated next to her, busy with her own box. "Do you not like it?" She took a bite of the fish roll. "I think it's fine. A lot better than some of the things we had in the creche." She felt a sense of anxiety thinking about that, a mental image of looking at those sterile trays coming into her mind. "The food on the boat was good too, but the best thing was those shrimps."

"In Quebec?"

"Yes."

It seemed so long ago. Jess smiled, and bit into her fish roll. "We'll get back there again," she said. "Y'know they have a winter festival in a month or two. We can go for that. Most of the citadel does."

"Is that like a party?"

"A little." Jess felt herself relaxing. "But it's more fun."

Dev remained quiet for a while. "I think I'd like that very much," she finally said, when they were almost finished. "I hope we get a chance to do it."

"We will. I promise." Jess put her wrapping away in the recycling bin and unzipped her jumpsuit, stripping it off and letting it hang from her waist. She sat down on the edge of the sleeping platform and pulled the aid kit from the drawer underneath it, removing a cleaning pad and wiping off the almost healed wound on her shoulder.

Dev finished her tea, setting the cup into the holder and walking over to the sleeping shelf. She pulled the catches down on her over-suit and took it off. That left her in her under-suit, and she sat down on the shelf, letting her legs dangle as she waited for Jess to finish. "Your cut is almost gone."

"Yeah." Jess had smeared some antiseptic cream on the jagged line. "Just don't like to take chances, 'specially after that damn stab in the back."

Dev reached out and stroked her arm, tracing the burned in patterns. "Jess, can I ask you something?"

"Sure." Jess eyed her.

"Can I get one of these when we get back?"

Jess stopped moving. "One of what...one of these?" She pointed at her markings, watching her partner nod. "You don't have to do that, Dev. Techs don't."

"I know. You said that," Dev said, in a calm voice. "But, if they do end up sending me back, I would like to have one so I can remember it." She looked away. "And remember you."

Jess sat there, stunned. Both by Dev's words and by the gut wrenching upset they stirred in her. She opened her mouth to deny the possibility and then stopped, finding herself unwilling to lie to Dev. Or to herself for that matter.

"Sometimes," Dev continued quietly, "they take stuff from you. In programming. They erase stuff." She gazed thoughtfully at her feet. "But I don't think they can take one of those things away from me."

"Dev."

"Doctor Dan said he'd make sure I could keep everything but..." Dev paused. "I don't know what's going to happen now."

Jess let her hand fall and exhaled. "Yeah, okay. If you really want one I'll do it for you," she said. "Give you one for the last run we did, and this one even though we didn't finish it out."

Dev nodded in what looked like relief. "Thank you. I'm sorry if that caused you discomfort."

Jess finished her tending. "Yeah well it's gonna cause me a lot more discomfort if they try to send you back, because they're going to have to go through me to do it." She pulled up her under-suit and stripped out of the jumpsuit, draping it over the bars and hoisting herself up onto the sleeping platform next to Dev. "Discomfort to the point of blowing my head off. Lay down. Let's get some rest."

The lights dimmed as they both settled down next to each other, the soft rumble of the engines sending a rhythmic vibration through them. Jess folded her hands over her stomach and looked up at the overhead, visible in the dim lighting as a blur of gray dark weave.

After a few minutes she turned her head, to see Dev curled up on her side, head resting on her arm, eyes closed. As she watched Dev's face, those eyes opened and met hers. She felt the physical sadness there, and reached out to put her hand on Dev's arm. "We'll be okay, Dev."

Dev smiled and put her fingers over Jess's, letting her eyes close again.

Jess closed her own eyes and let her mind go still, only to be nudged by a memory that surprised her. Her father joined her for an unexpected dinner at the citadel.

She hadn't even known he was visiting. He had just shown up at the entrance to her quarters that night and she'd been so happy to see him she hadn't thought to ask him why he was there.

Plain dinner, just talk about home, and family, and her progress in the corps. She'd said something about them, and us, and her father had swirled his drink in his cup and sipped it, watching her over its rim.

"Jesslyn. Those are powerful words, us and them," he'd said. "Be careful. One day you might find yourself to be the us, and this—" He'd circled his finger to include the citadel. "Might be them."

She hadn't understood then. But now, lying here in the dim light, she suddenly did. Because when she'd just said, "We'll be okay." Her and Dev had been we, and Interforce had somehow, become them.

Chapter Three

DEV TOOK THE controls as they came within range of the citadel. From the outside, the huge cliff side looked unharmed, and in the pale gray light of midday there was little action to be seen around it. "Control, this is BR270006, inbound," she enunciated carefully into the comms, once the short-range beam had come up.

"BR270006, acknowledge." Control came back in response. "Standby for deck open."

"Sounds normal," Jess said, from her fully strapped down and activated position. She had her hands on the weapons controls and the guns had power, but were for the moment quiescent.

Having little to compare it against, Dev just nodded. She curved the carrier around the craggy peak and then slowed to hover, as the hanger roof started to peel back.

She felt well, and rested. They had slept almost all the way back, and she'd woken to find herself tucked into Jess's arms, which had surprised her but in a very good way.

It wasn't even raining. Hadn't been for several hours, and Dev wondered if they might have a minute or two to go to that little shelf and look out at the sea.

The roof finished retracting, and Dev tipped the carrier forward a little, inspecting her path before she settled lower and engaged the landing jets. "We're entering the bay."

She saw the weapons active indicators switch off, as she gently moved lower into the cavern, descending through the rings of lights. "Control, this is BR270006 requesting a landing pad."

"Stand by, BR270006."

Dev could see a lot of activity around the cavern, there were at least ten carriers on pads, and four more in tech prep, more than she'd seen there before.

"BR270006, please land pad 67, stay to taxi path."

"Acknowledged." Dev located the slot and boosted a little, sliding over and then descending to the pad where she could see a tech team waiting for them. She let the carrier down lightly and then cut the jets, shunting power back from the engines to the battery store.

Despite how discomfiting it all was, she was glad to be back in the citadel. There was a safety there that made her relax, having the solid walls around them. "Landed."

"Felt it." Jess shut down her station and released her restraints. "Send the logs and let's get our gear off."

Dev waited for the hookup to latch on, and the lights went out briefly as they switched to ground power. She ran through the shutdown process and saw, from the corner of her eye, the crew coming in to service them. No foam spray this time, just quiet, serious faces intent on the external ports and the engine servicing.

Jess chuckled. "Bet they're glad we brought it back in one piece this time."

"Almost. There is some damage to the rear, and one side," Dev said. "But not like last time." She saw the incoming log request and set up the sync, then shut the comp down. "Done."

Jess was standing in the rear, stuffing things in her pack. "Busy outside."

"Very." Dev finished putting her things away and swung her pack to her back, cinching the straps tight and walking back to join Jess. "Okay to open the hatch?"

"Sure." Jess got her pack closed and ran one final check on the weapons rack, making sure all the portables were shut down. She got behind Dev as the hatch opened, blinking a little at the flood of mechanical chaos that flooded in. "Wow."

A speaker clicked on overhead. "Drake, NM-Dev-1, to debrief, urgent."

"Ah." Jess felt paradoxically relieved. "Let's go, Devvie." She followed Dev down the ramp and onto the walkway, lifting a hand to return the greeting of some of the senior mechs. "Let's find out what the hell's going on."

Dev paused and stepped a little to the side to let Jess get ahead of her, and then she followed down the hall and through the gateway into the security passage that led to the debrief rooms. There was no one else heading that way, and they didn't meet anyone.

Jess paused before the door and put her hand on the pad. "Drake, NM-Dev-1 for debrief."

The door slid open and they went inside. A fraction of a second later, Stephen Bock and Bain entered from the other door, both looking harried and upset.

"Stephen." Jess greeted their supervisor. "Sir." She gave Bain a nod, as she sat down in one of the comfortable chairs. "Sorry it took us so long to get back here. We were far outland."

"So you said." Bain leaned against the table. "Glad you are finally back." He turned his attention to Dev. "And you too, my dear."

"Sir," Dev replied briefly, folding her hands on the table.

Bock sat down and rubbed his temples. "Where do I start."

"Agent Drake already knows part of the matter," Bain said. "She saw the transports, and I assume by the way she said it, the unwilling passenger aboard."

"It's in the comp," Jess said. "But yes, we saw Doctor Kurok."

Bain studied her. "And you didn't go after them?"

Jess leaned back in her seat. "We weren't in our carrier at the time," she said. "We were in an old rig being used by ice pirates to give Interforce a bad name. Wouldn't have lasted five minutes in chasing them."

Both men stared at her.

"Ice pirates?" Stephen Bock repeated. "We got a squirt about that from Northern. Said you'd gone crazy looking for ice pirates in the Northlands."

"So crazy I found them," Jess said, in a mild voice. "More to the point, they found me, attacking a fishing craft halfway through no man's land."

"I added the information to the comp transfer," Dev spoke up for the first time. "I got it on the portable scanner."

Bain and Bock looked at each other. "This rather changes matters," Bain said cryptically. "Drake, how close did you get to target?"

"We'd just left Market Island when we were recalled," Jess said. "So probably...six hours?"

"Shit," Bock cursed. "It was a double cross."

Jess looked from him to Bain. "Mind telling us what's going on?" she asked. "We were damn close to terminus on this." She indicated the screen. "Roll comp. See for yourself."

Bain grunted and sat down. "As Bock here said, where to start."

"I don't even think the beginning will help." Bock covered his eyes with one hand. "Shit."

DEV REGARDED THE stone wall in her shower, the slate dark in contrast from the water she was standing in the path of. It felt wonderful, hot and mineral scented as it warmed her body and rinsed all the travel stains off her. She soaped herself clean and rinsed off, then shut the water down and got out to dry herself.

She put on fresh under things and a clean off-shift jumpsuit and settled behind her workspace, regarding her quarters and thinking about everything she'd just learned.

The transports had been an envoy from the other side, coming to talk a truce, caused by the destruction she and Jess had caused. Scientists, they'd met with Bain, and Doctor Dan too. Doctor Dan had agreed to go with them, along with some other Interforce people, to a place to sit and talk, in a neutral area.

So Jess had been right. Exactly right when she'd said they didn't know everything.

They had been recalled along with all the other teams so that nothing bad would happen while they were talking. Dev understood that well, and Jess had nodded, too. That would have put the people talking in danger, and if they had reacted then maybe Doctor Dan and the others would have been killed.

So Jess had been doubly right.

But then they had gotten a message, short and desperate, saying it was all wrong, and Doctor Dan and the others were being taken back to the bad guy's place.

And then the people at North Base had tried to stop them.

They didn't know what happened there, but no communication had been received from that base since.

Jess had been very angry at all of them, asking how they could have believed the other side wanted a truce? Bain just said that sometimes you have to take a chance.

Take a chance? Dev exhaled. So now Doctor Dan, and the people from Interforce were somewhere being held and they couldn't do anything about it because everyone thought they would be hurt if they tried to get them back.

So they were trying to figure out what to do, and that's also why they hadn't just sent them after the transports.

It would have been very wrong for them to chase the transports. Dev felt a little humble, remembering what she'd thought about letting them go, and why they hadn't just gone to help.

But all the teams were here now. Surely they would make a plan, and just as surely, that plan would include her and Jess. Bain had even said they'd been waiting for them to get back to decide what they were going to do about it. The man, Bock, said it was a shame they'd recalled them, because if they had finished their mission, they would have something to bargain with, and now they really didn't.

Bain said he thought the whole thing was to get them to stop Jess from her mission, and that Jess should be very flattered because they had turned over half the earth in the assumption that she'd have been successful.

Jess did seem happy about that, in a reserved kind of way. Dev just found herself wondering why Doctor Dan decided to go with them. He was smart. Wouldn't he have realized how unusual the request was?

Dev left off thinking for a while and got up, going to her dispenser and retrieving some kack and a package of the small seaweed crackers. She took them up to her relaxation area and lay down on the couch, very glad to have a few minutes just to sit quietly and, what was it Jess had called it? Decompress.

Which was really strange because where she came from, decompression was definitely not something anyone would find relaxing.

She sipped her drink and opened her crackers, nibbling on them and stretching her body out along the comfortable couch with a sense of contentment.

She paused as she heard sounds in the next room, the door closing and two voices.

Jess's, of course, and she thought the other one might be Jason.

Maybe Jess was getting her mark. Dev considered that, and hoped Jess would remember that she'd asked to get one too. She wasn't sure Jess really approved of it, but the more she thought about it, the more she really wanted one. If nothing else, if she ended up going back to the creche, for sure she'd be the only one there with one.

Unique. Dev regarded the ceiling. Unique even if they made another of her set, because that other Dev wouldn't have this mark. Only she would have it and she wanted that.

She faintly heard Jess laugh, and the male voice raise in exasperation. Then she pulled her book from her jumpsuit pocket and opened it up, bracing it against one upraised knee as she sipped her drink and started to read.

After a few pages, her comms beeped. Surprised, Dev regarded the small, embedded unit, then she put her cup down and reached over to trigger it. "Hello."

"Ah, hello, is that Dev?"

"Yes," Dev responded. "Clint?"

"Yeah, yeah, it's Clint. I heard you guys got back and just wanted to know if there was anything special you needed checked on the bus."

Dev considered that thoughtfully. "The port side took a pretty big hit and the rear panel," she said. "We escaped a cone and ended up in an ice cave for shelter."

"A cone?" Clint sounded confused.

"Yes, a big round thing in the storm, that made a lot of wind?"

"Oh. A tornado. Got it, we'll check. Glad you're back safe and sound."

Dev smiled. "Me too. It was a very exciting trip." She mentally marked down the tornado word, so she could call the cone the right thing the next time. "Thank you."

"Okay, well, later!" Clint said. "Bye."

"Bye." Dev closed the comms and nodded to herself. "He is a nice man." She decided, and then went back to her book, smiling when she came to one of her favorite parts.

"JASON, DON'T START with me." Jess dropped into her chair and indicated the one across from her. "It's not my damn fault I was halfway across the planet when this all went down."

"It was crazy." Jason sprawled across from her. "I thought the whole friggen base had chewed weed. Peace talks? Truces? I mean, what the fuck?"

Jess lifted her shoulders in a shrug. "Maybe they thought they could game them," she said. "Bain didn't say why he did it. Just threw the facts at me."

"Crazy." Jason shook his head. "I hear maybe they went for North?"

"I passed North on the way in. No comms, no scan, no nothing," Jess said. "Dev couldn't even pick up a sideband."

Jason shook his head again. Then he eyed Jess. "How's the kid doing?" he asked. "See she brought your bus in right side up this time."

"She's fucking brilliant," Jess said bluntly. "Best tech I've ever seen."

"You shitting me?" Jason leaned forward. "She's been here two weeks."

"Drives the bus." Jess ticked off her fingers. "Drove an antique bus probably older than I am, that neither of us could have started up. Drove a damn fishing boat. Rigged the damn portable scanner to penetrate the water and find a god damned school of fish big enough to fill their whole tank."

"No shit."

"No shit." Jess picked up her steaming cup of grog and sipped it. "Started off thinking this was bullshit, but no more. Wouldn't trade her for nothing."

"Huh." Jason grunted. "At least the whole tech thing's settled down. No one thinks they're going to get a knife in the back so much. Everyone figured he was turned and that's it."

Jess considered that. "Or that's what everyone wants to believe, either to avoid getting another bio alt, or just because that's what they want to believe."

Jason shrugged. "We're working again," he said. "The other newbs are settling down." He studied Jess. "Sandy didn't respond to recall."

Jess straightened up. "What?"

"Was out on a recon south. Got a positive accept on the recall, but no response. No one's heard from her for two days. Comp lost contact with her signal after the recall. Bock's going to send a team out to see if they see anything at her last coordinates."

"Damn." Jess frowned. "I saw a couple of the regulars at Quebec. Couple more at Market Island, and the old shark was at the fishery. No one came after me though. Market boys made me, and I offed Brenegan."

"Yeah?" Jason looked surprised. "Didn't hear that on the recap in ops."

"Just filed." She indicated the pad. "Wanted to make sure Dev got all her props. She handled being in the out lands like an old timer."

Jason smiled a little. "You like her."

Jess looked away, then back at him. "Yeah, I really do," she said in a straightforward tone. "Never worked with another female before. A lot less of that competitive crap." She opened the desk storage and removed a bag, opening it and pulling something out. She tossed it to him. "Here. Fell all over the deck of the boat when Dev got us out of that damn volcano going off on Market."

Jason whistled, and his eyes widened. "Wow. Nice one!" He held the black diamond up to the light. "Clean!"

"Big blast."

He glanced at her. "For me?" He held the stone up, grinning when she nodded. "Sweet! Thanks, bud." He tucked the diamond away. "You give one to Dev?" he asked, with a teasing tone to his voice.

"She's got her own bag," Jess said dryly. "I split the take with her. Only fair since I'd be fish food if she hadn't figured out how to out power two long guns heading out after us."

"She's allowed to own that stuff? She's a jelly bag, remember," Jason said. "I don't think they own stuff."

"She's a field tech and they do own stuff," Jess said. "Let 'em argue with me about it. Can't have it both ways, Jase—if she's got her life on the line for us, and doing the job—you can't come back and say she's just a bio."

"Huh." He grunted. "Well, anyway, you want your mark? I figure we're all gonna be headed outbound real soon so might as well do it now." He removed the heat gun that had been holstered at his hip. "Too bad you didn't get to go all the way on it, Jess. I heard talk in the mess it would have been a real big score."

Jess stood up and came around the side of the workspace, unfastening her jumpsuit and pulling it down. "Yeah." She took the seat next to Jason and braced her arm. "So give me two kills, and two levels. Leave the third level blank. Who knows, maybe I'll get to go back?"

"No med for you this time, though."

Jess smiled. "No, just this hit." She touched her chest, and the fading wound. "And that was my own stupidity, on the boat. That's where the first kill was."

"Guy you asked for ident on?"

"Yeah. He was with the pirates. Led the attack on the boat." She indicated the bag. "I brought back his tags. Was he active? Name wasn't familiar."

"Disappeared. Used to be one of Sydney's boys." Jason heated up the gun and put his hand on Jess's arm, picturing the pattern he was going to burn into her skin. "Way I heard it, there was some kind of three way action going between this guy, Sydney, and his tech."

"Huh." Now it was Jess's turn to grunt, and she did, taking a deep breath as she heard the gun trigger. "They were working the Northlands. Maybe he was doing it to trash old Syd's rep."

"Ready."

"Go." Jess closed her eyes, as the heat and pain started. "Maybe that's why he shut down when I asked him about the pirates."

"And why he sent that squirt." The soft sizzle of burning flesh was loud between them. Jason carefully traced the outline of the mark. "Bastard's always had it in for you."

"I screwed him over." Jess kept her breathing even. "He has reason."

"Does he? Way I heard it he brought it on himself," Jason said. "Color."

The buzz changed slightly and the burn became more intense. Jess kept her head down, the pain bothering her more than usual. Maybe she was still tired. "Yeah maybe." She exhaled. "Dev wants me to give her one of these."

The buzz stopped and Jason leaned forward to look her in the eye. "What?"

"What part of that didn't you get?" Jess asked. "Finish the damn thing so I can stop sweating."

The buzz resumed and she closed her eyes again, and the silence extended until it was finally over. Jess straightened up and ran her fingers through her hair, glancing at the red raw burn on her arm "Thanks."

Jason put the gun down. "Did I hear you right? Your rag doll wants a mark?"

Jess erupted up out of her seat so fast it startled both of them, and the loud crack as her fist hit his face echoed harshly against the walls. "Don't fucking call her that!" She lunged at him and took them both to the floor, seeing red in her vision as a growl emerged from her throat.

"Jess! Jess!" Jason rolled onto his back and put his hands flat on the floor. "Jess! Hold it! Stop! I'm sorry!" He kept his breathing steady as he saw the ice cold eyes bore right through him. "I'm down. I'm sorry, Jess. Sorry."

For a moment the mask didn't change, and then Jess's eyes blinked and she released him, rocking back to take the weight of her knee off his chest. "That's my partner," Jess rasped. "Don't you say crap about her like that."

"Okay." He held his hands up. "Sorry, Jess. Didn't mean to trigger you."

Jess half stood and dropped back into the chair. "Yeah, been a long couple of days." She rested her elbows on her knees and exhaled. "Just don't be an asshole, okay?"

"Hey." He got up cautiously and sat in the other chair. "Maybe I'm jealous." He watched the tremors in her hands until they started to ease. "I'm not used to them being more than custodials, Jess. You've worked with her, I haven't."

"Yeah, I know." She slowly leaned back, feeling exhausted. "If we go out together, you'll see." She glanced at him, then got up and went to the sanitary unit, grabbing a cloth and wetting it, then bringing it back over. "Here."

He wiped his face, studying the blood that stained it. "You always had a truly kick ass punch," he stated mournfully. "She must be good cause you never hit me for dissing a tech before, no matter where they came from."

A soft knock came at the inner door, and after a pause it opened and Dev poked her head inside. "Everything correct in here?" she asked. "I heard a noise."

"You heard your partner breaking my nose," Jason said. "And I'll be on my way to med to get a reduction kit and plas." He got up and reached for the burn gun, but Jess put her hand over it. "Right. See you folks later." He kept the cloth against his face as he left, and the door slid shut behind him.

Dev crossed the floor with a diffident expression, sliding her book into her thigh pocket. "Are you all right?"

Jess gestured her toward the other chair. "Yeah, I'm fine. Just got ticked off at something he said." She propped her arm upon the desk. "He just finished giving me this."

Dev leaned closer to examine the mark. "Oh." She clasped her hands. "Can I get that one?"

Jess grimaced. "You really want one?" she asked. "It hurts. Really hurts."

"Yes, I do," Dev responded at once. "Will you do it? I'd rather if you would." She reached over and put her hands over Jess's. "That would make it very special."

Jess felt her heart rate settle, and her body relaxed as she looked into Dev's eyes. The anger finally leached out, and with it went the twitching and the urge to hurt something. It had surprised her, that reaction, but now seeing the look of somber affection bathing her, it didn't surprise her any more.

She was caught. A faint smile appeared on her face. "I'll do it." She leaned forward and brushed her lips against Dev's. "And maybe we'll get lucky and we'll get a night at home tonight."

Dev's eyes brightened, and she grinned. "I'd like that."

"Me too." Jess picked up the burn gun and adjusted it. "Take your suit down, partner. Let's make you a marked one."

Dev felt a sense of crazy pride erupt in her. She undid the catches on her jumpsuit and pulled it down to her waist like Jess's was, straightening in the chair and tucking her boots under it. "Go ahead."

Jess put a hand on her shoulder and looked her in the eye. "It's really going to hurt." She warned her. "A point of pride with us is, you don't scream."

"Okay," Dev said. "I'm ready."

"I hope I am," Jess muttered, as she got the gun into position. "Hang on, here we go."

Dev heard the buzz a brief instant before it touched her arm, and then she blinked, as a searing pain lanced into her skin. It built faster than she'd expected, and she only barely had time to focus past it before her body reacted. She concentrated on her own heartbeat, hearing the hammering in her inner ear as the buzz grew and faded, and then grew again.

It did, as Jess had warned, really hurt. But she'd learned how to deal with that in the creche, in the long hours and days of various tests and trials, and the brief training on what it would be like if they did wrong and had to face discipline. So she thought of other things, of the things she'd shared with Jess, and their missions so far, and the cones, and the shrimps at Quebec and...

The buzz stopped. The pain didn't, but Jess put her hand on Dev's knee and she knew it was over. She opened her eyes and looked at her. "Did I do okay?"

Jess's lips tensed into a smile, one that warmed her eyes as well. "Like you'd been taking them for years," she said. "Let me get some cream for ya, and for mine too." She got up and went to the sanitary area, disappearing for a moment.

Dev took that time to look at her arm, which now had two areas of horribly reddened, burned skin visible. The pain was vivid, but it was now a throbbing ache rather than being on fire, and she examined the pattern with a sense of lightheaded fascination.

They started at the tip of her left shoulder, one set with some colored balls and bars, and then the second, with only two colored balls and an empty bar on the bottom. It was fuzzy and indistinct looking, due to the swelling, but she could see when it healed it would look like the brown marks that patterned Jess's arms.

That made her very happy, happy enough not to mind the pain. She looked up at Jess as she returned, and studied her new marks. "It's almost the same except for this bit." She indicated a small area on her skin.

"Uh huh." Jess carefully smeared some healing cream on herself, then turned her attention to Dev. "That little bit is mine. It means you are."

Dev felt lightheaded again. "I'm...yours?"

"Yes." Jess gently treated the burns she'd made on Dev's arm. "You are my partner, right?"

"Absolutely."

Jess finished putting a light gauze bandage on her, and handed her a small jar of the cream. "Put it on often. It'll help it heal," she said. "Hungry?"

"Yes."

"Let's go get some chow." She eased the jumpsuit up over Dev's shoulders and fastened it. "Know what?"

Dev flexed her hands a little, and gave a small nod. "No, what?"

"Glad you did that." Jess leaned forward and kissed her again and this time it went on for a while and she felt her breathing shorten as Dev's hands fit themselves along her ribs making her nape hairs prickle. It felt insanely good and it was very hard not to unfasten her suit and move over to the bed.

So hard. Dev's breath tickled her collarbone and then their lips met again and she knew she either had to pull back or take it forward and finally the newly scorched skin on her arm tipped the balance. Jess let her head rest against Dev's and savored the moment, as Dev very gently put her arms around her and gave her a hug.

That made her smile. She exhaled regretfully and stepped back, fastening her own suit and running her fingers through her hair. "I sure hope we won't be heading out until tomorrow."

Dev produced a rakish grin. "I hope so too," she said. "But I think it would be good to hurt a little less first." She regarded her arm. "You were right."

Jess ruffled her hair.

Dev shifted her gaze back to Jess. "You were also right about going after Doctor Dan. I'm sorry I gave you discomfort over that."

Jess rested her arms on her shoulders. "Trust me, Dev. I learned the hard way so you maybe won't have to." She grinned briefly. "C'mon. Let's go to the mess, then you can come back here and help me unpack this stuff of my father's my brother had sent here."

Dev regarded the bags and containers tucked against the wall. "Sure." She followed Jess out the door. "What is it?"

"What was left in the house." Jess evaded the moving bodies in the busy hallway. "Maybe you'll get lucky and get to see a picture of me as a kid."

Dev smiled and put the ache of her arm aside. "Excellent."

IT WAS LATE. Dev had put the cream on her arm, and was settled back on her relaxation couch in her tank top and short pants, after another shower, and dinner with Jess.

They were expecting some information. No one knew when that would happen for sure, and Jess was in the control place trying to figure it all out. There were two teams investigating, one that had gone north, and one south, and everyone was waiting for them to report.

The techs, herself, and the others, were sent to get some rest, so here she was, very comfortable and relaxed, glad to get some time to just be quiet.

Instead of reading, she had her headset on and she was listening to a comp report, items that had happened while she and Jess were gone. Updates to schedules, maintenance notes, a running inventory of detail she was glad to absorb and digest.

She'd gotten through one report, and halfway through another when the door between her quarters and Jess's opened and her partner stuck her head in. Dev waved at her and a moment later, Jess was trotting up the steps to join her in her space. She took her headset off and stopped the report. "Hello."

"Hey." Jess took a seat on the floor. "They got some real senior guys involved in talking to the other side. Trying to work out a deal."

"For Doctor Dan?" Dev felt heartened.

"For all of them," Jess said. "There were six of them who went."

"I see."

"So in the meantime we're just cleaning stuff up. They don't want me to leave the citadel, don't want a chance of the other side either grabbing me, or me causing a situation," Jess said with a brief grin. "So I guess we get some downtime."

Dev smiled back.

"They found Sandy," Jess went on, her face sobering. "Looks like they ran their carrier into an EMF swipe. Nothing much left of it."

Dev studied her. "They died?"

Jess nodded. "Both of them." She drew in a breath and let it out slowly. "Carrier was fizzled to nothing. Both of them inside. They're bringing the bodies back for ident and disposal."

That took a bit of thinking. "You said flying in that was dangerous."

"It is," Jess said. "Sandy knew that. Not sure what happened there." Which wasn't exactly true. She suspected Sandy decided to respond to the recall regardless of the danger and pushed it, figuring to get back first and pull whatever prime slot the emergency offered.

She, on the other hand, had stopped to rescue drowning polar bears. What did that really say about both of them?"

"That's very sad," Dev eventually said.

Jess grunted softly. "Anyway, wanna come over to my place?" She gave Dev a somewhat rakish grin. "Help me unpack those trunks?" She waggled her eyebrows. "Have a cup of grog?"

"Sure." Dev removed her headset and swung her legs off her couch. "That sounds excellent."

They crossed into Jess's quarters, which were lit with a quiet cool light around her workspace. There were the boxes that had been delivered earlier, and Jess pulled one closer to the chairs, gesturing Dev to take a seat while she diverted her own attention to a pair of mugs and a bottle.

"What are all these things, Jess?" Dev asked, regarding the dull gray cases. "You said they were from your family?"

"Not exactly." Jess poured out, then handed Dev a cup as she took a seat next to the box. "My mother decided she didn't want all the reminders of my father around the house. So she had my brother send them here. He figured I'd appreciate them, or something like that."

"Oh."

Jess took a sip from her cup then put it down. "So let's see what we got. I figure most of this is from his office in the house. He used to keep all his souvenirs there." She touched the panel on the box, which glowed briefly and then retracted, and the top of the case slid open.

A puff of air emerged, full of the smell of paper, and steel. Jess peered inside, and lifted out the first thing in it. She put it on the worktable and went back for a second. "That's a fishing award he got from the compound we lived at."

Dev picked it up and looked at it. It was a piece of stone or rock, carved into the shape of a fish, half curved around. "An award?"

"Yeah." Jess studied a worn blaster, side mount and very old, covered in rakes and scars. "Every year they had a competition who could free-dive and catch the most. He won that time. I remember it, sorta.

Dev put the item down. "Is that like the fisher people on the boat?"

"No." Jess put the blaster down and dug for something else. "That's with nets and mech and stuff. For this, you just dive into the sea and catch the fish with your hands."

Dev's eyes opened very wide. "Really?"

"Yeah." Jess opened a folio, stiff and aged. "He was good at that. Could stay down forever." She leafed through a few pages of notes, handwritten, and almost illegible. Just common stuff, things they had to do around the house, stuff he had to pay off. "Ah." She opened the other side and saw color and images. "Here ya go."

She handed one of them over to Dev. "That's me, on leave, around fifteen I guess."

"Ah!" Dev examined the image. It was Jess, but a slighter version of her in a gray jumpsuit like the ones the new people had arrived in. She had close cropped hair and a grudging smile in the picture, outside a structure. "You appear attractive."

Jess chuckled. "I look like a goon." She was sorting through the pictures. "Here, I was four in this one. You'd never know it was me."

Dev looked at the square, seeing a child with wild, curly dark hair dressed in a brief outfit that appeared wet. "What is that you have in your hand?"

"Conch shell," Jess said absently. She opened a folder tucked away in a back pocket of the case, finding a couple of very old plas images inside. "Here's one of my father at field school grad." She found herself smiling a little at the tall figure, standing with his hands clasped behind him with three other classmates.

Dev craned her head around to see it. "Oh," she said. "You look like him." The man in the picture had Jess's height and her dark hair, and their faces were shaped alike. "You smile the same."

"I do." Jess acknowledged. "He had gray eyes though, not these funny blue marbles." She put the picture down and went on to the next one.

Citadel, this one. "Must have been the intaking here," she mused. "Looks so different. That was before they rigged up that deck on top."

Her eyes tracked to the next picture in the stack, her eyes fastening first on her father's tall, relaxed form leaning against an old style carrier, and then drifting up to look at the second person in the picture.

She blinked.

She blinked again, a chill running down her back as she studied the shorter man, who was standing with arms folded. He was dressed in a techs dark green, blacked piped jumpsuit with her father's elbow resting casually on his shoulder.

Slowly, she turned the plas over, searching the back intently and finding a small, scrawled, handwritten note on it.

`Me and DJ, too young to know better.`

"Oh." She exhaled.

"Jess?"

Jess looked up, to find Dev watching her, brows knit a little. "Yeah?"

"Are you in discomfort?"

"Am I in discomfort," Jess repeated. She turned the plas back over and looked at it, then, with a little sigh, put it down on the table between them. "No. But I just figured out why your friend Doctor Dan reminded me of someone I thought I knew."

Dev gave her a puzzled look, then glanced down at the image and her eyebrows hiked almost to her hairline. Next to the man she now recognized as Jess's father was a much younger, but definitely recognizable, Doctor Dan himself. "Wow!" she blurted. "It's him!"

"It's him," Jess said in a quiet voice. "Must have been the first or second year after my dad came out of field." She touched the plas. "He was a tech, like you are," she added. "I knew he was one of us, but I didn't..." She fell silent. "Why the hell didn't Bain say something?"

"It was a long time ago." Dev was staring in fascination at the image. In it, Doctor Dan didn't look any older than she herself was, but she could see the look that was so familiar to her on his face, that half smile. She could almost see the twinkle in his eyes.

"Explains why you're so damn good at what you do," Jess said. "It wasn't some random programming. He knew what to give you because his gut knew it."

Yes, of course. Dev suddenly felt a mixture of emotion, relief and gratitude chief among them. "He was confident I could do this."

Jess studied her profile. "This wasn't a last minute project I bet." she said. "He had this in mind."

Dev nodded slightly. "Maybe," she said in a quiet voice. "I hope they get him back. I'd like to ask him."

"Yeah, me too." Jess sat back, still a little stunned. Not that Kurok had turned out to be Interforce, she'd known that for a while. But she hadn't expected him to come in that close.

Her father's partner.

His first partner, not the one who'd been with him when he retired. Jess remembered Janie. She'd retired two years after Jess became an agent, and she'd never liked the woman. Kurok had been his first, the one he rarely spoke of, but when he had, he'd always smiled.

DJ, he'd called him she now remembered, the very few times he'd called him anything at all.

She looked back at the plas. "Let's see what other surprises I can find in here." She went back to the images, but her mind lingered on the previous one, questions starting to surface she wasn't sure she really wanted to ask.

JESS LEANED BACK in her chair, finally finished sorting. On her workspace, she had the folder full of pictures, the blaster, a small hide pouch of old style coins, and a crypto locked recorder awaiting her attention.

It had been a somewhat weird, slightly uncomfortable ramble through her father's past. Aside from the surprise of the pictures, she'd found things he'd brought back from the field from sketches on pieces of slate to a heavy knit pullover she knew had come from the other side that even now held a faded bloodstain in the fabric of it.

Now there was the recording. Jess picked up the small device and touched it to her hand, feeling the faint twitch as it accessed the chips embedded under her skin, and with a tiny click an interface appeared.

Amiably, Jess attached it to her comp and waited as it spooled. It was keyed to her, but it could be anything from his recipes for fish to field notes. After a minute or two, the screen flickered on and presented her with a page full of text.

That surprised her, a little. It was not only text, but handwritten text, scanned in and cropped. She leaned forward and rested her elbows on her knees to read it, feeling a touch of unexpected anticipation.

Her relationship with her father had always been complicated, but maybe he'd left her a—Jess blinked and focused.

`Jesslyn.`

Well, no doubt it was for her.

`There's so much we'll never talk about that we should have. I hope this gets to you soon after I'm gone, but whenever it does, it does. It's the coward's way out, since I'll write things here I'd never have the courage to say to your face.`

Jess felt uncomfortable. This didn't sound like it was going to be fun, and she almost reached up to turn the comp off before her conscience got the better of her and she clenched her hands instead. Her eyes lifted and went to the door between her quarters and Dev's, and she suddenly wished her partner was there next to her.

And then she was embarrassed to even think that. She forced her attention back to the screen and picked up her grog cup to take a sip from it.

`You had no choice in what you became, Jess. Your mother and I bred knowing there was a good chance one` or more of you would take my genes. It hurt her when it was you because you were her little girl. She always figured it would be one of your brothers, but I knew from the start it would be you.

I had an inside look, after all. So if you're sorry it ended up like this, then I'm sorry because I knew it would. Luck of the genetic dice and all that. You never knew your grandfather, but I remember him showing up at my field school graduation and he gave me a piece of advice I'm going to pass along to you.

He told me to take life one day at a time, and enjoy it to the fullest because the bad times are a lot more frequent than the good ones.

That's true, Jess. I never realized it until it was too late. I was always too busy looking out for the next op, working the next angle to look life in the face and savor it. Don't make that mistake. I couldn't tell you that when I was still around, because the hypocrisy woulda killed me. Maybe you know what I mean by now.

Jess read and reread that, thinking hard about it.

You never took my path, though, so maybe not. When I last saw you, you were going your own way through the corps. I figured that it was at least your way, and you were showing signs of an independent mind. I can't tell you how sad and proud that made me.

She stood up and went to the dispenser, punching the code for some tea and waiting for it to come out. The message was more confusing and painful than she'd figured it would be, though she took some solace from the last little bit of it. She'd been so sure he'd thought she'd disgraced him.

Jess took the cup and sipped from it, waiting for her breathing to settle before she went back to the desk and settled into her chair behind it.

Anyway. I don't really have that much to say to you besides that. I don't know what got me in the end, or how it happened, or why, except I know it's them, that they finally got their revenge, that all those missions came home to me and I probably went in a room full of hateful sorts in a hell of a lot of pain.

Mark of my doing a good job for them, all those years, Jess, and with any luck, you'll have the same fate. I don't say that to be mean, kid, it's just what we are.

It was just what they were. Jess felt a little sad, reading that, and she remembered, sometimes, seeing that look of sadness in his eyes too.

> But I wanted to tell you this. If you're as much like me as I think you are, you'll never need to use it, but if you ever decide to go dark, and get lost, and you realize there's no place deep enough to hide you, then find an outpost and steal enough coin for a squirt up to bio station two. Ask for Dan Kurok. Tell him who you are.
>
> You'll be something to him. He'll help you. He's smart as hell and one of the best people I've ever known. He was a tech, and my first partner. And if I'm honest, he was also truly my last. Maybe I was just young, or maybe it was just one of those things, but I trusted DJ like no one else, and if I'd had as much courage as he did, my life would have been very different and you might never have been born.

Jess sat back and thought about that, not really sure what her father was trying to tell her. On the one hand, he would probably be amused to know that far from having to find Kurok, the man had actually come and found her. On the other, she wondered about trust and courage, and what all that really meant.

> At any rate, don't regret anything you've done, or will do, Jesslyn. You are who you are and you're from a long line of hell raisers and ass kickers, so do your best to fight like a devil and make no apologies. Maybe you and I can have a drink together wherever it is people like us end up.
>
> Dad.

Jess read the whole thing through again, and then she disconnected the reader and set it to one side. She picked up her cup and leaned back in her chair, and dimmed the lights a little, taking some time to just sit, and think.

DEV WOKE TO find herself in warm comfort, but a little surprised to find herself not alone in bed. She was on her side, but pressed up against her back was a still sleeping Jess, one of her long arms curled around Dev's body. It felt nice, and she remained still, enjoying the sensation.

It was just before dawn. The lighting in her quarters showed that, the faint hint of pale light reflecting what she would see outside and it reminded her again to ask Jess if they could maybe have a sandwich together out on the little ledge where they could see the water.

Or maybe, Dev considered their options. Maybe they could go swimming in the gym, after they got some rad.

Maybe they would hear some news about Doctor Dan.

Jess stirred behind her and then Dev felt a gentle pinch in the skin of her neck, putting a prickle up and down it. She lifted her head and peered behind her, to see Jess's eyes open, glinting softly in the dim light. "Hello."

"Hi, there," Jess rumbled back. "You mind me stealing half your bed?"

"No," Dev responded definitively. "Not at all."

"Good." Jess pulled her closer, and closed her eyes again. "Dev."

"Yes?"

"I'm going to try and talk Bain into letting us try to go and get your buddy back," Jess said. "I think we're the ones who can do it."

Dev's ears perked up, and she turned onto her back so she could see Jess better. "You do?"

"Sure. Don't you?" Jess propped her head up on her fist, leaving her other arm draped over Dev's stomach. "You want to see him back?"

"Absolutely! But I thought they said you should stay here, that we could cause trouble."

Jess nodded slowly. "Oh I'm sure we can cause trouble." She grinned briefly. "Anyway I'm going to ask him later. See what kind of mood he's in." She put her head back down on the pillow. "Worth a try anyway. If he'd send us out there, and we make good, that's a lot of props."

"I see," Dev mused. "That would be a good mission, wouldn't it." She fell briefly silent. "But I really don't want us to get in trouble, Jess."

"We won't." Jess tightened her grip. "Not if he sends us, right? I'm sure he wants to get him back. I just have to think of some good plan to get Bain interested." She studied Dev's profile. "You scared of having to go back up to station?"

Dev nodded silently.

"Didn't sound that bad when you talked about it," Jess said.

Dev wasn't really sure what to say about that. She felt bad about how she felt, and she didn't want to disappoint Jess. "I just like it here better," she said in a quiet voice.

"You like being a natural born better," Jess said, smiling faintly, watching the furrow appear between Dev's eyes. "Who wouldn't? I don't blame ya." She reached over and very gently traced one of Dev's fine, pale eyebrows. "Besides, I don't know what I'd do without ya anymore."

That felt nice. Dev felt her heartbeat, which had gone up, settle down. "We're not supposed to feel like that," she admitted. "We're not supposed to want to be like you."

"Dev." Jess touched her chin and turned her face so they were eye to eye. "You are like me."

It was wonderful, and it hurt. Wonderful because Jess was there, so close, looking at her with such a beautiful expression, and saying those things was wonderful. And it hurt because Dev knew it wasn't true. She reached up and touched the collar around her neck. "Not really."

"Tell me the difference between that, and these." Jess pointed at her arm. "At that, or this." She indicated the room around them. "You any more owned than I am?"

They were both silent for a while. Then Dev's expression shifted a little and she shook her head slightly. "That is an interesting question," she said. "But I still think we're different, Jess. I don't feel like I'm natural born."

Jess exhaled a little. "Then maybe I don't either." She felt strangely adrift, her mind still disturbed by her father's notes from the night before. "Maybe I always felt a little different."

Dev regarded her gravely.

"Or maybe I'm just being an asshole this morning," Jess said. "Let's get up and go mess around. I need some rad. Maybe that'll knock the gloom off me."

And so they did. An hour later Dev found herself dressed in an off-shift jumpsuit standing behind Jess in line in the mess. It was mostly empty this early and they claimed a small table on one of the upper levels, facing a tray full of processor provided items and hot kack filled mugs.

They were halfway through when Jason and Brent entered, waving casually at them as they went through the line and picked up their own breakfast. They came over carrying the trays and sat down at the table next to them. "Hey," Jason said, briefly.

"Hey," Jess answered. "What's the word?"

Jason shrugged. "Haven't been in ops yet today. You taking a turn?"

"Might as well."

Brent cleared his throat, and turned his head toward Dev. "Tech depot delivered yesterday," he said. "They got new mods in."

"Really?" Dev's ears perked. "Did any navigation comp boards come in, do you know? We need to replace ours."

Brent nodded. "Heard they did, and some gun systems tie ins. Gonna go scrounge after this. Interested?"

Jess's dark brow lifted sharply, and she gave Jason a look. He returned it with a mild expression and a half shrug.

"Sure," Dev readily agreed. "I wanted to run some system tests anyway, after our mission." She observed her now empty tray to make sure she hadn't missed any edibles, then she sipped her drink as the room started to fill.

Working on the carrier seemed like a good way to spend the morning. She could make sure their machine was optimal, in case Jess's plan worked out and they ended up going out again.

Elaine and Tucker entered, and plopped down next to them. "Well that sucked," Elaine said. "Just got off-shift in ops. I got the honor of doing the comms to Sandy's family."

Jason grimaced.

"Shuttle inbound," Tucker said. "Got some big shots coming about the swipe."

"Oh yeah, like we need more of them around," Jason grumbled. "I can't believe they haven't pulled together a response yet. I thought they'd be on it like sea lice when you got back, Jess, not put you in the can and sit around waiting for some gold suit to show up and tell us what to do."

"Huh," Jess said softly. "Bain must have something in mind."

Chapter Four

DEV GATHERED HER things, and looked over at Brent. "Would you like to go to the hangar?"

Brent nodded, and stood up, following her as they made their way across the getting crowded mess and headed out the corridor toward the hangar. As they cleared the intersection they heard boot steps hurrying after them and Brent paused and looked behind him. "Ah."

"Hi." Doug, one of the new techs caught up with them. "You all headed to the carrier bay? Mind if I tag along? Still trying to find my way around here."

"C'mon," Brent said gruffly and continued on his way.

Doug fell in next to Dev as they walked along. "So...uh...Dev...I heard you all were over on the other side. See anything interesting?"

"Yes," Dev said. "We saw polar bears, and sea lions, and some dolphins. I thought they were amazing." She glanced sideways at Brent, who had almost soundlessly chuckled.

"You did?" Doug looked at her with a quizzical expression. "What was so special about them?"

"I'd never seen any before," Dev said. "So it was a very interesting experience for me."

"Ah hah." Doug nodded. "So that was all?"

"Everything else is in the comp log," Dev said. "My programming instructed me to refrain from relating details outside that."

Doug studied her. "It did?"

"Yours did too," Brent told him. "Don't run your mouth off in the halls. Not everyone's field ops here." He paused and looked at Dev. "Maybe they should send the next class up in space for a while."

Dev assumed that was a compliment, and smiled in response. She reached up and palmed the latch to the hanger, pausing to let the other two techs go ahead of her as they entered the huge space. Even this early, it was very busy inside and the noise nearly made her cover her ears.

"Nice to have everyone busy again," Brent commented, as he observed the activity. "Hey, move over. They're opening the roof."

They all moved to one side and continued walking as the huge hatch ground its way open above them. They were halfway to the service bay when a klaxon blared out, and after a frozen second everyone blurred into motion. Techs on the floor dove for the protection of the service bays and anyone near an already open hatch jumped into it.

Dev found herself close enough to her own carrier to bolt for it, palming the hatch open and turning to wave Doug and Brent in. "This way!"

The two techs didn't hesitate an instant. They scrambled in and Dev followed, sealing the hatch as they heard a set of loud rumbling bangs.

"What the fuck?" Brent hopped forward to the front, so he could see out the wraparound windows, with Doug close behind him.

Dev went to her seat and sat down, powering up the carrier with automatic motions, bringing up comp quickly and starting an all scan. "What's going on?"

"Can't see." Brent flipped upside down so he could look up. "Get the screens on."

"Yes." Dev shunted power to the display systems and started her preflight check. "You should sit down," she told Doug. "In case we have to move."

Doug scrambled back to the gunner's seat and half fell into it, just as all the screens came live with a full view of the cavern around them. "Wow!"

Hovering overhead, limping down, was a carrier so battered and blackened it was hard to distinguish its outline. There were erratic flares emitting from its engine pods, and the landing jets were only partially firing. It was listing to one side sharply, and drifting erratically.

"Oh crap." Brent went flat on his back on the floor of the carrier, watching the screens. "If that thing blows it'll take half the cavern out."

Doug peered intently at the screen at Jess's station. "Can't even see the body number."

Dev put her ear buds in and retracted her seat restraints. "BR270006, central operations."

"Standby" The response came at once.

"What are you doing?" Brent asked. "You going to lift?"

"BR270006, centops. Status?"

Dev cleared her throat, programming kicking in strongly. "Centops, ready to fly if required."

"Standby."

All of a sudden Brent let out a yell as the half destroyed carrier near the ceiling pitched and rolled and headed groundward. Dev reacted instinctively, jettisoning the umbilicals and punching the landing jets hard, the carrier lunging off the deck and heading skyward at a steep angle.

Brent latched on to the console he was lying near and Doug snapped restraints in place as they took on multiple G, then Dev was leveling out and pointing the nose of her craft in a line bound to intercept the falling carrier.

There was barely even a moment to react, or be afraid before the impact. Dev flinched, but sent power to the jets as they both started groundward, feeling her carrier strain as a low rumble turned to a body shaking roar.

"Holy shit!" Brent curled himself around the console and covered his head. "You're nuts!"

Dev wasn't worried about that. She had her hands more than full with the carrier, fighting to keep control of it as the blaring horns outside rose to fever pitch and the shaking of the craft was making it hard for her to see as her eyeballs shivered from it.

She wasn't even sure what she was doing. She could feel the weight of the fractured craft above her forcing them down, and she knew she had only moments to decide what to do before they both crashed down onto the stone floor, or worse, onto another carrier.

She needed more power. There were voices clamoring around her but she stopped, in her head, and bore down hard for a second, just thinking. Then she ramped the forward jets up and killed the rear ones, the carrier nose tipping up for just long enough for her to kick in the mains.

"Holy shit." Brent whispered.

Now she had power. Dev concentrated hard, as their floorward drop stopped, and she let them hover briefly, playing the side jets with a careful touch as she moved them both over a clear spot and started to drop again.

Power increase here, decrease there, adjusting the thrusters and main engines in a delicate dance in three dimensions. She heard the klaxon cut off abruptly, then the low bong of the huge transport cranes in motion.

"They're gonna grab them off you!" Doug yelled, in excitement. "Stripe of a skunk!"

"BR270006." The comms bawled suddenly. "Hold in position! Hold! Hold!"

"Never heard ops do that before," Brent said, his eyes wide.

"Holding," Dev answered calmly, though she was panting a little, her own eyes big and round, her hands making adjustments almost every second as she watched the big crane swing over, its grapples dropping through the air with frightening speed.

A moment later, and they heard the clang as the grapples caught on, and Dev had just barely enough time to throttle back as the weight came off them and they nearly rocketed skyward. She tipped the carrier on its side and then rolled it over as she cut off the main engines and got the landing jets back in control.

"Ahhh!" Brent yelped, as he was spun in the air, his arms suspending him from the console as they inverted, then returned to standard orientation.

"Sorry about that." They were up near the ceiling now, and Dev tipped them forward a little so they could see the grapples moving the rescued carrier over to one of the service bays, where emergency teams were racing. "They got them!"

"Holy shit that was crazy making," Brent blurted. "How in the hell did you learn to drive like that?"

Dev waited a bit for her hands to stop shaking and then she let out a breath. "That was interesting," she muttered, before she triggered comms. "BR270006 to central operations, cleared to return to pad?"

There was a bit of silence before comms answered. "BR270006 cleared," they finally answered, with a roar of sound in the background, of voices and alerts.

"Thank you." Dev shut down the engines and adjusted the jets, lowering them back to their landing pad as quickly as she could, and feeling the intense tension in her body relax as they touched down and she could power down. She let her hands rest on the chair arms for a moment, then she started her shut down procedures. "That." She half turned to face Doug and Brent. "Isn't programming."

"That's crazy." Brent sat up and rubbed his elbow. "You mean you didn't learn it?"

Dev shook her head. "Programming lets me know what buttons to push and how to make things work, but when I'm doing this." She looked at her hands. "I just do it."

Doug released the restraints on the chair and leaned forward. "You know what?" He eyed her. "That's hot."

Dev swung around in her chair and regarded him, her head cocking to one side. "What?"

"That's hot," he repeated. "You're the bomb."

There was no real time to answer, because motion caught her eye and Dev turned to see Jess barreling toward them at top speed, leaping over bays and tools in a powerful flow of motion that immediately focused her attention. She released her restraints and stood up, her legs feeling a bit shaky as she moved across the floor of the carrier and triggered the hatch.

Jess bounded inside a breath later. "Are you all right?"

Dev looked around, then at her, then she nodded. "Yes," she replied. "I think Brent bumped his head, though, when we inverted."

"That was crazy." Doug hastily vacated Jess' s station.

Brent got up off the floor and dusted himself off. "No, that wasn't crazy," he said. "That was just mad skills. She's got them." He gave Jess a brief nod, then he slipped past her, with Doug at his heels, leaving Jess and Dev alone together in the carrier, the hatch sliding shut behind them.

Jess put her hands on her hips. "I think everyone in this place now knows you have mad skills," she said wryly. "Whole ops center nearly went out of their minds when you lit off the rockets."

Dev wasn't sure if this was all good or bad. "I had to," she said. "The jets weren't enough to keep us from crashing."

"I know." Jess grinned. "But pretty much no one would have had the guts to do that because you could have sent yourself into the cavern wall."

"I wouldn't have done that," Dev said, seriously. "Really." She looked past Jess. "Who was that? What was wrong with that machine?"

Jess turned. "Let's go find out." She paused, then turned back again, putting her arms around Dev and giving her a hug. "Glad you're okay," she muttered. "You kind of freaked me out a little."

Dev happily returned the embrace, reasoning it probably meant she did more or less the right things. "I didn't mean to," she said. "I just wanted to help that carrier."

"If anyone's still alive in that thing, you saved them." Jess turned and triggered the hatch. "Let's go see." She walked out with Dev right behind her. "You put a dent in the roof?"

"I hope not," Dev said.

They cleared the pad, and as they did, Dev realized they were the center of attention. Then she paused in her mind, and realized actually that she was the center of attention. All techs had been climbing up out of the pits and they were staring at her with wide eyes. Even the maintenance supervisors were standing there, watching them walk by.

"Was that incorrect?" she asked Jess, a little embarrassed by the focus. "What I did?"

Jess put her hand on her shoulder as they walked. "No," she said after a long silence. "You did the right thing. Everyone is just sort of surprised that you decided to do it."

"They are?"

Jess nodded. "But I wasn't," she added. "Let's find out what's going on, then we can talk about it."

Dev felt better about that. She didn't think she was going to get in trouble, or that Jess was upset with her. But she hadn't really thought about that before she acted, and that did bother her.

Think and then act. That was what Doctor Dan always taught them.

Safety teams were spraying down the damaged carrier, and as they arrived at the work pad Jason and Elaine joined them, along with two of the new agent teams. Doug's partner April was there, and Mike Arias came trotting up with his partner Chester as they all came to a halt beyond the safety zone.

"Holy crap," Jason said, after a brief pause. "Looks like that thing flew through a volcano."

A medical team raced past, ignoring the potential danger as they set up a triage point. Stephen Bock followed them, but paused at the group of agents on the ramp, stopping right in front of Dev. "They program you for flights into insanity?"

Jess bristled.

Dev took the question at face value though. "No, I don't think so," she said. "Just a lot about how to fly a carrier, and a little bit about parabolic dynamics." She paused. "And physics."

Bock looked at her, then looked at Jess, taking a half step back at the expression he found on her face. Then he shook his head and went up to the med point. "Let's just hope it was worth it," he called back over his shoulder. "And there's something still alive in this thing."

"He is in discomfort," Dev said, mournfully.

Jess relaxed, and chuckled softly under her breath. "All along, they've said you can't use bio alts in the force because they can't make a decision, Dev." She turned her head and eyed her partner. "And you just proved that wrong. He's not in discomfort. He's scared shitless."

Dev frowned, but remained silent as Jess draped her arm over her shoulders, not sure if she'd done that at all.

ALEXANDER BAIN SAT at the head of the ops table, elbows leaning on it, chin resting on his fists. The other chairs were filled with agents and ops management, with Stephen Bock taking an uneasy seat to his right.

Jess was in her usual seat at the other end, her hands clasped on the table in front of her, her eyes fixed soberly on her folded thumbs.

The doors sealed, compressing the air in the room a little, and Bain cleared his throat. "Well, people, every day seems to bring us new challenges, doesn't it?" He glanced at Bock and lifted an eyebrow.

"Five dead, two alive, both critically injured," Stephen said. "Med thinks Syd will make it. The other one, not sure."

Bain grunted thoughtfully. "Let's hope we get some information from one or the other, hmm? I'm told the carrier systems are nonfunctional."

"That's true," Stephen said. "Everything gave out just as they cleared the bay roof."

"So I hear." Bain looked over at Jess. "I hear your charming companion intervened to assist, saving us from a good deal more messiness."

Jess nodded. "Dev launched and caught them as they dropped, kept them up long enough for the grapples to take hold," she said, in a matter of fact voice. "Good piece of flying."

"Never saw anyone do anything like that before," Elaine said. "Not inside a space that small."

Nods and murmurs. "Dev says, she got used to dealing with three dimensional movement up in space," Jess said. "So maybe that has something to do with it. She's not oriented the same way, I don't think."

"Hmm." Bain considered that. "I wonder if we could contract time on station, perhaps? As part of training."

"Why not just get all our techs from there from now on?" Jason spoke up, in a mild voice. "I'm sold. I like Brent, but holy crap."

Bain smiled thinly, and exchanged looks with Jess. "That's for the future," he said. "Right now, it seems, we have a great deal of destruction to account for at Northern." He glanced to his right. "Mr. Bock, please assemble a recovery team, and start there at once. Find out what you can."

"Sir." Stephen nodded.

Jess drew breath to protest, then stopped when Bain's eyes swiveled back to her, and his eyebrow hiked. She kept her tongue still, rewarded with a brief smile from him.

"If the damage is as I expect," Bain said. "It will not go un-countered."

Jess relaxed, and settled back in her chair, sure in her own mind who'd be picked to execute that plan. She had no love lost for Syd, or any of his people, but the corps was the corps and she'd take vengeance for them as readily as if they'd been part of Base Ten.

"In the meantime, find out what you can from the condition of that vehicle," Bain said. "The damage seems...ah...more extensive than I would expect from the armament we saw on the transports." He waved his hand. "Go." His gaze drifted over. "Ah, Drake, stay behind a moment."

Jess felt no apprehension about the summons. She waited for the room to empty then she got up and went around the table, settling in a seat nearer to him, but not in the front row. "So."

"So," he echoed. "We begin to see the potential of your biological alternative team mate."

Jess smiled briefly. "Didn't surprise me," she said. "I don't think Bricker had any clue what he was introducing in here, but it works."

Bain nodded. "She does indeed, which could put her in some danger."

"I'll watch out for her."

"I suspect you will." He studied her. "I've received communication from our friends on the other side. A message arrived on the shuttle that recently landed." He folded his hands over his stomach and leaned back. "To send back the four men from science sector, and Doctor Kurok, their price is you."

"Me?"

"You. They've agreed to a midpoint exchange tomorrow night. They'll hand over their captives, we hand over you, and they'll take you and likely do horrible things to you before you die a slow, and no doubt very painful death."

Jess considered this thoughtfully. Then she looked up and into Bain's eyes. "Shoot me."

After a second, his face split into a smile.

"Or let me go, and see if they can take me down, or if I'll take them out," Jess said. "They tried that the last time. Didn't work out so well for them."

"Ah, my dear." Bain looked affectionately at her. "You did, indeed, breed true. No we can't do that, as one of the conditions would be to turn you over immobilized, and they would then inject you with something to keep you that way. They're taking no chances."

"Then?" Jess watched his face closely.

"I've sent back an answer rejecting their request," Bain said. "I told them to go ahead and grind them up for fish. That they weren't worth the price to me."

Jess felt a little lightheaded. She took a few breaths, trying to absorb the words. "Hard on them," she finally said. "Our guys that went."

"Yes," Bain agreed. "But that's why they pay me the big bucks. I get to make those kind of decisions.'

They were both quiet for a bit. "Kurok's a good guy," Jess said.

"He most certainly is."

"He's one of us." She looked at Bain. "He was a tech."

"Mm. Yes. He was actually much more than that." He stood up and paced a little "He was as revolutionary in his own way as your charming companion is," he said. "But going was his choice. Not mine, and not yours. He knew there was a chance this would be the outcome."

Jess grunted softly.

"I think he believed if he went, his presence would give some kind of safety to the rest," Bain said. "He always was an idiot that way."

Jess considered that. "Do they know who he is?" she asked. "Aside from a scientist from the bio station?"

"That's a very good question," Bain said "I suspect they're most interested in his current persona. They might know of his earlier one, but one never knows. I haven't revealed that to anyone. Have you?"

Now it was Jess's turn to get up and pace. "Everyone who saw him in the shuttle bay knows he's got something to do with us. But I haven't told anyone but Dev who he was because I didn't know myself until last night."

Bain turned. "Last night?"

Jess nodded. "My family sent me a few trunks of my father's things. There were some plas vid in there." She leaned her weight on the back of a chair. "He and my dad."

"I see." Bain sat down again. "Well, it's irrelevant in any case. I regret abandoning him, and them, but we don't make bargains, and we don't sell our people." He watched Jess's reaction sharply. "Do you agree, Agent Drake?"

"I do," Jess said, after a brief pause. "You start there, where does it end? No deals, no quarter. It's always been that way."

Bain looked both relieved, and pleased. "Excellent. Now." He shifted a little. "Let's discuss the future, shall we?"

Jess sat back down and rested her elbows on the table. "Sure."

IT SEEMED LIKE a very long walk from the ops hall to rad. Jess felt like the stone walls were endless, though it gave her time to think as she made her way through the crowd.

She was confused. Being told she'd be taking Bricker's place should have made her bounce like a crazy person. It was everything she'd ever wanted, or desired, though she felt sorry for Stephen, who Bain was going to send to rebuild Northern.

Awesome, right? She'd be in charge of the whole base, never have to put her ass out on the line, never have to sit in pain as yet another mark was burned into her arm, never end up in med for months or have to argue with the other agents.

The hitch, of course, was Dev. She'd be assigned to another agent, and Bain seemed to think she'd excel and not to worry about it. He was pleased with her, pleased with the program, and had already sent communication up to Life Force for them to proceed with producing more.

So yeah, it had all worked out great, for her, and for Dev, right? Bain sure seemed to think she should think so, and she'd done her best to respond like he expected.

But.

Jess reached her rad station and entered, acknowledging comp and stripping off her jumpsuit. She winced a little as the fabric rubbed against her new mark but then she was free of it, and she walked into the open area, feeling the warmth as the system came on and bathed her in its calming glow.

She sat down and exhaled. She didn't feel right about it. She just wasn't sure why.

After a moment, she got back up and went to comms, pulling a pad over and requesting Dev's whereabouts. Not unexpectedly, Dev was in the mechanical store and Jess hesitated, then entered the key for that area. "Let me talk to Dev," she said, when it was answered.

A moment later, Dev's voice echoed softly down the link. "Hello?"

"Hey, it's Jess. You done down there? C'mon over to my rad."

"Absolutely," Dev responded, then clicked off.

Jess let her hand fall, and then she went back over to the couch and sat down. Dev deserved to hear it all from her, didn't she? At least she could reassure her that she wasn't going to head back up to the creche. Jess was pretty sure her partner...

Her partner.

Jess sighed. "I knew I shouldn't have done that," she chastised herself. "Screwed myself over. Now I—" She thought about Dev partnering with someone else, going out in the field with someone else, and to her surprise it made her really, really angry.

That was just wrong. Dev was a tech, and she was a really good tech, so why not want her to be successful?

Why not?

Jess stared at her hands, a brief flash of memory filling her mind's eye with waking up that morning in Dev's bed. Why not? Because she wanted Dev to be with her, not out in the field with someone else, someone who might want to share a sleep sack with her and then what would Dev do?

Her stomach hurt. Jess couldn't remember feeling this confused and in mental turmoil for a very long time. It was unpleasant and she thought she might even throw up.

A soft knock came at the door, and she ran out of time for that. "Come."

The panel slid open and Dev ducked inside, a smudge of silicon grease across the bridge of her nose. "Did you need something? It sounded urgent."

Jess took a breath. "Yeah, c'mon in," she said. "Let's talk."

Dev shed her work suit and joined her in the rad area. "Some excellent parts came in. I got some of them for our carrier, and I'm going to see about getting them installed."

Something abruptly crystallized in Jess. She realized just how important to her that one word *our* meant, and as she did, she felt the tension in her relax. "So let me tell you what's going on," she said. "First off, Bain's really happy with you."

Dev smiled immediately.

"He's happy with me, too, so happy he offered me a promotion," Jess said. "He wants me to be in charge of this place. Take Bricker's job."

Dev's eyes opened wide. "That's excellent!" she said. "Oh, Jess!"

Jess smiled at Dev's delight in her good fortune. "Yeah, except I'm gonna turn him down."

"You are?"

"I don't want to be in charge of this place."

"You don't?"

Jess shook her head, feeling an odd, disjointed peace in herself. "Means I have to come in from the field," she said. "Means I have to sit at a desk, and get a poof head." She hesitated. "Means I have to give you up to someone else." She caught Dev's quickly indrawn breath. "I'm not going to do that."

Dev eased down on one knee and put a hand on her arm, her bare body almost glowing in the light from the rad. "But Jess, isn't it what you wanted?"

"I thought it was," Jess admitted. "I mean..." She shifted and rested her elbow on her bare knee. "It's what we're all supposed to want, you know? You can only be in the field for so long. You get too old for it. Then what? If we didn't want to be directors, or heads, what would they do with us?"

Dev felt highly unsettled. She realized rather quickly, though, that she was far more unsettled thinking about becoming someone else's partner than she was about anything else, even leaving the citadel. Nevertheless, she sorted through her thoughts trying to find something to respond with. "I don't know," she said. "When we get to where we aren't useful anymore, they put us down."

Jess studied her. "Really."

Dev nodded. "What else are they going to do?" she asked, in a quiet voice. "There's only so much room up in station, unless they move a lot of sets out. I remember when it got crowded once." She looked down at her hands, turning one over and studying the fingers of it. "It was just...one night it was really packed in the dining hall and then the next morning it wasn't."

Jess felt a chill go up and down her spine. "Wow."

"So you should be in charge if you can, Jess." Dev gave her an intense look. "Because only the people in charge can say what's going to happen. The rest of us just have to wait to be told."

Oh, wow. It had come around the corner and surprised her. She hadn't expected Dev to... "You want to go out with someone else?" Jess asked, cautiously. "Tired of me already?"

Dev's jaw actually dropped. She reached out and grasped Jess's arm. "No." she managed to get out after a brief, shocked pause. "I don't want to be with anyone else. For anything. But I also know it's good to be able to tell everyone else what to do."

Jess exhaled. "I'm really confused," she admitted. "I don't know what the hell to do now." She felt both better and worse at the same time, a sensation that almost made her hiccup. "I don't want to give you up, but I don't want someone else to take over and tell me what to do."

Dev smiled faintly. "I think I should say I'm very flattered," she murmured. "Anyway, please think about things, Jess. If this is an excellent opportunity it's important for you, isn't it?"

Jess gazed thoughtfully at the ground. After a moment of silence her head lifted. "Is it?"

The questioning in her voice made Dev pause.

"Anyway," Jess said. "The other part of the news is they heard from the other side. The price on your friend's head is my life."

Dev actually stopped breathing. Then she started again with a choked gasp. "What?"

"They wanted me delivered to them in order to let the rest of them go," Jess said. "As a price, I guess, for what we did over there." She touched Dev's hand and stroked the top of her knuckles. "Bain told them no. We don't bargain." She looked up into Dev's eyes. "Sorry."

Dev let out her breath. "What will they do?" she said. "Will they hurt Doctor Dan and the rest of them?"

"They'll kill them."

Dev felt like someone had hit her hard on the chest. "Oh," she murmured softly. "Why? Why would they do that?"

Jess exhaled and lay down on her back on the couch. "Because we didn't give them what they asked for." She let her eyes close, feeling the warmth of the rad on their lids. "Don't even know why they asked. They know better."

There was a very long silence. Eventually, Jess cracked her eyes open and turned her head, watching Dev's still, silent face. "Sorry about your friend."

"Yes, me too," Dev whispered. "Is it all right if I go back to my space?"

"Sure." Jess touched her knee. "Go chill."

Without a word, Dev got up and went to the locker, slipping into her jumpsuit and picking up the toolkit she'd been carrying. She left the rad chamber, the door sliding shut after her with a sense of metallic finality.

Jess folded her arms over her chest, at a loss for what to do with all the churning emotion going on inside her. She thought she'd settled on a course of action, and found peace with it, only to be shaken out of her comfort by Dev's unexpected reaction, and her stolid common sense about what it meant to be in charge of something.

Of course, a bio alt would understand that at a gut level. Dev had lived her whole, young life with the knowledge that anyone and everyone around her held power over her. Of course she'd look at Jess's opportunity as a good thing.

Even if it didn't seem like a good thing for her. Even if it meant she would end up being a part of someone else's life instead of Jess's.

Surprising, really, how much that thought hurt her. Literally hurt her. Here she thought she was being so noble and self-sacrificing, turning the job down to stay with Dev when Dev had turned out to be more mercenary than she'd expected.

Ow.

Well, maybe it would turn out for the best for both of them. If she was in charge, Jess pondered, she could make sure Dev got a good partner, and good assignments. And she could look out for her, right? Maybe that was Dev's point after all. Maybe she saw a good opportunity to make a place for herself, getting close to Jess.

It's what Jess would have done, right? What she had done, in a way, in sucking up to Bain?

Jess suddenly found herself feeling very sad. It was a dull melancholy that she remembered from her recent convalescence, and rather than give in to it, she got up and shook herself, going over to the console and punching out.

"Session not complete," the comp complained.

"Later." Jess got into her suit and pulled her boots on. It felt better to be up and moving, and she headed out in a determined march into the hallway. Maybe she would go to ops and get a head start on that high level view Bain spoke of.

Maybe she'd go to the gym, and get the kinks out. The memory of that goon wiping the deck with her rankled, and she figured at the least she should end her time in the field by being in good shape. Otherwise all that chair duty was gonna catch up fast with her.

So the gym, and then ops, and then maybe the other half of rad.

Jess nodded her head decisively, then looked up to find herself standing outside her own quarters, as surprised as anyone that her steps had taken her here despite her best intentions.

With a shake of her head she entered, and looked around, trying to keep her eyes from being drawn to the door that connected her quarters with Dev's.

At least for now it did, until Bain put the change through, and she moved from the agents' compound, up a level to where there was thicker carpet on the floor, and carefully inlaid tile on the walls. Where everything was plusher, and more comfortable.

She'd leave her blacks behind, and the heavy blasters, and use her mind more. Get hurt less. Not have to put it on the line every other day.

Great. Jess sat down in her work chair and rested her elbows on her knees, feeling sick to her stomach, with an ache inside she scarcely understood.

"Why in the hell do I feel like this?" she muttered. "What in the hell's wrong with me?"

With a sigh, she leaned back and pulled over the bound case that had been her father's. She opened it and leafed through the plas, the irony of knowing the position she'd just been given had been so coveted by him, and yet one he'd never quite reached.

She flipped through the images at the end, slowing and stopping when she came to the one of him and Kurok.

A fragment of memory. Just a moment of time that had captured an image of two people in harmony with each other, body language relaxed and comfortable, secure and confident.

Comfortable like she and Dev were.

Jess regarded the plas in silence for a while, then slowly closed it, got up, and walked over to the door between her and Dev, watching the door shiver into motion as she reached it and moved past into the darkness beyond.

THERE WERE TOO many emotions happening for her to cope with them. Dev was seated on the ground in the back of her quarters, her back to the wall. She had her arms folded around her upraised knees, and she was fighting hard to keep herself from throwing up.

What a contrast. She had left the service bay in very good spirits, having spent her time discussing the new mods with Brent and Doug. She'd felt a sense of acceptance from them that made her feel very good. The summons from Jess even made her feel better, and she'd been looking forward to joining her in rad and maybe telling her about the new gear.

Now she felt horrible. Really horrible.

Thinking about Doctor Dan was making her cry. The thought of never seeing him again hurt so bad she couldn't stop the tears from running down her face.

She knew the bad guys who had him would hurt him, and it was heartbreaking to think of him suffering.

She didn't want to think about it.

It was hard to think about anything else though. Dev exhaled. She understood why Interforce didn't want to make a deal for him, and there was nothing in her heart that would allow the thought of trading Jess, even to get Doctor Dan back.

There was no good at all in it. There wasn't any good even in Jess's opportunity for her, save that maybe it would mean Jess might make sure she could stay at the citadel.

Working with someone else.

The tears kept coming, and Dev rested her head against her forearm, feeling her chest heave in silent sobs.

Bio alts weren't supposed to cry. They were taught that in school, from the very earliest, that showing natural born emotions was a bad thing. It made them uncomfortable, and Dev remembered clearly that grip on her face, and finger to the lips, of the proctor when she'd slipped once after a hard fall.

But none of them ever really stopped feeling things, you just learned how to hide it, to keep it inside until you were alone, or in your sleep pod and no one could hear you.

She quieted after a few minutes and took a breath, releasing it as the hiccups eased and she felt the throbbing in her head lessen.

The door opening startled her, and she jerked upright, her shoulders hitting the wall as a tall figure entered and stopped, looking around. "Jess?"

"There you are." Jess came over to where she was crouched. "You sitting in the dark for a reason?"

Dev wiped her eyes, and sniffled. "I was just thinking."

Jess sat down and leaned on the wall next to her. "You okay?"

"I don't think so."

Jess sat there quietly next to her for a while, not saying anything. Then she cleared her throat a little. "You feel bad about your friend?"

Dev nodded, her throat aching too much to speak.

"He's pretty sharp. He probably knew it could happen."

"I know," Dev whispered. "I just feel bad about it." She cleared her throat and wiped her eyes. "I'm sorry."

"Why?" Jess's voice held a note of gentle inquisitiveness.

Dev had to think about that before she answered. "Why do I feel bad or why am I sorry?"

"Both."

"I feel bad because I like Doctor Dan a lot, and it...it bothers me to think of him getting hurt or killed," Dev said, after a long pause. "And I'm sorry because I don't want to cause you discomfort. Or you think less of me for it."

Jess reached up and rubbed the side of her nose. "Well." She leaned against Dev a little. "I don't really understand it all. But I know it bothers me that you're upset."

Dev sniffled.

"I know this guy was a friend, and all that, but you can't do anything about it," Jess said. "It's not your fault what happened, so try not to freak out about it." She patted her thigh in an attempt to comfort her. "Take it easy."

"Jess?"

"Hmm?"

"How would you feel if it was me?"

There was a long moment of absolute silence. "If it was you what?" Jess asked, cautiously.

"If it were me, being captured," Dev said. "Would it bother you?"

She waited for Jess to answer, but a very long time seemed to go by and her partner didn't. She looked up at her and saw her profile, very still and quiet, and intense, and after a second, Jess turned and returned her gaze.

"Would it bother me," Jess mused. "Boy that puts it in perspective, doesn't it?" She went on, in a slightly wondering tone. "I wouldn't have let you go. It was stupid of Bain to let him go, or the rest of them. Anyone wet out of field school would have known there was something off."

"Oh."

"But if you had I'd..." Jess paused. "I think I'd have to do something about it." She sounded surprised. "Even if it meant our trading places and me croaking." She regarded Dev. "So all right, maybe I do get how you feel about it. A little."

Dev thought about that, in silence.

"It would bother me a lot if they took you," Jess added, after a while. "I like you a lot." She hesitantly put her arm around Dev's shoulders. "Kinda sucks they made me the price of his ticket. Does that freak you out?"

Dev shook her head.

"It freaks me out, a little," Jess said. "That's a pretty big target on my back. Makes going out in the field pretty risky. Job's hard enough without half the planet gunning for ya."

"You should take that new job, Jess," Dev murmured. "I don't want you to get hurt."

"Yeah, I should," Jess said. "Better for me, maybe better for this place. Better not to piss Bain off with his itchy trigger finger."

Dev felt a sense of additional sadness. "I'll do my best to do good with the other person you put me with, Jess. I want to perform excellently for you."

Jess exhaled, feeling a cascading torrent of conflicting emotions she had very little experience with. It felt gut wrenching and cleansing at the same time and it made her body tingle from it. "I bet you'd perform excellently no matter what happened to you, Dev.

You're just that kind of person."

Dev smiled briefly, and looked away. "It's the way I was made," she said quietly. "I don't really have a choice about it."

"But I'm not ready to give you up," Jess concluded. "And I'm not ready to join the powers that be." She drew in a deep breath. "Leaving those guys out there to croak just to save my damn skin is wrong, Dev. No matter what Bain says, I can't just sit here and let them die."

Dev turned her head and stared at her, a little open mouthed. "But...uh...Jess..."

"But Jess what?" Pale blue eyes twinkled a little. "Life's short, Dev. You can't hold onto it. But I want you to know you've got a choice now to make. You get involved in a rogue op with me, you're done." Her face turned serious. "If you don't croak with me doing it, that is. You don't have to. I don't have to tell you anything else. I'll just disappear, and you won't know anything so you can't admit to anything. They'll keep you. You're good."

Dev gazed steadily at her.

"You've got a lot more to lose than I do," Jess said. "Dying has always been on my horizon. You've got a chance to make a new life for yourself here." She paused a moment. "Listen, I know you don't want to go back topside. I don't want you to screw yourself up just because I am."

Dev's eyes shifted and looked off into the darkness, then moved back to Jess's face again. "Are you saying you are going to go and try to help Doctor Dan?"

"If I can figure out a way, I might," Jess admitted. "I might just do that despite what Bain wants."

Then she waited, watching the dimly seen face next to her, faint illumination from the room's controls outlining Dev's gentle profile as she looked intently at her.

"Then take me with you," Dev said into a small, charged silence that had fallen between them. "If you go to do that, I want to go too."

"Even if it means you get in trouble?" Jess asked. "Or end up back up on station, or dead?"

"Yes."

Jess nodded slowly. "This could be a big mistake for both of us," she said. "But you know—I don't give a damn. I'm not going to end up like my father did, toeing the line all his life and ending up with what? A blaster up his ass and a long, hard death." She stared off into the dark shadows of the room, understanding that the instinct driving her was that same one she'd felt in the field, that she knew was perilous to ignore.

Insane as it often appeared. She felt that peace inside that had always guided her choices, and now, it seemed, Dev's choices as well. Hearing Dev's words brought a relaxation across her frame that she felt the twin of in Devs shoulders under her arm.

Take me with you. Jess grinned a little, thinking of how shocked anyone would have been to hear a bio say that. She felt the warmth as Dev's cheek pressed against her and just like that, the whole—us and them—thing came home to her again.

They sat there quietly together in silence, the sounds of the citadel penetrating dimly through the walls. Jess remembered the long weeks recovering from her injury, not that far in the past, and how that same remote echo had made her guts clench. Now she only felt a sense of anticipation.

"Okay," she finally said. "So the first thing we need to do is go back to what we were doing. Act normal."

"Okay," Dev replied. "What is acting normal?"

Jess chuckled wryly. "I'll go back to rad. You go back to wrenching," she said. "Then I'm going to go to ops and get some intel." She paused. "See what you can get out of your buddies in the pits down there. Details about what went on."

Dev nodded.

"Find out everything. What rig they took, who went, what they loaded. What I want to find out is, was this a real deal, or just a game?"

"A game?"

Jess nodded slowly, and lowered her voice, even though they were alone, in the back of the quarters furthest from anything in the whole citadel. "Something's behind this. Maybe we can figure out what it is and whatever that is, will keep us alive."

"I see."

"Maybe it is on the level, and legit. Just a bad choice. Maybe it isn't." Jess got up and extended her hand to Dev. "Let's go see what we can find out."

"I think I should wash a little first," Dev said. "This being sad thing is messy."

Jess pulled her up and wrapped an arm around Dev's shoulders, guiding her toward the sanitary chamber. "Do my best to limit that being sad thing then."

"Thank you."

"Sure you want to do this?"

"Yes."

DEV FELT A lot better. She slipped back under the carrier's open engine, settling onto her back as she brought the portable comp around to take readings on the new mods.

Though there now seemed to be a much greater possibility of something bad happening to her, at least there was a hope that something better might happen to Doctor Dan, and she knew if Jess could make it all come right, she would.

Her head hurt, from all the discomfort and sadness. But her heart hurt less, and she was able to concentrate on the comp, studying the results of the tweaking she'd done.

"Hey, Dev!"

Dev turned her head to find Doug trotting up. "Hello."

"Hey listen." He flopped onto the ground on his belly, extending a hand held monitor. "Do you know what this is? I'm trying to tune that rust bucket they assigned us and I've never seen it before."

Dev put her own comp down and half rolled onto her side to look. The small screen was displaying a diagnostic readout and after a blank moment, she felt programming kick in for it. "Oh." She leaned closer. "That's very strange. It's the homing sensor but— "

"But it's pointed in the wrong direction, right?" Doug said. "It's transmitting somewhere else, not locking on here."

"Yes." Dev nodded. "That's exactly right." She looked at Doug, who was frowning at the device. "That doesn't make sense. Does it?"

"Nah. Ah, well, now that I know I'm reading this right, maybe it was just screwed up and needs to be reset." He got up onto his feet. "They told me that carrier hasn't been used in forever. Who knows how long that thing's been bleeping."

"Let's go look at it." Dev grabbed on to the engine cowling and pulled herself up to her feet, pausing to grab her comp. "Maybe there are other things incorrect."

Doug seemed quite happy for the company and they crossed the busy cavern over to the service bay the new team had been assigned. A carrier perched atop it, its sides battered, scorch marks evident on most of its skin surface. It was the same model as her own though, and had what appeared to be updated engine pods.

"Inside's a mess." Doug worked the hatch and ducked inside. "They told us maybe they've got some new ones coming sometime, but April figures we'll be stuck with this one for a while."

The inside was a wreck. Not as bad as the old carrier they'd seen on their last mission, but it was evidently neglected and most of the racks and stations were being replaced. Dev crossed over to the open pilot's console and set her comp down, configuring it to read the mechanics inside. "It seems this needs all new boards."

"Yeah." Doug came and peered over her shoulder. "Thanks for taking the time to check it out with me. The rest of those guys act like they're doing a favor to answer a question," he grumbled. "I know we're newbies but sheesh."

Dev studied the readouts. "It took a few days for me to get settled as well."

"I bet."

Dev glanced at him, one eyebrow lifted.

"I mean, I'm just new," Doug said. "But I came in the regular way. I know those guys must have freaked out about you, right?"

"A bit." Dev went back to her comp. "But after a few days things got better. There was less discomfort." She looked at the console log, and her brow creased. The last entries were dated prior to her arrival, and she noted the irregularities as she copied the contents into her portable mem.

"We heard about you." Doug seemed content to watch her. "We heard rumors, and then, before we went for grad, they pulled us in and told us about you."

"Really?" Dev considered that. "Why?"

"Well, us, the ones who were coming here, I guess because they knew we'd meet you," he said. "I guess so we wouldn't freak out. They said you were just an experiment they were trying out. Everyone at field school thought it was a gag, or something. Or some rig for a mission, to try and fake out the other side or whatever. No one really thought it was real."

Dev closed her comp and turned, facing him. "So what do you think now?"

He grinned. "After that flight you took us on? I got no questions." He held a hand up. "I don't know how they did it, but I'm all right with you."

"That's very nice of you." Dev smiled briefly. "Since I have no control over what I am or how they taught me, it's good that some people think that's not so bad." She indicated the comp. "If I were you, I would replace this unit, not just reset it. It seems to have a lot of old data in it that might disrupt your systems if you keep it on there."

Doug grinned. "Glad to have the second opinion. I told Clint that, and he told me when he wanted my opinion he'd give it to me. If I tell him you said it, he'll hand over the part." He winked. "So thanks, Dev! I appreciate it."

"No problem." Dev returned the smile, and slipped out the door, pausing a moment to decide what to do next. There was a lot of activity in the bay, and instead of heading back to her own pad, she detoured by where the damaged carrier she'd rescued was being held.

There were groups of bio alt techs around it, all of them working on salvage. The carrier was in such poor shape it was hard for them to find things to save, but they kept at the task and didn't look up as Dev paused to study the rig.

Only two people had survived. But they'd told her that those two wouldn't have even had a chance if it hadn't been for what she'd done. Looking at the carrier now, it was hard to believe it had survived long enough to get as far as their bay, and Dev was very cautious in her approach as she moved toward the open hatch.

One of the bio alt techs looked up, and hastily got out of her way as she eased inside. "Take care, tech." He said, in a soft voice. "It's very unstable."

Dev paused. "Thanks, Kaytee," she replied. "I just want to look inside. I will take care."

He smiled at her. "It was a big thing you did, NM-Dev-1," he answered. "Everyone was talking about it, downstairs."

All bio alts lived downstairs in the compound, except her. Dev nodded. "It was an unusual thing," she said. "I am glad it didn't put any of you in danger, and it assisted the injured people inside."

"It was good," the Kaytee said. "Many were surprised. I think it gave some of the natural born discomfort." He kept his voice very low.

Dev nodded. "I think so too. However, I am not going to perform with less than excellence because of that."

"No." Kaytee smiled again. "That's not your programming." He lifted a hand and moved off, as two of Clint's supervisors approached. "Have a good day, tech."

"You too, Kaytee," Dev said, watching him leave before she turned and stepped very carefully up into the carrier. The Kaytee set was the most advanced set, she remembered, before they had sent her. They had a lot of specialized programming for mech, and she remembered some of them talking before they left the creche, proud of their advanced status.

Well, so was she. Dev paused and examined the inside. The smell of blood was strongly evident, and she could see the stain of it on the floor and on the weapons console. There were panels hanging from the walls, and mixing with the bio scent was the smell of fried electronics that made her nose wrinkle.

With so many people, it must have been terrible inside. Dev triggered her comp and did a scan, most of the systems dead and unresponsive. The only boards that showed any readings at all were the main engines, and the damage to them was extensive.

But what had made it? Dev adjusted the comp. The outside had shown huge fire scores, but not from any of the known blaster types. It was more as if they'd flown the carrier through one of the big electrical storms. It had that kind of disruption pattern to it.

Would they have done that? Dev remembered very clearly how cautious Jess had been about flying in the storms, preferring to take shelter no matter how much of a rush she'd been in. Maybe they had little choice, though, with all the trouble, and those other people dead, or dying.

A signal caught her attention and she turned, moving over to the pilot's station and dipping the comp down. She observed the results and frowned, checking the settings twice, before she ran the test again.

Then she flipped back to the readings she'd gotten from Doug's carrier and compared them. "This is unusual," she muttered, saving the data and tucking the comp under her arm. Then she went over to the console and knelt, working the dead control panel off the side of the carrier, and setting it to one side.

She drew a small light from her pocket and turned it on, peering inside and then, sticking her whole head in the panel. The stench was awful, but she studied the burned boards intently, before drawing herself back out and resting her elbow on her knee.

Hmm. Dev tapped her thumb against the side of the light. Was this something like what Jess had been talking about? Finding out what had happened? This wasn't really part of Doctor Dan's problem—or was it? She glanced up at the pilot's seat, its surface stained with a coating of blood, the backbone of it snapped in two places.

"Hello, my dear."

Dev nearly jumped out of her skin. She turned to find Alexander Bain in the hatchway, regarding her with those cold, sharp eyes. "Hello, sir," she replied politely, feeling more than a little apprehension as the old man climbed into the carrier and approached her.

He sat down on the half destroyed weapons station and folded his arms over his chest. "What brings you here, hmm? Was there not enough to do on your own machine?"

Dev settled on the floor, crossing her legs under her. "Well, sir," she said. "I was just wondering about this one."

"Ah, I see."

"I want to understand what happened to it," she replied. "I don't want anything like that to happen to ours. It seems to be very damaged."

Bain nodded. "It is indeed, my dear," he said. "What do you think happened to it?"

Dev looked around the inside of the carrier. "It appears to have passed through a high degree of electrical disruption," she said. "I think they flew through a storm."

Bain smiled. "They did indeed, young Dev. They had little choice, it seems." He straightened up. "If either of the two survivors regains consciousness, we can ask them why. Until then, the why is a mystery. These were all old timers. Certainly they knew better."

Dev nodded.

"Thank you, by the way, for your very brave, and hmm...expeditious action," Bain said. "It was most appreciated, especially by me."

"I'm glad it helped. I hope we find out what happened to them." She paused, and then stood up, tucking her comp into the big leg pocket designed for it. "Please excuse me, sir. I have to calibrate a new module for my system."

"Certainly, my dear." Bain stood and moved out of her way. "By the way, did Agent Drake tell you about the deal I turned down on her behalf?"

Dev paused. "Yes," she said, in quiet tone.

"Do you, perhaps, think I should have proceeded with it? To get your friend Doctor Kurok back with us? He seems an innocent victim of our machinations, no?"

Dev looked him right in the eyes. "I don't think that, no," she said, honestly. "It just makes me sad."

Bain studied her for a long moment. Then he nodded. "It makes me sad too, Dev. I'm quite glad you understand the situation. Gratified, in fact." He gestured for her to precede him from the carrier. "These things happen in our business, you know. Can't be helped."

Dev watched him walk off toward the control center, everyone scrambling to get out of his way. Then she turned and instead of heading back to the carrier, went to the inner corridor and started up the hall toward central operations. Hopefully, she would find Jess there.

Hopefully.

Chapter Five

JESS ENTERED OPS and took a seat at one of the big consoles, lifting her hand in brief greeting to the board runners and exchanging a brief grin with Jason.

"Hey," he said.

"Hey." Jess pulled a pad over and keyed in a request. "Anything interesting?"

"After that whole thing earlier? What could compete with that?" Jason remarked. "Stephen almost pissed himself, y'know. Didn't like it one bit."

Jess shrugged. "Would he have liked that thing coming down on top of everyone more?" she asked. "Dev did what she had to." She studied the reports on the boards, and leaned on her elbows. "Any word on Syd?"

"He's in the tank. Broken back, both legs, dislocated shoulder, and neural disruption," Jason recited. "No idea how he flew that thing in. Dom's pretty close to flat line."

"Huh." Jess read through the ops logs, recalling the ones from days prior. "He was a jackass to me when I was out there, but no one deserves that much med."

"He's always a jackass to you." Jason got up and came over to the console she was seated at, taking the chair next to her. "So."

"So." Jess kept her eyes on the screen.

"I hear Bain's going to put Stephen out at North on a permanent basis."

"Someone has to do it," Jess muttered. "Don't envy him. That place is a pit. Was a pit." She corrected herself. "Wonder if the damage estimates were as bad as they think." He didn't answer, and she looked over to see him watching her, one eyebrow lifted. "What?"

"What?" He echoed back. "You and Bain talk?"

"Sure." Jess went back to her screen.

"And?"

Jess glanced at him. "I'm not stupid enough to flap my jaws about his business. If he wants everyone to know, he'll put out a bulletin."

Jason grinned. "He has." He slid a bit of plas over to her. "Congrats."

Shit. Jess glanced at the plas, which had about six lines of text on it, and Bain's creds. "I hadn't formally accepted yet. Bastard."

Jason chuckled, but kept his voice down. "Only went out to upper grade field ops and at that, just to need-to-know so they'd hike your creds in here. You're still under cover to everyone else, so you've got a little time before the shit hits the intake tunnel." He bumped her shoulder as she let out an aggrieved sigh. "C'mon, Jess. Who else would he pick? You know he likes you."

"And that's the reason you should pick a director?" Jess kept her voice low also. "Because you like someone? Best I was hoping for was Stephen's gig. I wasn't looking for that much crap this fast." She glanced around. "Maybe I don't think I'm ready for that, or even want it."

He grunted. "Good thing Sandy croaked. She'd have split a lung right in the mess if she'd lived and gotten this note." He tapped the plas. "We all figured he had an eye on you when he talked you down at the shuttle. Otherwise, why care?"

Now it was Jess's turn to grunt.

"Most of the old timers are gone," he said. "Syd was the last of them anywhere near us. Seriously, Jess, who else? The active agents here are either from our class, or the kids who just came in. We lost a whole damn generation the last couple months."

Something about the words stirred something in the back of her mind.

"Anyway, consider my sucking up to start right now." Jason drummed his fingertips on the console. "Just like everyone else, except what I want is your driver." He nodded a little, giving her a sideways look. "Please don't hit me again. I'm still aching like crap from the last time."

Jess studied him in silence for a minute. "I won't. What made you change your mind?"

"You hitting me when I dissed her," Jason replied in a straightforward way. "Something you value like that. One thing about you, Jess, you don't bullshit. I trust your gun at my back and your likes and dislikes."

"Except Josh."

"Really?" Her fellow agent cocked his head. "You trusted him? Or even liked him? For real?"

Jess remained silent, but her nose twitched a little.

"That's what I thought." Jason drummed on the table again. "Well I'm just the first to ask. Won't be the last, but at least you know me."

"I know you," Jess said. "But I'll take my time making that decision. I like the kid."

Jason chuckled. "Yeah, we guessed." He nudged her. "I always said you had good taste. Glad the whole jel...bio alt thing didn't inhibit stuff."

Jess frowned, "It's not like that."

"It's not?" He seemed astonished. "You've been hanging all over her. You didn't take her in the sack?"

"Jason." Jess shifted, and looked up as the outer door opened, surprised and then relieved when she recognized Dev's slight form entering. "Hey, Dev. Over here."

Dev crossed over to them at once, her eyes flicking to Jason before they settled on Jess's face. "May I show you something?"

Jess nodded, but put a hand on Dev's wrist. "Excuse us a minute, Jase."

"Ssssuuure." The tall, muscular man stood up and meandered off, winking at Jess before he disappeared behind the main console.

Jess sighed.

"Is there something not correct?" Dev asked, softly.

"No," Jess said, gruffly. "Well, yes...maybe." She amended. "Anyway, what's up?"

Dev pulled her portable comp from her leg pocket and turned it on. "I saw something interesting and I thought you might want to see it too." She set the machine down and moved a little closer. "I was taking readings on the new mods and one of the new techs came to ask me a question."

"Them too, huh?" Jess rested her elbow on the console, her chin on her fist.

"Excuse me?"

"Go on."

A soft bong interrupted them. "Standby," Jason's voice echoed softly. "This is Base Ten, copy." He paused. "Ack, standby." He stepped back and looked over at them. "Jess?"

Jess felt a jolt of surprise. "What is it?"

"Call, for you."

For her? "Put it here." Jess grabbed a set of ear cups and slid them in place, as a tracer lit up on the board. She triggered it and leaned closer. "Drake."

"Jess, this is Jake..."

Her youngest brother. "Yeah, what's up, JJ?" Jess felt a chill, and she sucked in a breath, feeling a warmth on her arm as Dev put her hand there. "Everything all right?"

"Not so much," he replied. "Mom's air bike slammed into the rock face in a storm. She's gone."

Jess felt her mind go blank with shock. Of all the things she'd expected to hear, that was the last of them. "Damn," she finally said. "When?"

"Two hours ago. They just finished clearing the paperwork," Jake said. "Jimmy's making arrangements. He wanted me to call you, let you know they'll process her out tomorrow morning." He cleared his throat. "In case you wanted to show up."

Hard to fathom. Hard to accept. The last time she'd even seen her mother was two years back. Quick visit home, on the way out to the west coast. "Yeah. Thanks, Jake," she said, softly. "I'll see if I can get out there."

"Right. I'll tell him. Bye." The comms cut off, and she closed the channel out.

"Jess?"

The room suddenly sounded too loud around her. Jess turned her head to find Dev watching her with a concerned expression on her face. "Yeah, sorry," she muttered. "Got some bad news."

"What's up?" Jason had come back over, and was leaning on the console. "You okay? Trace said that came from the Bay."

"It did. Family stuff," Jess said. "I have to go talk to Bain." She stood up. "Dev, meet you back at our place." She patted Dev on the shoulder. "You can show me your comp then." She ducked around Jason and headed for the door, leaving him and Dev gazing at each other in silent puzzlement.

Dev finally shook her head and put her scanner back in her pocket. "Excuse me."

"Wonder what that was all about," Jason said. "I haven't seen Jess get that pale since she lost a drinking match with me, and barely made it back to her rig in time."

Dev didn't even have any intention of wondering what that bit of strange language was all about. She felt that something bad had happened, and she was anxious to get back to her quarters and wait for Jess to tell her about it.

Her quarters. Their quarters. Their place? Dev counted the hallways as she walked along, Something was going on.

JESS STOOD BRACED, with her hands clasped behind her back as she regarded the man behind the desk. "My brother just made the call."

Bain pursed his lips. "You put me in something of a quandary, Drake. Experience tells me that putting yourself out there as a target at this time is a mistake."

"Probably true," Jess said. "But I missed my father's. Family doesn't mean that much to us, but you only have one set of parents."

"That is a fact." Bain sighed. "I know you have your rights to ask this, you know. It just concerns me. Have you considered this might be a trap?"

"Yes," Jess said, in a quiet voice. "That did occur to me on the walk over here."

Bain nodded. "It just seems too much of a coincidence. But sometimes things are." He leaned forward and rested his hands on the desk. "You will not take transport. You will go in a carrier, with an escort," he said. "The escort will stand off armed until the processing's done, then I expect you straight back here"

Jess nodded. "Agreed."

Bain nodded back. "Take care, Drake. We need you."

"I will." She turned and left, heading right out of Bain's inner office and making her way out to the main hall. Her mind was still tight focused, and it took a full minute of walking before her surroundings started to take on color and the sounds around her filtered into her consciousness.

Another minute or two and she found herself outside the airlock, and then cycling through it, not bothering to check the weather before she triggered the external door and then was outside.

It was windy, but not raining. Jess let the stiff breeze blow her hair back as she leaned against the damp wall, her eyes staring almost unseeingly across the ruffled dark sea.

She wasn't really sure how to feel. Now that the shock was wearing off, she kept hearing Bain's voice in her head, warning of traps. She had to wonder if that had, in fact, been why her mother died.

The other side was as unfeeling as they were. Killing a family member to draw her out? Trivial. She'd done it herself, to them. But it made her angry anyway and she was caught between hoping it wasn't true, to save her the guilt, and hoping it was to bring on the vengeance.

So she'd go and see. Put herself out there, on the ledge, and see what happened.

Jess exhaled. She hadn't been close to her mother, not for a very long time. Not since she'd been taken. And their last conversation, after her father had died, hadn't been either cordial or friendly. So did she care if this random, somewhat selfish, old woman had died?

Jess let her hands rest on the wall, and had to admit she really didn't care. The only reason she was going to the processing was to make a presence for the family. If it was a trap, then she'd take the opportunity to turn it around on them. She had to concentrate hard to even remember what her mother's face looked like.

She stared out at the sea. And if not a trap, then she'd be out there, with a carrier, and Dev. That opened up all sorts of possibilities, once they lost their escort. Jess smiled faintly. Or maybe talked them into joining her.

DEV FOUND HERSELF pacing, her ears cocked for the sounds of Jess's return next door, as anxious and stressed out as she could remember being for quite some time.

She couldn't even sit down and do a sim.

It was a very strange and very unsettling feeling. She really wished she could ask Doctor Dan about it, about why she felt so strange about someone else's problem, and why it was causing her a deep sense of anxiety that wasn't at all excellent.

With a sigh, she detoured to her workspace and forced herself to take a seat and pick up her comp. She set it into the dock and synced it, bringing it up on the bigger screen above her desk and studying the results. She was halfway through it when the inner door opened and she looked up to find Jess leaning there against the sill. "Jess!"

She stood up, but Jess waved her back and came over to join her, perching on the edge of her workspace and reaching over to ruffle her hair as she sat back down.

"Jason was right. I do hang all over you," Jess commented mildly. "Does that freak you out?"

Dev studied her. "No," she said, after a pause. "Not at all."

Jess brushed her fingers across Dev's cheekbone. "Good." She changed the subject abruptly. "We're going out tomorrow. We're going to my family's home."

"We are?"

Jess nodded. "There was an accident and my mother died in it," she explained. "Tomorrow morning, they'll process her body out into the sea, and we'll be there to watch that."

"Oh." Dev studied Jess's face, but she didn't seem to be very upset about the news. "I'm sorry about that, Jess."

Jess sighed. "Yeah, me too. I was never close to her, but a mother's a mother. You know how it is." She paused, watching Dev's expression alter a little. "Oh, wait. No, I guess you don't."

"No. I can't even imagine that," Dev said. She tried to think about what it would feel like to hear someone had died that you were close to, and all she could think about was the proctor she'd seen once, getting that news. Maybe it felt a little like she felt, hearing about what could be Doctor Dan's fate.

That felt very sad. But Jess didn't seem to feel sad at all about it, so it was strange. "We'll go see that, and come back?" She looked up into Jess's eyes, and slowly, the right one winked at her.

"Yep," Jess said. "And we get an escort to make sure nothing happens to us." She got off the desk and sat down in the chair across from Dev. "I was going to ask Jason, but he'd be better off staying here. You like that Doug guy?"

Dev considered that thoughtfully. "He seems functional," she said. "I only spoke to him a little. "

"Be good to take out a set of newbies." Jess leaned back and laced her fingers behind her head. "Pretty tame run, get to see how he flies a bus. Good opportunity."

There really didn't seem anything to say to that, so Dev kept silent.

"So it's good. You'll get to see where I came from," Jess said. "We'll leave at dawn, if the weather cooperates. Bring our formals with us." She studied the ceiling. "Interested in chow? After that I can show you the caverns down below."

"Yes," Dev said. "I would like both things very much."

Jess stood up and stretched, and jerked her head toward the door. "Let's go." She waited for Dev to join her and then casually draped an arm over her shoulders, leaving it there even when they exited into the central corridor and headed toward the mess.

People noticed, and Dev noticed them noticing. She wondered if there was something incorrect about it. The natural borns' eyebrows lifted, but Jess ignored them and steered her into the dining hall before she released her.

Dev picked up a tray and studied her choices, tapping in a selection and waiting for it to be dispensed. She heard the hum of conversation behind her, and as she turned around to find a table, she noticed everyone's eyes moving away to find something else to look at.

Hmm.

"Over here." Jess nudged her toward one of the tables on the upper level, settling her tray next to Dev's and sliding into the seat next to her. "Notice anything?" She asked in a near whisper.

"Everyone's looking at you," Dev replied. "Did you do something?"

"Not yet." Jess smiled briefly. "Everyone knows Bain's been talking to me. He sent a note out to the senior agents, so they know about my job offer, but nothing's official."

Dev studied the faces near them without looking directly. "There seems to be some discomfort."

"I bet." Jess dug up a forkful of stringy seaweed and munched it. Then she glanced up briefly. "Call your buddy Doug and his partner over here."

Dev lifted her eyes and caught the attention of the new tech, making a little gesture with her hand to the empty seats at their table.

Visibly pleased, Doug bumped his partner with his elbow and they made their way over and sat down. "Hey, rocket star. Thanks for the invite."

"Doug." April gave him a look. She was a serious looking woman, a little taller than Dev, with curly light brown hair and somber hazel eyes. Next to Doug, who was tall and muscular, she seemed slight, but the body beneath the jumpsuit had that elastic strength developed in field school. Tucked along her hip was a blade with a carved, old style hilt that was worn and visibly well used.

"It's a compliment!" Doug protested. "You weren't in that bus when she turned it upside down, were you?"

Jess chuckled. "I've been there," she commiserated. "When she says sit down, she means it."

April relaxed. "I saw that from the simulation room," she said, glancing at Dev. "It was pretty amazing."

"Thank you," Dev replied, turning her focus on her tray. "I'm sorry if I caused any discomfort to anyone. I was just trying to help the other carrier."

Jess used the distraction to study the surrounding tables. The mixture of attitudes made her smile, and she picked up her cup of kack and took a swallow. "You get that carrier of yours running?" she asked Doug, abruptly.

"Um. Almost," Doug said. "Have to replace most of it. Dev saw."

Dev nodded, her mouth full of fish.

"Finish it in time, you can go out with us tomorrow." Jess caught the intense, eager gleam in April's eyes. "Nothing exotic, I just need an escort team on a trip home. Up for it?"

"We will be," April said, forestalling Doug's response. "It'll be an honor."

Jess smiled and lifted her cup in her direction. "Hope that's all it'll be."

DEV COULD FEEL and hear the ocean as they made their way down a long, slippery rock staircase in the very bowels of the citadel. The air was full of salty moisture and she licked her lips as she followed Jess closely on the steps, lit by the odd phosphorescent block set deep in the stone.

"Long way down, huh?" Jess commented.

"In the creche, the upper levels were where the natural born lived," Dev said. "The very lower levels were where the space workers stayed, and it was like this a little, when you had to climb down through the core to there."

"Humans are the same everywhere." Jess's voice sounded wry. "Even in the outlands where shelter's a dug hole, there's status and fights over it." She reached the bottom level and turned to the right, where a large metal door had been fitted into the stone.

"Yes, that's true," Dev said. "Everyone wants to have more or better stuff or a better assignment than anyone else. Even we do."

"Even?" Jess worked the manual lock and put her shoulder to the door, shoving it open. That revealed a long, narrow tunnel, and without hesitation, she headed into it. "C'mon."

It was dark and mysterious. Dev resisted the urge to reach out and take hold of Jess's jumpsuit as she followed her through the tunnel. She heard a rumbling, wild sound ahead of them and a moment later, they were out of the tunnel and into a huge, huge cavern.

Jess stepped to one side so she could see past her.

Dev stopped in surprise. "Wow."

Jess leaned against the wall and regarded the space before them. The wall of the citadel came down to the water, over the edge of the sea that roared and surged through it, sending a volume of water through a tunnel underneath their feet. "It's one of a dozen of them," she said. "Flow dumps through turbines behind that wall there." She pointed to their right. "Then goes back out a raceway over there."

Dev stood on her tiptoes to see the outflow on the far side of a thick ridge of stone smashing against the low wall before it escaped back to the sea. "This is amazing."

"It is," Jess said. "Too bad we didn't think of this before we sucked half the planet dry of fossil fuels, but then, there are a lot less of us around now to need it." She went to the edge and pointed down.

"That's where we swim, there where it breaks off. And those long waves there are great to surf."

Dev edged up next to her and peered at the surging whirlpools created by the in rushing water. Then she looked at Jess. "Are you serious?"

Jess nodded. "See that stairwell there?" She pointed at the side of the wall, where roughly cut steps led down to a long, open rock surface that was continually washed over by water. "We go down there, and dive in. It's past the intake for the water, so you don't get sucked in, but it's a great ride, and you end up on that little beach there."

Dev could hardly imagine it.

"See? We chain our boards to the wall there. Let's go down." Jess headed for the steps. "Getting in the water feels great."

Knowing more than a moment of doubt about that, Dev nevertheless followed her partner down the steps, her entire body vibrating from the force of the water's motion. They reached the bottom platform and she stayed near the wall as the water surged up around her boots, glad of their thick and waterproof construction.

Then they moved around and were in a surprising dip in the wall, a three quarter round space that oddly cut off the roar as Jess pulled her closer against the long vaguely oval objects she'd pointed at. "Oh."

"Oh." Jess folded her arms across her chest. "This is one place you can really talk in private." She said.

"Why is it quiet here?" Dev turned around in a circle.

"Quirk of acoustics," Jess said. "So. Listen. Let's talk about tomorrow." She leaned against one of the boards. "And then I'll show you how to surf."

Dev eyed the boards, and hoped the tomorrow discussion was a long one. "Tomorrow for our trip to your home?"

"That's one part. But after that's done, we're not coming back here. We're going to get lost up over the white, and come down on the other side. I think I know where they're holding the team," Jess said, in a calm tone. "Once we leave Drake's Bay, we'll be renegade."

"I see," Dev responded. "That sounds incorrect."

"It is." Jess looked out over the water. "I just have to decide what to do about our escort."

"Do about them?"

Jess turned and met her eyes. "They either have to agree to join us, or I'll have to take them down."

Take them down. Dev felt a little chilled. The serious woman, and her fellow tech, who had eagerly jumped at the chance of coming along on their first mission, and Jess was talking about making them dead. "Jess, are you sure this is a correct thing to do?" she asked, after a pause. "Because I'm not sure Doctor Dan would think it was."

Jess studied her for a long moment. "You don't?"'

"No," Dev answered honestly. "I don't think he would want us to get into this trouble, and hurt our colleagues, to provide him with assistance. I think it would make him sad."

Jess looked intrigued rather than upset. "He doesn't want to be rescued? He would rather be tortured to death? Really? Because that's what'll happen to him, Dev. I've seen it. They'll string him up and take power poles to his entire body until his brain fries."

Dev thought very hard about that, but sad and hard as it was, she thought she knew the truth of it. "I remember once we were in class, and we were doing a lab. One of the people in class did something wrong and the lab broke apart and the stuff in it went flying."

Jess waited without speaking.

"Doctor Dan stepped in front of it, so it hit him, and not us," Dev said. "It hurt him a lot, but he just stood there and let it hurt him."

"Ah."

"Dr. Doss came and he yelled at Doctor Dan, because he said we were replaceable." Dev folded her arms. "But Doctor Dan said he didn't care."

Jess pondered that. "You may be right. He may not agree," she said. "But I'm going to go rescue his ass anyway. Offer still stands, Dev. I'll leave you and maybe those kids at Drake's Bay. Go myself." She put a hand on Dev's shoulder. "Could be one way."

After a pause, Dev exhaled. "Whether or not Doctor Dan thinks this is good or bad, I want to go with you." she said. "Because..." She paused for a long time. "Because I think it's the right thing to do." She looked up at Jess. "It's what I want to do."

Jess smiled. Then she leaned closer and kissed Dev on the lips. "Thanks," she said. "That made the one way thing a lot less likely, because you're a lot better driver than I am, and I need you." She eased back a little. "So now that we're over all this serious, self-sacrificing bullshit, let's surf."

There was really no question in Dev's mind that she would rather go practice that sex thing than try surfing. However, she nodded anyway. "It's going to be cold, isn't it?" She regarded the water mournfully.

"Very." Jess unchained her board and set it to one side, then pulled a thick jumpsuit from the rack and started to unfasten her own. "But I promise I'll warm you up later."

Ah. Well at least there was that to look forward to. Dev regarded the suit she'd been handed, and resolved to at least try to enjoy it.

IT WAS COLD. Dev held on to the rocks as the water rushed around her, almost overwhelming her with the smell of salt and the rich scent of the water itself.

She was in a shallow curve of the rock, somewhat protected from the roughness of the surf, but it was still more than enough to have tossed her around if she wasn't holding on.

Very different than the pool. She shook the wet hair from her eyes and watched as Jess got onto her board, and paddled across the surface of the water, heading for the outer wall. When she got there, she turned, and as the next surging wave came in she got up onto the board and stood up, as the water picked her and it up and rolled toward the little shore.

Wow. Dev watched in fascination as Jess balanced gracefully, her body relaxed as the wave rushed along. She could feel the pulse of the sea herself, its surge alternately sucking at her and shoving her against the rocks she had tight hold of. It was like nothing she'd ever experienced.

Jess waited for the board to reach the little beach she'd launched from and hopped off, grabbing the handhold and hauling the oblong item with her. "See?" She turned and called out, spreading her arms. "Easy!"

Dev released her hold and waited for the next surge to shove her beach-ward, practicing her newly learned swimming skills as she made her way toward Jess.

It wasn't easy. The pull of the water made progress tricky, but she kept at it as Jess stood there leaning against her board, watching her. Eventually it was shallow enough for her to stand, and she slogged out of the water onto the beach, trying not to shiver too much as the cool air hit her.

"Doing okay?" Jess asked, as she joined her. "Not like the pool, huh?"

"No," Dev said, rubbing her arms through the heavy stretchy fabric covering them. "But it's interesting."

"Okay, so grab that board." Jess pointed at the second one. "And just follow me."

Dev obeyed, lifting the oblong object, a little surprised at how light it was. "Oh." She hefted it. "I thought it would weigh more."

"Hollow." Jess headed for the surf. "This beach used to be three times the size." She lamented. "Then the water rose. Made for better waves, but all the erosion's knocking part of that wall down."

Dev waded into the water after her, towing the board. "Didn't that man at the North base say something about the water level dropping? Was this the beach he meant?"

"Sure is." Jess paused as they got into water deep enough to start pulling her off her feet. "Okay, so now lay down on the board and just start paddling with your hands. Watch me."

Usually, watching Jess was a pleasure. In this case, however, Dev had her hands full just keeping herself upright and it was actually something of a relief when she managed to get on top of the board and the water stopped pulling at her. She lay down on her stomach on it, and copied Jess as best as she was able.

The water kept coming over the edge of the board and hitting her in the face. Dev sneezed and shook her wet hair out of her eyes, arching her back a little to keep her head up.

They neared the outer wall, and she got a glimpse of the outside, a roil of whitecaps that flashed before her eyes before the surge came in and the view was blocked.

"Okay, now watch," Jess yelled, as they turned around. She pressed herself up and got her feet under her, standing up on the board as the wave started to gather speed. "Stand up and just go with it!"

That seemed to be very easy for her to say. Dev was struggling just to hold on to her board, but gamely, she pushed up and nearly fell off, before she managed to get her feet under her in a weird sort of crouch.

"Stand up!" Jess called back. "Or you'll end up tipping over!"

Uncertainly, Dev released her grip and felt the board slide around as the water came up under her. She remained in a crouch though, holding her arms out for balance as she tried to adjust to the erratic motion. "Okay." She took a breath. "I think I can— "

A cross wave smacked into her, and the next thing she knew she was flying off the board and into the water, plunging under the surface as the shifting forces pulled her under.

It was dark, and frightening. She struggled to get herself moving in the right direction, not entirely sure what that direction was. She felt a smack on the back of her head and waved her arms around to find the source of the attack, then was pulled in a circle as she fell into a whirl of surf.

She fought to not breathe, feeling a burn in her chest as she kicked with her legs, trying to get to the surface she didn't know the exact location of. The desire to suck in air was overwhelming, and just as she started to give into it, she felt something grab her and yank her upward.

Her head broke the surface and she gasped, feeling Jess's iron grip on her upper arm. "Ugh!"

"Easy!" Jess had a good hold on her now. "I forgot you don't goddamned float. Even with this thing on." She stroked sideways through the water, pulling them both toward the shore. "Sorry about that."

Dev saved her breath for fighting the water, doing the best she could to aid the effort as they both ended up being shoved ashore by the surf, covered in sand.

"Buh." Jess sat up, her long legs sprawled on the beach as the continuous waves washed over them. "That was kinda stupid."

Dev coughed, spitting out a mouthful of sand. She rolled over and pushed herself up to a seated position. "That was interesting," she said. "I'm not sure I would be good at it." She glanced behind them at the churning surf. "I do like this place though. And I liked the little bit over there to swim in."

Jess chuckled wryly. "Did they program you for optimism, Dev?" She examined a scrape on the back of her hand. "Yeah, I come down here and swim a lot. It reminds me of the bay near where I grew up, I guess." She hiked her knees up and circled them with both arms. "Not as rough though."

Dev leaned back against the stone wall that bordered the small beach. Here, out of the wind, the cold wasn't so bad, and she could imagine Jess here in the dim light of the phosphorescent blocks, reliving earlier memories here in the water she seemed to be very much attracted to.

Which she wanted Dev to share, apparently. "I would like to try this again," Dev said, catching Jess's eyes as they lifted to her face in some surprise. "I will try to float better next time."

Jess glanced around, then back at her. "You sure?"

"Yes." Dev felt the whole thing was worth it, seeing the sudden, big grin on Jess's face. "Should we go find the flat things?"

Jess stood up and held her hand out. "Let's go," she said. "Don't know when we'll get another chance with all that's going on."

Dev let herself be hauled to her feet, and sloshed back into the water, spitting a little bit of extra sand, and what she suspected was some small animal, out of her mouth, determined to collect yet another thing that would mark her as unique.

Just in case.

THE SHOWER ITSELF felt amazing. Dev stood quietly under the hot water, feeling her body slowly thaw. But even more amazing was Jess's presence behind her in it, scrubbing her skin with the clean smelling soap. "I think I swallowed some seaweed."

She hoped it was seaweed. She tried not to think about the vaguely wiggling sensation it had provided her, going down. It was a little unsettling to think about that whole swallowing live animals thing.

"Happens." Jess was humming softly under her breath, as she worked. "Glad you got something out of it, Devvie. Ya did good, those last two runs."

Dev supposed she had, somehow remaining standing long enough to get to the shore, in a flail of waving arms and wavering legs that nevertheless still stayed upright. "I liked it."

"Did you? Or are ya just humoring me?" Jess brought her arms around and soaped the front of Dev's body, making her completely forget about what she'd just been asked. "Hmm?"

It felt so amazing. "I'm sorry. What?" Dev finally asked. "Did you ask me something?"

Jess chuckled, and kept up her soaping.

After a moment, Dev turned around in the circle of her arms and started reciprocating. "I like this also," she said as Jess ducked her head down and they kissed.

"Yeah me too." Jess slid her hands up to cradle the back of Dev's head, feeling the gently exploring touch across her body make her breathing shorten. "Let's dry off and continue this in a more comfortable spot," she said, but found herself not budging, as Dev traced a curious path down the centerline of her torso.

Her skin felt sensitized, and the shower pounding against it only made it worse. She had to force herself to shut the water off and reach for the towel, all the while touching and nibbling Dev, the surroundings starting to fade out.

Somehow, they made it over to the bed. Jess was glad to feel the cool, soft surface under her and started to return Dev's attentions in earnest.

Hard to remember, really, that Dev had so little experience. Jess felt a thigh slide between hers, and was glad they were in the citadel, where security was someone else's problem for a while. She said that, stifling a sound as Dev's curious touch fastened on a nipple.

And then Dev went suddenly still. "Jess," she said, on an irregular breath. "I found something in the carrier bay."

Jess felt her chest heaving. "What?"

"I brought it to the big place to show you. Before."

Jess opened her eyes to find Dev's pale ones looking back at her. She could see the flush on her face, and she was on the razor's edge of just telling her to forget about it.

That it could wait for later.

But training, deep as bone, paused that. "You have damned inconvenient memory, NM-Dev-1." She rolled over and scrubbed her face. "Oh, boy."

"Sorry." Dev cleared her throat. "The whole thing with the water made me forget. I remembered when you said that about security." She got up out of the bed and walked over to the door between their quarters. "Let me get it and show you."

Jess rolled flat onto her back and glared at the ceiling.

A moment later Dev came back with her portable comp, climbing back into bed with it, still completely naked. She focused on the screen, reaching up with one hand to push the still damp hair out of her eyes. "I was doing a reading on the new people's carrier, then I was in the damaged one, and look." She held the comp up so Jess could see it. "This was present in both of them."

Jess rolled onto her side and looked at the screen. "What is that?"

"It's the recall beacon," Dev said. "Except its polarity's reversed. It's sending out a signal on that sine wave. Not receiving one."

Jess slowly straightened up, lifting her body up on one elbow. She reached for the comp and pulled it closer, the readings standing out with a surreal clarity in the dimness of the room. "You said this was in April and Doug's bus, and the one Syd was driving?"

"Yes."

"What the hell?" Jess's brow creased. "That old bus they're driving wasn't..." She paused. "Check the comp. When was it last used?"

Dev got up and retrieved her under jumpsuit, slipping it on before she sat down behind Jess's workstation and pulled a pad over to her.

It was a shame, of course, that the sex practice had to be interrupted. They had been well on their way to feeling excellent, but after all, they did have their job to do. She typed in the request and waited. Of course, she was hoping the question could be answered quickly.

"If they went out like that, they'd be a target a walrus could have hit with a hairball." Jess was studying the portable unit. "Did you check ours?"

"Yes," Dev answered. "That unit was last in service six standard, seven day weeks ago. Assigned to Mr. Bock, and someone called Callie."

Jess got up and walked over, coming around the back of the chair and leaned on the desk with one hand. "Is that so?" she mused. "Now where were you going, Stephen? Pull the nav on that." She triggered comms. "Mech ops, Drake."

A crackle. "Mech, this is Clint." The tech supervisor sounded wary. "What can I do for you, Jess?"

"Dev found a glitch on April's bus, in the beacon. You hear about it?"

Clint sighed. "Yeah, that new tech was bugging me for a new one. I told him to get out the soldering iron. Why?"

"Run a scan on every carrier in the bay for that glitch, Clint," Jess said, in a quiet, and serious tone. "Now."

He was briefly silent. "Ack," he answered shortly.

"Let me know what you find."

"Ack." He triggered off.

Jess exhaled. "Sure hope he doesn't find anything," she said. "Got nav back?"

"It was unregistered, according to this," Dev responded. "Is this all incorrect?"

"Two teams went out this afternoon," Jess said. "If they had this same alteration, they're flying wide open." She exhaled. "Glad you remembered this."

Dev felt bad. "I should have thought of it earlier," she said. "I got distracted."

Jess kissed her on the top of her head. "Another sign of your humanity, Devvie. C'mon." She reached over and unzipped the zipper on her under-suit. "Let's finish what we started."

Ignoring your duty wasn't good. Dev could feel that intensity starting again and she stood, letting Jess peel the suit off her. But she wanted this and Doctor Dan had been right about that too.

She hoped he wouldn't be too disappointed if he ended up finding out.

DEV SETTLED INTO the tech seat, hitching it forward and bringing up the boards that would activate the carrier's systems. She was dressed in her flight suit, her formal one stashed in one of the cabinets at her left hand side. The carrier hatch was propped open, waiting for its second occupant and all around her things were in motion as the busy bay carried on.

It was early. Dawn was just cracking outside, and above her, the hatch was already open, revealing a dull gray sky that was thankfully still rain free.

Over to the right she could see bio alts scurrying around April and Doug's carrier, their freshly painted names clear and sharp against the machine's mottled skin. As she watched, she saw Doug enter, and knew he'd be shortly performing the same checks as she was, having worked all night to get his systems ready for flight.

She'd helped, after she and Jess had gotten a late meal in the mess. With all the swimming and everything else though, she'd only been able to help him for so long before she was tired enough to wish Jess would come and retrieve her.

Doug had gotten far enough with her help that she thought he might finish, and she had only felt a little guilty about leaving with Jess and crawling into bed with her to get some sleep.

So now she felt good, having gotten sufficient rest, and she ran through the preflight checks with confidence.

Everyone seemed a bit somber. No one made jokes with Jess in the mess during breakfast, and one or two of the other agents had come up to offer her condolences, or wish them a safe flight.

She heard footsteps, and glanced behind her as Jess entered the carrier, putting a gear bag with her formals into the rear cabinet. "Hello."

"Hey, Devvie." Jess closed the cabinet and then sealed the hatch, coming forward to Dev's position with a small pad. "Here's the coordinates. Go ahead and plot it, then file the flight plan with ops."

Dev accepted the pad and set it down, calling up the nav system to program it. The system accepted the coordinates and drew her a wiremap, outlining a long concave route to the south and west. She reached over and settled her ear cups on her head. "BR270006 to central operations for comms check."

"Standby BR270006," Centops answered.

Dev used the time to connect the carrier's systems to her suit inputs and run the pre start sequence on the engines. She observed the response of the systems carefully, plugging in her portable comp and comparing results there. The beacon subsystem had been looked at last night, but theirs, unlike some but not all of the others, hadn't been altered.

Jess sat down in her gunner's position and started activating her controls. "Give me some juice."

Dev balanced the batteries and shunted power to weapons, seeing the aux weapons boards come live near her station.

"BR270006, go ahead for comms check," Ops came online. "Standing by for flight plan."

Dev sent the nav plot over. "Comms check midband and sideband alpha," she said. "Requesting steady comms throughout the flight plan."

"Confirmed," Central ops replied. "Comms check cleared, flight plan accepted. Standby for clearance."

"Open a side band to April's rig," Jess said, as she settled the restraints around her and snugged them tight. "Send her the coordinates from your output."

Dev complied, requesting the contact from the other carrier. "Jess, carrier supply is asking if we need any supplemental."

"Tell them no," Jess said. "Tell them short trip, no need for anything special."

Dev nodded and pressed an ear cup more firmly to her head. "Standing by." She muttered softly.

Jess arranged her boards and settled back, letting her hands rest on her thighs. Now that they were on the verge of flight, she had time to think about what they were doing and it made her grimace a little

But it did get her out of the citadel, on as legitimate a flight as she could have invented. And as far as she was letting on, this was just a routine family obligation, with nothing in her planning that might indicate anything else to anyone who happened to be checking on her.

She suspected there were a few, including Bain.

"Jess, we have clearance," Dev said. "We also have a connection to the other carrier."

All regulation. All normal. All as expected. "Great. Go ahead and lift. Tell April and Doug to meet us topside." Jess ran another set of checks on her boards, and then set them into quiescence.

"Releasing umbilicals," Dev announced softly, as the power shift went from external to internal, and she spooled up the landing jets. "Launching."

Jess felt the motion, and she settled her head against the padded rest of her chair, watching on the screens as the carrier lifted and turned, sliding sideways and then moving up through the open hatch into free air.

As she expected, the carrier rotated in a complete circle, then moved off to one side as they waited for their escort to follow. "Give me comp and comms wouldja, Dev?" She saw the indicators, some almost instantly, on her console and set her ear cup in place. "Thanks."

She keyed up the bio scan and set to work, humming slightly under her breath.

Dev set a scan in motion and looked around at the thick clouds overhead. They were dark and dense, but the wind had dropped and there wasn't much motion to them. She shifted the carrier back a little to clear air, and watched as the other carrier rose up from the bay.

"BR270006, copy." Doug's voice echoed softly in her ear. "Copy good. Standby to transit." She glanced in the mirror. "Jess?"

"Huh?" Her partner looked up. "We ready? Yes? Let's go."

"Proceed on nav coordinates," Dev told Doug, as she swung them around and boosted the engines into forward, then increased speed. "ETA one hour."

Jess nodded. "Yup. No long distance butt aching this time." She triggered a transmit and then relaxed, taking advantage of the transit, regardless of how short, to clear her mind of both thoughts and stress. "Going home."

Chapter Six

DEV ADJUSTED A setting, glancing up at the nav comp as it updated their position. They were running along the edge of a long string of islands and shallows, and she hadn't seen much sign of any life along the way.

The dull gray daylight was outlining the green surf, and in the distance, she saw a taller height rising out of the sea, long arms on either side descending down in a rough semicircle. "Is that where we're going?" She pointed at it.

"Yup." Jess was leaning on the console near her, drinking from a container. "That's it. That big half round area is Drake's Bay."

It was too far to really see any detail, but it looked big. "Are there a lot of people there?" Dev asked.

"Not like Quebec, but there's people there," Jess said, in a thoughtful tone. "Aside from my extended family, and the people who work the processing center down the coast, there's little haulers, and scavengers, lots of small caves and tuck unders you can survive in."

"I see."

"Most people work at the processors, but supplement that with after-hours work in the Bay," Jess said. "My grandfather wanted to make the place self-sufficient, be able to pay full time, but he never made it. My dad never even tried. But they can feed themselves. Don't really need to work for the processor but they're so scared they'd lose the place if they stopped."

Dev wasn't sure she understood all that. But they were coming within scan range of the half round area, and she started to pick up signals. "We're being scanned."

"I bet." Jess kept sipping from her mug. "Drake's Bay is not exactly like any other place we've been so far, Dev." She watched the coastline slip by. "Contact Doug and tell them to stay behind us, and keep cool."

Dev made the call, and repeated the instructions, hoping the last part made sense to their escorts. Then she saw an incoming signal and keyed to it. "Repeat, calling station?"

Jess smiled faintly.

"Incoming vessel approaching Drake's Bay. Identify yourself and your originating location or standoff. This will be your only warning."

Dev looked at Jess in question.

"Go ahead and identify us."

"This is BR270006, Interforce, flight outbound from Base Ten," Dev obediently supplied, then blinked as she felt a second, much more powerful scan sweep through them, making her skin tingle, and the chips in her hand itch. "Is that correct?" she asked Jess.

Jess half shrugged. "Is it approved? No. But I sent over our bio scans so with any luck that'll clear us and we won't have to engage in any more, who the hell are you, bullshit."

"So they know who we are?"

"They know who we are," Jess confirmed.

"Interforce BR270006, come ahead. You are expected," the comms sputtered. "Advise your following vessel to stay to your inbound pattern. Access bay twelve is available."

"Tell them thank you." Jess extended her legs and crossed them at the ankles. "Then go around that far wall there, midway up the slope you'll see the landing bays. Twelve's the second from the top."

Dev complied, sending the signal to Doug to stay on their tail. As they approached the tall, half circle wall of stone she could see that it sloped up away from the water and rose above it, but it had no flat wall like the citadel did. It was more like a cone, and it reminded her a little of the market island that had blown up.

The half circle bay at its foot was protected by the arching walls that came down from either side, and the water in the enclosed part was a lighter shade of green and blue. Dev thought she could see through it and see some rocks and things beneath the surface.

There were docks tucked into the inside of the curve, and there were boats there tied to them. And though the surf was choppy, it was far less rough than farther out. On the edge of the water was a beach like the one in the citadel, only this one was much larger, and wider.

Dev glanced up at Jess, seeing a thoughtful, and somewhat sad, look on her face. She was about to ask a question, then decided to hold it for later. She returned her attention to the rock wall, angling their course so they would come around the edge.

On the far side of the curved wall she saw the landing area. There were ledges and openings scattered over the bare walls, and zigzagging from them were steps carved into the stone, leading down to one large opening at ground level.

Dev found the second from the top and angled toward it, as two smaller craft dove into an opening two levels lower. She approached the entrance and slowed her forward speed, dropping down to make sure she cleared the ceiling and passed inside.

The interior of the cavern surprised her. It was more regular in shape than she expected, and the inner walls were flat, and straight, not like the walls of the carrier bay back at the citadel. She noticed there were people on the ground with bright colored sticks pointing at them.

"Over there, Dev." Jess indicated the flat area they were pointing at. "Just put her down, then we can change into our formals."

"All right." Dev gently eased the carrier down. She could see a landing crew waiting for her, none of their faces in any way familiar. "They know what to do with this vessel?"

"They know what to do with a lot of things," Jess answered enigmatically. "But yeah, you can let them hook up once you land. They won't do anything but put power up for us."

"Okay." Dev extended the landing skids and set the craft on the floor of the cavern, shutting down the engines as the tech team approached them, and with casual skill, connected a set of umbilicals to their ports. She observed the settings, then she switched over the power and watched for a moment as the leads evened out.

"Dev?"

Dev unfastened her restraints and got out of her chair. "Yes?"

Jess opened the back cabinet and started unzipping her flight suit. "There aren't any bio alts here," she said. "But they'll probably have heard of you."

Dev studied her, as she opened the small cabinet near her station. "Will it cause discomfort?" she asked. "Would you prefer if I stayed here?"

Jess slid into her formals, fastening the shoulder catch on the sleeveless under-suit. "You might prefer it," she said wryly. "In general, my family's just against the whole idea of bio alts. They'd rather build a bigger population base of natural borns. They think making what they view as servants is dumb and immoral."

"I see."

"On the other hand, you're a tech." Jess slid into her jacket and pulled the sleeves straight. "And one thing they do respect is Interforce. Probably give the whole lot of them indigestion for a year."

"I see," Dev repeated, making sure her insignia were in place, and fastened correctly.

"So no, I'd rather you not stay here. But try to ignore any jackassery you hear. Okay? I can't really start beating the crap out of my family for insulting you." She finished dressing and ducked her head to look at a reflective piece of metal, running her fingers through her hair.

"Of course not," Dev said. "They can say anything they want, Jess. I'm trained for that."

Jess rested her wrists on Dev's shoulders. "I know. But I'm not." She leaned forward and gave her a kiss on the lips. "And we Drakes have some odd ideas of honor. So hopefully they'll give you the respect a tech, and my partner, deserves." She patted her cheek. "Let's go."

Jess triggered the hatch open and the ramp extended, letting in a gust of sea air mixed with stone and silicon oil. She led the way down, glancing to her left where Doug and April were standing, braced, waiting for her. Bain had said to have them stand off, but Jess knew better.

Have a carrier, armed, hovering over the homestead? Not even she could pull that off. She wasn't even carrying a single weapon on her. Having the two newbies with her would have to be enough.

She motioned them to follow and started toward the inner halls, slowing when she saw her brother Jimmy's tall form fill the doorway. "Hey, Jimmy."

He held a hand up in greeting. "'Lo, Jess." He stepped out of the doorway and cleared space. "Sorry this had to be a homecoming occasion." He glanced at her companions. "Welcome to Drake's Bay," he addressed them.

"Sorry to hear the news," Jess said. "This is April Anston, and her partner Doug Sars." She half turned. "And this is my partner, Dev."

"Your new partner?" Jimmy asked.

"Brand new, and already notorious." Jess kept her gaze steady, and her eyes flatly expressionless in warning.

Jimmy kept his eyes on Dev for an instant, then he nodded. "Follow me." He turned and ducked back through the door, holding it open for them as they followed and then letting it close as he continued on.

So far so good, Dev thought. She walked along a pace behind Jess, looking around with interest.

Jess and her brother were headed down the steps and they hastily followed, down several levels and then through another hall that led to a beautiful archway into a big chamber beyond. Dev looked up as they went through, seeing a pretty design carved in the stone above it, a sort of diamond or triangle shaped outline with a creature in the middle, odd and strange, with its fish-like tail, and wings.

She put a reminder in her head to ask Jess later what it was supposed to be. Right now, her attention was captured by the space they were entering, a big room with stone floors and a beautiful arched ceiling, where there were a number of people waiting.

There was a table there, with trays on it, and glasses. The people in the room were all dressed well, and some were drinking from glasses, standing in small groups talking. Jimmy put a hand on Jess's shoulder and then left them, going across the room to talk to three men, who were in simple gray jumpsuits with colored bands on their shoulders.

People noticed their entrance, Dev realized. A lot of them were watching them, though most looked curious rather than in discomfort. As they milled around they exposed a pit with a heating element in it, round and stone cut, that had carved plaques above it going around in a curve.

"So, what do you think?" Jess whispered in her ear.

"This place is amazing," Dev whispered back.

Jess smiled briefly, standing with her hands behind her back. "Yeah, it's not bad for an old rock pile," she said, in a nonchalant tone. "Couple of families of stone masons and steel wrights have lived here as part of the extended homesteads for a few generations. We use barter for life staples, works out pretty good for both sides."

Jimmy moved to the center of the room and cleared his throat. "Okay, folks, thanks for being here. Processing is set to start soon as we get to the viewing station. This way." He indicated a door in the back of the chamber. "Wake lunch'll be in the dining chamber when it's over."

Jess indicated for them to hold off going until most of the room had emptied, then she led their little group into the back hall. She knew a number of the others there, but she hadn't seen most since she'd been very small, and she didn't really expect any of them to come up and talk to her. Service family or not, it was true once you were taken, you became part of something else and she'd stopped being a part of Drake's Bay's life a long time ago.

Didn't really bother her. Right?

She walked along the halls she'd last really trod as a child, and as they turned a corner and the corridor started downward she felt a gust of the rich salt air she remembered so well.

"So you made it."

Jess turned to find her brother Jake walking next to her. "I made it."

Jake nodded. "Glad you did. Even if you and the old woman didn't get along."

Jess sighed. "I don't think it was that. I think she just wanted things to be different and I couldn't change that. I think she always figured I could have said no to this at some point."

"Crazy woman." Jake shook his head. "Lucky it was only one of us."

"Yeah." Jess slowed as they reached the lock to the outer platform, which was set in the open position. She followed the last of the guests out of the lock and then they were facing the bay. After a brief pause, Jess circled the crowd and eased over to one side of the platform, moving through the other guests until she was up against the wall.

She put her hands on the top of it, and waited, drawing in a breath of the air coming off the bay. Jake came up to stand next to her, and she was aware of Dev's presence at her elbow. Dev keeping very quiet, and sticking very close.

It was a very impersonal process, really. Jess regarded the outflow station three levels below. There was no place to put organic garbage, no use for its components in the holding, so they did what made sense, grind it up and expel it into the sea where it became a meal for the creatures living in it.

Human bodies were just large pieces of organic garbage, once life had left them. They got the same treatment as any of the kitchen refuse, and now, though not in the beginning, it was common and accepted. Her mother would have a memorial plaque set in the wall of the family chamber, and her name added to the remembrance ceremonies held once a year. But nowadays the thought of keeping a body around just to remember someone would horrify anyone alive.

It was, what it was.

"Standby," Jimmy said, quietly, though his voice echoed softly in the viewing station. "Processing underway."

A soft rumble, the sound of a hatch, and a rush of darkish matter into the blue green water. The fish saw it, and a moment later there was a frenzy, a roil of fins and silvery bodies thrashing the water.

There was something still, of that corporal reverence. But then life would go on, and they would continue to live in the way they had for generations now, the only way they'd been able to manage.

"So." Jake shifted. "That's done."

"Bye, Mom," Jess said. "Sorry we never got a chance to be human to each other, there at the end."

"Sorry you never got to see me spawn," Jake said, giving his sister a sideways glance. "Finally got an allotment. Sagra's pregnant."

Jess smiled briefly. "Congratulations."

The crowd was breaking up and going back inside, already talking of other things. Jimmy came over to them, folding his arms across his chest and glancing briefly out to sea. "Glad you could make it out, Jess," he said. "Let's go have lunch. Trade some stories. Tayler wants to see his aunt. I think we've all had a lot of changes lately."

His eyes flicked to Dev, who returned his look with bland politeness.

"Sure," Jess said. "We'd love to." She spoke for her three companions, who were really in no place to argue about it. "You can give me all the details on what happened to Mom."

"And you can tell us all about those gold bars and the new recruits," Jimmy countered. "After you?"

"After you."

JESS RESTED HER wrists on the big, old table, salvaged from who knew what, how many generations back in Drake history. It was wood, which was rare enough, but it had patterned inlay and a decayed, stately elegance that was now very rare. It had been the dining table she remembered from her childhood, big enough for a dozen or more to eat around it and close to the big kitchen with its baking pit and cook tops.

Here it was private lunch, bowls of food passed around the table and her brother's families along with two old aunts and an ancient uncle seated around sharing it.

Little Tayler was there, sitting next to her left hand side, with Dev on her right. He was busy showing her a starfish, found apparently just that morning on the reef. He had a tangle of dark brown curls and a snub nose, and no idea what was about to happen to him.

He would probably miss the same things she had.

She felt unsettled, as she usually did here. Aware at some level of a sense of faded familiarity, yet aware that people watched her constantly, perhaps waiting for her to lose it and get crazy on someone.

Strange love hate relationship, with both the idea of, and the reality of Interforce. "That's a nice starfish, Tayler," Jess told her nephew. "Find it at the point?"

"Yes." Tayler put a finger between the arms of the petrified thing and moved it in a circle. "I like it."

"Me too." Jess reached over to help him turn the item, remembering sitting at this table, younger than he was now, doing more or less the same thing.

Tayler looked past her at Dev, and gave Dev a shy smile. "Hello."

Dev smiled back. "Hello."

"You like my starfis?"

Jess was glad of the distraction, and she was content to watch the kid engage with Dev, who being closer to his size, apparently was a fascination.

"I do," Dev said. "I have a vid of a bear. Would you like to see it?"

Tayler's eyes lit up. "A bear? A real bear? Daddy! Daddy! She saw a bear!"

Everyone looked up and over at the excited child, then Jimmy eyed Dev warily. "She did, huh?" He looked over at Jess. "You all up in the white? Hadn't heard that."

Dev got up and came around to where Tayler was bouncing in his chair, pulling her comp out and calling up the vid. "The bear was really amazing. We saw baby ones too."

"We were up in the white," Jess said. "Just got back. I saw great uncle Jacob, matter of fact."

"That old coot?" Jake spoke up. "Haven't seen his fishy ass in years. He still remember you?"

"Oh, wow!" Tayler was glued to the comp screen, as Dev ran through the vid she had of the bears, ending with the three animals watching them as they escaped into the cavern, the baby's tiny faces and cupped ears outlined against the ice. "That's cool!"

"He remembered me," Jess said. "They're doing all right. Should trade more on this side of the fence though."

"They pay more," Jake commented shortly. "Got plenty of hard cred over there."

Everyone looked a little uncomfortable, watching Jess closely. She was aware of that, but shrugged. "I know. I sold them a hold full of one of his boat's catch. Made more than I take a year." She chewed a mouthful of leaf seaweed and mushrooms, along with a forkful of the whole fish fillet on her plate. "There's a reason market island's over on that side. That's where the cred is."

"Maybe not now for a while," Jake said, glancing at her. "Heard they had a big loss half month back or so. Whole research processing center gone."

"Yeah?" Jess looked mildly at him.

"Trading boat came through yesterday, early," Jimmy said. "Telling a story of some crazy ass lone gun shooting out half the damn side of Gibraltar."

It got quiet. Everyone focused on Jess, who stolidly kept chewing. She eventually swallowed, and then looked at Dev, who was kneeling next to her. "You think I'm crazy ass?"

Dev regarded her solemnly. "I don't think I'm programmed to comment about your ass."

April stifled a laugh.

Jess looked back across the table. "My first mission with my new partner," she said, briefly. "Let's just say it was a payback for turning Josh."

"So you got 'em there, little Jessy?" Uncle Matt spoke up. "Kicked 'em where it hurt? Good on ya." He nodded to himself, munching on his fish. "More of 'em dead, the better."

Jess smiled, and Mari, Jimmy's wife, changed the subject. There was a lot of that around family dinner tables, when you were part of an in-service clan. Uncle Matt could be excused though, because he'd lost everything to the other side, a wife, three kids, and a homestead along with his left arm and a foot.

Matter of fact Jess was glad to have taken a piece out of them for him. "So where was the old woman coming back from?"

"Council meeting," Jimmy said. "They had a vote up for the east flats. A bunch of lower caverners petitioned to open a station there. Vote went for them. I'm not sure it's worth it though."

"Not enough shells?" Jess asked.

"They're trying for independent status," Jimmy replied. "There's no facility out there."

"Uh huh. So she was headed back here after that, just after the vote? No stops?" Jess asked. "Any comp from the flyer?"

"Nothing left of it," Jake said. "She probably tied one on before she left. You know what she was like." He studied Jess. "Hey, well maybe you didn't. She went for the bottle last couple years."

"So they figure she splatted from that? They'll take her benefits," Jess said. "Didn't she have shares in this place?"

Everyone now looked very uncomfortable. Dev had gone back to her seat and Tayler was playing with his food, ignoring what was going on around the table. "C'mon, people. I don't have a stake in it," Jess said. "I'm just asking."

"Right now they're calling it a weather related accident," Jimmy said, stiffly. "Her benefits come back to the family pool. She hadn't made a formal arrangement with anyone else."

"She was never part of this family." Auntie Grace spoke up. "Only made the arrangement with your father to get her hands on a piece of this place."

April and Doug looked vaguely embarrassed, but Jess lifted a hand in their direction. "Sorry. Shoulda warned you," she said. "My family's as assholish as I usually am."

Doug cleared his throat. "My dad's a senior councilor out on Rainier Island. I know the drill," he said. "He's had women after him for years, after my mother passed." He glanced at April. "Not your gig, I know."

"No," April said. "Not with a bunch of traveling nomads. No land, no fighting over it." She had a low, intense voice. "But I know all about asshole families, thanks."

"Anyway." Jimmy pushed his dish aside a little. "So yeah, it ended up good for us. She'd have taken a thirty percent share out, and I don't know what she'd have brought back in here." He lifted his gaze and met Jess's. "But now, either way, it's not an issue."

Jess nodded.

"Can I talk to you a minute in private, Jess?" Jimmy said. "We don't get much chance."

Jess stood and moved around her chair, putting a hand on Dev's shoulder and pressing it before she joined her brother at the back door to the dining hall. They passed through and down a corridor, then into a smaller room lined with shelves. One section of the back wall of the chamber had a clear block in it, and past that you could see the bay.

"So." Jess took a seat in one of the chairs, and put her elbows on the arms. "What's up?"

He went over and perched on the workspace at the back of the room. "Before I call you out as bullshit, I'd like to know why the hell you just put out that crap about you having no stake in this?"

It wasn't often Jess found herself completely dumbfounded, but in this case, she was. "Huh?" She managed to get out, her brows knitting over a creased forehead. "What the fuck are you talking about?"

"The shares." He glared at her. "Your shares."

Jess looked around as if trying to find some other person he could be referring to. "Are you stupid?" she asked. "I have no shares. Remember? I had to sign away my homestead rights when I graduated field school. I have no more stake in this place than I have a horn growing out of my head."

He stared at her. "You don't know?" he said, after a long pause. "He never told you?"

"Told me what?" Jess spread her hands out. "What are you talking about?"

Slowly, he straightened and got up, walking behind the workspace and sitting down behind it. "You really don't know," he repeated, in a half exasperated, half wondering tone. "Son of a bitch." His hands fell to the chair arms. "Well here see it for yourself." He reached into one of the workspace pockets and drew out a pad, keying something up and handing it across the desk at her. "We all thought you knew."

Jess got up and grabbed the pad. "I don't know shit about..." She paused, as her eyes scanned over the screen and she absorbed its contents. "What in the hell did he do here?" She slowly sat down again. "He can't have processed this. I'm not eligible. He knew that."

"He didn't give a shit," Jimmy said. "He told us we were a bunch of losers, and the old woman was a thief. He coded all his shares out of the pool and locked them to your civ profile."

Jess studied the readout, running through it a few times. "Well." She tossed the pad back on the workspace. "I'll never transition to that profile, so it makes no difference anyway. I'll never survive to fully retire. He was just being an asshole."

"He survived."

"I'm not him," Jess said, in a clipped tone. "I'm crazier than he was, and we both know it."

Jimmy exhaled, and slumped a little in the chair. "Seeing that thing with you I believe it. He'd never go for that." He looked up to see the icy look directed at him. "They looking to make sure you don't survive?"

"She got me these gold bars." Jess touched her throat. "That thing's for real."

"Really?"

"Really. And you call her a thing to her face and I'll break both your arms," Jess said, in a mild tone. "Now that I've relieved your avaricious ass and you don't have to worry about me tossing you and your useless brother and these suck-ons that live here out, we done?"

Jimmy had the grace to at least look embarrassed. "Sorry, Jess," he said. "I really thought you knew."

"And I was just laughing at you?" Jess snapped back. "Fuck you."

He exhaled. "The old woman thought you knew. That's why she was so damned pissed off at you these last years. She wangled it all so she could get controlling shares, and he screwed her." He said, "She finally gave up, no way to get around his lock."

"She wanted controlling shares of this place?" Jess felt her anger sidetracked.

"We all do," Jimmy said, straightforwardly. "This place gets directed by committee right now. Who we trade with, what we trade, who gets to stretch out, who gets to take the boats—pain in the ass. One person has all the shares, they make the rules."

Jess thought about that, then laughed. "Our father knew what the hell he was doing. Tie up those shares in me, and no one wins."

"Unless you sign them over."

"Fuck you." Jess got up. "One, I can't unless I'm a civ, and two, I'd rather ram my head through that door." She headed for the aforementioned portal.

"Jess." Jimmy stood up. "Before you storm out and slam the door behind you, can I ask you a question?"

Jess turned, and waited.

"When you finished field school and were going into service, you ever think about turning it down and coming home?"

Jess tilted her head a little, and studied him. Then she came back across the room and stood on the other side of the desk, leaning forward and resting her knuckles on the surface. "You don't get that choice, Jimmy," she said, in a very quiet voice.

"But they told us—"

"You get to the end of field, and the grad ceremony, and then, late that night, they take you, one at a time, Bain does, to Eagles' Point and he tells you the bitter truth of what you are. And you can either accept that, and go into service, or he kills you."

Her brother stared at her in silence.

"You put Tayler on that transport, he's never coming home," Jess said, after a long pause. "Now that's something daddy really should have told you." She straightened and walked quietly to the door, opening it and passing through, letting it shut behind her with a gentle click.

THEY WERE BACK in the carrier, the hatch shutting with a thump as they cleared the opening. "That's that." Jess went to her station and sat down. "Let's get things buttoned down and get out of here."

Dev sat down in the tech chair. "Jess?"

"Hmm?"

"There's a lot of discomfort here."

Jess sighed and sat back. "Yeah, it's pretty fucked up. Reminds me again why I don't come here a lot." She let her hands drop to her thighs. "So now what do we do?" She looked at Dev. "Ditch our escorts and head east?" she asked. "Ready to go destroy our careers?"

"If you mean we're going to go help Doctor Dan, I agree with that," Dev said. "But I hope we don't cause our teammates discomfort. They seem agreeable people."

Jess chuckled softly. "Ah, maybe we'll just go back to base." She sighed. "I don't really have a plan, and they're all gunning for me. Not really much chance of our getting in there."

Dev was ready to accept that decision too. The entire day had been very unsettling, and the only moment she'd liked was showing the vid of the bear to the little boy. Everything else had been tense and uncomfortable, and she was really glad they were leaving now.

Doug and April were too, they'd said as much as they walked back to the shuttle bay. Dev thought about it and decided she would really like to go back to the base, and relax and not get into trouble. "I like that idea more," she said. "Maybe we can practice—"

"Sex?" Jess grinned at her.

"I was going to say surfing, but that would be good too." Dev smiled back.

"Yeah, all right," Jess said. "Get this pony on the road. Let's go home."

Dev swiveled her chair around and started up her systems. Outside the window, she could see Doug doing the same, and though she couldn't help thinking of Doctor Dan, and what he was doing, she also couldn't deny she was glad they were going back to the citadel.

She thought maybe Jess was glad too. "I do think your place here is very nice."

Jess chuckled briefly. "Yeah, it's probably the oldest, and the most developed homestead in the east. They've got a few that old on the west coast. Jason's Rainier Island place is one of them, but Drake's Bay's a good place to live." She leaned back and waited as Dev booted the bus. "It's the biggest trading center in the area. Got nice big turbines down below, generates a surplus of power they sell to the battery plants, and is pretty much self-sufficient. "

"I see."

Jess folded her arms over her chest and sighed. "Stupid family."

Dev wisely refrained from comment, settling her ear cups in place and activating her restraints. The chair gimbaled forward and she started to make adjustments, reaching over to disconnect the docking umbilical and switching to internal power. She'd heard Doug and April discuss their families, seen Jess's, and remembered hearing Jason gripe about his. She was starting to ponder the possibility that being a bio alt, and having no family, wasn't entirely an awful thing.

They eased from the shuttle dock and formed up over the bay, as Dev triggered the nav that would take them on a course north and east. "Jess? We just got a weather warning." She shunted the met alert back to her partner's station.

Jess keyed up the report and studied it. "That's a big one coming over the citadel," she said. "We'll just go a little slow and come in behind it." She dismissed the met and leaned back. "Tell the kids to follow us."

Dev glanced in the mirror. Then she opened the sideband channel and hailed the other carrier, as she gave the engines power and they moved offshore and away from Drake's Bay.

Jess twiddled her thumbs idly and listened to Dev chat with Doug, already thinking ahead to what her options were next. Should she have taken the chance to go rogue? Should she—

Jess turned her head as her comp caught sight of something and started tracking it. "Dev?"

"Yes?"

"Give my board power." Jess moved her seat a bit closer and put the target on the big board, the comp resolving it into not one but two images. "We've got something coming at us."

Dev relayed the message to Doug, then took control from the autonav and turned the carrier in an arc, to face the west where the images were heading from. She started a long range scan, checking the status of the shields and shunting power to them.

"Tac 2, Tac 1." Doug's voice burred in her ear. "We see target. Engage standby."

"Acknowledge," Dev responded. "Wait for ident."

Jess felt her adrenaline kick in. She snugged her restraints and kicked on the guns, the targeting boards coming live on either side of her as the head's up display appeared, and centered on the two incoming spots. They had no patrols west, so likely they were not friendly.

"Profiling in process," Dev reported quietly. "Long range reports energy outline indicates high rate weapons."

"Ah." Jess got her hands on the gun triggers and flipped the switch that put all the scan input to her leads. "Dev, if they make a run at us, take us up and over and do your thing."

"Yes." Dev already had full power spooled up to the engines, and her hands were curled around the throttles. "Scan reporting they are reacting to our presence, course has changed due north."

"Chase 'em." Jess wiggled her fingers in muted delight. "Go get 'em, Devvie!" She felt the whump as the engines kicked in and she was smacked against the back of her chair, the restraints curling around her as they took on G-force in a high rate turn, and then went full speed to the north.

"Scan return showing TK300 series heavy cruisers," Dev reported. "Weapons systems are powering up according to comp." She pointed the nose of the carrier at them and sent Doug a quick status update.

"Ohhh, real bad guys." Jess shook her head. "What in the hell are they doing out here? How did they get past..." She let the thought trail off. "Dev, send a squirt to Base Ten. Just a status, what we found out here."

"In work." Dev reached over to key in the long-range comms. "Stand by to transmit."

Jess calculated several trajectory solutions, and put the long scan on tight resolution. After a moment, it came in and she could see a rough picture of the two fleeing crafts.

TK's all right. She could see the distinctive profile, and she checked the range, then programmed two plasma bombs and ejected them. "Time to intercept?"

"Five minutes," Dev reported crisply. "We have plus ten on their speed."

"That because of your tinkering?" Jess smiled. "I know these carriers are not supposed to be able to catch those suckers."

"We did some adjustments," Dev admitted. "I think we are causing them discomfort. They are going into an evasive pattern." She shifted and watched the comp, then adjusted the trajectory and sent more power to the engines. "Four minutes."

Jess watched them eject a backscatter, which drew off her bombs, and they ignited behind the craft. "Overshoot them and then do a 180, Dev, come at them head on."

"They will fire from their front cannons," Dev said. "I think we should come to zenith, then from the left."

In the silence that followed, Dev looked in the mirror and met Jess's eyes. Slowly, a grin formed on Jess's face, and she lifted one hand off the guns and touched her forehead. "You're the driver."

"Was that incorrect?

"We'll find out in four minutes."

"Three."

DEV COULD SEE the outflow from the enemy craft's engines with her own eyes now and made a picture in her head of what she wanted to do once they caught them. She flexed her fingers around the throttles and leaned forward a little.

"One minute," she warned Jess, who was reading her guns, the soft whine of the energy spool up audible to her outside the ear cups.

"Got it," Jess said. "Tac 1, Tac 2, keep to aft, match."

"Ack," Doug's voice came back, sounding tolerably steady.

"Welcome to Interforce," Jess added, suppressing a grin as she tuned her aim. "Dev, tell our friends to haul up and surrender or we'll blast them."

Dev switched comms to broadband all hail and repeated the threat. Then she closed the channel and prepared to maneuver. She could see the two sets of engines flaring bright at full power ahead of her, but the new mods they'd applied to the carriers left her with reserve, even though she was catching them.

Excellent.

"No answer." she told Jess, somewhat unnecessarily.

"Hehehe." Jess chuckled audibly. "Take us in, Devvie."

"Hold on." Dev kicked the side jets and put the carrier on its horizontal axis, boosting up and over the trailing carrier in a rush of speed and then dumping over to its port side as it swerved.

"Hehehe." Jess repeated, releasing her triggers and sending a barrage from the lower guns across the side of the vessel. She watched the scan intently as Dev came around and saw a sudden flare of energy across the boards. "Holy shit, Dev get us a—whoa!"

Dev saw the same thing, and instinctively hit the back jets and hauled up, sending them cloud-ward and then upside down, putting the heavily shielded bottom of the carrier toward the enemy just as the energy surge exploded toward them and swamped comp and scan, blowing them sideways through the air.

Engines cut out as a wash of energy flowed over and through them, safety systems blaring with sudden vibrant screams.

It was hard to keep control. The carrier tumbled through the air and started to drop, before she got her inputs sorted out and got the engines back online. "What happened?"

"Damn thing blew up." Jess sounded rattled. "I couldn't have blown their shields that fast. Should have just tickled them." She looked at the screens. "Can you get comp back? Where's Tac 2?"

Dev kept them high, but boosted the back jets to pitch them forward giving them a view. "Chasing the other one," she reported, "they're shooting." She ran the repair programming and started recycling the boards. "Standby for comp and scan."

"Get after them. Anything left of that tank?"

"No." She brought the engines up to full power and started after the fleeing second craft, just as Doug dove at it, and April let loose a set of plasma bombs aimed at the front of it while the enemy vessel returned fire, sending a blast of fire along the port side of the Interforce carrier.

Scan came back, and a moment later, comp as well, screens coming alive with alerts and warnings. She spared a glance for them, then concentrated on catching the other craft, feeling the energy release as Jess fired the forward guns.

The beams stitched a line across the top of the enemy as they dove toward it, then once again scan screamed a warning. "Plasma flare!" Dev yelled, as she yanked them sideways and then in an arc.

"Tac 2 evade!" Jess hit the comms and then held onto her console, as the carrier rolled in the air and boosted skyward. "What in the hell!"

This time they were far enough away to weather the wave unharmed, and Dev finished her roll out and got them back on heading, looking intently through the energy wash and blinking to clear the brightness from her eyes. "Tac 2, Tac1." She triggered comms. "I don't see them."

Jess dropped weapons scan and picked up standard to her console, running sweep. "C'mon, you raw little kids. Don't croak your first run on me."

Comp crackled hard. "Tac 1, Tac 2." Doug's voice sounded breathless. "Nadir."

Dev dipped the nose of the carrier and headed down, dropping altitude rapidly as a layer of thick clouds rippled around them and then cleared, giving a view of ruffled waves and shoreline beneath them.

"There they are," Jess said. "Near the escarpment."

"I see them." Dev moderated her drop, and leveled, coming even with the other carrier.

"Open sideband local," Jess said. "What the hell was that? No way either of those strikes should have skunked them."

Dev opened the channel and sent the encodes, waiting for the sideband shortwave to come up and let them talk to each other in long speech. "BR270006, BR36024, copy."

The line opened. "BR270006, we copy." April's voice sounded relieved. "We lost power after the target blew up. Just got it back before splashing."

"Copy that, 36024," Jess responded. "Your comp catch the explosion? I'd like to compare it to ours. Didn't have a standard outflow."

"What the hell were they doing this far in?" April asked. "Is that normal? They told us in-field engagements were in the mid zone."

Jess was momentarily silent. "Good question," she said. "First time I've seen them this far in. Dev, did we get a squirt back from Base Ten?"

Dev checked the comms board, running through the logs. "No," she said, after a pause. "No response from them at all." She re-keyed the request, and engaged long scan. "We received comp from Doug." She shunted the data to Jess's boards. "Everything else seems clean. No additional targets."

"Yeah," Jess murmured. "Let's get back on course." She engaged comms. "April, you good to move on?"

"Took a few dents, but yes," April responded. "We're picking up some debris on the surface there. Recon?" she asked. "Didn't think there would be much left but we're seeing some large pieces."

Jess stared unseeing at her console for a long moment. Then she lifted her head. "Yeah, Dev, take us down to the shore." She keyed comms. "Acknowledge. Let's take a look at what's left. I don't like what I'm seeing on these recordings."

The two carriers dropped down, angling for the beach and landing above the high tide line side-by-side. Dev ran the shutdown process, and unhooked her restraints. She stood up and removed the carrier links from her flight suit and turned, watching Jess as she got up from the gunner's chair. "This seems incorrect."

Jess seated her weapons, and triggered the hatch. "It is, Dev. I just don't know why or how it is." She walked down the ramp, as the wind blew in a gust of salt tinged air.

Dev followed her, stepping down off the carrier step onto the somewhat soft surface they'd landed on. It shifted under her boots, and she could see debris in it, pieces of stone or rocks and some glints of color. It crunched a little, under her. She stopped as Jess stopped, and they waited as April and Doug joined them.

"That was crazy," Doug said. "That thing blew itself up."

"That's not necessarily what happened," April said.

"Something happened." Jess continued down the beach until she reached the first piece of debris. She circled it warily, and Dev pulled out her portable comp and started a scan on it. "Look at those edges." Jess knelt next to one and studied it. "This was blown out."

April joined her. "From the inside?"

"It has a high emission of positive electrons," Dev said, after a pause. "There is residual in the atmosphere also. It appears something released a lot of energy."

"Engines?" April speculated.

"Not this type." Jess had gotten up and went around to look at Dev's screen. "Your driver might be right. Sure looks like an internal explosion to me." She went over to the next piece of debris, which was hardly larger than her two hands put together. It had a bit of steel skin attached, which was curled and burned like it had been plastic.

"Are you saying they blew themselves up?" April asked, in a surprised voice. "They never mentioned that in school."

"Never mentioned it in the field either, since I've never seen them do it before." Jess frowned. "They're not martyrs, any more than we are." She nudged the piece with her boot. "Unless they had something on board they weren't willing for us to see."

"And they brought it all the way over here? That doesn't make much sense," Doug said.

"It would if it was something they were going to use against us." Jess stood up. "I can't think of any other reason they'd want to prevent us from capturing them, aside from sheer embarrassment. We should send a squirt with this back to Base Ten, and get moving."

"Let's go, people." Jess headed back to the carrier, and April was winding up taking an image of the debris. "Let's get back in touch with base. Something doesn't feel right."

Dev trotted after Jess, triggering the hatch as she entered the carrier. She went over to her station and sat down, putting restraints in place before she triggered comms. "Should I send a message?"

"Yeah." Jess was busy at her own console. "At least get a status through to them, squirt them the vid of the blow up."

Dev got her comms set settled and took the engine systems off standby. She saw a flashing light and paused, reaching over to accept it. "Jess, there's an alert here."

She barely heard the release of the restraints before Jess was hanging over her shoulder, and she keyed up the automated alert for her to see. "I think it's weather."

Jess studied it. "Met over the base. Damn it. Maybe that's why they didn't answer. Too much damn EMF." She absorbed the message. "That's a huge storm cell." she said. "Look how far it extends." Her finger touched the screen. "They must be getting the shit kicked out of them."

Dev tried to make a picture of that in her head, then quickly stopped. "Should I keep trying to send a message? I'm not getting any response."

"Keep trying. Get us up in the air before we find something else around here that doesn't belong." Jess sat down in her station. "I'm going to send a warning back to Drake's Bay."

Dev engaged the landing jets and moved off the sand, sending a blast of it out everywhere from beneath the carrier as they rose up off the ground. She heard Jess behind her speaking softly into her comms, and paused to watch Doug lift before she put the message system in automatic loop and engaged the main engines.

There were a lot of unusual things happening. She had the feeling that things were moving very fast, and that Jess wasn't really sure what direction she wanted to go.

It was unsettling, and it made her uncomfortable.

"Okay, later." Jess closed comms, then opened them again. "April?"

"Here." April's voice came back on the inter-ship intercom. "We have a met warning."

"Us, too," Jess said. "We'll come in from the north, top side of that met's moving faster. Keep your eyes open for more of the bad guys."

"Ack."

"I have the squirt on loop," Dev said. "So far, no response."

Even with the met, that started a ball of worry in Jess's gut. This close, they should have gotten, at the very least, a reject of the message no matter how bad the storm was. She unlocked her restraints and got up, moving over to the lockers and opening them up. "Just in case."

Dev glanced in the mirror. "What is a case?"

Jess managed a brief smile, as she got out of her standard jumpsuit and into her heavier gear. The light armor settled into place as she sealed the openings, tightening the fit around her body. "I'm putting this on in case it's all gone to crap at base and I need to drop and start shooting people in the halls."

Dev digested this. "I see."

"Been kind of a crappy day so far. I'm betting that's not changing in the short term." Jess slid her small arms in place, adding a set of throwing daggers in the small of her back. "Any response to the squirt? What's the time in?"

"No, and twenty minutes." Dev inched the throttles forward, and ran a check on the power systems. They were racing fast for both the edge of the storm system and the base. She could already feel the buffeting from the wind against the outside of the carrier in minute shifts of the controls against her hands.

She felt the nervous energy building inside her and heard Jess take her seat again, the sound of a heavier body thumping against the padded surface, and the soft whine as Jess activated the restraints that would hold her in place.

From the corner of her eye she saw all the targeting systems come online, and for a very brief moment she thought about the people who must have been in the two enemy craft that had been destroyed.

Had they gotten ready, been doing the same sort of tasks she and Jess were doing right now?

"Tac 1, Tac 2." April's voice filtered over the comm. "Review of comp shows they got a message off, and it was answered, about sixty to one-twenty prior to the first one exploding."

Jess nodded slowly. "Tac 2, ack," she answered. "I think this kid's gonna be good. Sharp. Check the timestamps. See if that message went out before or after we threatened 'em."

"After," Dev responded at once. "Was that April were referring to?"

"Yeah," Jess said. "Always a crapshoot with women in the corps. Either you're an asshole like me, or an asshole like Sandy usually."

"If the definition of asshole is what you seem to mean it is, I don't think you are one." Dev adjusted setting, and increased torque to the engines to counteract the increasing wind. "That other agent seemed a lot more unpleasant."

Jess chuckled. "You only say that because you like me." She set the scan on long range and directed it at the base. "Ask anyone else at base, even Jason, and they'll tell you different. I treat them all like crap."

"You treat me very nicely."

"Yeah, well." Jess reran the scan, her muscles starting to twitch when it refused to return anything to her. "You're different."

Dev sighed. "That is true. Ten minutes. No response to the squirt."

"Nothing from scan either." Jess drummed her fingertips on the console. "Know what the most different thing about you is?"

Dev knew perfectly well what the most different thing about her was. "Yes," she said. "I'm a biological alternative and I was born from an egg in space. But I don't know why that either makes you treat me nicely, or makes me not think you're unpleasant."

"Ah." Jess tweaked the scan a little, filtering out the spiking frequencies she knew were from the storm. "Actually, what makes you different for me ain't that." She peered closely at the screen. "It's the fact you're the first person I let myself fall in love with."

Dev's eyes went to the mirror, staring at the dark head bent over the console. "What?"

"Yeah, you can look that up later. I think we've got some real problems here." Jess keyed comms. "April, we're getting a lot of disruption from base. You get that?"

"Ack." The other agent came back immediately.

"We may need to drop."

"Kitted up."

Jess gazed fondly at the comms, very glad her instincts had read true on her pick of escorts. "Follow us down. There's an emergency dock midway on the backside that's keyed to my bus. Manual in."

"Ack."

Jess cut off the comms. "Sending you up the coordinates, Devvie. Not big enough to land, just do a pass and drop me." She studied the comms. "Something's disrupting base systems to the point they're nonfunctional. Don't think they can even open the bay."

She looked up after a moment of silence, to find Dev watching her in the mirror, those pale, gentle eyes completely intent. "You okay?"

"Yes," Dev said. "If the disruption is causing so many problems, won't it also affect the carrier?"

"Yes. That's why we're coming in on the backside of the ridge. It'll clear the storm front first." Jess got up and went to the drop chute, turning and backing into the pack and locking the frame in place. She reached over and grabbed her blaster rifle and seated it, then she swung the comp pad next to the rig in place so she could see their progress. "Drop down so we come in low, Dev."

Dev exhaled, then focused on the fast moving wasteland beneath her. She cut their altitude by half, and now the ground—a vast plain of rocky gravel and deep gorges—was clearly visible. Ahead of them, she could see the line of storms, black thickness shot through with almost continuous lightning strikes.

The clouds were low enough to cover the escarpment that contained the citadel, not a bit of the structure was visible and she could now hear low booming cracks rippling across the ground. There was still no response to their comms hails, and just as Dev wondered how the citadel was reacting to that, the threat scan blared alive. "Jess!"

"I see it." Jess unhooked herself from the drop rig and leaped into her gunner's seat, slamming the straps in place and bringing the guns live. "How in the hell are they flying in that!"

A line of enemy craft were coming over the ridge right through the storm clouds and heading their way, already firing. Just as abruptly a small, thinner craft came arching up from the base itself, streaking toward them at top speed.

Dev evaded the incoming bolts and steeled herself to fly into the barrage, tightening her grips on the throttles and picking a line between the diving enemy and the streaking flight coming from the base.

That, at least, was blaring an ident the carrier recognized.

"Drake!" The comms crackled alive, weird and skewed sounding though they were. "Get out of here!"

Jess let loose a full release of her guns toward the enemy. "Sir!" she yelled back, recognizing Bain's voice. "We'll cover you!"

"No! They've got something that shields them from energy. Get out of here. Go find it! Or we're all dead! I'll draw them off! That's what killed North!"

"I can feel interruption in our systems," Dev warned. "I don't think we can get closer until the storm leaves."

Jess took a breath, as the carrier spun in midair and arched up through the enemy with the guns on automatic repeat, sending them off in different directions. "Ack," she finally said. "Dev, get us out of here. Go up and get over the clouds and head..." She paused. "Go polar. Due north."

Dev reacted at once, pulling the carrier up into a hard arc, turning sharply to one side as a barrage of fire came at them. She got them leveled and threw in the afterburners, blinking a little as the rear scan blanked out white as Jess kept up a continual fire.

Blasts came back at them, impacting the rear shields and shoving the carrier violently to one side as she felt the rippling boom of them clearing the speed of sound. Then they were up through the first cloud layer and she was fighting to arc them over before they ran out of air to fly in.

The enemy came roaring up after them, but only two of them. They spun off, heading back down, leaving the two carriers to streak on together alone.

After a moment of silence, Jess exhaled. "Guess they wanted him more than us." Her hands started to shake as battle tension relaxed. "Shit."

Dev kept all power on, driving the engines to full speed and more. "Did they damage our place?" she asked softly.

"Probably isn't much to go back to, yeah," Jess said. "They probably just did to Base Ten what I did to Gibraltar. They had no way of fighting back. I could see it on scan, no power anywhere. The generating mains were off line."

Dev thought about all the people there. Were they all damaged? Dead?

"But who knows," Jess finally added. "We've got work to do ahead of us." She glanced at comp. "Those guys behind us?"

"Yes."

"All right, let's move. "

Chapter Seven

THEY WERE CLEAR of the storm and Dev had them on auto nav, while they sat quietly together sharing some rations. Long-range scan was set to detect anyone approaching. Only the carrier flying port side aft of them was considered friendly.

Jess had been very quiet since they'd left the base's airspace. Now she was sitting on one of the arming benches, elbows resting on her knees as she munched her way through a fish roll. "We need to get somewhere we can set up a plan, and get our bearings."

Dev swallowed. "Will we go to one of the caves?" she asked.

"Sort of," Jess said. "There's an old met and science station near the Pole. We used to keep it stocked. It was North's responsibility, so who the hell knows if they did. We'll try that first." She finished one roll and started a second. "Now I know why those other two carriers blasted themselves. Probably were told to."

"To keep us from capturing them and finding out what their new thing is?"

Jess nodded. "Didn't expect us to be out there." She bit a mouthful off. "Freak chance we were. You and I would have probably been there, in rad, or...something."

Dev thought about that. Then she studied her partner's face. "You seem in discomfort." She put her hand on Jess's arm. "Are you angry? Did we do something incorrect?"

"Nah." A faint smile appeared on Jess's face, then faded. "I just get the feeling like I've been...that there's some big plan going on we don't have any clue about. I hate that."

"Ah."

"Anyway. When we get up to the old station, I'll see if the powerhouse is still running. If it is, we can alert the rest of the force. Our ship coms won't do squat. Not enough transmit unless we bounced it off a base, and the two closest are now dead as a doornail."

Dev felt a lot of discomfort about that, the bases not responding. "I hope they just turned everything off," she said. "There were some nice people at our place."

Jess sighed. "Yeah. My promotion sure didn't last long, huh? I'll probably end up low on the totem in some outpost if we make it through this."

Dev considered this, as she finished her fish roll and chewed a dried mushroom cake. "Will I get to go with you?" she asked, in a very quiet tone.

"If I have anything to say about it. Maybe that's my dark cloud's silver lining. I don't have to worry about being promoted out and losing you."

Dev felt warm and good hearing that. She thought about what Jess said before, about the love thing. She wondered if that was connected to this. What did that mean? She said she'd fallen in love. Was that like falling down?

"I hope so. I want to stay with you. I don't want to be with anyone else."

"Not even April or Jason? They're both okay."

"No," Dev said, definitively. "I don't think Jason likes me and you're much more attractive than April."

Jess looked up and smiled. "You think so, really?"

"Yes."

"Thanks. I don't usually hear things like that," Jess said. "Especially not from someone I want to hear it from." She put the remains of her box into the trash compactor and remained seated, lacing her fingers together. "Did I freak you out with that falling in love comment before?"

Dev put her trash away and edged a little closer. "No. I don't really understand what that means," she said, apologetically. "I think it's a good thing. Right?"

"Is it good or bad? I don't know either," Jess said. "I think from a job perspective it's not good. You get trained not to think about that, not to get involved in that way with people because it makes you really vulnerable. You know?"

"Um."

"No, I guess you don't." Jess sighed. "Doesn't really matter anyway."

"It doesn't?"

"They tell you not to do it, warn you about it, but forget to mention you can't do a damn thing about it when it happens." Jess leaned against her and rested her head against Dev's. "They do their best to suck the souls out of us, Devvie. Then something like this happens, and you realize how much of it is bogus."

Dev's brows knit a little. "Jess, is this good or bad?"

"What do you think it is?"

"I have no idea," Dev answered honestly.

Jess scratched the bridge of her nose and shrugged lightly. "I like it. I look at you and it makes me feel good. I really like feeling good. Don't you?"

Dev considered solemnly, then nodded. "Of course."

"So there we are," Jess said. "It's good, Dev. Even if it ends up bad for us, it's still good. You get that?"

Now, Dev smiled. "I do get that."

"Good." Jess sat there for a bit, leaning against Dev's warm body, letting her mind slip a little. She felt Dev rest her head against her shoulder and something in her just let go, appreciating this human contact in a new and surprising way.

Dev circled her arm with her own and gently rubbed the skin on

Jess's forearm in an absent sort of way.

Jess focused on the sensation, warm and friendly and tending to make her heart skip a little. She wished it could continue on, and that they weren't in trouble, weren't running from some new terror, were tucked away in their quarters or in a cave, or...

Or anywhere.

She could feel the thrum of the engines through the frame she was sitting on, images of the recent past shuttling through her internal eye. She took a breath, and a second, and let the past go, consciously shifting her focus to the present, and the near future.

"We have to find out how the bad guys are flying through EMF." she said, after a few minutes. "Otherwise, they can attack us at random, and we can't fight back."

"Yes."

"So we need to either capture one of their rigs, or get into the developmental science center. If we get one of their trucks, you think you can dissect it?

"Yes," Dev said, with surprising confidence. "I have programming on that."

Jess turned her head and looked closely at her partner. "You do?"

Dev nodded. "On the type of system we saw earlier, and some older models, and also, a bigger one they use for transporting a lot of people," she said. "I can fly them, or take them apart, whatever it is you need."

Jess blinked. She looked around the carrier, and then back at Dev. "We don't know how to do that. How did they get the programming for it to give you?" she asked. "We've captured a few, but they program them to short out if one of us boards—just like we do."

Dev shrugged slightly, looking a touch sheepish. "We don't know, most of the time, where the programming comes from," she said. "But I know the big blocks of it. I've done sims for the other side's stuff."

"Wow," Jess murmured. "I bet your buddy knows where that came from."

"Doctor Dan?"

Jess nodded. "So you know, there's definitely a reason we need to get him back."

"Didn't we have a reason before?"

"You and I had a reason." Jess turned her sharp gaze on Dev. "He's your friend. He was my father's partner. But that wasn't enough for Bain. He wasn't going to make a deal for him, not only because we don't make deals, but because there wasn't anything compelling for him to do it for."

Dev considered that. "I thought they were friends," she said, with a touch of sadness in her voice.

Jess shook her head. "I don't think so. I think...I think they respected each other. But finding this out, finding out how that kind of information got processed—he'd want that."

Dev got up and went to her station, settling in her chair and starting a report running on their status. She checked the course they were on, and also the comms for any messages, finding it all quiet, and aware of Jess watching her. "Does that matter about why we would go help him?"

Jess went back to her seat and dropped into it, folding her hands over her stomach and looking up at the ceiling. "Not to you," she said. "But I'm a selfish bastard, Dev. I want to go help him, but I want there to be something for me in it, too. I break the rules and go after him and end up being locked up or thrown out, it ruins my day, and yours, too."

"I see."

"Do I sound like an indecisive ass? I feel like one. I tell you I'm gonna go rescue him, damn the consequences, and then I back out and go pansy on you until I don't have a choice. I'm such a jerk." Jess sighed. "I feel like my head's in ten different places."

Dev turned around in her chair. "I'm sorry you're in such discomfort," she said. "I'm sure we'll figure out how to make everything come out right."

The comms set buzzed gently, distracting them. Jess reached over and closed the connection for the intercom. "Yeah?"

"Um." Doug's voice sounded hesitant. "We're picking something up on scan. Looks like one of ours, but not answering squirt."

Dev turned and lit up the comp board, setting up a long-range scan and starting it.

"So you sent out an automatic ident?" Jess asked.

"Yes."

"It's at the very edge of the band," Dev said. "Outline does show as this type of vehicle."

"Probably Stephen and his team," Jess said. "We're just passing the edge of North's territory." She studied her own screen. "Now why isn't he responding to comms, and where are the other two buses?" She coded in her own ident to comms. "BR270006 to incoming, acknowledge."

There was no response. Jess frowned, and changed frequencies, moving to a reserved high encrypt one. She repeated the message and waited.

Still nothing.

"BR270006 to incoming, acknowledge or standby for enemy action." Jess enunciated the words carefully and loudly. "Dev, give me power please, then slow down and hold steady."

Obediently Dev shunted power to the weapons, and felt the soft rumble as the guns came online and the protective covers slid back, exposing them to the wind outside. She cut their forward momentum and turned, hearing the guns move as she did

"Standby," the incoming craft said, briefly. "Hold for shortwave."

Jess kept the hatches open, swinging her aim around and plotting a targeting choice on the craft moving toward them. "Tell our friends to stay behind us."

Dev keyed the intercom. "Doug?"

"Here."

"Jess says to keep behind this vehicle."

"I'm keeping way behind the direction she's pointing those guns at," he said. "No worries."

"Excellent." Dev studied the clouds they were between, the thick surface off to the left flickering with lightning below. Scan was detecting the disruption from the flashes, but they were far enough away not to be affected. "Do you think those people are correct?"

"They're either correct, or about to try and shove their guns up my ass," Jess said. "Hard to say which one it is at this point in the general miasma of craptasticness today's been."

Dev turned around and looked at her, then she swiveled back and took a better grip on her throttles. The incoming carrier was now visible, and she felt her heartbeat speed up when it appeared to not be slowing down. "Hmm."

Jess audibly released the safety shields on her triggers and leaned back, bracing her boots against the console. She'd played chicken before, but rarely in such an uncertain situation. She took a breath and let it out, then focused on her target, looking past the screens and past the front window as the carrier came into range.

Her fingers tightened.

"Incoming request on shortwave sideband six, Jess," Dev said, calmly. "BR27004 channel setup acknowledge."

The comms crackled, and Jess let her hands relax, but not completely.

"Jess?" Stephen's voice came over the intercom. "That you?"

"It's me," Jess answered. "You want to travel with us before the storm backs up and kicks our asses?" she asked. "You know what happened?"

"I know what happened to North." Stephen's voice sounded grim.

"It might have just happened to Base Ten," Jess said, in a quiet tone. "Just got out of the area in time."

Silence. "Oh shit," Stephen said. "That's why I can't get a squirt through. I thought it was just met."

"We're going to the pole station," Jess said. "Have to get a plan going. Bain said they've got something that lets them fight in met. I think it's something that makes met worse."

"Bain got out? Figures."

Jess shrugged, even if he couldn't see it.

"No sense going to North. Everything inside's burned to a crisp and it stinks from dead bodies," Stephen said. "Pole sounds good. Any clues what the new tech is?"

Jess started to answer, then paused, and keyed the mute. "You got any ideas?" She asked Dev. "What could fry all that stuff?"

Dev watched her in the mirror, as she piloted the carrier on their original course, at a very slow speed. "It might be useful to see what it did. I can see if it matches any programming."

Jess nodded. "Stephen, let's take a quick tour of North. See what we're up against."

"If you want. Hope you haven't had lunch," he said. "Follow me. Got the two buses with me sitting on top of the next ridge waiting."

His carrier pulled ahead, and curved to the left, and Dev changed course to follow him.

"Let's see where this takes us." Jess capped her triggers and pushed the targeting system back off its axis. "And get the—who's the boss—knock down drag out over with."

Dev glanced behind her, brows contracted.

"You'll see. Want to make a few cred? Bet on me." Jess leaned back and closed her eyes, content to let the crosscurrents carry them for now.

Bet on her. Dev increased power to the engines and pulled the comp pad over, typing in the statement and waiting for it to regurgitate its meaning.

SEEING NORTH BASE was shocking. Jess had come up next to her and they were both looking out the front wraparound windows.

"Holy shit," Jess said. The pinnacle and mountainside that they'd been to only a week prior was now shattered and blackened, the stone cracked away and a third of the rock wall collapsed down the side of the slope and littering the valley at the bottom.

Where they'd entered the bay there was only a smoking hole, gray mist still emitting from it.

"I'm getting a complete null on scan," Dev said, in subdued tone.

"I bet." Jess was leaning against her chair. "See if you can get the bus in near the entrance to the bay. Shine some light in there." She held on as the carrier dipped and dropped in altitude, the powerful front lights coming on and splashing against the smoke dulled granite.

It was creepy. Dev approached carefully, slowing their speed to almost nothing as she drifted in front of the bay, and the interior became visible. "Oh," Dev murmured, seeing the destruction inside. "That is not good."

Jess let out a long breath. "No. Get closer."

Dev did, easing the carrier into the gaping opening. Inside she could see carriers in complete wreckage, and lumps on the floor completely black that she suspected were people. "It's like everything touched a live wire," she said. "I saw that happen up in the creche once. They were moving the leads from the solar arrays to one of the batteries. No one really knew what happened, but it was like that. All black."

Jess reached over to key comms. "Stephen, it like this everywhere?"

"Yeah," he responded shortly. "Worse inside. Central ops looked like a bomb went off in it."

Jess stared at the interior of the cavern in near disbelief. "Dev, go ahead and land. I want to get a look firsthand at this."

Dev inched the carrier in and then rotated a half turn, putting the edge of the craft over the ledge. "I don't want to go farther. There's a lot of debris. Can you get out now?"

Jess fastened the catches on her suit and seated her weapons, then she triggered the hatch. It popped open and she stopped in her tracks, blasted by a gust of stench that took her breath away. "Ugh." She glanced back at Dev, whose face was scrunched in an expression of distaste. "Sorry." She stepped onto the ledge and keyed the hatch shut, hearing the air handlers cycle behind her.

Jess had seen a lot in her time. She'd seen dead people of all types, many made that way by her own hand, but the charred, crisped black remains she was carefully stepping over were horrible even to her hardened senses. A flash of this cavern not a week ago when they visited appeared in her mind's eye, busy and full of techs and bio alts, all going about their business as they had for years.

Now there wasn't a sound around her save the faint rattling of bits of rock falling out of the walls. Jess turned on her light and moved farther inside, coming up next to what was left of a big transport. Probably the largest craft assigned to North. It was charred like everything else was, the walls blown out and panels melted into nothing but hard lumpy slag.

There had been a tech inside working. His burned body was half in and half out of the service bay, testing probe still clenched inside his fist.

No warning. Jess picked up a piece of the burned panel and examined it, flashing her light on the tracings inside. It meant little to her, but she kept it as she walked on, intending on showing it to Dev.

Everywhere she looked was horror. As she stood in the center of the cavern and slowly turned, she noticed a faint pattern on the floor, lines that angled out from a more or less central point not far from where she was standing. Jess moved over and set her boots over the point, looking to her right and left, and seeing the destruction flaring out on all sides.

Something had blown up from where she was standing, and caused the damage. She could imagine the stark terror of the few who'd gotten out, direly wounded, leaving all their colleagues and friends behind.

Interesting perspective, since they were so often the ones bringing the terror, not facing it.

Jess turned around and started heading back to the carrier, waiting patiently at the edge of the cavern for her. She'd already gotten used to the stench, and as she moved closer to the opening she spotted something against the inner wall. Curious, she diverted her steps and walked in front of the humming carrier, patting its nose as she moved past and played her light along the inside rock surface.

Nothing very remarkable, just a toolbox. Jess stood next to it and studied it. Just a plain metal casing with drawers and cabinets, slightly dented and dinged with use.

But altogether strange in its whole, un-scorched plainness the only item in the cavern that escaped the blast.

Jess studied it for a long moment. Then she took hold of the handle and started back around the carrier, dragging it behind her. As she got to the hatch it opened, and she boosted the case inside, then climbed in after it. "Let's go, Dev. Faster we get under cover, the better."

IT WAS FULL dark by the time they got to the old station. It was quiet, they hadn't seen anything on scan for hours, and Dev had dipped below the lower cloud layer and flown with nothing but gray over her, and white below for quite some time.

Jess had spent the time examining the box she'd dragged on board, sitting cross legged on the floor next to it as she patiently took it apart piece by piece.

"Jess?" Dev called quietly. "We're almost there."

Jess hoisted herself to her feet and came up to the pilot's station, still holding an adjustment tool in her hand. "Yeah, we are," she said. "Look at that place. Nothing but ice."

"Really?" Dev studied the wire map, showing a low, craggy outline. "It's built from ice?"

"Built from ice," Jess confirmed. "Back in the old days, they built it after the end times, cause they figured nothing was going to end up habitable and it was a last chance bunker for the governmental big shots who are now long gone. Interforce took it over after that all ended, and for a while it was a training center. Then they moved the school out to Denali where at least they had elevations to work with."

"I see," Dev said. The wiremap showed almost nothing but the outline, scan reported only ice. "There's not anything operating there."

"No, we shut it down," Jess said. "Remains to be seen if we can start it back up again." She put her hand on the back of Dev's chair. "If not, we can land the carriers in a circle and make a rough camp, but I'd rather be able to charge bats. They sunk a heat sump a mile deep up here."

Dev started a slow descent. A glance at the comp showed her a chilling temperature outside, and the darkness they flew through was complete save the faint glow from their engines. She wished she'd brought her lined suit with her, and after that, she realized it was possible it no longer existed.

That her whole space no longer existed, including the one thing she'd brought, her book. She felt very sad thinking of that. "Where do you want to land?"

"Good question." Jess enlarged the wiremap with a swipe of her fingers. "Try here." She pointed at a flat area on the left of the structure. "Once you get to this point, turn the lights on."

Dev trimmed the engines and started up the landing jets, coasting over the blurry white surface to the spot Jess had indicated, slowing to hover as she turned on the bright lower lights.

Instantly, the area blared into reflective relief, a level ice field covered in a layer of fresh snow. It was large, and very desolate looking, and Dev selected a spot near the wall of the structure to land on, delicately letting the extended skids settle and leaving the landing jets activated until she was sure the surface was going to bear the carrier's weight. There was one slight lurch, then the craft seemed stable, and after a pause, she shut things down save the exterior lights.

Around them, the other carriers were landing, and in a moment the area was lit up brightly with five sets of lamps as they settled around in a rough circle.

"Glad I forgot to take these out of here." Jess had the equipment case open, and she pulled out their heavy parkas and ice boots.

"Yes." Dev agreed wholeheartedly as she exchanged her flight boots for the heavier ones and stood up to shrug into the thick jacket. She dropped the portable comp into one pocket, and her diagnostic scanner in the other, and fastened up the catches as Jess moved toward the hatch.

She weaponed up and slapped the latch, waiting for the door to open and the ramp to extend.

A solid, cold, startling blast of air came in, and Dev immediately got her hood up and the flap over her mouth as she drew in a breath and felt the inside of her nose freezing.

"Brr." Jess went down the ramp, bringing up her own hood. "Hope like hell we can boot this place."

Dev got her gloves on and followed her, blinking as she felt the chill against her eyeballs. She paused to extend the spikes on her boots then advanced over the ice, moving toward the center of the open lit space to join the rest of the agent teams.

As they closed in, she recognized Stephen Bock, and then the other two teams, one the newcomers Mike Arias and his partner, and the other an older pair she wasn't sure she remembered the names of. Doug and April came up on their right hand side, having landed just behind them.

"Jess." Bock nodded at her.

"Hello, Stephen." Jess had her hands in her pockets, her breath a steady stream of fog. "First things first. We should see if we can commission this place. Let the techs get their hands on the gear." She finished talking, then paused, waiting for a response.

There was a little silence. Then Bock exhaled. "Sounds good to me. Let's go." He nodded at the two pairs with him. "Place hasn't been used in years. No telling what we'll find."

Jess started toward the structure, and Dev fell in at her heels. The rest of the group followed, and they climbed a small hillock of ice toward a rounded arch packed with snow.

"I'll get that." Mike pulled out his small blaster and steadied it, moving a step past Jess and firing carefully at the doorway, melting the ice in the center of the opening. The pale blue light of the weapon disappeared in a fog of vaporized crystals, and after a few minutes the doorway was exposed.

Jess moved forward. "Thanks, Mike." She examined the door and touched the panel, but it was dead and didn't produce even the faintest twitch of a response.

"Dead?" Stephen edged in next to her. "You ever been here?"

"No." Jess took a step back. "My father was." She gestured him to get out of the way. "So let me see how much we're going to have to destroy before we get in here. Dev?"

"Yes." Dev wormed her way over.

"Take the rest of the wrenchers and go over that lump there, that's where the plant is. See what you can do with it."

"Yes." Dev backed out and started across the ice. "Please follow me." She told the other techs. "We have a task."

"Right behind you." Doug tugged his hood a little tighter. "Holy crap it's cold here."

Mike's partner, Chester, was right behind him, along with the older tech, a man named Oscar. They all climbed over the snowdrift and down into the next hollow, which seemed to be a semi-protected alcove.

The snow came up to Dev's thighs, and she plowed through it gamely, moving across the bowl toward the wall of the enclosure. "I am not sure using a blaster on this is correct," she said as they came to the power plant, encased in a solid wall of snow and ice.

"Maybe on the outside layer," Chester said.

"Get too close and it'll break its bits." Oscar was standing with his arms crossed, observing the surface. He removed his light from his belt and shone it on the wall, shaking his head a little. "Anyone got an ice ax?"

The techs all looked at each other. Then Dev cleared her throat. "I think we might. We took an ice kit on our last mission and I think it's still in there." She turned and started back, and after a moment, Doug plowed after her.

Chester pulled out his hand blaster and set it on its lowest setting. "I'll see how much I can trim off."

"I'll start here." Oscar moved to the other end. "This is all so fucked up the most normal thing I seen is that bio alt tech today." He shook his head. "Now we get to try and shelter inside an ice ball."

"Not having a great first month of service myself." Chester carefully started working down the edge of the structure. "Maybe I should have stuck to oyster harvesting back on Rainier Island."

DEV KEYED THE hatch open and ducked inside, glad to be out of the cold wind for a moment. She waited for Doug to follow her and then palmed the door closed. "It seems we're in for a lot of difficulty."

"You can say that again." Doug pushed his hood back. "I figured three of us trying to melt that ice back there would mean at least one of us losing a finger."

That made Dev chuckle a little as she opened the big equipment locker and dug out the ice axes she and Jess had used in the white. She handed one back to Doug and took the second for herself. "Jess said in the worst condition we could move the carriers together and make a shelter that way."

Doug hefted the ax. "At least no one's likely to go looking for us up here. Last thing I'd wanna see is some death ray from the other side hunting for me. That base was ugly."

"Yes." Dev tightened her hood again. "It makes me feel a lot of discomfort to think about our place looking like that."

Doug was briefly silent. "Yeah, me too. I hadn't been there long, but it was okay, you know?"

"Yes." Dev turned and headed for the door. "I feel the same way."

Doug followed her out and they started across the bowl, where snow was starting to drift in flurries outlined in the work lights from the carriers. "You do?" he asked. "Not to be a jerk or anything, but I never met any bios that cared about much before."

Dev thought about that as she walked, the ice crunching under her boots. "Well," she blinked against the cold. "They teach you not to show a lot. It makes natural borns feel discomfort. But we do." She paused. "I do. Jess told me it's all right to say that."

"Huh." Doug tugged his hood a little closer. "On the other hand, you're the first one I've ever talked to for more than, like, ten seconds. It's kinda weird."

Dev climbed over the ice hill. "It's strange for me too."

They reached the wall and both Chester and Oscar moved aside to make room for them. Dev took hold of her ax and studied the surface, selecting a spot where Chester had been burning a groove and starting to chop at it. With all four of them together it cut the chill down and soon she was completely absorbed in the effort to expose the power inverters.

She hoped Jess was having good success as well.

"OKAY, THAT'S OPEN." Jess clipped the light to her hood and

pulled her gloves off, grimacing as she eased the entry panel from its pocket and turned it over. "We get in there and they get the juice flowing, maybe we can figure out what the hell we're going to do."

Stephen was patiently chipping the ice from the door edge with a screwdriver. "Thought you had that figured out already," he said.

Jess chuckled dryly.

April and Mike were clearing ice from the front of the structure and Oscar's partner Carlos was in his carrier, keeping a scan running to make sure they didn't get surprised.

All under Jess's direction, which Bock hadn't made a move to countermand yet. Jess wondered briefly why, then decided to just take her good fortune where she found it.

She shook her head and returned her attention to the panel, which now under the warmth of her hand had revealed the tracing of its circuitry.

Very old. Jess breathed gently on it, studying the etched pathways. "Okay," she said. "Stephen, give me your insignia."

"Huh?"

"Give me your insignia," Jess repeated, slowly. "The thing on your collar."

"I know what my damned insignia is." He unfastened the throat flap on his coat and fished beneath it. "What the hell do you need it for?"

"You never really took any of the tech ops classes, did you?" Jess took the insignia from him and bent her head over the tracings. "Or have you just forgotten it all already?"

"Don't be an asshole, Jess."

"I'm not, for a change." She delicately touched the edge of one insignia post to one trace, and licked her lips, half closing her eyes as she touched the second to another.

Nothing.

"Saw the squirt from Bain when he bumped you," Bock said unexpectedly. "Kind of burned my ass."

"Wasn't my choice." Jess tried another combination, with an equal lack of success. "And it didn't do me a damn bit of good seeing as they torched Ten." She studied the board. "Matter of fact I didn't even officially accept."

"False modesty?"

Jess sighed. "Now who's being an asshole?" She tried a third trace, and paused, then selected another at random and touched it.

Her hand twitched, as a residual jolt went through the card. She almost screwed it up, but it held long enough for a low, anticlimactic groaning click to sound in the door next to her, though it didn't move. "Pry it."

Bock got the edge of the screwdriver into the gap he'd been chopping and put pressure against it, leaning his muscular body against the end of the driver as Jess let the circuit card rest against its holder and turned to help him. She picked up a bit of metal they'd pried loose and went to a knee, jamming it into the ridge and shoving hard against it.

With both of them prying, the door moved an inch, reluctantly.

"Hey, that's progress," Bock said. "Nice."

"Larcenous youth." Jess reseated her makeshift pry bar and leaned on it again. "I used to break into storage silos at school."

He snorted, then wryly chuckled. "Figures."

The door opened a bit more, and then they could get a grip on the edge of it with cold stiffened fingers. "Mike, April, c'mere," Jess called to the two rookies, who joined them at once. "Grab this thing and pull."

Four sets of hands gripped the door and hauled backwards, metal grudgingly giving way to powerful bodies as the door screeched open and thumped against the ice.

"Least we'll get out of the wind," Steven said. "Lead on, Jesslyn."

Jess obligingly drew her blaster and set her light to high, then cautiously stepped inside.

Wasn't really much to see. The facility was a series of long, corrugated metal boxes set end-to-end to make corridors, all covered by tons of ice and snow. Containers, Jess remembered they were called, which had once held stores of whatever stacked on a cargo ship or carried on trains.

They were rusty and the air smelled rancid, but she kept moving on with the other three behind her. They came to a cross corridor, the square blackness extending to either direction. Far off, they heard faint bangs and scrapes, echoing softly in the darkness.

"Hope that's the tinkers," April said.

"Me too," Mike muttered. "This place is complete ancient bad news."

Jess moved on past the side corridors and continued down the main one. Another five minutes walking and they entered a big, dark area that seemed to be six or so of the containers all welded together. There were consoles on shelves welded to the walls, but nothing was live. Not even the faintest hint of power was evident in the center.

"I guess this is ops," Stephen said, turning around in a circle. "Or something."

"Main control room for the facility," Jess said. "I remember seeing the plans for this place somewhere."

"Not going to be useful to us without power," Mike remarked. "Could we power this place off the carriers?"

Jess went over to one of the consoles and touched it. The shelf was clean and the control surfaces looked in reasonable condition. "My tech can probably power it off three salmon and a glow worm, but we draw all the power from the carriers we don't have power we need to go get that weapon."

"At least it's warmer in here," April said. "Can I ask? Does anyone really know what happened to our base?"

Jess undid her jacket and folded her arms over her chest. "You saw the same thing I did."

"Which was?" Stephen asked. "Since I didn't see any of it?" He looked at April in question.

She cleared her throat. "We were coming back from Drake's Bay."

Bock swung around to face Jess. "You giving guided tours now?"

"My mother died," Jess said flatly. "I attended her processing. Bain mandated I take an escort."

He lifted a hand. "Sorry," he said, gruffly. "Didn't know."

April studied him with a dour expression. "We noticed that standard status messages weren't getting acknowledged, and then we encountered two enemy targets heading east."

"Two? What kind?" Stephen asked.

"TK300s," Jess said.

Bock folded his arms over his chest. "Just flying in our airspace?" His tone was incredulous.

"We chased them, and when we were on top of them, they blew themselves up," April said. "At least. That's what we think happened."

Bock frowned. "That makes no sense."

"Not to us either," Jess said. "I got a hit on their sideboard and next thing I knew scan was showing a blowup. We just got clear in time."

"They were hiding something," Arias suggested. "Maybe this new weapon?"

"Maybe." April walked over to one of the consoles and studied it, directing her light on its surface. "But if that was the case, why did they attack the citadel in force? Didn't they fear the same thing from them?"

Jess was standing, just staring off into the shadows. "Storm was over them. They were flying free in and out of it. Must be tied in to whatever this new thing is."

"You sure of that?"

Jess felt the raw prickle of temper rise at the skepticism in Bock's voice. "I'm sure I saw at least six TK300s flying through a storm front coming across the range," she said. "We could feel the EMF disruption. Dev was adjusting for it."

"Oh, the wonder child." Bock snorted a little.

"We felt it too," April said quietly. "And with all due respect, Mr. Bock, given the crap we've been through today, no one needs to be slighted here."

Jess had turned and her back arched under her jacket, but relaxed a bit at the words. She gave April a brief grin, and then turned back to the console. Hopefully Stephen would stop being an ass and rubbing her temper the wrong way.

They were in the field, after all, and all kinds of things happened out here.

Bock gave April a sour look, but refrained from commenting. He walked over and joined Jess at the wall. "Well if that's how it is," he said, in an undertone. "You collecting supplicants already?"

Jess looked him full in the eye. "Why not? She's apparently a hell of a lot smarter than you are." She knew he heard the slight rasp in her voice, and he took a step back away from her, his hands coming out of his pockets and lifting up between them.

"Don't get crazy on me, Jess," he said. "It's not the time or place."

"Take your own advice and shut the fuck up then."

Footsteps behind them made them both turn, as a light entered followed by a short, slight figure in arctic gear. "Hello." Dev removed the cover over her mouth. "We have revealed enough of the structure to determine its functionality."

"And?" Jess moved closer, watching the grave, pale eyes focus on her. "D'ja fix it already?"

Dev produced a brief grin. "It will require a power boost. I instructed Doug to bring his carrier over so we can use it to restart the batteries," she said. "However, I do not know if resuming the heat exchange will allow all of this equipment to function. It has stage six degradation."

"That's pretty bad," Mike said. "My grad sim was to re-commission one of these old stations. Never did get it all the way right."

Dev nodded. "It's not optimal. I would like to suggest that you vacate this facility while power is applied. I do not know what result it will have on these systems."

"So you think it's going to blow everything up?" Jess only just kept from reaching up to push the pale hair out of Dev's eyes. Her hand and arm twitched, in fact, and she clenched her fingers into a fist to keep herself still, surprised at how much effort it took.

"I don't know, but I don't want to take a chance having you be in here," Dev answered honestly and loud enough for everyone to hear her. "It would be better if you were outside."

"Fair enough," Jess said. "All right people, let's go outside and see what trouble we can cause." She put her hand on Dev's shoulder and steered her back toward the entrance, clearly expecting the rest of them to follow.

April and Mike promptly did, turning their backs on Stephen, who waited almost until they were no longer visible before he reluctantly started moving. "Fucking ridiculous," he muttered, as he cleared the entrance and pulled his light from his pocket. "Absolutely fucking ridiculous."

Chapter Eight

JESS USED THE back of the ice ax to tap down the stake clenched lightly in one gloved fist. There was now a roughly made tarp over the outer panel, protecting it from the snowfall that was slowly burying everything else.

Under the tarp Dev was kneeling with Oscar next to her, connecting up a set of power leads on the laboriously cleared external interfaces and behind them parked precariously with its forward skids on the ground and the rear ones up on the snow ridge was Doug and April's carrier.

Oscar picked up the leads and walked over to the front of the carrier, which was also providing a convenient shield for the wind and snow. Doug was already in front and opening an access hatch, running a scanner over the interior.

"Better hurry up before this thing freezes," he told Oscar. "Holy crap it's cold."

Stephen had retreated to the carrier he'd piloted alone, but Mike and April were standing next to Jess, their cold suits fastened all the way up and eye shields in place. Inside the suits it was bearable, despite the sixty below zero temperatures, but any exposed skin suffered immediately.

Dev stood up and stuffed her now gloved hands into her pockets, coming over to stand next to Jess. "The ingress is prepared," she said, her voice muffled by her face cover. "Application of sixteen point five volts across the terminus will stimulate a response."

Oscar got the leads connected then turned, giving them all a nod.

"Go on, Doctor Dev." Jess bumped her with a hip. "Give the sign. Let's see what we're going to get out of this so we can either go inside and get warm, or get into our buses."

Dev hopped in place a time or two then trudged over to where Oscar and Doug were standing. "Go ahead," she said. "Please make sure it's exactly sixteen point five."

"Roger that." Doug tuned his comp, and pressed a small relay inside the hatch, resulting in a slight whine and thump, as the leads went from leaden gray to purple, and power surged across them lighting the snow and then hitting the power panel of the facility.

"Cease," Dev said.

The purple faded, and then for a moment it was all dark and gray again. The wind blew a gust of snow into their little alcove, dusting them all with a covering of ice.

Then with a crackling bang that made them all jump, the power panel came to life, and a second later, lights came on and outlined them all in the old fashioned green tinted glow.

That was followed by a series of bangs and thumps, and a moment later a puff of discharged air came rolling out of the entrance behind them, spraying dust and ice crystals almost to the back of the open space.

"Interesting," Dev said.

"Glad we weren't inside the damn thing," Jess said. "Wouldn't like a faceful of that crap."

Oscar was studying a hand scanner. "Power readings coming up," he said. "Looks like things are trying to boot. Good job, Dev." He glanced at Mike. "Want to see if your sim'd work?"

"Let's all move inside." Jess noted Dev was shivering. "Nice work, Devvie." She casually draped her arm over Dev's shoulders, and started toward the now lit entrance.

Stephen met them as they reached it, hunching his shoulders in his parka as he entered the squared off portal after Jess and Dev. "One good thing. No one's around here for a thousand miles," he said, as they trooped down the hall. "If any of this comes up, we can get a high level long range scan going from here."

"We can open a channel with home base too," Jess said. "Let them know what's going on."

Stephen eyed her. "Let everyone know how screwed up we are?"

"This isn't some blown mission, Stephen." Jess's body relaxed as she felt the air moving in the hallways, already warmer than the outside. "Two bases are blanked. It's not like Bain doesn't know."

They entered the central space and it already looked far more friendly. Panels were showing some kind of life, and there was an audible hum around them.

"Okay." Mike pushed his hood down and moved to one of the panels. "Let me see if I remember any of this from class."

Oscar sat down at one of the scan consoles, and the rest of them drifted around, getting a better look at what was, to them, ancient technology.

But there was power, and a very gradual warming of the air, and that was all to the good.

There was an awkward moment of silence, then Jess drew in a breath and straightened. "Okay," Jess said. "Let's split up and see what we've got to work with here. Check for stores, and weapons. I doubt anything's going to be useful, but you never know. We're going to have to stay here long enough to put a plan together to insert."

It was the tipping moment, and she knew it. Stephen could choose to challenge her at this point, or follow her lead. If he challenged her, she also had a choice—to step back, or fight. He'd gotten the note from Bain, and knew the old man's intentions.

But even if he didn't, she intended to take command. If she had to fight him, there was no doubt in her mind she would.

"Sounds reasonable to me," Bock said, somewhat anticlimactically. "I'll check the central stores." He pointed at the back of the central space, opposite the door they came in, then headed toward it, shrugging his hood back.

Jess actually had to admit to a guilty sense of disappointment. April and Doug started off without comment toward the front corridors, leaving her and Dev standing in the middle of the control center together.

Dev gave the room a speculative look, then tipped her head back and looked up at Jess. "If the precipitation continues the carriers are going to be covered. I don't think that would be optimal."

"Me either. Let's go look." Jess indicated the front entrance.

OUTSIDE, THEY FOUND the snow slowing down, and the carriers only buried up to their skids. Jess studied them, then turned to Dev. "Doesn't look like that much of a problem yet."

"No," Dev agreed. "I really didn't think it was, I just wanted to talk to you and didn't want everyone else listening."

Jess looked at her in surprised delight. "For real?"

"Yes." Dev smiled a little.

"You going to tell me I'm good looking again?" Jess asked hopefully.

"If you want me to, of course," Dev said. "But what I wanted to say first is, that man Bock seems to me to be incorrect."

"Ah." Jess stuck her hands in her pockets. "What do you mean by incorrect?" She glanced across the now lit central opening, where the carriers were parked in their orderly circle. She could see the internal lights on in Carlos and Oscar's bus, where the older agent was keeping watch until they got the base systems working.

Dev thought about the question. "He does not wish you well," she said, slowly. "I think he wants to cause you discomfort."

Jess nodded. "He's jealous. He heard about Bain wanting to promote me. He wanted that job."

"But that's not your fault."

"No, of course it isn't, but he's not man enough to be mad at Bain, and I'm within reach." Jess sighed. "I didn't care when he was promoted. Not sure why he cares that I am. He was going to get a directorship at North when he rebuilt it."

"That's not really what I meant." Dev frowned. "I think he wants to do bad things. I get a bad feeling about him."

Jess crossed her arms and leaned her shoulder against the metal entranceway. "Bad things, as in, you think he's on the wrong side?"

Dev looked disturbed. "I'm not really sure what I mean, but something—maybe it's programming—tells me not to trust him."

"Ah." Jess straightened. "Okay that's different." She considered, reaching a hand out to capture an errant snowflake. She cupped it in her hand and showed it to Dev. "Every one of them's unique."

"Like you," Dev said.

"Like you." Jess smiled in response, then sobered. "Stephen was the one who told me about your project," she said. "He kept nudging me. I wondered...but then I forgot about that after we met."

Dev watched her with alert eyes.

"We kind of got distracted by you. The whole issue of trust and our techs and the leak kind of got pushed under the rug," Jess mused. "I forgot about Stephen. He was all ready to escort me to the shuttle, too."

"The day we got there?"

"Yup."

Dev caught a snowflake herself and examined it. "I don't think the man Bain trusted him."

"I don't know about..." Jess paused, as a memory surfaced. "Huh. When we met on the shuttle..." She remembered the moment, Bain seemingly sure if they left Stephen alone long enough he'd go and tell—go and tell what? To who? Bricker? Or someone else? "Maybe," she said.

"At the first lunch thing we had, he seemed okay," Dev said. "But now, he's saying incorrect things about me. Remember he spoke sternly to the agent Sandy?"

Oh. Crap. Jess gazed intently at Dev. "You're right."

"I don't understand why it's different now. I didn't change."

"No, you didn't. But," Jess tapped her on the nose. "That was before you showed your stuff. Maybe as long as he thought you were just an experiment, one he thought would fail, you were okay, but now he's scared of what you can do."

"But why would he be? He's already in charge."

And that was true. Jess shook her head. "I don't know. But anyway, let's go back inside so your nose stops turning blue and see what we can find stashed away in this place. Probably nothing but long frozen whale crap, but you never know." She put her hand on Dev's back. "I'll keep your idea in mind though. He's being a prick, no doubt about it."

Dev exhaled in some relief, glad she'd told her thoughts to Jess. The uneasiness she'd felt around Bock seemed quite strange to her and she now felt much better having expressed the oddness to Jess. "What's a prick?"

Jess chuckled. "It's slang for a male sexual organ." She steered Dev down the right hand side corridor as they headed toward the control center.

"I see," Dev said. "Why would you say he was acting like a male sexual organ? They showed us vid of that as part of the sex class. He wasn't going up and down," she said. "At least, not that I could tell."

Jess closed her eyes and stifled a laugh.

Dev wasn't really sure what was funny. She shrugged and studied the walls instead, spotting a door in one of them. "Is that a storage space?"

"Yeah. Stand back." Jess didn't bother with the archaic locking system. She drew her blaster and shot the hatch with casual accuracy, leaning back and kicking the door open with one booted foot. A puff of dusty air emerged into the hallway, and she waited for it to clear before she poked her head inside and shone her light around. "Nothing."

They continued down the hallway, discovering another corridor at the end that was set at right angles. Everything was lit with the weak, green glow and it made distinguishing things difficult. There were old signs on the walls, and Jess let her fingers trail over them as she walked, feeling the roughness of the corrugated metal walls.

The words on the signs were almost meaningless. Jess wasn't sure what most of the signs were for, save the ones that marked muster stations, and one that seemed to have something to do with weapons. "There's another door. Let's try it." She studied the roll down hatch, then aimed and fired at what appeared to be a latch at the bottom center of it.

The door abruptly let loose and flew up, sending Jess hurtling backwards, her arms wrapping around Dev and hauling them both against the far wall.

With a boom, the door hit the roof, and a thick cloud of rusty dust invaded the hallway, bringing a taste of dry, rancid age on the back of the tongue.

"Pah." Jess cautiously looked around, her back turned toward the door as she set her body between Dev and the opening.

"That was exciting," Dev commented mildly, apparently content to stay where she was, wrapped up in Jess's arms. She really didn't think the dust was dangerous, but she had no intention of protesting.

"Sorry." Jess straightened up and released her, dusting off her jacket. "Wasn't sure what that was." She cleared her throat and turned to study the now open, apparently inoffensive door. She walked back over to it and turned her light on, making a show of inspecting it carefully.

Dev joined her, putting one arm around her and giving her a quick hug. "Thank you for ensuring my safety," she said. "What's in here?"

"Good question." Jess edged inside. "Let's find out." It was definitely a storage chamber of some kind. The inside walls were lined with locked cabinets, and plastic boxes were lined up on pallets up and down a narrow space with two aisles. "You check the containers, I'll open those cabinets."

Dev willingly went to the first one, studying it intently. On the top there was a piece of plas, but the characters on it had long faded off. The container was closed by a hasp and a lock, and she drew out her multiple tool and applied it to opening the device.

Programming was strong here as she lifted the lock and held the tool in her other hand. She felt the patterning driving her motions and inserted a small, thin probe into the bottom of the cylinder, a picture coming strongly to her of what the inside looked like.

A moment later, and it was open. She removed the lock and opened up the container, shining her light inside.

"Did you just pick that lock?" Jess asked from across the chamber.

Dev nodded. "Yes. There are some kind of frozen units in here."

"Frozen units everywhere." Jess joined her and looked inside. "Ah hah!" She hauled out one of the packages, knocking it against the edge of the container. "Rations."

Dev picked one up and looked at it. "Quite old."

"Probably completely useless," Jess said. "But we'll take some back. You never know." She closed the container and went back to the cabinet. "C'mere and pick this one. I'm lousy at it. I'd rather use my gun." She held the cabinet door still as Dev applied her skills to it. "And there's armament in there that could ruin both our days."

"Yes."

"Been a long enough day already."

TWO HOURS LATER, they were gathered back in central ops. Cases had been dragged in to make worktables, and two portable heaters had been located and were adding their warmth to the room. Oscar had gotten the comms systems online, and he was patiently reworking the radio bands to match the ones currently in use.

Parkas were strewn about the space, draped over boxes and hanging on console edges, the dark black and green of standard jumpsuits standing out against the glare of the phosphorescent light and the dusty gray of the consoles.

Jess entered from the corridor, an old style brown pack on her back that she unloaded onto one of the boxes. "We got power up to everything?"

"Yes." Dev looked around from the control console she was seated under, her head halfway inside the metal structure. "There are a lot of ruined components. It's not very optimal."

"No, I would guess not." Jess peered inside the pack. "Okay, so I dug up enough of these things to give everyone a feed if we can figure out how to heat some water."

"There's a dispenser in that second chamber," April said. "I turned it on when I went through. It might have done something since then." She came over and peered at the packs' contents. "What are those?"

"Rations. Old style." Jess held one up. "Really old style. They used to dehydrate cooked stuff and zap it into these bags. You add boiling water to them and they become something."

April looked skeptical. "Really?" She examined one. "All these years, you sure they're not just dried seal barf?"

"Not sure at all." Jess readily confessed. "But all I've got in my bus is two days' worth of fish rolls, so if we can use some of this stuff it'll make life easier."

"Yeah, us too," April said. "Mike, did you take a bigger stock?"

Arias was paging through a personal pad on the desk, his jaw resting on his fist. "Got five days' worth on board," he said. "We were going to make a stop in Quebec."

Jess paused with her hands on the pack and looked around. "Where'd Stephen go off to?" she asked April casually. "Thought he came back here."

"He was just here," April replied. "Said something about starting up the backup generators, maybe charging the carriers off it."

"Ah." Jess picked up the pack. "Well, that'll be useful." She headed toward the bare, half lit convenience chamber in the section past the control center. "Might as well make myself useful too. Want to give me a hand?"

"Sure." April caught up to her as they reached the chamber. "You have any idea what the plan's going to be yet?"

Jess put the pack down and examined the dispenser. It had dusty lights lit on the front and she pressed the hot water tab, jumping back when it started sputtering and spewing liquid everywhere. "First, we let the corps know what the story is," she said. "Then, we find a hop point closer to the target."

"In the white?" April removed one of the food packs and fitted the spigot to the small plas intake valve on it and carefully triggered it to fill. "So is your theory the new thing is dangerous when it's mixed with met?"

Jess filled a second pack, and set it aside to do whatever it was it was supposed to do. "That line turns red when it's ready, according to comp."

"Uh huh." April retrieved more rations.

"I think they've got the advantage when it's mixed with met, or those two wouldn't have blown themselves up when we caught them. They were two on two, no reason not to turn and fight if they had the better weapon," Jess said. "Not sure where the jump point needs to be yet, but probably."

"Shorter route," April said.

"I found this too." Jess pulled out a stack of cups and some packets. "I don't know where these guys hid all this stuff, but that's freeze dried coffee."

"Coffee?" April's eyes opened wider in surprise. "I had an elder who claimed he tasted that once. No one ever believed him."

"Excuse me."

They both turned to find Dev entering the space, Dev's face smudged with dust.

"Hey, Devvie," Jess said. "Want to try some coffee with us?"

"Actually, some water would be good," Dev said. "I heard there was a dispenser in here?" She wiped her hands off on a cloth clipped to her belt. "This air is very dry. A little like the creche."

Jess filled a cup with cold water, and handed it over. "Between snow and the desal, they always had plenty of water here. Just like we did at the base," she said. "I found showers and sleeping quarters. Pretty basic, but not bad."

Dev's eyes lit up at the mention of showers, but she silently sucked her water down.

"Must have been hell, living up here though," April said, carefully opening one of the coffee packets into a cup and smelling it. "Oh, that's weird." She applied some hot water to it, and set it down, observing it as it bubbled a little and emitted steam into the air.

Jess duplicated her motions and swirled the water around a little. "Kinda looks like mud."

There were crates lined up against the walls. They took their cups and sat down on them. "It's late," Jess said. "Soon as we get comms up we should get some downtime while comp updates from HQ."

April nodded, taking a cautious sip from her cup. She mouthed the substance and then swallowed it, licking her lips thoughtfully. "That's not bad."

"No, it's not," Jess agreed. "Got a kick to it." She half turned and offered Dev her cup. "Want a taste?"

Dev took it and swallowed a little, then handed the cup back. "They gave us something like that in the creche," she said. "They said it was chicory or something. Some bark they'd replicated. It didn't last though, some fungus killed it."

A soft rumble made them all jump a little, then Jess put her hand on the wall. "Generators," she said. "Guess Stephen got them going." She walked out into the hallway and stuck her head in the central ops area. "C'mon in and get some of this fantastic grub."

Then she went back and sat down on the crate next to Dev. It was, by her internal clock, well after late watch and they'd been on the go since before dawn. She was tired, and there seemed to be really no end to the tasks ahead of them, and as of yet she had no solid plan.

She could, of course, turn the whole problem over to Stephen, but she knew she wasn't going to do that.

The rest of the group entered, and everyone took possession of a food pack, using their multi tools to open them and studying the results.

"What is this?" Chester asked poking at it.

Dev looked at the partitioned tray under the stiff plastic. "Those are carrots," she said, in a surprised tone. "I think."

"Carrots?" April picked up a small, orange item. She put it in her mouth and chewed it. "Huh."

Jess picked up a chunk of brown something and sniffed it, then bit into it. It was, to her surprise, some kind of solid with a rich, pungent taste. "That's meat."

"Meat?" Dev tasted it cautiously. "Meat of what?" She stopped chewing. "Jess, this isn't bear, is it?"

Jess chuckled wryly. "No." She picked up the packet and read the almost faded to illegibility label on the bottom. "Pot roast. Well that's damn helpful."

"I think this is beef." Mike had been chewing his meal thoughtfully.

"Beef?"

"Cow meat," he said. "I had it once. They found a deep freeze where I lived when I was home on leave. Unfroze some of it and cooked it. Tasted like this."

"Huh." Jess ate another piece. "It's all right," she said. "Different than fish, anyway."

"Yeah, not bad," April said. "This white stuff is okay too."

Dev investigated the white stuff. "Those are potatoes," she said. "They grew some of them in the synth dirt but we never got to taste them. All of them went to the senior admin food service."

Jess poked hers. "Why?"

"I have no idea," Dev replied. "I just remember the proctors being mad about it because they wanted some."

"Huh." April swallowed some of hers. "To each their own, I guess."

Chester entered, wiping his big hands off. "Got scan up." He looked satisfied. "Syncing the crypto keys from my carrier now. Should be ready to go in about ten minutes." He picked up a tray and sat down with it. "I told Carlos to head on in. Bet he could use some grub."

Stephen came past the doorway then paused, and entered. "There you all are," he said. "Got the gens up. Plenty of power to spare." He entered and went over to the processor. "Found their weapons store too. May be something useful there. Things are looking up, huh?"

Jess watched his back, seeing the tension in his posture. She recalled Dev's suspicions, and felt a prickle of her own chase up and down her spine. "Yeah, sure are," she said into the almost uncomfortable silence. "We're right on track."

Stephen turned and smiled briefly at them, taking a seat on a box, drumming his heels on the side of it.

"SYNC'S TAKING LONGER than I thought," Jess said, studying the screen. "What do you figure, two more hours?"

"Yeah," Mike agreed. "About that, and the charge up should be done by then too." He glanced around. "What is it, near mid watch?"

"After." Jess dusted her hands off. "Get some rest if you can, people. We got two hours before we can transmit. I want to make sure HQ knows what's going on before we go on the move." She waited a minute after she finished talking but no one commented back, accepting the plan without question.

Good sign.

Carlos made a final entry, then stood. "I'm going to bunk in my rig," he said. "Just in case." He ran his fingers through his dark, dense black hair. "I'll build a link to comms in here and relay," he told Jess. "Everything looks pretty good though. Old, missing a lot of progs, but it'll compile."

He stretched and twisted his body. "See you in two hours."

"Aw, who's gonna see us up here?" Stephen protested. "It's white out for a hundred miles. Pack's taking two inches per hour. No one can fly in that."

Carlos studied him. "No one was supposed to be able to fly in charged met either." He paused. "No offense." He motioned his partner to join him and they left the control center together.

"Probably just want some private bunk time," Stephen called after him, in a wry, meant to be overheard tone. "Well, I'm not. I found a nice hammock and I'm going to grab it." He got up and sauntered out and down one of the back corridors.

Jess watched him until he disappeared, and then she spent a moment exchanging looks with the rest of the teams still in the center. The two younger agents gazed stolidly back at her, April folding her arms over her chest in a shift of body posture that told its own tale.

The nomads were like that. Silent and suspicious most of the time, never trusting anyone's motives but their own.

That turned Jess's thoughts back to her own situation. Nominally, Stephen was the ranking op. Bain had given him control over the rebuild of North, and hadn't removed him from his position at Ten, and that position, at least on paper, put him in charge since Bain hadn't filed an official change of rank for her yet.

Interesting, that he wasn't claiming that. Jess mulled that over. Maybe avoiding blame if it all went sour?

Yeah. She was disappointed, expecting more from someone she'd considered a friend. "Hmm," she grunted audibly. "I'm going to go stake out a bunk. Dev?"

Dev was busy at a console, and turned in the chair and faced her. "I would really enjoy going to find a bed with you," she said, in a very serious tone. "But I'm working on a mod for this system, and it will be about another ten minutes or so."

Jess was glad the lights were half-assed, because she knew she was blushing. She hadn't expected the frankness of the answer, but she reckoned she probably should have. Dev was just like that. "Well thanks, Devvie," she drawled. "Take your time. You're worth the wait."

Dev accepted the compliment with a smile, and turned back to the console.

"We'll go grab some rest," April said and cleared her throat. She pointed at the forward corridor. "I guess what was, sometime, a ready room is up there. Mike?"

"Right behind ya." Arias picked up his duty pack and slung it over one shoulder. "Be back in two." He gave Jess a faint salute. "Have a good rest, boss."

The two young agents made a show of parading out with their techs behind them, leaving Dev and Jess alone in the control room.

No doubt at all what they were thinking. No doubt at all that's why she was blushing even harder, to the point where it was making her a little lightheaded.

To cover that, she walked over and dropped into a chair next to Dev, rubbing her face and clearing her throat. "What'cha doing?" she asked. "Aside from talking dirty to me?"

Dev studied her face. "Was I doing that? I didn't mean to." She frowned. "What part of that was incorrect?"

Jess blinked and felt the heat fade a little. "It wasn't...um." She glanced around despite knowing they were alone. "It's okay. I don't care if they know."

"Know what?"

Jess nearly bit her tongue. "Uh...well, I mean, you know. I don't mind they know we hooked up."

"Hooked up?" Dev tilted her head. "What did we hook up to?"

It made Jess laugh, in an almost helpless way. "Aw, hell. What did I just get myself into." She sighed, rubbing her face again. "I meant it's okay that they know we practice sex with each other."

"Ah." Dev's expression cleared. "If that's so, then why are you in such discomfort?" She put a hand on Jess's knee. "I'm glad it's okay. I just don't want to get us in trouble in any way."

Jess edged a little closer. "I'm not really in discomfort," she said. "It just caught me off guard. We don't usually share personal stuff with each other in the field. At least most of us don't. Sandy never cared."

"I see."

They were both silent for a moment, then they looked into each other's eyes at the same time. Jess smiled and dropped her gaze. "So what are ya working on?" she asked again, in a quiet tone. "Looking for bears again?"

"No." Dev acknowledged a surprising sense of confusion, and felt a heating on her skin that made her blink. "No, I was calibrating the scan." She indicated a screen. "It was set to only thirty or forty degrees from azimuth. I imported wire maps from our carrier to give it three hundred sixty range."

Jess leaned her elbow on the console and rested her chin on her hand. "You sound so damn sexy when you talk like that."

Dev felt the heat increase. "W...what?" she asked, softly.

Jess got up and ruffled her hair. "Let me get out of here before I get us both in trouble. C'mon back to that set of racks I found just behind the wall over there. I'll set up some padding."

"Okay," Dev said, confused but not displeased. "It won't be long. I just want to set up a long range scan. The amplifiers in this facility are quite powerful."

Jess grinned at her. "Sexy," she said, winking before she turned and left.

Dev leaned her elbows on her knees and clasped her hands together, having little to do except watch the mapping schema on the screen while the blood slowly faded from the surface of her skin. It left her feeling a little weak, and a little chilled, a very strange sensation she really wasn't sure she enjoyed.

What had Jess meant? And, was it good or bad? Dev rubbed her fingers together. From her parting smile and wink, she supposed it was good, but it made her feel strange, and it looked like it affected Jess the same way.

She wondered if it had anything to do with that love thing, and if it did, did that mean she'd gotten the same thing too?

With a sigh, she straightened up and turned her chair back around to the console. The program she'd just finished entering now seemed unimportant and boring, when her body was urging her to get up and go follow Jess to the space she'd found, wanting the door to be closed behind them so she could explore this whole sexy thing some more.

They only had two hours to rest, after all. She studied the readout, and then reached over to make an adjustment, finding it very hard to focus. But she drew in a breath and released it, wanting the scan in place before she abandoned her post. There were many things she felt around them that weren't optimal, and though Carlos was watching from the outside, the carriers had limited scan and they were stuck in a relatively unprotected space.

She wanted them to be safe. She felt very uneasy about things.

A soft noise made her look up, and she half turned to see Stephen Bock entering the space again. He went over to the comms set and leaned on the shelf, peering at it.

"Hello, sir," she greeted him quietly.

He jerked in reaction and swiveled, spotting her on the other side of the room. "Oh," he said. "Thought you went to get some rest?"

"I will," Dev said. "I am almost done with this routine. Then I will go."

Bock watched her warily. "What are you doing to it?" He jerked his head in the direction of the console.

For a moment, she paused, studying his face. "Just importing the scan routines from the carrier," she answered. "The ones here were very old."

His shoulders relaxed. "Yeah, I'm sure they are, kid," he said. "So, how are you liking working with Jess?"

That, at least, she could answer readily, and did. "I like it very much," she said. "I find Agent Drake very competent and pleasant to work with."

"Really?" He walked toward her. "C'mon, kid. We all know Jess. She's no picnic."

"What's a picnic?" Dev asked in a mild tone. "I don't know what that is, so I can't comment on whether or not Agent Drake is or is not one of those."

Bock stared at her. "She screw you yet, kid?"

Dev regarded him quietly. "The only reference I have to screwing is attaching something with a metal fastener using a hand tool. So I would have to say no, she has not done that." She paused. "Nor can I really imagine a situation where she would be required to. Bio alts are biological organisms, sir. We don't require screws or bolts or fasteners of any kind."

Bock looked intently at her. Then he took a step back and laughed briefly. "Okay, whatever, kid." He turned and lifted his hand in a wave, disappearing back down the corridor he'd come from.

That, Dev considered, had been interesting, but not in a good way. Her eyes flicked to the console, glad to see that the programming had run its course, and the scan routine was starting up. She pulled the pad over and keyed the alerts to her portable scanner, then coded the console to lock, putting in her own ident and clearing the screen.

She got up and shook herself, turning to look carefully around the room before she finally and gladly quit it, heading around the corner and hauling up short before she crashed right into Jess. "Burfp."

"Sh." Jess touched her lips. "I was just being psychotically overprotective and making sure Stephen behaved." She leaned forward and removed her fingers, then replaced them with a quick, gentle kiss. "I loved the screw and bolt comment. Nearly gave myself away laughing."

Dev reasoned that she'd done something quite right, and returned the kiss, a very pleasant jolt of warmth in the never-ending chill of the station. Then she felt Jess's arm encircle her, and they walked along the hallway only a few steps before Jess triggered a door and they ducked inside.

"You handled that pretty slick," Jess said, as she paused to survey her scrounging. "How d'ya like this?"

This turned out to be what looked like a watch station. Her pack and Jess's were on a metal table bolted to the wall, and there was a big, deep shelf built into the opposite wall that was covered in layers of some kind of springy material.

Dev studied it. "I think I would very much like to lay down on that."

"Good, me too." Jess seemed pleased with her reaction. "Let's shower off, and get a power nap."

The watch station turned out to have a wash down chamber. Jess knowledgeably started it up, and the small space was filled suddenly with the bright smell of water hitting steel and a blast of steam that tickled Dev's face.

She was glad to see the shower. While Jess retrieved both of their sanitary packs she unfastened the catches on her jumpsuit and started to take it off.

A moment later, and her fingers were being removed from the fabric and Jess's took their place. "Let me do that."

It seemed strange to Dev, but she didn't object, feeling her body relax as the warmth of the steam heated the space they were in and the fabric was peeled back from her skin. "That man was not happy talking to me."

"No," Jess said. "I don't really know what got up his shorts either. When we talked about it I was the one who went ballistic over the idea. He was just talking Bricker's line. Wonder what made him turn like that." She smiled as Dev undid the catches on the front of her jumpsuit, an adorably serious look on her face. "Or was he just putting feelers out to see if you were going to jank me."

Dev looked up, one pale eyebrow hiking up a little.

"If you were going to play the game," Jess explained. "Be political with him, and try to suck up." She stepped out of her suit and steered Dev into the shower, carefully testing the temperature with one hand before pulling them both under.

"Jess."

"Yeah?" She started to playfully scrub Dev with a handful of soft soap.

"I didn't understand one word of what you just said." Dev said. "This wasn't like the shell thing, was it?"

Jess laughed. "No. He was testing you. To see if you'd say something bad about me."

"Oh!" Dev got a handful of soap and spread it on Jess's bare chest. "Okay, I get that!" She was glad to put the conversation in perspective. "Did he really think I would say something bad about you? I would never do that. I think he's very incorrect."

"I think maybe he's a little jealous." Jess cupped her face in both hands and ducked her head to brush her lips against Dev's. "He never got along with any of his partners. Never was that successful in the field." She gently rinsed the soap out of Dev's hair. "He got the position more by sucking up to Bricker than skill, and he knows it."

That sounded sad to Dev. She didn't much like Bock, but she thought it was a bad thing to be so unhappy. "You were with him when we got to the citadel."

"I was." Jess rested her arms on Dev's shoulders. "He was walking me out. I thought," she paused, "He told me he was doing it as a friend. That he'd miss me." She gazed thoughtfully at Dev. "Now I wonder."

This time it was Dev who stepped forward, finding the soap covered, powerful form in front of her becoming far more interesting than

Stephen Bock. She touched Jess's skin, and felt the water hitting her rapidly sensitizing body. "He doesn't want me to succeed," she said, before Jess pressed against her, and she lost track of why that had meaning.

"Forget him." Jess bit down gently on the edge of her ear. "We've got two hours. Let's just lose our minds."

Dev tried to make a picture of that in her head, and then erased it, after she got past the stuff inside her skull leaking out her ear, or possibly being sucked out of her ear by Jess's nibbling.

It felt very good. "Okay." She stepped with Jess into the flow of the water, watching the liquid sheet off Jess's body, studying it in the off color light as Jess ruffled her hair and washed the soap out. She reached out to run her fingers over the pale golden surface, tracing a long scar from her ribcage down to her hip.

It looked old, and faded, but prominent amidst the lighter, fainter tracings scattered over the surface. Aside from that, Jess's skin was smooth, and soft, fitting tightly around the bone and muscle that was evident just underneath.

Jess observed this exploration with a mild and wry expression. "Wanna know how I got that one?"

Dev leaned closer. "I'm sure you were doing something excellent."

"I'm sure I fell down the side of a pier piling back home like a dork and ripped myself wide open on an old and rusty nail." Jess gently nudged her out of the water and shut it down. "Drenched half of Drake's Bay in blood running back into the lower caves, screaming my fool head off."

"Really?" Dev removed one of the flat, compressed towels from her pack and opened it, drying her skin off.

"Yeah, my first leave from school." Jess sighed. "I told them I wrestled with a shark when I got back. Got cred points for that, at least."

Dev smiled, imagining it. "I saw a picture of a shark." She toweled her hair dry. "Have you seen one really?"

Jess smiled back, tossing her towel over the bolted shelf and plucking Dev's from her fingers and sending it to join hers. She moved to the padded platform and sprawled on it, extending her long legs out and crossing them at the ankles. "I've seen one," she said, as Dev joined her. "I've swam with them."

Dev considered that. "The one in the picture had very big teeth."

Jess rolled onto her stomach and reached around to point at the back of one shoulder. "Look there." She waited for Dev to hike herself up on an elbow and inspect the spot. "That's what their big teeth leave when they bite you."

"Oh. Wow." Dev looked at the triangular scar, deep and thick, and knotted. "That must have been very uncomfortable."

Jess shrugged. "About as much as any of them." She let herself back down. "We were fighting over a four foot long grouper. I won."

Dev's eyes went wide, in silence.

Jess grinned. "Lesson for you, Devvie. Don't get between me and my dinner."

"I will absolutely remember that." Dev curled her arm around and put her head down on it. It was tolerably warm in the chamber but she was glad when Jess pulled the lightweight cover over them both from her service pack and then squirmed closer, bringing a welcome warmth as she settled against Dev.

Something was niggling at her conscience, some detail was pecking gently at the back of her head, but just when Dev went to focus on it, Jess's hand touched her hip and her body reacted, driving the niggling back out of her mind.

She felt her body react to the touch, a gentle pulse of desire filling her guts. Then Jess's lips brushed against her shoulder and she put aside all thoughts of sharks and scars. She pressed closer and started her own, gentle and hesitant nibble on the edge of Jess's ear, amid a waft of soap scent from her still damp hair.

A sound made them both go still. Jess's hand moved from Dev's hip to her shoulder, and she lifted her head, ears cocked. "Shh."

Dev remained silent, and kept her hands still. The sound was mechanical in nature, and she wondered if it was just something in the systems they'd just recently restarted.

Dev frowned. She decided she actually felt discomfort from the interruption. She wanted to continue their touching and the rest of it, no matter the fact that she knew they were in a non-optimal place.

Doctor Dan had been absolutely right about that.

There were no more sounds, and after a minute more of silent listening, Jess half shrugged and leaned forward, kissing Dev on the lips and starting that feeling up all over again.

Probably was just a piece of machinery. Dev stroked the skin on the inside of Jess's leg, and felt the muscle tense lightly under her touch. Jess shifted a little and curled an arm around her and she moved closer, pressing her body against Jess's.

It felt very good.

She wished they had more than two hours.

Chapter Nine

THERE HADN'T BEEN time to sleep, but Dev felt good and her body seemed rested, or at least contented, as she lay in the circle of Jess's arms listening to her soft breathing.

In twenty minutes, or thereabouts, they would need to get up and go send the message, and after that, Jess would tell them what the plan was.

Dev felt sure there was a plan. Jess seemed relaxed before they'd retired, and she seemed relaxed now, her hands open and at ease and no hint of tension in the body pressed up against her own.

It was nice to just lie here quietly together. It made it possible for her to set aside the fact they were in a strange place, and in the middle of a lot of trouble. Dev idly observed Jess's arm, the burned marks faded in the dim light and that made her turn her head slightly to look at her own shoulder.

The mark had healed, mostly. It was no longer an angry red. Instead, it was taking on a darker hue that was lighter than Jess's, but seemed to look all right against her pale skin. It was still a bit sensitive, but it made Dev smile, knowing there was one almost just like it on her partner.

Made them part of each other, sort of. Dev drew in a breath and released it, setting her head down on the folded packing that made their pillow just as her portable comp let out a soft complaint.

Dev reached quickly out and grabbed it, stifling the noise as she drew it close to her and triggered the screen, waiting for it to clear and resolve.

She looked at the data, then her body tensed at what she saw. She felt Jess stir behind her, as Jess lifted up and peered over her shoulder.

"What's up, Devvie?" Jess blinked and cleared her vision, focusing on the screen, now held closer where she could see it. For a moment, she stopped breathing, as a prickle of alarm lifted the hairs along her spine and her muscles tightened. "Oh shit."

"That does not sound good." Dev was already sitting up and moving out of the way as Jess bolted upright, and a moment later Jess's naked body was flickering past her and heading for her jumpsuit. "It appears ships are heading in this direction."

"Wrong kind of ships." Jess was already fastening up her suit and reaching for her weapons. "We gotta get out of here. Someone ratted us."

Oh, that was really not good. Dev got her jumpsuit on and slung her portable comp over her shoulder as she reached for her boots to tug them on. "Those are enemy targets?" She glanced again at the screen, which was just a wiremap at long range, and not that discernible to her.

"Oh, yea." Jess got all her weapons in place and moved for the door at a gathering run. "I can tell by the pattern. Not ours." She drew her hand blaster and as she came out the door she slapped a dusty panel on the wall about a foot over her own head.

Instantly, a klaxon blared, and the lights changed to an odd shade of gray green. "Stay behind me, Dev." Jess ordered. "Only people who knew we were here are here with us."

"Suboptimal," Dev said. "Do we need to get away from here?"

"Oh, yeah."

Dev started a program running as she moved quickly behind Jess. They ran down the hall and around the corner into the control center, met a moment later by April and Chester coming from the other direction.

"What the hell?" April saw the gun in Jess's hand and drew her own, making a tight circle and shoving Chester back against the wall.

"Trouble coming." Jess went to the comp and flipped it through its screens. "Battalion inbound, ten targets, KRs."

"Shit." April, rookie or no, got it. "We have to get moving." She grabbed her jacket as Mike Arias came into the center, taking one look at her and grabbing his own outer gear. "Need to get the buses running."

Mike stepped forward one more step, April got her arm in her jacket, Chester rebounded from the wall he'd been bumped into, and a breath later the room was full of blaster fire.

Full of yelling and motion and the sizzle of ions hitting metal.

One moment Dev was tapping on the screen, the next moment she was grabbed and held, a rough tension and violence that made her throat catch. She heard Jess yell, and then realized it was Stephen Bock holding her when his voice answered.

"Don't move, bitch. I know you don't want me to waste her."

"I'll waste you regardless, Stephen." Jess's voice sounded cold, and rough. "The rest of you, out of here! Move!"

"Stop!" Bock yelled over her. "Just give it up! It's over! You're done! Interforce is done!

This was not good. Dev grabbed the arm holding her and shoved outward, bowing her body as she turned and pushed herself backwards, taking him with her as they both crashed into the console.

It surprised him. She felt his grip shift and she twisted, slamming her elbow back with all the force she could, feeling a clamp come down on her neck that cut off her breathing.

She shoved backwards again, lifting him off his feet and throwing him against the wall, as she heard motion and a blood curdling howl, whose very primal rage made her hair stand up on the back of her neck.

He yelled, and then coughed, and she felt a hot spray of something hit her as she ducked away from his suddenly released grasp and dove for the floor, tucking and rolling as she got behind another console and out of range.

"Go, go, go!" April yelled, and then a blast of icy cold air blew into the command center, as the klaxon suddenly got a lot louder. "They're almost here!"

Dev started out from her hiding spot only to find herself grabbed and surrounded again, this time by more familiar arms and the rough heave of Jess's breathing. "Jess!"

"Okay?"

Dev shook the hair out of her eyes and blinked them, focusing on her partner. "Yes."

"Let's go." Jess's voice was surprisingly hoarse. "They're gonna blow us ten miles out if they catch us here." She turned and shoved her blaster into its holster, reaching for and tossing Dev her jacket and stopping briefly over Bock's slumped body to yank something free from it. "Fucker."

Dev got into her jacket as they kept moving, only then realizing she was covered in a thick, coppery smelling liquid she belatedly recognized as blood. It spattered her skin, but she didn't have time to worry about it. She got her parka fastened as she caught up to Jess's rapidly moving body. "He was incorrect?"

Jess let out a snorting laugh as she pulled her hood up. "Mother fucker," she said, in a crisp tone. "He called them down on us. Figured to catch us sleeping and let them evaporate us." She glanced behind her. "Only thing that saved our ass was that scan alert."

They reached the door and plunged into a dark and icy night, full of fast falling snow that had built up around the door and covered the carriers midway.

"Definitely not excellent." Dev could now see the other agents digging out the hatches on their rigs, save one that was dark, and black, and open. "What hap..." She paused, realizing it was Carlos and Oscar's.

The carrier next to theirs had a hatch propped open, but was empty. It was Bocks, she remembered.

"Killed them," Jess said. "Poor bastards. He was a year from being able to retire." She plowed powerfully through the snow, shoving her body through the thick ice as though it was water. "Stupid mother fucker. Almost as stupid and clueless and jackass as me."

"You?"

"Me." Jess stomped over to the small rise Dev had landed the carrier on, jerking to a halt as the snow evaporated under her feet and the cleared hatch opened. "Hah." She turned and lifted her arm, rotating her fist in a circle and giving it a pump, before she jumped inside with Dev right behind her. "You do that?"

"The hatch? Yes." Dev shed her coat and stowed it, getting to her chair and settling into it quickly. She started the preflight checks as she sealed the hatch, comp already up and showing her rising energy levels in the other carriers. She kicked the heaters on for the engines and activated the batteries, a hum of power starting to surround her.

"Just get us up and out of here, and headed east." Jess got herself strapped in and pulled comms over. "Sideband Six, open all."

"On."

"Here."

"Follow us. We're going to the dark side and killing as many of them as we can." Jess shook her head as she got her systems prepared. "Stupid son of a bitch."

"Check."

"Ack."

The two responses were quiet, but confident, and Jess stopped kicking herself long enough to take a breath, and let it out, the residual dark energy and rage slowly fading out of her.

She felt the carrier come to life around her, and felt again the rush as she'd had that one chance, one slim moment to put her knife in Stephen's throat before he shot her.

Would have shot them all. Would have killed Dev. Jess felt her heart start to race again and she closed her eyes, erasing the memory of his scornfully triumphant face and his hands on Dev's body. Triumphant until he felt the slim form in his clutches lift him up and toss him like a rag doll, giving Jess her chance.

She'd certainly taken it.

Fucker. "How could I have missed it?" She growled, under her breath. "I knew something was wrong with him, and I just..." She slammed a fist against her console. "Shit."

Engines came live. Jess felt the vibration.

"Jess—incoming"

"Lift," Jess said. "They'll blast us."

The carrier moved under her and she was thrown back in her seat, tightening her restraints as the carrier lurched and then turned on its side. She strained against grav and got a screen pulled over. "Keep an eye on the kids." She got her boots braced against her console. "Gimme power."

Dev was busy trying to keep the carrier level as she came up and around the ice escarpment that hid the pole base. She couldn't see the enemy, but the scan was sounding warnings in her ear cups, low anxious tones mixed with the incoming chatter of the shortwave from the other two rigs.

It was snowing hard, and it was dark. She relied on the comp to tell her where she was in space, and leveled the carrier as she shunted power back to the weapons systems. Jess had said east, so she quickly laid in a track and transmitted that as comp to the other two, punching up the engines to full power.

The force sent her thumping back in her gimbaled chair and she curled her hands around the throttles, shoving them forward as they rolled up to speed. She kept her eyes on the forward scan, watching for obstacles as she kept a low profile track, skimming over the ice in near total darkness.

"Standby for bangs." Jess got her targeting up and the scan immediately pinpointed the incoming enemy sweeping up and over the horizon though not yet even visible to IR or UV.

There were a lot of them, though, and she reluctantly put off cursing at herself to focus on the task at hand, now aware that not only had they lost the chance to advise HQ about the attacks, they also couldn't tell them there were squads of bad guys roaming the land with impunity.

Life was just completely full of suck at the moment.

But there was no time for that. She set up targeting solutions and readied the rear guns, bumping the shields up and moving juice from the front systems she hoped she wouldn't need.

"Chester and Doug are in line with us," Dev said calmly. "Intercept in two minutes. They have an angle on us."

"So I see." Jess flexed her hands and settled them on the gun triggers, her fingers fitting into the metallic half gloves, whose inside surface was full of controls.

Each finger controlled one of the main guns, the knuckles positioned to release ion torpedoes. Coordination had to be instinctive—at some level there was no real way to even learn how to do it. Just something you felt your way through. Jess exhaled and tightened her focus, the wiremap on the scan now showing a solid outline of their pursuers.

Ten of them.

Had Bock been right? Was it all over? Was she just prolonging the inevitable?

Jess watched her reflection in the screen, seeing the smile appear on her face. "Ready, Dev?" She wiggled her fingers. "Time to make the doughnuts." She took her eyes off the screen long enough to glance up at the pilot's station, where she found Dev's pale eyes meeting hers in the reflective mirror.

Dev, though harried, had that expression that indicated she was puzzling something out.

"Doughnuts are bits of cake they fried in oil back in the day," Jess said. "You'd like them."

Now a faint twinkle entered Dev's eyes. "I do like them," she said. "We would have them once a season, up in the creche. I just wasn't aware that was something we produced downside. Intercept, one minute."

"You've had doughnuts?" Jess tore her attention away and put it back on the targets, uncapping the triggers and getting ready to fire "You little lucky monkey. I've only heard of them." She triggered comms. "Standby for battle. Keep moving. Don't let them take a bead on you or they'll fire at once and your shields are toast."

"Ack."

"Ack."

The two other carriers shifted a little, moving away from hers to give them space to fire and she got herself ready, feeling the sudden change of motion as Dev wrenched them out of plane and curled in a tight U, plunging down again toward the ice as she let off a barrage from the rear guns.

They cut between the leading two enemies and Dev rotated them along their axis, a move Jess was getting used to. She took advantage of it and held her fingers down on the center guns, firing in a circle as they dove down again.

"Holy crap," the sideband erupted in a crackle. "Stay clear of them!"

Them meaning her and Dev, Jess realized, their aerobatics as dangerous to their allies as to the other side. She ducked instinctively as they took a broadside hit, hearing the thump against the hull as the shields reacted and then she was upside down again as Dev spun them.

It was disorienting, but she tightened her focus to the screen, her hands reacting automatically to what her eyes were seeing, firing incessantly as they swerved to miss a direct impact ahead of them.

Two enemy rigs peeled off to either side, firing their own midship guns at them point blank. Jess flinched, but then left her stomach on the floor as the carrier peeled straight up and then angled down and around to come up behind the two that had just been shooting at them.

She let off a blast from the forward guns, hastily transferring energy to them, watching it splash back at her as it impacted the left enemies' rear shields.

There were clouds overhead and in a moment they were in and through them, as the KRs chased them, firing all the while. Blasts hit them on the side, and she heard alarms start to blare up in the front. "Whoops."

"Please hold on." Dev abruptly cut the power to the engines, and they fell down back through the clouds like a rock. Jess squinted and just started firing in all directions, hoping her blasts didn't hit their own people.

The enemy scattered out of their way, and arched off, and then Dev fired up the mains again, sending them rocketing to the left on their original course.

Jess checked scan and saw eight targets instead of ten, and spotted the distinctive maps of her colleagues coming up from the ice almost right at her. She let off a steady stream of torpedoes to the rear, and followed that up with a barrage that caught one of the chasers with shields fluctuating and had the satisfaction of seeing it blow apart in a blare of sudden light that outlined the stark ice below and lit the clouds above with orange.

The rest of them scattered, diving out of her way and arching off.

Three down. "Let's see if we can out run 'em now, Dev."

"Yes." Dev was very busy up front. "Running our damage control now."

"Check in." Jess opened comms. "Damage?"

"Shields seventy five," Doug responded. "Ack?"

"Ack," Jess said. "Tac 3?"

"Standby," Mike answered for his tech. "Running comp."

"Full speed, on course," Jess ordered. "Red line it. Let's leave 'em."

"Ack, Tac 2."

"Ack, Tac 3," Chester said. "We have full power to engines, but lost scan and some steering."

Jess felt the shove as they came up to full power and moved back into line with their original course. She watched scan carefully, seeing the enemy pull themselves together and form up, but they were still gathering as the three of her force were speeding off, already losing sight of them on visual.

The wiremap formed and showed her their images, and she held her breath, then cursed as they started after them, spreading out in a search and destroy formation. "Dev, you're gonna need those tweaks."

"Yes," Dev agreed. "However, Chester's machine does not have the improvements. He can't keep up with us."

Ah. Well. Jess tossed that plan out and studied her options. "Okay." She sent a set of coordinates up to Dev. "Head there, and send that to the other two. Let's see if we can out fly them if we can't outrun them."

Dev nodded, and tapped the configuration in, adjusting the throttles with a twitch of her fingers.

"Tac 2, Tac 3." Jess cleared her throat. "Stay low, follow tight."

"Tac 1, Tac 3." Mikes voice came back. "Ack, but we can keep rear."

Jess understood the message. At some level, she even admired it. "Stay low, follow close," she repeated. "We'll turn and pick them off if we have to."

"Ack."

She looked up, not surprised to find Dev looking back at her in reflection. She could see the spattering of rust stains on Dev's skin, from Bock's blood, but the gaze remained steady, and there was a little smile on her face. "Stupid cocksucker didn't hurt you, did he?"

Dev's brows tensed, then relaxed. "The man Bock?"

"Yeah."

"No." Dev adjusted trim, and edged the speed up a little. "They will overtake us plus ten, or perhaps twelve," she said. "I was just surprised he took hold of me."

"He knew I'd..." Jess paused to release a barrage of torpedoes to seed their path. "He figured I'd stop."

Dev studied the wiremap intently, making a picture in her head of the next maneuver she wanted to try. "You would stop?" she asked, after a moment's distraction. "Why?"

Jess held off answering for a minute, the roil of emotion the thoughts incurred surprising her. "I did stop," she answered at last, in a subdued voice. "I didn't want you to get hurt."

They were both silent for a few minutes, adjusting things, making changes. Jess sent another barrage out, Dev changed their course just slightly. "Did that man do something incorrect?" Dev finally asked. "To cause this attack now?"

"They must have paid him off," Jess said. "He sold out to them. I don't know if he told them where we were, or they just found us and he didn't warn us, or what." Some part of her really didn't want to believe Stephen had turned.

But... Jess watched the screen, seeing the wire-mapped enemy moving closer. Dev had been right about one thing—Bain hadn't trusted him.

Had he known?

Jess exhaled. "Glad we got the kids out with us," she said. "Dev, we'll let them get close then break up. Have the other two go out to the right and left and try to get around in back of them, we'll go topside and do the same."

Dev nodded briefly.

"Unless you've got a better idea," Jess added. "Since you're flying instincts are a hell of a lot sharper than mine."

"Five minutes to intercept," Dev responded. "The location you requested us to go to is about six to eight minutes away."

Jess sighed. "Story of my life."

"How accurate are the maps for that?" Dev asked, somewhat suddenly. "Of that place?" She had a scan up and was looking at it. "It appears irregular."

"They're fjords," Jess said. "Deep valleys with ocean at the bottom, or sometimes ice, or sometimes just gravel. They were made by glaciers a long, long time ago." She paused. "Why?"

Dev studied the screen. "If these are accurate, I think we could try to lose them in there," she said "Or perhaps we can make them crash."

Jess straightened up in her chair. "Crash?"

"Yes," Dev said. "That's why I asked about the accuracy." She glanced behind her. "So we can avoid that."

"Huh."

"So are they accurate?"

Jess half shook her head. "No guarantees."

After a moment of silence, Dev cleared her throat. "Want to try it?"

Did they have a choice? Jess felt her body settle. Did it matter? "Go for it." She tightened her restraints again. "Fly your ass off, Devvie."

"Well, okay." Dev glanced in the mirror. "But it will make it really hard to sit, won't it?"

Jess chuckled, and triggered comms, shaking her head as she composed her words for her erstwhile troops.

No point in worrying about it anyway.

THE CARRIER SHUDDERED as they were hit by a blast along the topside and Dev only kept from ducking as she felt the craft swerve in response.

Alarms were blaring all around her, and she glanced at the comp screen, seeing the shields on the port side almost nulled. "Jess, we are exposed on the left side up to the hatch."

"Nifty." Jess was busy trying to avoid hitting the other friendly craft while targeting the six enemies that were swirling around them, taking shots at will. "How long to the coast?"

"Two minutes." Dev could see the rapidly approaching outlines of solid structures, and once again hoped the scan was accurate.

Another blast shook them, and she felt the shift as one of the engines cut out. "Jess, we lost a pod." She adjusted the trim but they lost speed, and after a second, she dove for the surface of the sea, rolling over and presenting the bottom of the carrier to the ongoing attack. "Hold on please."

"Sure." Jess was hanging in her restraints, holding off on firing until the carrier allowed her guns clearance again. She felt the hits on the bottom, but that was where their heaviest shields were and they were only muffled booms, not the crackling pops the ones on the sides had been.

Her ears were throbbing from the blood rushing to her head and she held her breath a little, watching her screens intently. She saw the other two carriers crisscrossing overhead and she realized after a second that they were drawing fire away from her and Dev.

Good, kids. She felt them start to right and got off a quick burst, tracking across the absolute darkness when she spotted a shadow against the clouds.

Lucky shot. She watched the enemy craft come apart in midair as her unexpected hit impacted a weak spot and the parts went spiraling out, two of the other attackers swerving out of the way and bringing themselves into her line of fire.

She took advantage of that, of them being distracted, by sending some blobs their way and then she had to stop when they went upside down again. "Hey, I got one. I was doing good."

"Sorry," Dev replied. "We're about to go into the...what did you call them?"

"Fjords."

"Yes. And I wanted to complete a repair cycle on the engine or we were not going to have enough maneuverability to get through them."

Jess took the opportunity to remove one hand from her firing gloves and scratched her nose. "You really are cool under fire, you know that? I bet you're not even sweating."

"Please standby." Dev watched her scan intently, then nodded in relief as they reached the edge of the land and the engine came back online. "The only time I have really experienced sweat is when practicing sex with you," she said. "We are at the fjords."

"Is that good or bad?" Jess felt them rotating and then she was right side up, and then they were pitching down and she had a sense of enclosure. "Never mind, don't answer. Tac 2, Tac 3, follow."

"Ack."

"Ack." The responses came back at once.

"Stick to our tail," Jess added. "Will be tight maneuver."

"Ack."

"Ack."

And then they went to hell. Jess felt the sudden and violent buffeting of the wind against the carrier as Dev slowed it, and plunged into the narrow space between the fjord cliffs. "Whoa."

Dev kept her eyes glued to the scan, watching the wiremap outline of the space around her. The valley was very narrow, and she set the carrier in the very center of it, aware that in some spaces, the walls were only a wing length from her wing.

Comp showed both other carriers right behind her, and behind them, the staggered flood of enemy.

"Just lead 'em, Devvie," Jess said. "Don't worry about what's on your tail."

That was easy. Dev slid her chair forward and concentrated on her work. This was hard, and she felt her breathing quicken as she made slight adjustments, keeping the carrier even between the walls. She flinched a little as a blast hit the wall on her left hand side, blowing rock off and sending bits of it over to scatter on her front windscreen.

The walls were very stark, and very craggy, even in wiremap. In light they would be awesome. Dev pondered if she would get to see the light when another blast hit on the top of the carrier, nearly sending the nose of it pitching down. She only barely kept it even, and saw the damage alerts start flashing.

"Not nice." Jess patched in the vector and sent a blast back up and to the rear.

Dev adjusted a setting and let their altitude drop a little more, forcing their pursuers to enter the valley to chase them. The blasters only had a certain range, and she kept the angle going, studying the topography. To the right there was an even narrower crevice, and she ran a quick calculation.

"Bastards," Jess grumbled under her breath. "They're gonna tank us, Dev. I don't want them to tank us. I'm not done here yet."

Tank. Tank. Dev frowned and keyed in a route, then squirted it to the two other carriers. She snugged her straps more tightly, then took a deep breath. "Please really hold on."

Jess had just shot off a few blasts, now she turned and regarded Dev. "What are you going to do?" She looked at the forward scan. "That's a dead end. We going back up?"

"No," Dev said. "There is a space there, to the side."

Jess blinked. "Dev, we can't fit in there."

"Not going straight, no." Dev glanced in the mirror. "Do you wish me to stop?"

Jess looked at the scan, then at Dev, then back at her scan. "Oh boy." She released her guns and yanked her restraints tight.

"Tac 1, vector impassable," the sideband erupted.

Jess slapped at the comms. "Just stick to her tail," she ordered. "Be kickass, or be dead. Your choice."

Dev took that as an agreement on her plan, and she settled herself, then she smoothly tipped the carrier onto its side and turned, arcing out of the main channel and heading for the slit.

A curse trickled through the sideband, before it was cut off. Dev heard the sudden rattle of blaster fire around her and she felt a thumping impact on her topside wing, making the carrier swerve and shudder under her touch. She gripped the throttles harder, and bore down, adding speed to even out the path.

"Incoming!" Jess yelled.

Dev could almost sense the closeness of the attack, the wall before her abruptly lit up with plasma, showing her a real time view of the wiremap she was using as a guide.

Really small. Her heart started to thump a lot faster, and she bit her lip, almost closing her eyes as she reached the opening and the enemy reached her at the same time.

The explosion nearly did them in. Dev barely kept control of the carrier and she felt the skin scrape the rock, making a grating, keening sound that set her teeth on edge. The craft started tipping over, veering dangerously toward the rock walls and she hit the side jets with a rapid touch.

Then the enemy craft imploded over them and she was blinded by the flash, losing all sense of sight and flinching at the barrage of sound all around her.

Terrifying. "Jess! I can't see."

"Notgoodnotgoodnotgood." Jess released her restraints and climbed up onto her console, leaping across the open space and landing with her arms around Dev's chair and she got her hands on the controls just as they were about to smack into solid rock. "Yow!"

Dev blinked furiously, trying to get her vision to clear.

Jess tilted the carrier back up on its side and sprawled over the chair, the arm of it digging a dent in her ribcage making her short of breath. "Notfuneither," she said, reaching around Dev to grasp the throttles. "You okay?"

White spots on black, the sound of imminent destruction all around her. Dev felt a moment of angry frustration. She could feel the tension in Jess's body, and the strain in her breathing and knew things were seriously not good.

Jess was sweating. She didn't really have the skills Dev had in flying, and she could barely see the outline of the crevice they were in on the wiremap past Dev's shoulder. The action was happening too fast to absorb and she heard warnings and sirens all around them.

They were running out of sky, and the collision alert sounded. Jess frantically tried to judge which way she had to turn when hands fitted over hers and moved the controls. A quick look showed her Dev's face, her eyes wet with tears, and her pale lashes moving as she blinked, but with a clarity there that made her take her own fingers off the throttles. "Got it?"

"Yes." Dev nodded, dodging and twisting in between craggy outcroppings and then dropping suddenly and twisting the carrier in midair to send it half falling and half under power, boosting the landing jets and ducking under a thick ledge of stone that scraped the top of the ship.

"Good." Jess just hung on, getting her elbow down to lift her ribs up off the chair just as they took two Gs and she wrapped her legs around the chair to keep from being thrown across the carrier. "Oof!"

"Sorry." Dev spotted a wider space and headed for it, at last able to tip the carrier back onto its axis as she shot out of the narrows and into a valley that opened up on either side of them. "Are you all right?"

"Peachy." Jess got her feet under her and leaned against the console, flipping through comp. "Kids are still there," she said, triggering the comms. "Tac 2, Tac 3, stat?"

"Holy fuck!" A blast of static carried the words through the sideband.

"Stable," April's voice came through in calm counterpoint. "Comp shows no targets."

Dev ran the damage assessment programs. The carrier was running very rough, a heavy vibration rattling her bones as she worked to even out the power grid. "That was difficult."

"No kidding." Jess eased her way back over to her seat and dropped down into it. "My stomach's killing me." She put her hand on it, flexing the fingers of her other hand. "What in the hell was that flash? Damn good thing I wasn't looking at it like you were."

"I don't know." Dev ran comp on the logs and studied them, glancing at the nav that plotted their course, spreading out in a wide V shape before them. "There's a flat space ahead there. Should we stop?"

"Do we need to?"

Dev checked comp. "I would like to examine the outside of this vessel," she said. "Many sensors are not reporting."

Jess pulled over her own pad and scrolled through a set of readings with impatient fingers. "They really not back there?" She studied the report. "Or are they just hiding?" She pressed the comms. "Tac 2, squirt comp."

"Ack," Doug responded. "Got rear cam action."

Jess waited for the transfer, then she injected the squirt into her comp. She ran the vid, mostly darkness overshot with blaring light, then quickly shielded her eyes as the blobs erupted into a hellish white over flash, briefly outlining the rock edge, blasting it to nothing but an implosion of vaporized powder.

Only the narrow slit they'd been flying through had protected them. Jess felt a chill go down her back, and she anxiously searched the comp to make sure none of the bastards were following them. "They tried to fry us."

Dev glanced in the mirror. "Is that what that light was?"

"Must have been," Jess said, after a pause. "Go on and pick a spot to put down, Dev. Let's make sure we can maneuver. I get the feeling we're gonna need to."

THEY FOUND A gently sloping side valley and landed on it, the carrier's skids crunching and slipping a little on the loose rock, then coming to a halt.

Nestled between the high walls, they were protected from the wind and when they all stepped out into the faintly visible dawn light it was almost eerily quiet.

Overhead, dark clouds were moving, their edges shredded and packed with moisture. Far off in the distance they could hear thunder, but at the moment nothing was falling on them.

Jess was grateful for that. She turned on her hand light and studied the ground, leaning over to pick up a bit of the loose gravel and let it run through her fingers. It was sharp and hard, and had thick veins of color running through it. "So."

Dev was busy drooling over one of the engines, the cowling pulled back and her body half buried inside it. "There was intense disruption," Dev said, in a muffled tone.

"No kidding." Doug came over, his hands clasped around a burned out piece of hardware. "Fried my comp."

April had just finished a walk around her carrier and came over to join her partner, her jacketed figure emerging from the shadows into the circle of Jess's light. "Was that their new weapon, really?" She looked grave. "Went right through our shields."

"Looks like it," Jess said. "We lucked out." She handed over the rocks. "Metal content in that must have been high enough to have reflected the blast on them."

"Two of them flew into the cliff," Chester said, dusting his hands off. "The other two, yeah, my back cam got them getting backlash.

Guess the aims a little off still."

Mike joined them. He folded his arms over his chest and regarded their little group gravely. "Wasn't how I was looking to start my hitch out," he said. "What do we do now?"

Everyone looked at Jess, save Dev, who was still head first down in her engine pod.

Jess turned and leaned back against the wall of her bus, putting her hands inside her pockets. The air was cold, not the killing chill of the pole, but still enough, and she felt her skin warm as she flexed her fingers. "What do we do now," she repeated the question. "Well, we could just find some place and hide out until we hear from HQ."

April frowned.

"Or," Jess went on. "We could surrender."

Mike joined in the general, though silent, disapproval.

"But we'll probably be of more use to our oath if we find a way through these Norwegian fjords and sneak across into their coastal base, just east of Gibraltar." Jess's voice was quiet and very serious. "Then we can get into the developmental sciences center and find this thing."

Both rookie agents nodded in immediate agreement.

"And turn it on them, and make that center look like North. Maybe if they realize it can bite them in the ass as much as us, they'll stop using it."

"I like that idea," April said. "I'm not hiding. That's not what I came here for."

Jess smiled a little.

"Besides it won't do us any good," Mike said. "We can't hide forever, and when we come out they'll be there waiting for us. What would be the point?"

"Glad you both think that way," Jess said. "Because I'm not surrendering and I'll shoot anyone who tries. Let's get ourselves patched up as best we can, and then Dev'll find us a way to navigate through these cliffs. They'll block scan, at any rate."

The light was growing, and they could now see the steep, stark valley they were in. The stone walls rose on either side, folded in naked, sharp relief, their once green sides gray and featureless. "I've seen pictures of this place," Mike said, after a moment. "It was pretty."

Behind them a solid, ruffled surfaced black water spread out, covering the ground between the cliffs they were between and the next set of escarpments. It was deep water, Jess knew, and a little farther north it was ice and snow, glaciers filling the spaces between the walls as they inched down toward the sea.

Glaciers had made the slope they were on, unremembered eons ago. Jess exhaled and leaned back. These slopes would have been covered in green trees before the change, rich and fragrant as they towered over the waters below. It would have been pretty, indeed.

Now there was only raw rock, and the same dark waters, and as the dawn light touched the walls and brought out the veined patterns that had likely saved their asses, Jess still found it so.

The slope they were parked on stretched out in a long finger, ending in another sheer cliff that then branched off to the east into the distance.

"I like the idea of us sticking it to them," Mike said. "It bothers me to think about my—our classmates in the citadel, toasted."

Jess nodded. "Bothers me too."

April stuck her hands in her pockets. "Funny," she said. "We were always told it wouldn't." She studied Jess gravely. "You weren't supposed to worry about anyone else."

Dev hopped out of the engine and sealed the cowling. She came back over to the group with a somewhat relieved expression. "I think that will be all right," she said. "The repair sequence did enough."

"No," Jess answered April's comment softly, her eyes fixed on her partner. "You weren't. But that's not how life is." She switched her gaze to April. "Even for us." She let her arm rest on Dev's shoulders. "So. Here we are. We only have us to work with, so we should get working."

The four rookies nodded. "I'll see what I can do to get this sorted out." Doug held up the card. "I think I have a spare in the back box." He turned and headed for his carrier. Chester joined him, and after a moment, April and Mike also turned and walked toward their respective crafts.

Jess let out a long breath. "This sucks, Dev."

"Does it?" Dev asked. "I am glad the carrier is not as damaged as I thought. That's good, isn't it?" She moved a little closer to Jess, glad that the bone chilling cold had moderated to just the damp temperature she'd started to become used to in the citadel.

This cold didn't freeze her eyeballs, at least. That let her keep them open so she could watch Jess's face, now outlined in pale gray morning light. Jess looked like she was in discomfort, and Dev wanted to make that not so, but she wasn't really sure how.

"Yeah, that is good," Jess said. "We're going to need these carriers." She paused and chewed the inside of her lip. "We need to get in there, and get this done."

Dev considered that for a minute. "I will continue mitigating the damage," she said. "But this all seems very difficult, and dangerous." She found Jess's hand inches from her face, and studied it briefly, then touched her cheek to it.

The fingers moved, brushing her face gently.

"It's dangerous and difficult, and probably we're going to die doing it, Dev," Jess said. "I'm sorry. Maybe I should have just kept going onto that shuttle when we met. You'd probably have ended up living longer." She gave her a brief hug, then she released her and headed for the hatch. "Let me work up some kind of half-assed plan."

Jess left the hatch open and walked inside, dropping into her seat and for a minute, just sitting there staring at the screens. Part of her knew that she should start bringing up met and nav, and getting the plan started. Another part of her was just looking bleakly into fate, not wanting to do a thing.

She had to wonder, given how her luck was running, if going a mile farther was even smart or just heading into the inevitable.

She found herself wondering, for the first time, if what she was doing had a point. Was the battle for a purpose, or were they just so used to conflict it had become an indelible part of their psyche. Had Dev's question, about why they didn't just work together, asked in all open innocence not had a point?

Did it even really matter anymore?

Jess exhaled, feeling a sense of exhaustion she thought she'd left behind with her injury. She honestly didn't feel like even moving, much less forcing herself to go be a leader of her little, battered force.

She heard footsteps, and looked up to see Dev climbing up the ramp and into the carrier. As she got inside she looked up and their eyes met. Jess had the uncanny feeling Dev knew everything that was going through her head. "Hey," she murmured.

"Hello." Dev came over and sat down on the floor next to her seat. "I think the outside's okay."

Jess studied her, guiltily glad of the distraction. "You look bummed."

Dev tilted her head back and regarded her. "I do? What does that look like?"

Jess remained silent for a minute. "Like you're sad," she finally answered. "Or, what do you call it? In discomfort?"

"I am," Dev said. "They teach us not to say things like sad, or mad though. It reminds natural borns that we're people." She pulled her knees up and wrapped her arms around them. "So we say we're in discomfort, or incorrect. But I really am sad. I feel bad about the big place, and what happened to the others, and about Doctor Dan."

Jess reached over and touched her head, stroking her soft, straight hair in an almost hypnotic pattern.

"And because you're sad," Dev continued. "I like it a lot more when you're happy. I don't want you to feel bad."

"Is that because you're programmed that way?" Jess asked, in a mild tone.

"No," Dev responded immediately. "It doesn't feel like programming. I just hurt." She touched her chest. "When I see you feeling bad."

"Do ya?"

"I do." Dev scooted around a little so she was facing Jess. "Isn't it strange?"

Jess smiled a little. "I don't think so. I feel bad when you're sad too." Jess felt a certain sense of something altering inside her that eased her breathing and made her shoulders shift a little and relax.

Dev studied her gravely. "Could it be part of that love thing?"

"In me?"

"In me." Dev's face edged into a faint smile. "I looked it up in comp. I'm not really sure about all the contexts, but I think it's possible that I love you."

Jess sat there blinking.

"Is that okay?" Dev put a hand on her knee. "You seem in distress. Was that incorrect of me to say?"

Jess felt her whole body flush, bringing a sense of warmth that made her slump back in her chair and gaze at her companion with slightly widened eyes. "I don't know. Was it?"

"I don't know either." Dev chuckled a little. "But I don't feel bad when I say it."

Jess smiled back at her "I don't feel bad when I hear it." She plucked at Dev's sleeve. "C'mon up here." She edged over and made space for Dev in the chair next to her, a squishy but very comforting situation. With a sigh, she put her arms around Dev and hugged her.

Dev hugged her back, putting her head on Jess's shoulder, despite the awkward position. "This feels good."

"It does." Jess willingly surrendered the gloom of her thoughts for the pleasure of the contact. With everything so bad, this bit of friendly affection almost bowled her over with its potent appeal, and though she knew nothing would change because of it, she wanted it anyway.

Wanted to hear Dev say that, about loving her. It made her crazy happy for no really understood reason, since she'd never really wanted or thought about feeling that way. It wasn't really encouraged, in the corps. Too much baggage.

Too much death. "Dev, you're the one good thing in my life right now," she said softly. "How did I let that happen?" She sounded melancholy even to herself. "I don't want all this to be happening. I wanted to have some good times with you."

Dev wasn't at all sure what to say to that. This was all so outside her experience all she could really do was go along with it. Certainly, the words made her feel good inside. Jess seemed to be saying that she was important to her, and that she was valued and that was all good.

It did feel good, too, to hug Jess and be hugged by her, and Dev considered that this was different than the whole sex thing. That was good, and she liked it a lot, but this was something else. "I think I do really love you," she said. "I can't imagine what else this could be."

"Lucky me." Jess exhaled softly. "At least I got to know what that felt like."

Dev felt unhappy about that. "You think bad things will keep happening," she said, not quite a question.

Jess swallowed an unexpected lump in her throat. "Dev, we're so screwed here. I don't know what the hell to do," She said. "I know we have to go try and attack them but, shit. What's the point?"

Dev considered this question at its face value. "Well," she said. "The point would be that we could stop them from hurting more people, and rescue Doctor Dan." She looked up at Jess's profile, half hidden in the hood of her parka. "Correct?"

Jess blinked at her again.

"Not correct?"

Jess let her head rest against Dev's and closed her eyes. "I'm an idiot. Keep thinking for me, willya, Dev?" She let the moment go on, absorbing the unexpected grace and the surprisingly pragmatic advice. "I know we have to go and do it. I'm just..."

"Tired?" Dev suggested. "I am. We didn't get much rest."

"Yeah," Jess said, after a moment. "Tired, and pissed off, and kind of discouraged." She felt Dev's hands fold around one of hers, and without thinking, she lifted her hand up and kissed the back of Dev's knuckles. It caused a flash of memory, confusing and vivid, and she remembered then seeing her father do that one time.

Was that inherited? Jess wasn't sure, but the gesture made her smile anyway. "We should move our asses and get this show on the road," she said. "We're too close to where they last saw us. Don't want them showing up on top of us."

Dev untangled herself and stood up, moving around the console and heading for her station. She sat down and started calibrating her systems, still leaving her heavy jacket on.

Jess reluctantly pushed herself to her feet and went to the hatch, looking out over the landscape as she listened to the clanking and thumping of Doug fixing his sensors. The cold wind blew into her face, and she smelled rain on it, the torn clouds overhead heavy with moisture.

She scanned the towering walls of rock around them, figuring if she wanted to she could find some cave to hide out in, but aware that this would only be delaying the inevitable. She didn't want to do that. "Doug," she called out, waiting for his head to appear. "Time?"

"About ten minutes," Doug said. "Just making the connections."

Jess nodded, and stepped down from the carrier, hearing the rising hum of its systems as Dev brought them online. She spotted April and Mike talking on the far side of Mike's carrier and motioned them over to join her in the middle of the triangle made by the three crafts.

They did.

Jess pushed her hood back and regarded them. "Those things going to hold together?" She motioned at the carriers.

April nodded. "Yes. They were really going after you. We only took a few hits."

"We lost two backup systems, but Chester put a patch in," Mike said, when she finished. "What's the plan?"

Jess crouched down and the others did too. She brushed aside the gravel and got down to dirt, using a piece of the rock to draw with. "I checked comp. We're here." She sketched in a rough outline of the fjords, continuing around to fill in the land between them and the target. "This is approximately where their central command is."

"Approximately?"

"They move it around," Jess said. "We usually pinpoint it not by where it is, but how they protect it."

"Ah." Mike nodded. "Got it." He touched one of the lines. "This lets out just north of the line where you think they might be."

"Exactly. We stick to ground level, follow the land," Jess said. "Try to stay out of scan, give us a chance to get close before we hit the deep water here." She juggled the piece of rock in her hand. "We can't depend on met to hide us. We'll get our asses blown up."

"New game," April commented.

"New game," Jess agreed. "But the advantage of a new game is, you get to make the ground rules," she said. "So we pause here." She marked the spot. "And we see what we can see. If this storm overhead sucks snow down we might be able to use that as cover."

"So the strategic ops center is here, you think?" April put her fingertip in the dusty surface. "On the edge of the landmass, there?"

Jess nodded. "But I think that's where this new tech comes from." She touched a different spot. "Doesn't do us any good to go to the ops center and try to kill it there. This is where it comes from. There's a big, sprawling complex spread out over this area near the river delta. Hard to get at."

"Flat, no target to dive at," Mike murmured.

"No target. It's half underground. Hell, it's mostly underground. Can barely see it except for the sump towers. We've been trying to get in there for years."

April rested her forearms on her knees. "So what makes you think we'll get in this time?" she asked. There was no sarcasm or challenge in her tone, just bare, raw interest.

"Because we have to," Jess said. "Before now we just wanted to."

Both agents nodded in understanding, and smiled. Jess smiled back at them, understanding their understanding of the situation and bleakly glad she'd ended up with these two, who seemed to have that same animal spirit she knew in herself.

Agents were supposed to have it. But they'd been scraping the barrel for a while, taking in kids who were on the margins, who took on the veneer and became killers, were trained to be, but didn't have it in the gut. She did. These two did. Jess grinned a little wider.

Maybe they'd make something of this fiasco after all. You never knew. "Okay, let's get buttoned up and rolling." Jess stood and casually scraped out the marks with her boot. "When we get to the edge, we'll see what the situation is. Maybe we'll go right in, maybe we'll wait a bit and watch."

April nodded in satisfaction. "Sounds good. Let me just say before we leave, I'm glad you put that knife in Bock's throat. My gut said he was compromised." She gave Jess a direct look. "But I know you knew him a while."

Jess's lips twitched. "Dev told me the same thing. She said something changed in him since we left the citadel, that he wasn't right."

Mike's eyebrows lifted. "Pretty bold for a bio."

"She's not a regular bio," April said before Jess could say it. "I know you told us that, but you can see it. No bio I ever heard about would have ordered the techs around like at that base. That's outside." She studied Jess's face. "That a scam? You can tell us. We're probably going to die together."

Jess regarded them for a moment. She didn't feel any temper at the question, just curiosity and she spent a bit of time thinking about what she thought about Dev being a scam. "Are you saying maybe she's not a bio?"

April nodded. "Yeah. Something like that. Maybe they were just trying to sell Interforce on the idea. Put in a ringer."

Was that possible? Jess wasn't sure if she felt excited or disappointed by the thought. "Dev thinks she's a bio," she said. "I'm gonna guess only Kurok knows for sure. But what she told me, she went through the regular deal with them."

"Could be lying," Mike said.

Now that caused a temper flare, but Jess held it down. "I don't think so. Some of the things she's said, some of the things she's done, wasn't a natural born acting as a bio. It's too..." She considered. "It's too layered."

April nodded again.

"Besides, Kurok was one of us," Jess said. "Ops tech," she added. "Partnered with my dad. Very out there in terms of fate, eh?"

Both junior agents eyes widened. "Really?" Mike said. "He left Interforce and went up topside?"

"I think he more like created the bio station. Created the bios. That's why they grabbed him. They want him to do that for them." Jess dusted her hands off. "So now you know. I want to get him back, not so much for our side, but for me, and for Dev."

"Got it," April said. "More going on than we knew." She stuck her hands in her parka pockets. "School said there'd be days like that."

Jess chuckled, remembering being given the same advice. "Been a while hearing that, but yeah, there are days like that." She turned and regarded the sky. "Here it comes." She felt the first patter of icy drops against her skin. "Let's go."

They parted, and returned to their vessels, Jess hopping up into hers and shutting the hatch as the thunder rumbled softly overhead. It wasn't a bad storm, not like the ones they'd been seeing, but any met now made her more than slightly nervous. "Hey, Devvie."

"Hello." Dev was standing by her chair, holding a steaming cup.

Now that the hatch was closed, she put the cup down and stripped off her jacket and stored it. "Are we ready to go?"

"In a few minutes. Doug's just buttoning up." Jess went and got a cup for herself, feeling the warmth start to gather around her as the air handlers kicked in. "I think we've got the start of a plan."

"Excellent." Dev sounded confident. She picked up her cup and sat down in her chair, swiveling it around to face Jess. "I hope we can do good work and rescue Doctor Dan," she said. "I have a lot of things I want to ask him."

Jess chuckled. "I bet you do." She went to her own console and dropped into her chair, lifting her cup and toasting Dev with it. "We're going to give our best shot at this, Dev. No guarantees, though."

Dev nodded. "I know," she said. "We can just do our best."

They drank quietly together, with the occasional glance at the screen that showed Doug finishing up his work. Then Dev put her cup into its holder and turned her seat around, fastening the restraints around her and swinging her chair closer to the controls.

A very natural motion, even after so short a time. Jess watched her work, part of her mind casting back to what Mike had asked. Dev's speech was, still, consistent with her origins, the turns of phrase coming naturally to her and completely unaffected.

It was layered. Jess felt her own trust ring true, and catching Dev watching her in the mirror, that cute little grin on her face, made her almost believe it had nothing to do with how she felt for her.

Almost.

Jess tried to be honest with herself most times. She knew she didn't want to think any ill of Dev and she knew she'd allowed a very soft spot for Dev to form in her heart, but she also knew, or wanted to make herself believe, that the reason she felt that way was because some innate instinct in her said it was okay.

She'd never felt this way about anyone before. She'd always kept everyone at an arm's distance, understanding that people were people and they all had their own personal stories and motives.

But not Dev. She'd felt from the start that Dev was true, and she knew damn well that Dev trusted her wholly—and liked her—no, apparently loved her with a full hearted honesty that in itself seemed unlike the rest of humanity that Jess had encountered.

Now, that could be true, or it could be the strength of her own desire to believe making it true, but Jess found herself not actually caring. To her it was true. She didn't want to believe otherwise. "Hey, Dev?"

"Yes?" Dev was doing the last of her preflight checks.

"What's the first thing you remember?"

Dev considered for a moment. "You mean, of anything?" she asked. "I think it was of the play ring." She went on without waiting for Jess to answer. "We were all in the ring and they had just fed us, and we were tumbling around in the sun." A smile crossed her face. "I remember going near the plas and seeing downside through it."

Definitely the memories of someone spacer born. That at least was true. Jess relaxed, and settled back in her comfy chair. "What was that like?" she asked, as she started getting her boards up. "I think the first thing I remember is going in the water. The sand and rocks and what it smelled like, and getting water up my nose."

"I don't remember thinking anything about it, really. I was very small," Dev said. "Just a huge gray and white thing rolling under us. I didn't know what it was." She settled into place. "Should I lift?"

"Sure," Jess said. "Stay as close to the ground as you can, and follow the valley heading south." She got her screens in place and set up scan, feeling the carrier shift underneath her as the landing jets kicked gently in. "Send the track you're going to use to the others."

"Yes." Dev squirted the track and brought the main engines online, glad the coming of daylight now let her see where she was going in something other than a stark black and green wiremap. She started down the valley, keeping low along the slope they'd been landed on.

It seemed quiet, but she slipped in her ear cups and turned on the external sensors, listening to the soft whistle of the wind and the shift of the gravel they were flying over.

Behind her she heard Jess get up and start rattling around, but she focused her attention on her route. She was aware of the two other carriers swinging in behind her, and they flew along in single file between the towering walls.

It was nice, sort of. There was almost no wind, and only a mist of icy, freezing rain and after a few minutes she felt her body relaxing into the flight.

"Hungry?" Jess asked. "I'm going to break out some rations."

"Yes." Dev's stomach rumbled. "That would be very nice, thank you."

Jess removed two sets of rations from the store. "When we stop at the south escarpment, we should do a little fishing. This stuff's not going to last and we didn't have time to load on that beef stuff from the base."

"I wasn't sure I liked that," Dev said. "I have to look up what a cow is. I hope it's not as appealing as that bear." She adjusted a settling. "I like the fish better."

"Me too," Jess said. "So we should catch some fish, and I'll make you my one specialty." She brought over one of the plas trays with their utilitarian meal, two fish rolls a dried shrimp cake and shredded mushrooms with a dispenser of kack. "Here ya go."

"Thanks, Jess." Dev reached out and touched her leg, giving her knee a squeeze. "I would love to try your special thing."

Jess laughed, blushing, then cleared her throat. "Yeah and the fish isn't bad either." She winked and then settled onto the low bench next to the console, resting her own meal on her knee as she put her cup down on the floor of the carrier.

Now what did that mean? Dev wondered. Was it something to do with sex? It seemed so, based on the blush that still colored Jess's distinctive cheekbones. Well, that was all right with her.

Dev put the cup in one of the holders and studied Jess from the corner of her eye. She could have gone back and eaten comfortably at her own station, not sitting here on the narrow bench. But she seemed content to be where she was, her elbow only inches from Dev's hip. "I think it will take about three hours to get to the stopping point," Dev said. "I don't want to go too fast since it's so narrow here."

"Fine." Jess munched her fish roll. "Tell you what, I'll get some sack out time while we're underway, then I'll spell ya." She extended her legs, and gently bumped the back of Dev's calf, leaning back and watching Dev's profile. "Since we can't sack out together tonight."

There was a faint flush of color on Dev's cheeks, and a moment later, Dev glanced aside at her, a tiny little wry grin appearing on her lips, her pale brows scrunching down a little.

Really cute. Jess picked up a bit of shrimp cake and offered it to Dev, grinning back as Dev opened her mouth to accept it, feeling the tickle as her teeth bit gently on the edge of her fingertips.

No, she was sure. Jess gently traced the shape of Dev's lips. If she was sure about anything, she was sure about this. About the raw honesty in those eyes watching hers.

"That's really too bad," Dev said. "It would be nice to be in an ice cave."

Jess chuckled softly. "It would."

They were on auto nav, but Dev was keeping one hand on the controls and an eye on the comp, because of the closeness of the walls. Shyly she broke off a piece of her fish roll and returned the offer, feeling her heart beat a little faster at the slow smile on Jess's face, and half closed eyes watching her.

Oh, that felt good.

Dev found herself feeling happy again, despite how terrible the last little while had been. The look and that smile filled her heart and she felt an almost ache in her chest from it.

She hoped she got to ask Doctor Dan about it, but she thought surely this was what love was, and no matter what happened to them she was very glad she'd gotten to experience it.

Chapter Ten

THE FREEZING RAIN turned to snow by the time they got to the edge of the fjords and they could see the deep, dark waters beyond it, black under a mist of white, thick flurries.

It seemed eerily beautiful. Dev slowed their speed as they reached the edge of the U shaped valley they'd been traveling down. As she did, Jess came forward and put her hands on her shoulders. "We are here." She glanced at her console. "These are the coordinates you gave."

"So they are," Jess said. "On the very edge of the horizon there..." She pointed in the distance. "That's the coast where the center is, but farther east. I don't think they picked us up yet."

Dev studied the scan intently. "No returns," she said. "It does not seem we have been detected." She paused. "Yet. Are we going to land somewhere? If we clear that edge we will be in the open."

"I know. Slow down. There," Jess said, pointing to a shadow at the edge of the slope. "There's an overhang there, get under it if you can. There should be room for us."

"You have been here before?" Dev asked.

"Yes. Once," Jess replied shortly. "Wasn't one of my better memories."

"I see." Dev angled that way, dropping their already low altitude to skim over the snow covered gravel and shallow, iced over channels of water heading down into the sound. It seemed a very sparse and desolate place. There were no moving things anywhere to be seen, and at the very edge of the ice she saw waves breaking in a mix of white froth and gray.

The ruffled white surface indicated a stiff wind, and as Dev wrapped her hands on the controls she felt it against the carrier's skin. Compensating with the side jets, she fought to bring the craft in line to the far wall.

The shelf Jess had spotted was actually bigger than it first appeared. It was a crack in the rock wall that had fallen away long ago, and once had probably been undercut by the powerful waves. Now, the water had receded a little, and the shelf was almost a cave, the ceiling high enough to admit the carriers, so long as they were careful.

Dev slowed further and engaged the landing jets, floating just above the ground as she moved them forward with brief, gentle bursts from the side trims. It was a relief to be out of the snowfall and she moved to the back of the shelter and cleared space for the others.

The carrier bumped softly down on its skids, and she killed the jets, stabilizing the flight systems and shutting down the mains. Ahead of them was the edge of the shelf, and past that, the sound.

Waves rumbled up and crashed below the entrance of the cave, releasing a light spray into the air.

The edge of the rocks was rimed with ice, and Dev opened up the sensors on the outside of the carrier, letting in the low booming of the waves, and the hiss of the surf. She released the controls and flexed her hands, letting out a faint sigh, glad to be out of the wind and down. "We are stable."

"Tired?" Jess was still perched behind her, gazing out at the water over her head. "Been a long day, huh?"

"Yes, a bit," Dev said. "So much happened today. It's hard to absorb it all."

"Don't try," Jess said. "Think about what we're going to do next. We've got a lot coming up."

"Yes, I know. I think what I will do next is get a drink." Dev released the restraints and let them retract, then got up and stretched her body out. She felt stiff from sitting and it was good to move, even better when she walked around the edge of the console and Jess stepped in front of her and opened her arms.

The hug was nice, and she welcomed it. They hadn't actually gotten to have any rest during the trip. It went faster than Jess anticipated, and met and comp had come in that required her review.

So it felt wonderful to be gently rocking in Jess's arms, her back being kneaded as she savored the warmth surrounding her. "What are we going to do now?"

Jess patted her back and released her. "What are we going to do now," she mused, going to the window and looking out. The snow was coming down harder, making a white curtain that almost obscured the view of the sound. Past the water, in the distance, she could see the shape of the other side, and she pondered briefly about her plan's timing. "Pretty damn good question, Devvie."

Go now? Go later. Going now would preserve as much surprise as she could muster in this little attack. No one in their right mind would fly at the face of the innovation center in broad daylight after being chased down by a squad of hit men.

On the other hand, no one in their right mind would fly at the face of the innovation center in broad daylight, because they would be on full optical scan even if she managed to find a route in that would avoid digital. Probably get her ass blown out of the sky maybe even with the new weapon, her and Dev merely a scattering of ions freezing on the way down.

Not very appealing.

If she went under darkness, she'd give them a chance to prepare for an attack, after they got word of the failure of their attack on the pole base. She wasn't sure she wanted to do that, but she also wasn't sure she wanted to fly into their faces either.

Sucked to be her some days.

"Would you like a drink?" Dev asked, politely. "You seem a little unsettled."

Jess's lips twitched. "Sure. I was just trying to decide which of my bad choices I'm going to take. What do you think about flying out now, and getting it over with?"

Dev came over and handed her a cup, then leaned against her chair, considering the question in her serious, straightforward way. "Hmm."

"Hmm?" Jess's brow went up. "What does that mean?"

Dev cleared her throat. "Hmm means I really would rather practice sex with you," she said frankly. "And also, I think flying the carrier into a fight in the storm will likely end up sub optimal."

Since this was also what Jess thought, she smiled at Dev. "But we'd be a surprise," she countered, watching the faint twinkle in Dev's pretty eyes.

"Or we might get surprised," Dev said dryly. "Not in a good way."

"Or we might get surprised, not in a good way," Jess conceded. "And I hate surprises, unless I'm the one who's giving them." She sat down and sipped her hot seaweed tea. "So here's what we're going to do. We're going to wait until just before dark, and come in then, but not in a frontal assault. I want to do some recon and see if we can slip in through the service intakes."

"Okay." Dev didn't really know what that was, but it sounded plannish to her, and it meant they could get some rest. She was good with both of those things. "I think we are out of scan and visual here. It's a good hiding place."

It was. Jess watched the surf spray laying down an ice curtain, and figured in about an hour you wouldn't be able to even see the three carriers crouched under the ledge. They could stay there in safety and make sure they were ready to attack. Let the snowstorm go overhead, and coming in at twilight would neatly split the difference between daylight and darkness.

Maybe she would get lucky. Maybe they all would. Jess leaned on the console and put herself at peace with her decision. "Send a squirt to the others. Tell them to bunk down and get some rest while they can."

Dev smiled.

"You like that idea."

"I do." Dev turned and settled an ear cup as she reached for the comms key, setting her cup down on the edge of the console. "Tac 2, Tac 3, Tac 1 admin."

"Ack," Doug's voice echoed softly in her ear. "Here," Chester chimed in with somewhat surprising unorthodoxy. "Just got everything shut down and squared."

"We are to stay here until one hour to dark," Dev said. "Then we will proceed."

"Big old ack," Chester said. "Going to start a regen."

"Ack, seconded." Doug sounded relieved. "Syncing comp."

The screens flickered as the two carriers published their findings to her database, then Dev settled down to chew over the data, updating her charts with three metrics now. She clicked off and removed her ear-piece. "They confirmed." She paused. "Do you know what we are going to do when we get there? Or are we going to decide that then?"

There was absolutely no censure in Dev's tone, only curiosity, but Jess waited for her temper to spark at the question. After a moment she frowned when it didn't.

"Was that incorrect to ask?"

"Yes," Jess answered. "No," she corrected herself. "Shit, I don't know at this point. I thought we could come in at the waterline, and see if we could hide the carriers in the rocky escarpment that's at the shore there," she said. "Then find a way in. No way to know how we do that until we do it, but there's openings to the sea where they tunnel in water for the turbines."

"Like in the cave place, in the citadel?"

Jess nodded.

"It's too bad you didn't bring your board thing then," Dev said. "You were amazing with that."

Jess turned and regarded her, one eyebrow inching up until it was buried under the unruly hair on her forehead. "My board thing?"

"Yes." Dev got up and imitated what she'd seen Jess do, holding her arms out and wiggling her butt a little. "It was really interesting."

Jess clapped her hand over her mouth and closed her eyes. "Don't do that."

Dev straightened up. "No?"

"If I have to imagine myself looking like that I'll never be able to stay up on that board," Jess said, eyes still tightly shut. "Anyway, trying to get close to the shoreline on that thing would end up with me being fish food." She cautiously opened one blue eye then the other when Dev didn't seem to be inclined to repeat the motion.

"Okay." Dev went back to her tea and took a swallow, making a small adjustment in the carrier's systems. Now that they were out of the wind and the snow, the energy exchange at the skin of the vessel wasn't as drastic, and she calculated that the batteries would let them keep the environmental systems warming them until they were ready to go.

That was good. But she still wished she had her lined suit. Just looking at all the ice outside made her a little chilly and she moved around a bit, to get her energy back up.

Jess came up behind her and leaned her elbow on Dev's shoulder, just watching the spray turn into ice in front of them. They both watched in silence for a few minutes, sipping from their cups as the dull light from outside the overhang reflected through the frozen filigree.

"Know what I miss?" Jess said, suddenly.

"What?"

"Rad. The gloom all the time gets to me. Wish we'd found some of the old school pills they used to take in that base."

Dev tried to think about what she felt about rad, but she hadn't had the experience of it enough to really know. "I remember liking the sun," she said. "They also put us in the sun a lot during sleep, but you didn't know you were in it after you woke up."

"Rad cheers me up." Jess put her cup down and tickled Dev's ear. "Maybe if we take a nap together, that'll cheer me up. You think?"

Dev immediately grinned.

"Cheered you up already." Jess turned her back on the window and headed to the back of the carrier, setting her cup down on her console as she passed. She opened the gear trunk and unhooked the back latch, letting down the flap that would give them space to lie down on.

She was tired. Now that she'd laid out a plan that allowed for rest, she could admit that to herself. She spread the two sleep sacks out over the hard surface, imagining how good it would feel to lie down and relax.

The fifteen minutes she'd ended up with at the base didn't really cut it. Once she had the sacks sorted out to her liking, she stepped back from them and started undoing the catches on her half armored jumpsuit.

Dev had already stripped down to her gray under-suit and folded her uniform, putting it neatly away in the small locker assigned to her in the carrier. She eased into the sanitary unit and used it, aware of the metal and mechanics nearly brushing her skin.

"So, they put you in a capsule to sleep?" Jess's voice rumbled from outside the panel.

"Yes." Dev finished her business and emerged. "It was like an egg," she explained. "Oval shaped, and soft inside. They said it was supposed to remind us of before we were hatched. They were all on a rotating ring, that went along the skin of our part of the creche."

Jess came over and undid the neck fastenings of her under-suit, pulling down one side to inspect the burn mark on her arm. At the base, it had seemed a little inflamed, but now it was dark and apparently healing. "Looks good," she said. "I don't know what I'd do if someone made me sleep in an egg."

"It's comfortable," Dev assured her, as her sleeve was pulled back up. "The motion rocks you to sleep, like when we were on the boat."

"But you're closed in."

"Yes."

"Yuk."

They sprawled together on the platform, and Dev squiggled over against the back wall, while Jess extended her long length next to her. Jess exhaled, gazing thoughtfully at the ceiling of the carrier. "Wish I knew what the real deal is back at the citadel."

"I do too," Dev said softly. "I would like to know if everyone is okay." She turned her head and looked at Jess. "I miss having my book with me."

Jess's eyes widened a little. "You didn't bring it?"

Dev shook her head.

Jess regarded her with a perplexed expression. "Sorry about that." She said eventually. "I never..." She paused to think. Did she care about her possessions back in the citadel? Were there any memories invested in them?

Not so much. "Anyway. Sorry about that," she repeated somewhat awkwardly. "When we get through this whole crapshoot, we can go back and look for it."

Dev made a little face. "If it's like the North station, I don't know if I want to do that," she said. "It makes me feel bad to think of people like Clint and Jason all burned up."

Jess folded her hands over her stomach and tilted her head a little, thinking about Jason and the rest of the people in the citadel, dead and rotten on the floor.

It didn't make her feel bad, but then, she didn't expect it to. That's how people like her were made, after all. You just didn't care. That was the whole point of the battery. It found people who had no sympathy. Had no empathy.

Then she thought about Dev all burned up and felt the immediate, physical difference. Her stomach twisted and her heart gave a huge thump, and she felt a silent scream of horror assemble itself inside her head.

Her eyes popped wide open, and she stared at the ceiling. The sensation was so uncomfortable it felt like she'd been shot in the gut.

"Jess?" Dev put a hand on her arm. "Are you all right? You seem in discomfort."

"I am," Jess said. "I think my navel is going to explode."

Dev hiked herself up on her elbow and gazed at her in alarm. "Should I get a medical kit?

Jess sighed. "Nothing in there for this," she said, mournfully. "Tell you what, kiss me and it'll probably go away."

"Uh...what?" Dev looked confused. "What does that have to do with you being in discomfort?"

"Trust me." Jess rolled onto her side and tilted her head, as Dev, with a faint shrug, leaned in to kiss her. Sure enough, when their lips met she felt the turmoil relax, as her body found something else to interest it aside from thoughts of her partner toasted like a three day old fish.

Everyone could die, after all. Including her. She gently explored Dev's lips, the tension easing and moderating to a different type as Dev casually draped her arm over her hip.

They moved closer and she edged back over onto her back again, coaxing Dev with her until Dev was leaning over her, their bodies brushing through the gray under-suit fabric. She slid a hand between them and unfastened the catches on Dev's, rewarded with the touch of warm skin moving under her touch.

Somehow her own suit got opened, and she savored the heat as Dev pressed gently against her. She swallowed as a pleasant ache erupted in her gut and washed away some of the stress knotting her muscles. It felt good and she wanted more of it, stifling a smile as Dev's fingers started a curious exploration of her breast, the edge of her thumb brushing against her nipple.

Not really sure what she was doing yet, obviously, and yet that was part of the exciting raw edge of this new relationship of theirs. Jess had no idea really what her bio alt partner was going to do. Sometimes the surprises were great. Sometimes they just made them both laugh.

She slid the under-suit down off Dev's shoulders, blinking as the dim overhead light outlined her slim form and glared highlights off her pale hair. She rolled onto her side again and Dev agreeably adjusted, taking the opportunity to strip her under-suit off to her waist, exposing her back to the cool air.

Dev's attentions moved lower, tentatively nibbling her skin as Jess helpfully peeled the bottom part of her suit off. There was a faint hint of the pleasantly scented, but strange, soap they'd found in the base, the warmth of Dev's body altering the smell into something Jess found quite attractive.

She slid a hand across Dev's hip and a moment later Dev's thighs clamped gently around her leg. She leaned against her, bare skin now touching bare skin.

Worry about the mission evaporated. Her heart lightened and she gave herself over to the pleasure, sincerely hoping no alert, no squirt, or inopportune knock on the hatch interrupted them.

A SOFT CHIME woke them, Jess rolling off the platform and standing up before it sounded more than twice. She reached up and silenced it, feeling a restoration of energy that reassured her. "That felt good," she said. "You agree?"

Dev was curled up with her arm still wrapped around a folded blanket she used as a pillow. "Yes," she said. "And the sleep was nice too."

Jess half turned and folded her arms over her bare chest, one eyebrow hiking, and a rakish grin appearing on her face. "Why, Dev," she drawled. "I didn't know they programmed you for hedonism."

"Hedonism," Dev mused, unwinding herself from her sleeping sack and sitting up. "No. I don't think so. The only time I ever heard that word before was from some of the proctors talking about stealing fish eggs from the lab." She worked her way off the shelf and stood up, going to the storage shelf and retrieving a fresh under-suit from her pack. "I don't really know what that was all about."

"Ah huh." Jess put her hands on her hips and watched, a mild, amused look on her face. After a moment, this disappeared and she went over to her own pack and rummaged in it. She pulled out a thermal under-layer and slipped into it, the micro thin fabric almost sticking to her skin.

On top of that she put her under-suit, and then her half armored jumpsuit, sealing the catches around her. She could hear some soft sounds outside the carrier, and walked over to the window near Dev's chair and looked out.

April was already armed, and walking around the ledge they were parked on, a long blaster cradled in her arm. Her partner had an engine cowling open and was halfway inside. Next to them, Mike and Chester were just emerging from their craft, long streams of fog issuing from their mouths.

Jess ran her fingers through her hair and retrieved a bottle of kack from the dispenser. "How's the met look?"

Dev was fastening her flight suit. She sidestepped over to her station and pulled a pad over, her fingertips tapping lightly over it. "There is still some snow, and heavy fog."

Jess smiled. "Perfect." She shrugged into her parka and hit the hatch, letting in a blast of cold air that thoroughly woke her up, and nearly put frost on her eyebrows in the process. "Bitchin'."

April heard her, and detoured over. "Met looks good."

"Does," Jess agreed, her ears catching the sound of Dev exiting the carrier behind her. She saw April's eyes glance past her shoulder, then return and then heard the soft crunch of Dev's boots against the frosty iced stone ground.

Mike spotted them and was walking over, raising a hand in greeting to Dev as she moved past and joined Doug at his engine. "Good to get a rest," he said. "Haven't had that long a nap in years."

No, sometimes you didn't. Jess nodded. Sleep wasn't assumed. Even in the citadel, which was...well...had been safe, there were always night alarms, sounds, sudden assignments. You never could count on a full night's sleep. "Yeah, nice to get a shift in," she said. "Let's get a meal in, then we leave."

"Do we know where we're landing?" April asked, bluntly.

"No." Jess smiled. "I know there used to be a little, rocky flat at the tidal boundary, but it's a toss if it's still there. If it is, we'll make for that—if we make it in under scan. If not..."

"If not," Mike mused. "If not, we nose first, take out everything we can?" He watched Jess's face, alertly.

She shrugged. "Something like that, but I'd rather get out and get back with something worth the effort. I don't want this to be an end run."

April nodded in agreement. "You think they'll be expecting us, really?"

Jess nodded. "Sure," she said. "What they did, and my history?

They know I'm coming." She walked over and touched the ice covered rock wall. "But I'm betting they'll think I'll be coming for revenge. Heading for Dover base. Biggest of theirs, and a training center."

"For what they did to North?" Mike asked.

"For what they did to Base Ten." Jess turned and looked at him, her pale eyes taking on the sheen of the ice around her. "That's why they came after us, and wanted to blow us out. They knew I'd come after them." She smiled without any humor at all showing. "I have a family history of unrelenting insanity when it comes to revenge."

April studied her with a mild expression on her face. "I think we studied your grandfather in strategy at school."

"You did. So did I." Jess turned, crossing her arms over her chest. "Funny watching my whole class make the connection and turn around to stare at me." She released a faint chuckle. "Grandpa Jack and his cobbled up thermo nuke taking out three bases and half their control stations."

"That was the last one, wasn't it?" Mike leaned against his carrier.

"That we know of." Jess wandered over and peered at whatever it was Dev was wrenching at. "They've still got three headed fish coming out of that area. Made it useless to live in for a half million years. Dirty as hell. I figure if they'd come up with one to respond with we'd already know it."

She tapped Dev on the shoulder. "You done in there?"

Dev pulled her head up and shook her hair out of her eyes. "Almost. I'm giving Doug one of our spare sensors," she said. "This one's inoperative." She held up the part, which was crispy and darkened. "About two minutes more."

"G'wan and finish." Jess patted her hip. "Then let's get ramped up and go." She addressed the rest of them. "When we fly in, make sure you're both lined up right on my axis."

Both agents nodded, then turned and headed back to their crafts. Jess loitered around the engine until Dev hoisted herself up over it, braced on her hands, then hopped backwards off, landing with a tiny skid on the ice. "Okay, that should be optimal," she told Doug. "Try it and let me know."

"Yes, ma'am." Doug closed the cowling and locked it down then trotted off and hopped up into his carrier, the ramp already retracted by his impatient partner, the hatch thumping closed behind him.

"Good job, Devvie." Jess draped her arm over Dev's shoulders and steered her toward their rig. "You've become the queen of the wrenchers."

"The what?" Dev dusted her hands off and then stuck them in her pockets to keep them warm. "I'm glad I could help out with that system. The component failure in the tracking device would not be good if we need to locate them."

Jess stopped. "Tracking system?"

Dev also stopped, since she didn't want the warmth along her side to be removed. "Yes," she said. "It must have been damaged in the fight. The component board was completely destroyed."

Jess cocked her head thoughtfully. "Hmm." She continued on, climbing up the ramp with Dev at her side, and waiting for it to retract and the hatch to close behind them. "So now they have a component that's the same as ours?" she asked. "It's new? One of the ones that just came in?"

A little puzzled, Dev nodded.

"Have Chester and Mike check theirs," Jess said. "Do we have another spare if theirs is older?"

"Yes," Dev said. "But I believe that one is functional. They didn't say it wasn't."

"Uh huh. Well, if it's older, functional or not, replace it." Jess stripped off her outside gear, stowing it. "Tell them it's a precaution." She dropped down into her chair and pulled her console over, one hand skittering across the surface inputting data.

"Okay." Dev removed her jacket and heavy boots, putting them aside but not away before she went over to her station and settled an ear cup into one ear. "Tac 1, Tac 3." She keyed the sideband channel. "Requesting comp link, and diag."

"Ack," Chester responded amiably. "Standby."

Jess listened to the exchange with one ear, while she set up a battle plan in front of her. Details were now slowly edging into place, and the picture of what was happening was starting to form in the back of her head. Coincidences not really coincidental, facts and pseudo facts sorted themselves out and started to line up.

"Jess." Dev turned in her seat. "The component they have is a Model 12C2. Older than ours, and older than the one that was in Doug's system," she said. "That seems incorrect. That carrier was just retrofitted. It should have had, at least, the version we just replaced."

"Uh huh." Jess nodded. "Replace it with the new one you've got here, m'kay?"

"Of course." Dev put her ear bud down and got up to re-don her jacket. "I have told them to open the system for it. Would you like to examine the part?"

"Nope." Jess got up and retrieved a padded square insulation pack. "Put it in there, and leave it just outside the rock wall there," she said. "Slosh some water over it so it'll freeze down."

Dev was pulling on her boots, and she paused to look at Jess with a puzzled expression. "Is it correct to leave a piece of our systems in the open?"

"In this case, yes." Jess smiled a little. "I'll tell ya all about it later, Dev. Just do it."

"Yes." Dev straightened up and took the pack, reaching into the stores and removing a card from it that she put inside the square. "Be right back." She tugged her hood up and stamped her feet well into her boots then headed for the hatch, a determined look on her face.

Jess went back to her plan, nodding a little to herself.

THEY WERE UNDERWAY. Dev slid her carrier sideways out from under the ledge, doing her usual circle before she moved aside to allow the other two crafts to exit.

The lowering light cast very pale shadows past her, the sky already a dark gray on the horizon rather than the lighter dun they'd been before. There was still a steady snowfall going on, and the edge of the water crashing up against the ice was thickening into a slushy mass.

There was nothing else to be seen, save the channel they'd come down, and the far off edge of land. No living thing was in range of eye or scan, save some blips Dev caught deep under the water that seemed large, but solitary.

Maybe they were whales. Dev dredged up a smile for the idea, then she tugged her restraints a bit tighter and waited for the other two to form up behind her.

She had her course programmed in, and the carrier was as ready as it was going to be. Jess was behind her, setting up her weapons and whistling softly under her breath. "We are ready to go."

"Go, baby, go," Jess responded, glancing to her right to make sure her drop kit was secure. "Let's go do what we do."

Dev engaged the engines and they started forward, keeping tight to the waves as she skimmed just over the surface of a dark and frothy sea. She had the heaters on for the forward plas, and her view was clear, the clouds building overhead as they moved quickly along.

The trip would be relatively short. Dev had no idea what they would find at the end of it, but she realized she wanted to find something at the end, get some kind of final resolution to this task, and then...and then see what life was going to be like for them afterward.

She felt sure, inside, that they were going to continue. She didn't want to stop living, and she thought Jess didn't want to either. So it would be interesting to see what they would do if everything was gone where they came from.

She thought about Doctor Dan, and what he would do if they rescued him. Would he want to go back to the creche? Would he want Dev to come with him?

Dev thought carefully about that, and didn't like the feeling that created. She didn't want to leave no matter how difficult it was all turning out to be. Then another thought occurred to her. What if Doctor Dan asked Jess to come too? Would Jess want to go up to station, and see what it was like?

See the sun?

Dev frowned. She still didn't want to go back to the creche, but if

Doctor Dan was okay, and he asked Jess—and Jess wanted to—well, maybe she would have to go.

Anyway.

"Hey, Devvie," Jess called over from her station. "Get me a long range, wouldja?"

Dev set up the scan and told it to output to Jess's console. "Yes." She picked up a container of seaweed tea and sipped from it, while another thought occurred to her. "Jess?"

"Yup?"

"What are we going to do if our place is like North base was?"

Jess remained quiet for a time, then she cleared her throat. "You mean, if it's all gone there? Like, all gone?"

"Yes."

Another silence. "What do you want to do?" Jess asked. "If we can't go back there. You want to go back upside?"

"No."

"No?"

"No," Dev said firmly. "I do not want to go back to the creche."

Jess smiled to herself. "So you're sure about that now, huh?"

"Yes, I am very sure," Dev said. "However this event ends, I never want to go back there. Ever."

Jess considered that and wondered what exactly Dev's legal status was. "We'll work something out." she promised her. "Don't worry about it." Jess figured if they survived the raid, she'd have plenty of time to arrange—something.

She settled back in her chair and reviewed the scan, glad to see nothing on the near or far horizon that might intercept them, but now wondering if that in and of itself wasn't a suspicious warning. They should have patrols out. Especially on this coast, which was so close to their industrial heart.

So were they just waiting for them?

Maybe. Probably. She was probably leading them right into another trap, but this time, her eyes were open and she was waiting to see how she could turn the trap back on them. "Keep low as you can go, Dev."

"Yes," Dev said. "I'm getting the bottom of this craft wet."

"Lucky carrier." Jess snickered.

Dev looked at her in reflection, her face a study in bewilderment. "Excuse me?"

"Never mind." Jess wriggled into a more comfortable position in her seat and leaned back, her thigh muscles jumping a little in an unconscious release of tension. "I'll explain that all later, too."

Dev shook her head and concentrated on her controls, not leaving anything to the autopilot this close to the waves. There was no judging when the waves might roll up at them, and she kept a light touch on the landing jets, ready to elevate them if the water got too rough.

She checked her rear comp, and saw the other two carriers

obediently in a straight line behind theirs, sticking to their tail. It felt reassuring to have them back there, and let her concentrate on what was ahead of them.

The coastline was starting to become more distinct. She could see the darkness of slopes beyond the edge of the water, but they were gradual and in front of them a lighter colored surface that ran right down to the waves.

It was quiet. She had the external sensors turned on, and only the sound of the waves and the wind echoed softly in her headset.

Her pulse was starting to pick up, and she flexed her hands around the controls, already scanning ahead for the landing place Jess had mentioned. She saw a pinnacle of rock, and past that seemed to be a flatter area, and she adjusted their course slightly to angle toward it.

Scan was short range, and on rapid now. She kept expecting to see the enemy respond to them, and as the minutes went by and they didn't, it made her more nervous rather than less.

She heard Jess behind her, making a drumming sound, but she didn't dare look behind her to see what Jess was doing. "Ten minutes."

The weapons systems powered up. Dev heard the energy surge around her and focused hard on the route they were taking, lowering their altitude a little more, and steering the carrier around the waves rather than over them. Her breathing came a little faster as the land approached, the hills behind the shore now becoming more distinct.

The scan picked up life forms. Dev drew in a breath, then released it when they resolved into sea lions, perched on rocks offshore that comp identified as benign.

Now she could see the structures built into the mildly sloping shoreline, random vertical lines being wire-mapped by scan into vents and narrow towers, the front of the structure sealed and windowless facing the sea.

Like the base was, she remembered. Except for the one opening that she and Jess had visited.

The light was fading fast. The clouds overhead becoming indistinct, and the light snowfall that had continued following them across the water now seemed to be slacking off. Dev angled a little more to the east, so low to the waves that the carrier appeared to blend with the water, the skin melding its cover to the gray and white surface.

"Go, Devvie, go," Jess said softly. "Right to that beach, there, just past that big up thrust there, see it?"

"Yes." Dev put a dot on the wiremap. "There?"

"There."

A wave brushed the bottom of the carrier, rocking it a little. Dev kept them steady though, and a moment later the carrier came behind the rocks and she could no longer see the installation. The beach beyond was cut off from all sides by the cliffs, and a moment later she was over it, selecting a spot near a pile of tan boulders and setting the carrier down onto it with a rotation that put their nose back toward the water.

The other two carriers set down, their skins mottled and morphing from the slate and white of the water to the tan of the rocks and blending in rapidly.

They were down. Dev checked the shields, and did a quick burst scan to see if anything was approaching. "We are clear."

"Amazing." Jess was leaning on her elbows and staring at her screens. "We just fly in here, no one says anything, lets us land. What do you think, Dev?"

"I think it's probable they know we are here and are coming to get us," Dev said calmly. "What would you like to do? There does not appear to be a route to the facility from this location."

"There is one. But I'm the only one who's gonna like it." Jess got up, and came over, flicking on the sideband. "Tac 2, 3, meet waterside, bring water gear." She released the comm and turned to face Dev. "So here's the deal."

Dev turned in her seat and listened attentively.

"Just below that big pylon of rock?" Jess indicated the up thrust on the wiremap. "That's their sea intake. I'm going to take Mike and April, and ride the flow inside."

Dev digested this. "I can't go with you?"

The immediate agreement on Jess's tongue stuck there, as those clear, pale eyes met hers. "B— "

"I wanted to help you rescue Doctor Dan," Dev said.

"Yeah, I know." Jess felt a very uncharacteristic sense of confusion. "But you're not that great a swimmer, you know?"

"Yes, that's true. I haven't had much practice." She continued to study Jess. "But if something bad happens, I'd rather be with you."

Oh well, hell. "C'mon." Jess motioned her over to the stores locker. "You said you knew about their stuff. Maybe we'll need that." She pulled out a set of gear and then a second. Then she looked up. "If something bad happens, I'd rather be with you too."

Dev hopped up out of her chair and joined her, studying the gear. "Is this for going under the water?"

"Yes. So you can breathe under there." Jess handed her a suit. "Put that on over your flight suit. You're gonna need it. Water's a lot colder than the air is."

"I remember," Dev said, sorting out the new gear. "I got some programming for this. About the underwater part. How they made equipment to let you do that."

"Yeah, that's how most people do it," Jess muttered under her breath, as she sealed her suit and picked up the breathing pack and its mask. "Grab those." She pointed at two pairs of fins and hit the hatch. "Let's go. Every minute we wait here is one more minute they can kill us with."

The suit felt a lot warmer than she expected. Dev picked up the objects and followed Jess out into the chill air. April and Mike were waiting for them, both of them looking surprised at Dev's presence.

"Did you—" April started to ask, glancing at the hatch to her carrier.

"No." Jess negotiated the half frozen, half wet ground. "Dev's got special programming we're going to need." She indicated the edge of the water. "Tube's just around the point there."

"We're going in via the intake?" Mike asked.

"Yes." Jess glanced at him. "Do you have a problem with that?"

Unexpectedly, he grinned. "Nope. Rather do that then climb that cliff with my ass bare to a blaster." He indicated the rocks. "Just hope we don't get sucked into a turbine."

"Don't worry, Dev'll hang on to ya." Jess slipped her mask over her head and let it hang on her neck, while she strapped the breathing bladder to her side, pausing to do the same for Dev. "She's stronger than she looks."

Both agents looked at Dev, who blinked back at them without comment.

April remained silent, adjusting the straps on the weapons pack she was wearing and clipping her fins to the hook on the bottom of it.

"Let's go." Jess started for the water, as the light started to fade and the clouds lowered, snow starting to fall again and dusting their shoulders. Dev glanced behind her, reassured when the carriers blended in to the rock, then she turned and followed Jess toward the surging surf, considering that she might possibly want to find time right now to be afraid.

It seemed like a good time for that.

"Okay." Jess paused, and faced them. "Make sure the magnos are turned on for the gloves and the knee pads." She held her hands up. "Soon as we come around the edge of the tube it'll suck you in. Get a grip, and just follow me."

Dev flexed her hands and felt programming kick in hard, showing her the touch points for the magnets, and giving her the knowledge of when and how to settle the mask, and keep it tight to her. She nodded when Jess looked at her, then got right behind her and waded into the cold surf after her.

"Good luck," April said, sliding her mask down as she followed Dev into the water. "Let's go earn our marks."

"This'll end up shoulder to elbow," Mike said, as he brought up the rear. "We'll start right at the top."

IT WAS COLD, and frightening. Dev felt the water tug hard against her as she copied Jess, sliding the mask into place and holding onto the rocks as she fit the fins over her boots.

A wave nearly swamped her, but she had a good grip and after a second, she regained her balance and continued her task. The water seeped inside the outer layer of her suit, but the inner one remained secure, and now she felt the water between them insulate her a little.

It was now full dark. Jess braced herself against a rock and waited for them to finish gearing up. She then tapped her finger on her mask and tightened the fit, watching them do the same before she turned and motioned them to follow.

Dev leaned forward like Jess did, letting the water cover her. As it came over her head, she took a gasping breath in reflex, hearing the soft sound of the reaction from the canister strapped to her side, relieved when her lungs expanded and the mask provided clean air.

It was a simple device. It took in water, made breathing air out of it, and then recycled the exhaled breath into the process. Dev had programming on it, and she understood its workings, but she realized the programming was mostly to maintain and manage the devices, not so much about using them herself.

That was, the programming told her, one of the things the agents did, like the weapons she knew how to power and fix but not aim herself. She had only rudimentary knowledge of how to put the gear on, for emergencies.

Oh well. It was far too late to go back now. She would just have to use what programming she had and adjust to the situation. It was an emergency, after all, wasn't it?

Dev watched Jess closely, just a bare outline in front of her, and mimicked her motions as best she could. She waved her boots and felt the fins propel her, and she held her hands out in a balancing motion as she swam after Jess. It was quieter than she'd imagined, with just the rush of the water against her ears, and as they moved away from the rocks the water didn't pull so much at her and it became a little more comfortable.

They angled down and approached the tube. Now she could see the end of it, lit dully with a green ring, and in that light she could see outlined a metal grate that stretched across from end to end. There was a sense of pressure against her ears, and she swallowed in reflex, feeling it ease as memories of the creche surfaced, those times when they balanced the bio systems and the tanks would cycle.

As they rounded the edge, the force of the water sucked them against the metal with startling fierceness, and she grabbed hold of the grate before the force could suck her through it as April and Mike thumped against it next to her. She glanced at them, their eyes barely visible in the faint light from the helmets.

Jess moved cautiously across the grid, motioning them to follow. She mimed putting her hands carefully on the metal, and shifting her body over the cross pieces. Her knee pads gripped the surface, and she was able to move fairly quickly with her three companions sticking in her shadow with meticulous care.

When she reached the far edge of the tunnel, she stopped and waited until they clustered up next to her. Jess pointed through the square grid, the opening just large enough for her to squirm through it. She reached through with one hand and put it flat on the rounded wall of the tunnel, a faint blue light appearing around her glove after a moment.

She looked back at them.

April nodded and lifted a hand, flexing its fingers and causing it to glow blue for an instant. Mike and Dev nodded also, but kept both hands firmly in place.

Jess eased through the grate, twisting and getting her grip with a smoothly athletic grace until her entire body was inside, and both hands, and both knee pads were firmly anchored.

She moved a little further, and Dev went next, her smaller form transiting the grate with far more ease as she got her gloves in place and released her leg grip, pulling her lower body in and tucking it next to Jess's. The action was difficult, but she felt it was well within her strength, and now that she was getting used to the pull of the water, it vaguely reminded her of being under heavy G in the creche.

Her body adjusted to that, shifting and positioning to resist the force almost automatically.

The only lights were the faint ones from their gear, and the green ring behind them. Dev concentrated on following Jess, aware of the two agents behind her as they moved along the curved wall of the tube, deeper and deeper into the tunnel until the outer ring and the grid were invisible, and they were coming closer to the intake raceway that sucked the water through turbines they could feel vibrating under their hands.

It was amazing. Dev suddenly felt like despite the strangeness and the imminent danger, being there with the others and working this very difficult task was good and right, and she was glad she was doing it. She released one glove and moved it over as Jess did, aware that Jess had paused and looked back at her, only a slight reflection of her helmet light revealing her eyes.

Dev smiled and saw Jess smile back. Then Jess turned her head and moved further down the tunnel, pausing after about a minute and waiting for the rest of them to catch up.

Jess lifted her hand up and pointed toward a smaller tunnel, half hidden by the curve of the main one. There was a scoop at the edge of it, sticking into the flow and redirecting part of it into the smaller tube, and Jess transferred into it smoothly, this time lying on her belly on the bottom of the curve.

It was still more than wide enough to accommodate her, but she kept her head down and squirmed forward in a side-by-side motion Dev tried hard to copy. Now that the pressure of the water was behind her rather than at her side, the task was easier, and she got the sense that the flow was lessening.

Then they came around a slight curve, and Jess stopped.

Ahead of them was a solid ring of light, this one faintly purple. Jess turned as they came up next to her and released one hand from the tunnel, closing her fist, then opening it and fanning her fingers before closing them again.

Scan. Programming kicked in. The ring was a bio scan, like the one they used in the citadel. Dev eyed it, remembering what Jess had said about the ones there, and how they could kill you if you weren't correct.

She doubted any of them were correct right now. She suspected if they passed over the ring, they would be seriously damaged.

Dev studied it. The inner ring was smooth, there were, of course, no control surfaces available but in the purple glow, she could see a flush mounted panel behind it, with tracers of lights flickering over its surface. It seemed clear to her that if she could reach it, she might be able to do something useful.

It also occurred to her that of the four of them, she was of least value, and shortest association.

Without further consideration, she released all four magnetized surfaces that held her and let the water yank her forward, so suddenly that even Jess's excellent reflexes couldn't react fast enough to stop her. A flash of purple went past her, and she felt a strong tickle of scan, but then she was through it and activated the magnets to grab on just past the ring.

Excellent. Dev took a moment to look back, a little startled to see Jess's face outlined in the purplish light, so close to the scan she could almost see it reacting to her presence. Jess's eyes were wide and shocked, and her body was tensed as if she was about to lunge through the ring after her.

So Dev held up a hand, and waved it, then she moved over to the panel and started to examine the surface. Anchoring her knees firmly, she reached inside one of the leg pockets on the over-suit and removed her portable scanner in the water bag she'd sealed it in, and activated it with some difficulty due to the rubber and her gloves.

The scanner evaluated the system and returned results to her. She observed them, and felt another layer of programming surface, as the codes and outputs slowly came into focus and her understanding. She tuned the scanner and reversed the polarity of its beam, slowly matching it to the panel's algorithms.

It was difficult. She could barely see the scanner's screen, and the water was thrumming against her, making her waver in the flow.

She glanced to her right, seeing all three agents crouched just on the other side of the ring, watching her intently. Oddly, she felt herself blushing.

Then she returned her attention to the scanner. The codes weren't matching and she frowned, searching in her programming for hints of what to do. It occurred to her that the mission was counting on her to be able to do something useful, and she felt very uneasy about failing in that.

For a long moment she studied the scanner, then she recalled the change she had made to find the fish. She recalled that program in the device and put it in debug, reviewing the code she'd used. It wasn't the same, but there was something there that she felt might be interesting to try.

She made note of the code block and went back to the panel scan, instructing the device to change its matching pattern, referencing her previous block and after a moment, the lights tracing on the panel changed.

That was interesting, she hoped, in a good way. She retuned the device again and rescanned, and then reversed the polarity of the signal and the lights stuttered, then went out. She turned her head, and saw the purple ring sputter, then morph to a lower, light pink color.

Her eyes met Jess's and Dev had to shrug, lifting one hand and then returning it to the scanner. She shook her head, then sucked in a startled breath when Jess released her hold and sailed through the ring, without taking her eyes off Dev's.

It was over in an instant. Then Jess was grabbing hold next to her, a grin visible behind her mask. She touched the plas front of it to Dev's and gripped her neck, squeezing them together.

It almost made Dev lose her hold. But then the others were alongside and Jess released her, giving her a pat on the side of her head. She looked at both April and Mike, and they both held up one hand with a thumb pointed up at her.

Dev figured that was good. She returned the gesture, then tucked her scanner away and got ready to follow Jess along the tunnel again, now that the way was clear.

It was good. She'd done the correct thing. No one had been made dead. An excellent result.

Chapter Eleven

JESS HELD THEM up just short of the end of the tunnel. The water emptied into a large open space and there was enough light ahead for them to see each other by. Holding a hand up for caution, Jess removed a small reflective square from one of her leg pockets and positioned it, looking carefully up and to all sides to see what was outside the tunnel edge.

Satisfied, she climbed outside onto the wall, pausing for a long moment to gauge any reaction, before she lifted a hand off the tank and motioned them forward.

Once on the wall, the pressure of the water stopped, and the absence of the thrumming pressure was almost as startling as its start had been. Dev clung to the wall with one hand and a knee, looking around at the big space with interest. There were grates on one side of it, big and on the bottom. But on the wall there was a ladder mounted, and that's where Jess was heading.

It was still mostly dark. The light from within was a beam focused on the grates, leaving the rest of the space in shadow, with only the occasional reflection moving against the wall and across their bodies.

Jess reached the ladder and paused, motioning them to stay against the wall. She removed her fins and clipped them to a ring on her suit, getting her boots on the ladder rungs and moving quickly upward.

Dev watched her, seeing her approach the top of the ladder and remove one hand from the rungs and put it on her blaster grip. She felt motion next to her and saw Mike and April doing the same, both of their eyes glued on their leader.

But Jess released her grip and continued moving upward, the upper half of her body rising up out of the water. When only her boots remained in view, she reached down and motioned them up, and then disappeared completely above the surface.

For a moment, no one moved. Then Dev realized they were waiting for her to go first, and she did, not bothering putting her boots on the rungs just pulling herself up with her arms until she broke the surface, looking quickly around for Jess.

Jess was standing in a small, open space with her gun out but her body relaxed, apparently just waiting for them to join her. Dev climbed up and over the small wall at the top of the ladder, and let herself down on the other side, moving to the left to let the others out.

She removed her mask and let it hang around her neck as the breather ran out of water to convert, and drew a breath of air that was full of chemical smell and old moisture, abruptly replaced by Jess's scent as she found lips touching hers with gently insistent passion.

"You," Jess whispered in a barely audible tone. "Are a rock star." She straightened and took a step back as April emerged from the pool and climbed into the drainage area.

Dev resisted the urge to try and look up what a rock star was. She busied herself getting her gear sorted out, watching Jess and following her lead in draining the water from between the layers of her suits. It ran away down the drain in the floor and she checked her scanner, glad to see it hadn't come to any harm during their underwater entrance.

When they were all secured, Jess motioned them forward, then turned and lifted her gun from her hip, adjusting a setting, then firing at the ground they had been standing on.

Instantly, it was dried, as their suits had already done likewise.

Jess led them through a short corridor and into an area that held lockers lining both walls. Just as they reached it, the sound of a door opening made them all plaster themselves against a dark area to one side of the door, watching as two men entered and went over to different lockers.

They seemed disgruntled. They removed suits from the lockers not very different from the ones Jess's team was wearing, only they seemed bulkier and well worn. The men climbed into the suits and headed for the same place they'd come out of the tunnel from, cursing as they picked up a set of fins from the ones lining the walls.

"Going to fix your hack," Jess whispered into Dev's ear. "Hope you remember how ya did that for the way out."

"I do," Dev whispered back.

Jess smiled and ruffled her damp hair. "It's a good sign. They're not on alert." She kept her voice very low. "This is one of the first development centers on their side. Techs not razor edge, they don't figure this a target. It's just basic research." She paused. "At least, that's what we think they think we think."

"You thought they'd go check that," April said. "That's why you dried the floor."

Jess nodded. Then she removed a plas from her pocket and put it against the wall. Faint tracings showed up, and she indicated a path on one of them. "We're here," she said. "We need to get here, so Dev can sync in and find out where the targets are."

Mike nodded. "That looks like a remote scan station."

"It is. We'd never make it to central." Jess pointed at a part of the map. "Behind six or seven layers of bio. But I think they'd keep Kurok as far away from that as they could anyway, so we might get lucky."

"You think he's here?" April whispered. "Why here?"

"It's far away from their science center where we'd expect him to be, and my guess is, the project they want him to cough up data on is here," Jess said. "They want him to duplicate her." She indicated Dev. "The other side. They don't like bios. They buy them from our side, but they killed their program way back when."

"But would the other tech be here too? The met blaster?" Mike asked, glancing around. "Why here?"

"Isolation." Jess folded the map back up and stuck it in her pocket. "No one heard of that new tech. Not a whisper. So either it's all coming out of here, or I've fucked up and we're going to die for nothing. Ready to find out?"

Both agents paused, then shrugged, and gave her a thumbs up.

Jess smiled. Then she eased around the lockers and triggered the door, pausing a long moment before she slipped through and into the corridor beyond.

THEY WERE IN the lower areas of the complex, Dev realized. She could hear machinery behind the walls, and the corridors had a rough, utilitarian feel to them that reminded her of the base at the pole they had recommissioned.

So far only two people had appeared in their path, and both times Jess had somehow found a place to hide them and they had walked on by without looking in their direction, busy about their tasks, or talking to each other.

They passed several staircases heading downward, and as they passed the door, the sounds of life trickled up toward them. Soft clashes and bangs and the clatter of metal ware, and occasional voices, and once, a rapid thumping that made all three agents smile in a grimacing sort of way.

Then they turned down a long corridor that was more dimly illuminated, with doors on either side regularly spaced with vents in them that allowed the soft hum and clatter of machinery to leak out. Jess stopped about midway down this corridor and paused in front of one of the doors, looking quickly back and forth.

The sound of multiple sets of boots was heading toward them, from the top of the hallway they were standing in.

April and Mike drew their blasters, moving past Jess and braced themselves against the wall, cradling the weapons with their muzzles faced upwards, their eyes pinned on the direction of the noise.

Jess faced the door and put her hand over the lock, sliding a probe into the opening and half closing her eyes.

The noise got louder. Dev pressed her back against the wall on the other side of the door, admiring the calmness of her companions. Despite the relative newness of the two rookie agents, they were steady in their resolve, and ready to face off against whomever it was who was coming toward them.

Jess's hands were steady as she worked to pick the lock. The echoes got louder and now voices were heard, rough and male voices that matched the heavy booted steps they could hear just around the next corner.

"Okay." Jess pushed the door forward and stepped in, reaching out to grab Dev and pull her in with her, as Mike and April spun and joined them, getting the door shut just as the oncoming group cleared the turn in the hall and came down it.

Two men were inside the room and they stood as the four of them entered, one reaching back for a console keypad just as he was blown apart by April's blaster.

Mike took the other one out, his fire crossing April's fire in a neatly matched sending of death.

"Nice." Jess had pulled Dev out of the way, now she released her and crossed over to the console. "See what you can get, Dev. Let's get this trash put in the disposal."

Dev sat down at the half circle of comp and put her hands on it, looking from one end of it to the other and waiting to see what, if any, programming surfaced. There was a session open on one of them and she tapped in a common query, regarding the screen intently as the results came back.

The syntax was unfamiliar. She tried again, this time changing the query slightly. When the response came back this time, it was still wrong, but the error message triggered a memory.

"Any luck?" Jess was wiping her hands off on a piece of fabric.

"Not yet," Dev murmured, her eyes tracing the letters on the screen. Why did it seem familiar? Was it the—She paused and concentrated hard, closing her eyes.

"Dev?"

Jess's hand was warm on her back and distracting but she thought about the message and then realized why she knew it. "Oh." She opened her eyes and typed in the request again, changing the order of the words. This time the response came back readily and she exhaled, shaking her head. "I'm not sure if this is good or not, Jess."

Jess leaned next to her and looked at the screen. "What's wrong? It's answering you isn't it?"

"Yes." Dev went a level deeper, using a routine she dredged out of her earliest school memories. This brought up a page of code and she let her eyes run over it, feeling a strange sinking sensation in her stomach as the code triggered further programming and she understood the system she was using.

"And?"

Dev took a breath and started hunting in the system. "Let me see what I can discover."

Jess clapped her on the back and straightened up. "Dev's in," she told the other two agents. "You find their schedule?"

Mike came over and handed her a plas, taken off the wall on the far end of the room. "Shift change in about twenty minutes," he said. "Not much time."

"This stuff's old," April said. She had one of the floor-to-ceiling consoles open and was examining the machinery inside. "You were right, even have some digital converters in here." She crouched down in front of the system. "I saw some stuff like this in what was left of Cheyenne Mountain." She looked over her shoulder. "My clan sheltered there a while."

Mike came over to join her. "Yeah, that's not too much newer than the stuff we kicked in the ass up in the ice." He studied it. "Why the hell didn't they upgrade this place?" He turned and looked at Jess. "If this is where their hotshot stuff comes from?"

Jess shrugged. "Hopefully we won't have an opportunity to ask 'em." She went to the door and stood against it, listening to the sounds outside. There were more boots moving through, and she heard people talking. After a moment she relaxed as the discussion filtered through as one about fishing and the next supply run due in.

Nothing about intruders. Nothing about weird things happening to the perimeter defenses. Nothing about three Interforce carriers huddled just out of sight outside.

So far, it seemed they were undetected. Jess was still nervous though, since such an easy penetration raised immediate concerns in her gut. Was it really possible they'd flown in, landed, and inserted without tripping anything?

Really?

"Jess," Dev called, softly.

Jess left the door and ambled over to the console, letting a hand rest on the back of the chair Dev was seated in. "What's up. Found something?"

The screen was full of characters. Dev touched the surface with one finger and indicated two lines. "There's nothing in here about a new weapon."

Jess exhaled. Maybe that was why it had been so easy. Wild goose chase.

"However," Dev said. "This is a damage report on a part of the facility, and the damage appears to match what you saw at North base."

"Yeah?"

"A central point of explosion, with a three hundred sixty degree radius," Dev said. "This report is just a recap of equipment that needs to be replaced and a complaint that six persons were damaged during the event." She tapped in some codes, and the report appeared, in plain lettering that Jess could read. "There."

Jess studied the images and the text. "Seems the same," she murmured. "Are there labs around that area?"

Dev brought up a schema and wiremap of the site, her typing growing more confident. She indicated a semicircle around the damaged space. "These are research facilities."

Jess tapped it with one finger. "That's where we'll start," she said. "What's this?" She indicated a round chamber on the other side of the facility, one she hadn't seen in their research. "The intel didn't show that."

Dev sent a request to the system. Then a second. But the response was the same "There is no information on that area. Just that it's secured."

"That's where we'll end, then," Jess said. "Close it out, Dev. Let's get moving."

Obediently, she did, getting up to join them heading for the door. What else she'd found for now she kept to herself, hoping it didn't mean what it seemed to.

It always was right to get all the information first, wasn't it?

LATE WATCH, AND the halls were busier than expected. Jess pressed her companions back into an alcove for the fourth time, waiting for voices in a cross corridor to die down, only to have another set grow louder.

"Time's ticking," April muttered almost soundlessly.

"Getting blasted would make the time go faster," Jess remarked back. "Immediate gratification, yeah?" She cocked her head and listened. "Okay, let's go." She eased out into the hall and kept flat to the wall, moving quickly along the angle toward a side corridor about twenty feet down.

Halfway there a door opened and in a flicker of motion a man emerged into the hall, turning to close the door behind him and then back around to head right toward them.

April bounded forward and took him, getting him by the throat and breaking his neck in a swift motion as Jess bumped the next door she passed and, feeling it move, shoved it open and stood back as April dragged the body over and dumped it inside.

It was dark in the room, and Jess spared only the briefest of looks before she closed the door silently and they moved on. They got to the cross hall and turned right, spotting the door to the damaged area at the end of the hall, blocked off with warning signs.

It was quiet and dark here. None of the rooms they passed showed any signs of life and Jess ignored the barricaded door as she went to the lab door across from it and listened hard past it.

Dev went to the door that was blocked and studied it, bending her head a little closer and sniffing at the scent coming from it. She straightened and returned to her teammates, tucked behind the angle that prevented them from being seen by anyone in the hall they'd just come down.

The lab door opened to Jess's pick, and they slipped inside, closing it behind them. Inside it was cool and dark, and Mike quickly lit his hand light and moved to the center of the room. April followed suit, and they moved in a circle, revealing the contents of the room.

It was a lab no doubt. Dev recognized a lot of the equipment at once, and she went to the comp station and sat down at it, programming kicking in hard again as she picked up a pad and keyed it on. "The room over there smelled like it did in the base," she said softly.

"The burned smell?" Jess asked. "Or do you mean there's dead bodies in there?"

"Yes," Dev answered, looking up. "I don't know what is in there, but it's the same smell."

Mike grimaced. "Hope we don't need to go in there. Training or not, my stomach nearly kicked my ass when we were recon over at North."

April sat down at another console and started exploring it. "Looks like this place hasn't been touched in a while." She lifted a hand covered in dust.

Dev nodded. "This program was last accessed thirty days ago." She reviewed the screen. "I don't think this is what we were looking for. It's something to do with peas." She half turned and looked at Jess. "They attempted to grow them under rad. It didn't work out."

"Sure didn't." Mike had been examining a tall rolling cart against the back wall. It was covered in trays. He held up one. "Looks like dead seaweed."

Dev got up and went over to the tray, examining it. "That's synth biomesh." She poked a finger in it. "They worked with that up on station, but I didn't think they sent any downside." She removed a curled, brown crinkly thing from it and looked at it. There were tiny shreds of substance at the bottom of the item. "Part of it worked. They got roots."

Jess came over and peered at it over her shoulder, pressing her body against Dev's back. "Roots?"

"Roots." Dev's sudden smile had nothing to do with the roots. "Plants put them down into the dirt, and suck up nutrients. Sometimes in the creche, they would hang them upside down and spray vitamins and things on the roots to make them grow better."

The three agents regarded her with more than a touch of bemusement.

"Okay, well, anyway, let's go find the next lab," Jess said. "Dead plants aren't going to do a damn thing for us."

"Have you eaten fresh plants?" Mike asked Dev curiously.

"Yes." Dev put the plant down and dusted her hands off. "They tested everything on us. Some of it was interesting in a good way. Some of it wasn't." She added. "Sometimes people would get sick."

"You did once," Jess said, as they abandoned the lab and headed for the door. "Didn't ya?"

"I did. But most of it was pretty good, or at least, I didn't mind it."

They fell silent as they reached the door and Mike and April put their backs to the wall on either side of it, while Jess tilted her head and listened. "Dev, anyone out there?"

Dev removed her scanner and set it to bio, reducing the power. "I didn't want them to see this." She started a fast scan, half turning to direct the device along the outer hall they couldn't see. "There are two bio objects," she said. "About twenty feet from the door. They are stationary."

She shut the scanner down and pocketed it.

"Yeah I hear them." Jess leaned closer to the door, as quiet settled around the four of them. She closed her eyes and concentrated.

Her mind called up the hall outside. The T-junction they'd come down, and the curving corridor going the other direction directly opposed to the destroyed room. The two men were near the door on the other side of the junction, and Dev was right, they were standing still.

Talking? Jess carefully focused her ears, imagining herself outside the door but invisible. She was aware of the faint movement of air against her skin from the door vents and on that bare breeze came words.

Two men, definitely. One of them was angry. She could hear the sibilant emphasis, and it suggested to her mind that he was using a pointed finger, and firm gestures. She made an image in her head about it, and then, hearing the hesitant responses, imagined the other person as lesser ranked.

Scientists. She caught a word, project. And then another, alkaloids. Jess leaned against the door and pressed her fingertips against it, absorbing the vibrations as she strained to hear what they were talking about. Then she heard footsteps, and she straightened and opened her eyes as they came rapidly closer.

Jess took a step back and braced herself, as the steps came right to the door and stopped. She heard the keypad being accessed and took a breath, jerking a little as Dev appeared next to her. "Don't get in the way," she whispered, her body already tensing in anticipation of the kill.

"There's a cabinet there," Dev whispered back. "Maybe we could hide and listen to them?"

Split second. Jess made a low sound in her throat and pointed her light to the huge cabinet, door standing half ajar. The other agents moved silently over to it and slipped inside, as Jess and Dev followed, getting the cabinet door shut just as the main door opened and the two men came inside.

They flipped the lights on and walked right past the cabinet, going to the console and standing over it.

The door shut to the lab, and Jess let her hand casually rest on her blaster. It was awkwardly close inside, but none of them moved, staying alertly still as the men started to talk.

Almost still. Jess leaned against Dev, who was standing next to her, and, let her chin rest on her head. After a brief pause, she felt Dev lean back and a moment after that, a gentle touch on her leg almost made her forget what they were doing there.

They heard noises, then the sound of pad entry, and bodies seating themselves in chairs. No one spoke for several minutes, then they heard creaks, and the sound of a hand slapping metal.

"That is it. I told you, it was wrong," a deep voice said. "It's unstable. Look. It's right there, in the emitter results. How many have to die to prove it?"

"No one cares how many," a quieter, gentler voice answered. "Don't you understand, Gregory? They're past caring. All that matters is they can use it to destroy."

"They took our project!" Gregory shouted. "They took it, and put it to the wrong use, and now look! If they had just waited, we could have perfected it and it would have worked right!"

"And we would have ended up killing just as many people. Is that what you wanted?"

"It wasn't a killing device," the loud man said, and seemingly turned to face the cabinet. "It was meant to grow things."

The quieter man snorted. "Do you truly think anyone believes that? Oh yes, Gregory. Yes. A device to bring the light of the sun into a cavern, and it will grow peas. Yes," he said. "And oh by the way, it also blows up everything for a half kilometer around it."

There was a brief silence. "It worked," Gregory said, shortly. "You saw it."

"So did Denst. He just saw a better use for it."

Jess nodded silently. The two inventions had come so perilously close together she'd wondered if they were related. Finding them one and the same didn't make her job easier, but at least, she now only had one target.

Two if you considered Kurok.

"Well, Denst is on his way here." The loud man now sounded resigned. "I'm sure he'll get what he wants out of us."

"One way or the other." The other man sighed. "Look, Gregory, I'm sorry. It would have been a good thing, to be able to grow plants, real plants, downside once more. Maybe if it keeps blowing things up, they'll give it back to us, and we can try again."

"Maybe with a little more effort, they'll get the bio matrix out of our visitor." Now the loud man chuckled a little. "Save us all a lot of time."

"Peh. Let's go get some dinner. Leave these damn labs for tomorrow."

Jess could feel Dev's ears prick, the gently rounded surface moving a little against her shoulder. They listened to the men close up something in the room, then go to the door, shutting the lights and leaving. She waited until the echo of the door closing faded, then grunted very softly in her throat.

"What was that all about?" Mike whispered. "Who's Denst?"

"He's their equivalent of the old man," Jess said. "Okay, let's get out of here. Now we know at least we're on the right track." She eased the cabinet door open and paused, then slipped out into the dark room, going to the door. She heard the footsteps fading, and almost keyed the lock, then stopped. "Dev, scan again please."

Dev was at her side, and busy with her device. She ran a sweep, then another, edging the scope out a little. "It seems empty," she said. "However, there is a power fluctuation nearby." She showed the display to Jess, the light from it casting stark shadows on the ceiling.

Jess glanced at it. "We better get going." She opened the door and they moved out into the hallway, keeping flat against the wall as she moved past the intersection and along the labs on the opposite curve. The wall across from them was obviously damaged, big dents and protrusions marred the surface, and it was discolored.

The labs on this side of the half circle seemed to be still in use, faint lights showing behind the doorframes and inset plas windows, and finally one on the very end that was labeled "control".

Jess picked that lock quickly and they slipped inside.

They used their lights rather than turn on the overheads, and found a space that was in active use, with no dust visible. Mike went to the desk and sat down, and April cruised over to a tall data store, opening a panel in it and touching a screen inside.

Jess went to the back wall where there were shelves that had gear on them. She motioned Dev over, and pointed at them. "Check these out"

"This was the lab," Mike said. "Code name was Paprikash." He studied the screen. "Everything's locked down."

"Got any passwords?" Jess asked Dev casually.

Dev glanced at the console. "No," she said. "My programming says they change them often. There would not be much point." She went back to examining the devices, picking one up and studying it. It was roughly square, and covered in a grimy black dust that smelled of carbon.

Inside there was a flat plate, which was scorched and pixilated. She ran her scanner over it and touched one part, examining the gritty dust that came off on her fingertip.

The scanner came back blank. It had no idea what this was, which was interesting to start with. Dev set the scanner down and removed her multi-tool from her pocket, setting to work on the device and easing the sections apart.

"Be careful with that," Jess said. "I have no intention of scraping you off the walls."

Dev paused, and glanced at her. "This is inert," she said. "But I will be careful."

Jess hung around for a moment more, then went over to a cabinet and opened it. "Well, crap."

April scooted over and peered inside. "What the hell?" she said. "Is that a tunnel?"

"Interesting." Dev had stepped to the side and peeked past Jess's elbow. Where the back of the cabinet might be expected here was a roughly cut hole in the rock, its opening covered with a piece of cloth that half hung down exposing half the entrance.

It was interesting, and there was a damp, cold breeze coming out of it that held a hint of salt on it.

"Never look a gift horse in the ass, kids," Jess said. "Let's go see where this goes. If it's hidden in a cabinet, in the back of a lab that was doing black ops, chances are it goes somewhere we need to go."

"Not much here anyway without cracking the codes," Mike said, juggling his hand lamp. "That'll trigger an alert." He removed his blaster from its holster and started forward, edging past the cloth and entering the tunnel. April followed him, after a quick glance at Jess, and then Jess motioned Dev to enter.

"I'll bring up the rear," Jess said, taking out her own gun and cradling it between her hip and her wrist. She closed the cabinet doors behind her and paused, pushing one open again a bit and then re-closing it just to be sure they would have a way back out.

Never paid to take those kinds of chances. Jess flicked on her light and entered the tunnel, stepping carefully along the uneven ground as she followed Dev's slight form.

A tunnel in a cabinet made no sense to her, on the surface of it. Though she knew there were a few hidden hallways back in the citadel, they were purposely built and formed the same as the facility was. This thing looked like some guy had hammered it out step by step with a hand blaster.

"Not much dust in here," April said.

Jess ran her hand along the wall and examined it. "No," she said. "They used this recently."

"Yeah," April said. "But what's up with that? A tunnel into a lab?"

"Mm." Jess ambled up closer to Dev and ducked a little, as the tunnel got a bit shorter. She also got the sense it was going uphill, her thighs feeling the motion as she walked along. "No telling."

Mike paused up ahead, and held his hand up. He moved a pace or two more slowly, exploring the ground on the right hand side of the hall with his light. "Body."

Jess eased forward past Dev and came up next to him. Not quite a body, but a skeleton, the whiteness of the bones clear and sharp in the raw light from their handhelds. "Huh."

"Old," April commented.

Dev slipped in behind to get a look. "We had something like that in our lab in the creche," she said. "But it was on a stand. They taught us biology with it."

Jess nudged the skull over, and displayed a hole the size of her hand in it. "Probably wasn't a teaching aide any time recently," she said, studying the untidy pile of bones, before she leaned over and picked one up, running her fingers across the surface. "Not as old as it seems."

April focused her light on it. The surface was clean and bare, but nearly white. "Doesn't make sense to find this here." She looked down at the rest of the skeleton. "That was an open entrance back there. No way they had this body here and didn't know it."

"Interesting." Jess tossed the bone down and dusted her hands off. "Let's see what else we can find."

They left the skeleton behind and continued along the hall, now noticeably pitching upward. The tunnel got a little wider and in carved pockets they came upon shelves, long abandoned and half collapsed.

Around them, there was an almost constant soft patter of rocks and pebbles shifting, but none except Dev looked around on hearing it. She hadn't been downside long enough to get used to being inside stone walls to where parts of them coming down on her didn't bother her.

"Sh." April drew against the far wall. "Hear that?"

Jess cocked her head to one side and lifted a hand to push her hair behind her ear. There was a moment of silence, and April flushed a little, then the sound repeated. "Air handlers," she said, after a pause. "Cycling, maybe."

"That's a lot of compression," Mike said, after a pause. "Almost sounds like—" He went silent.

Dev considered the sound. "It's actually what it's like when you evacuate a chamber to space," she said. "That sound of rushing air just all at once."

The three agents regarded her somberly.

"But I doubt they're doing that here," Dev said. "Since there's a distinct lack of vacuum downside."

"Vacuum," Jess repeated. "Well, we're heading in that direction anyway." She edged forward and took the lead, one hand holding her light the other on her gunstock.

Dev hurried to catch up, as the other two brought up the rear. She stayed just behind Jess, and they made good time up the tunnel as the sound started to become very obvious, a periodic thumping boom that coincided with the bits of rock coming down around them.

It was getting colder, and as they moved up another steep slope, a gust of damp, chill air came down and dusted past them, making Dev glad they'd mostly dried out.

They reached a level area and in the faint glare of Jess's light, they could see a sharp turn ahead. They slowed and approached it cautiously, finding another bend, and a larger open area beyond it, stretching out in the darkness.

Jess proceeded inside, shining her light around to illuminate a large natural cavern with a series of tables inside it. Though the booming sound continued, it still seemed far away and she walked further inside and motioned the others to spread out.

Dev stayed at her heels, and followed her across to the center of the room, arriving at the tables and bringing out her own light and scanner. They were covered with trays, and she scanned the closest of them. "This is bio."

"Yeah." Jess walked slowly alongside the tables and studied the contents. "What is it?"

"Proto soil," Dev said, poking the substance with her finger. "I saw this in the creche in the labs. It's what they used to grow things." She ran the scanner over the next tray. "There is vegetable substance here." She dug in the dirt and extracted something, which she held up. "That's a plant."

Jess came over and looked at it. "Doesn't look like much."

"No." Dev put it back. "It's a bean, but it's dead. They tried a lot of stuff with beans." She made a small face. "I didn't like them a lot."

Jess studied the tray then she tipped her head back and directed her light straight upward at the ceiling of the cavern. There was something mounted there that was neither rock nor natural, and she blinked a few times, trying to force it into focus.

Dev came to stand next to her, running her scanner over it and regarding the results "This is the same shape as the device on the shelf, but much larger." She showed the wiremap to Jess. "Do you think it's the device they were speaking of?"

"Yup." Jess shut her light off. "Not taking that back with me." She turned and headed over to where April was examining an output schema. She was halfway there when a loud bang echoed through the chamber and then several voices were heard along with footsteps, getting louder fast, and coming closer.

"Back in the tunnel." Jess herded them out the way they came, everyone scattering fast as motion started in the chamber behind them and after a long moment, lights came on just barely missing their forms as they darted back past the bend and into the short hallway behind it.

A rising hum of power thrummed through the rock and Jess pressed herself flat against the rock wall, pulling Dev close to her as the sense of loose electrons made her grimace.

"Hair's standing on end," April said. "Something's got a lot of juice back there."

Dev shut down her scanner and removed the power pack, stuffing both in her pockets. She could feel the flow of power as an itch along her skin. "This is not optimal," she said. "Feels like a rad cleaning."

"Yeah? Then I know why you like water better." Jess closed her eyes. "Shut your eyes and let's hope this rock protects us from whatever the hell they're doing." Running back down the tunnel wouldn't much help, she figured, and at least here they could have a chance to get some intel.

She felt Dev press against her left side and without thinking, put her arm around Dev's shoulders. As the crackling energy surged around them, she heard voices yelling over it.

Dev stiffened. "That's Doctor Dan."

Jess kept herself firmly in place, her eyes tightly shut. "Save us the trouble of finding him. Today's going much better than I hoped," she said. "Now if we don't all explode, it'll be perfect."

IT WAS HARD for Dev to stand still. The waves of energy were thumping against her skin, producing a sensation that was a mix between an itch and a slap and it was growing more painful every second.

She fought the urge to jerk, concentrating on taking deep, even breaths and holding herself still.

"Hang on," Jess whispered, almost right in her ear. "Gotta stop soon."

Just as she said it, they heard yells, and an anguished scream and then a low throbbing thump that blasted against the rock wall and sent them all flying back down the tunnel, slamming against the far wall and reeling to keep their respective balance.

"Holy shit," Mike said, grabbing hold of the wall to keep his head from crashing into it. "What the hell was that!"

"Their super cooker." April wiped a trace of blood from her nose, which had come to a full halt against the rock wall. "Blowing up I guess."

"Let's go." Jess headed back to the wall and pulled her long blaster, coming around the edge of the rock as a roiling ball of black grit and dust boiled through the entrance to the big chamber and overwhelmed them. It was thick and pungent, full of particulate and almost impossible to breathe in.

Dev instinctively closed her eyes, as she half turned away from the particles. She heard Jess curse, and she shaded her face, forcing herself to look as the air around them turned into black unpleasantness. She took a quick breath and followed Jess's dim form as they charged through into the chamber, hearing chaos and loud bangs inside.

It was a nightmare. Lots of loud noises, and crackling sounds, and Dev was hard pressed to keep up with Jess as she bolted across the floor and dove for cover behind the big table in the center. It was half overturned, one corner crumbled into the floor and the trays of samples scattered everywhere, throwing the scent of synthetic dirt into the air.

Barely conscious of it, Dev felt a rumbling overhead and looked up, seeing traces of fire in the device hanging over them, it, too, hanging partially down with electrical sparks popping out from every direction.

Not good.

On the far side of the room men were yelling. There were two behind a console, and five or six more in a pile near the far wall. They were all struggling, and that's where most of the yells were coming from. As the device above them flared it cast the group in stark shadows before it faded out again.

"Get security!" One of the men yelled. "He's loose! Watch it!"

A second later a low howl started sounding, and the lights in the corridor outside turned from white to red.

"Uh oh." Jess peeked up over the top of the destroyed table, and spotted motion outside, coming fast. "Okay." She half turned to face the others. "It's crunch time. I'm guessing our buddy Kurok is under that pile. Let's get him and get out, and get as many of the other side as we can."

"Ack." April pulled a second gun from another holster, her face lighting up with anticipation. "'Bout time for some killing."

"You got it." Mike got off one knee and into a crouch. "I want lots of green dots on this one."

Jess glanced at them, and then shook her head. "Kids."

"Glad you asked me along, Drake," April said, giving her a brief grin. "Been a hell of a first mission so far."

"Dev, take this." Jess handed her a blaster. "Stay here while we make a distraction. You wait and try and get it into his hands so we've got another vector."

"To Doctor Dan?" Dev took hold of the gun and wrapped her fingers around it.

"Yup. He knows how to use it, and since it's keyed to us, it won't blow up on him," Jess said. "Be careful," she added, after an awkward pause. "Keep your head down."

"Okay." Dev put a hand on her knee. "You be careful too. I don't want you to get damaged." It was too dark to see Jess's face, but somehow, she knew Jess was blushing. Maybe because she was too, a little.

"Okay." Jess turned a little. "I'll go first, cover me, then come on. Ready?" She asked, watching both the younger agents nod. "Let's go do what we do."

It was time. She blinked, and focused and then in a flicker of motion surged up and over the table as the entrance filled with half armored bodies. "Yeahhh!"

Guns focusing on the pileup arrested their motion as helmets turned and saw her in midair and all of a sudden a security response turned into an intense firefight. Blaster fire erupted everywhere in an instant and amid the darkness and the dust blue and green flares cast intense shadows.

Dev took a grip on the gun she'd been given and watched the activity, half of her scared for Jess, half of her unsure of whether giving Doctor Dan the gun was a good idea.

She hoped he would really help them. It was so very unsettling to have seen his name, and his code in the consoles. As though he had worked there. But Jess seemed to have no reservations about him, and she supposed the one thing she could trust was Jess's judgment since, after all, she'd trusted Dev, hadn't she?

Yes, she had. She'd trusted her utterly, after only a very short time.

There was blaster fire overhead. She kept behind the table. With the air full of dust and debris it was hard to tell what was going on, though somewhere nearby she suddenly smelled flesh burning and heard a hoarse scream.

The alarm outside changed, going from a low howl to a klaxon, and as she watched, the other entrance filled with newly arrived bodies, behind half shields, all shooting inside. She felt a bolt come past her, and the heat made her blink hard.

It occurred to her that bad things could happen.

She edged around the side of the table and kept low to the ground, straining to see what was going on in the corner. She saw four people on top of the pile of bodies, their arms and elbows flying as they pounded what was underneath. Something they were hitting was moving, though, twisting and turning. Through a break in the dense air and the fire, she caught a brief glimpse of pale hair and a familiar profile.

She felt a sensation of shock, as though she'd jumped into cold water.

It was Doctor Dan.

They were hurting him.

Without thinking any further, Dev turned everything over to instinct. She scrambled out from behind the table and raced across the floor, hopping suddenly as a bright flash headed toward her.

The blaster fire hit the floor and vaporized a pile of dirt, but she was past it, tucking the gun under her arm as she reached the struggling group of people. She grabbed the nearest one and yanked backwards as hard as she could.

He came tumbling off the pile and smashed into her, but she hopped out of the way and let his body roll past her. She moved forward again to grab the next person.

Hands grabbed her, though, and she twisted, pushing her elbow into the dimly seen form behind her and hearing a gasp from the motion. She ducked past the figure's arm and it triggered programming, as her body responded automatically and pulled her adversary to the ground.

Then she went back to her task, and hooked an arm into the arm of a man hitting something. She turned and used leverage to pull him up off the stack and over her own back, to thump on the ground.

"Dev."

Dev saw a hand extending from the pile and she grabbed it, hauling backwards and yanking the owner of the hand with her, sensing something coming at her from behind.

She ducked and went to one knee, as a bolt came right over her head, sizzling into the now unraveling pile and sending body parts exploding everywhere. A hand bounced off her as she got her hands on Doctor Dan, who reached for her at the same moment. "Doctor Dan!"

"Sh." He looked bruised and in great discomfort. "Let's get under cover."

"Are you okay?" Dev asked. "I think you are bleeding."

"Probably." Doctor Dan wiped his hand across his head, and it came away with a dark stain. "Now I remember all over again why I switched to science," he muttered, ducking instinctively as something came hurtling over his head. "Move, Dev. Before we get squashed."

They half crawled, half scrambled, ducking bolts and running bodies as they got behind the big table, hearing more screams and something exploding.

Dev got the gun from under her arm and handed it to him as they crouched behind the fallen cover. "Jess said to give this to you."

He covered it with one hand and looked past her, then his eyes met hers. "She did, eh?" He managed a faint smile. "Hmm."

"Yes," Dev said, slightly confused. "She said it would be good to have another person on our side." She ducked as a blaster hit slammed into the table, and sent a shower of synth dirt over them. "This is very difficult."

"Yes it is." Dan exhaled. "Far more than I thought it would be." He looked past her again, then drew up the gun and leveled it, cocking his head a trifle as he aimed and fired. "Take that, you stupid bastard." He watched the bolt slam into one of the running figures. "So is there a plan to this, Dev?"

"They were going to distract everyone so I could get you the gun. That was about it," Dev said. "Jess didn't say what was supposed to happen next."

Doctor Dan, surprisingly, chuckled. "Some things never change," he said. "All right, let's go help. Stay behind me if you can, Dev. I don't want you to get damaged." He cautiously lifted his head up over the edge of the table and got both arms clear, leaning on the surface and cradling the blaster in both hands.

With the smoke now billowing out of consoles, it was almost impossible to see what was going on, or who was shooting at whom. But Doctor Dan was taking aim and letting off short blasts of plasma,

Dev wished there was something she could do. She spotted Jess and came half up on her knees, her eyes going wide as she saw her being slammed against the wall by three of the half armored men, one of them raising a blaster to shoot her.

She really didn't understand what happened next. One moment she was kneeling at Doctor Dan's side, the next moment her hands were hitting the back of one of the men, pounding on him, yelling her head off as she yanked on his arm as she attempted to pull him over and away from Jess.

He struggled, but she was past thinking about it and she pulled him away, and tossed him across the floor where a blue bolt intersected him.

His body exploded into several pieces. In the glare, his face was shocked, his helmet coming off and his eyes protruding from their sockets as he died.

Dev jumped over the flying leg that came her way and headed for Jess again. She picked up a piece of the table and swung at one of the guards holding Jess, feeling a sense of ferocious rage that shocked her—but not enough to make her stop.

She saw the man raise his gun toward her and she batted it out of his hands, whacking at his chest and head and anything she could aim at to make him get away from Jess. He went down and she leaped over him, heading for the third guard.

He turned as she approached and his gun hit her metal piece, sending it flying from her hands.

Then she was grappling with him for a minute before a loud sound happened next to her and then the man was just taken out of her grip and slung against the wall like a bag of silica packets. She ducked to one side and then was grabbed herself, but there was a friendly feel to it and the next second she had Jess's voice in her ear.

"Nice! Let's go before we all croak." Jess pushed her forward and let out a startling sound that was high pitched and clear, in a pattern that made everything in front of them shift.

Bodies moved. Somehow, Jess knew the difference between the good and the bad ones, as she hauled them all back toward the tunnel and pointed her blaster up over her shoulder, firing an intense, long burst at the device hanging over the table as a dozen enemy soldiers pelted toward them.

The device slowly lit up and then abruptly flared. As they reached the back corridor, a heavy, crackling sound suddenly filled the chamber and then yells followed it along with a booming roar that nearly blew them into the opening and flowed past them to rattle the stone.

The ceiling started to come down, on the room, and on them, and rock slid and pummeled them. They twisted and turned and fought their way through it to let it fall behind them and block anyone from following them.

"Shit!" Mike yelped, as a rock nearly smacked him in the head. "Did that thing blow up?"

"Hope so," Jess replied. "That was my intent. Now move!"

They half rolled half stumbled around the corner and pelted down the rocky tunnel, as it filled behind them with debris, hauling up for an instant as a dust cloud puffed at them and turned their dark suits grayish white

"They aren't following us," April said. "At least not this way."

"Let's get out the other way, and see if we can make it out of here,"

Jess said, in a short, gruff tone. "Doctor Kurok, you okay?"

"I'll live," Doctor Dan replied. "I'm very surprised to see you all here. Gratified, but surprised."

"I bet." Jess turned as she walked, glancing at April and Mike, who were now silent and covered in soot and burns. "You two all right?"

"Not bad for my first firefight." Mike held up a hand, which had a scorch from fingertips to elbow. His jumpsuit was penetrated, and there was some blood there. "Got four of them."

"Three here," April said. "But no hits," she added, with a touch of pride in her voice. "But I tell you what, Drake, I've never in my life seen someone move like you do."

"I have," Kurok said, dryly. "But not for a good long while."

Jess wiped her hands off and gave him a brief smile. "I'll take that as a compliment."

"You should," Dan said. "Thank you all, by the way. It was getting pretty gritty in there." He ran a hand through his dust-streaked hair, and there was a viable circular bloody bruise on his wrist. He was dressed in a nondescript jumpsuit, but there were rips and gashes in it that also showed blood.

"You need med?" Jess asked, briefly.

"You have med?" Kurok turned the question on her. "If not, then no." His eyes twinkled just slightly.

It was dark in the hall, and it was hard to see what was really true and what was just bluster. Jess understood that though, and she smiled to hide a grimace of her own as she twisted the wrong way. "You okay, Dev?"

"Yes, fine thanks." Dev was physically unhurt, but her head was filled with wondering about her attack on the people who had been hurting Jess and Doctor Dan. She knew she had programming not to do that. In fact, it was echoing in her head right now, bothering her as she tried to keep her footing on the uneven path.

Bio alts were not supposed to hurt natural borns. The programming was very, very clear. Even with the overlay of the tech stuff, it was one of the first programming basics they all got in their very first session.

Dev remembered it. She remembered coming up from it, and looking at the programming tech, and feeling almost ashamed, because of how powerful the lesson had been and how clearly it had been made to her it was a rule never to be broken.

And here she had just broken it. She had hurt a natural born. She had caused another to become dead.

She wasn't sure if she was in more discomfort about that, or about how little discomfort she'd felt in actually doing it.

"What if they know we're here?" April asked, after a minute's silence, as they walked quickly along the dark tunnel, using just the barest hint of light to lead the way.

"They know you're here," Kurok said. "That second klaxon was the intruder alert. The first one was just for me."

"Figured that. I know at least one of those guys recognized me," Jess said. "Just makes it more interesting." She slowed as they reached the end of the tunnel and approached the half cloaked entrance to the cabinet cautiously.

With the edge of her gun she moved the cloth aside, pausing to listen hard. Everyone went still behind her. Jess moved forward at a slow pace and put her hand against the inside of the cabinet door, pushing gently against it and opening it out into the lab.

It was dark, and still as they'd left it. Jess emerged into the room with the rest of them following, and she went right to the outer door and stopped to listen again.

Still quiet. She opened the door and they all flowed out into the hallway, turning quickly right and bolting down the corridor the way they'd originally came.

Then the klaxon burst into blaring alert and all around them echoed the sound of running feet. Jess knew they weren't going to get out the way they got in. She led them down a side corridor as they heard a patrol coming toward them. Going by instinct she ducked past a long, tall wall mounted ladder and saw a service hatch next to it.

Yells went up in the next hallway, and she heard the overhead in battle language, theirs, tracking them. Not good.

One touch on the blaster and the hatch burned open. She kicked it in and wormed her tall form inside, pressing her body flat against the wall as the rest followed her. She shoved the hatch shut and burned it closed, running a melt point along all three edges.

Then she indicated the narrow, panel filled space that had barely room for Dev to walk in, with lights and tracers on either side of them. "Careful. Most of that's live."

"Nice," April muttered.

"No one's gonna chase us through here then, huh?" Mike eased forward and took point. "We know where we're going?"

"Where are we trying to go?" Doctor Dan spoke up. He was just behind April, with Dev and Jess behind him.

"Going for the wet," Jess said. "Know a route?"

Kurok glanced over his shoulder at her. "The wet. Should have figured. We've got a Drake with us." His lips twitched, almost unwillingly, into a faint smile. "I know a route. Not going to be easy." He tucked the blaster in the back of his belt and motioned Mike back. "Let me go in front, if you don't mind."

"Sure." Mike amiably changed places. "You know this place?"

"I grew up in it," Doctor Dan replied in a wry tone. "But that's a long story we don't have time for now. So just follow me, and hope I remember this place as well as I just boasted I did." He moved cautiously forward, turning sideways to ease through the electrified walls.

Dev glanced at Jess, whose brows twitched, but otherwise didn't react. Instead, she tucked her own blaster away and put her hands on Dev's shoulders as they moved forward, Mike turning sideways as well, but April managing to edge through with just a finger-span clearance on either shoulder

It felt good to have that touch on her. Dev could also pass easily between the walls, but she felt Jess twisting behind her as it became too close for comfort.

It was warm, and she felt the electricity on either side of her raising the hair on the backs of her hands. "I'm glad we found Doctor Dan," she whispered to Jess, hearing her laugh very softly under her breath.

"Me too," Jess whispered back.

"He knows this place." Dev's voice went even lower.

"Figured he might. The stuff you got on the other side came from somewhere," Jess said, her lips very close to Dev's ear. "It's okay."

Dev nodded, falling silent. Jess surely knew what she was doing. Maybe she could talk with her after. If they came out of this undamaged.

"You all right?" Jess's breath tickled her earlobe.

Dev took a breath. "Yes."

"Thanks for whomping on those guys for me," Jess said, casually. "Shoulda seen the look on that one bastard's face when you body slammed him. Cracked me up."

Dev didn't answer, feeling a very uncomfortable twisting in her gut thinking about it.

"Okay," Doctor Dan called back at that moment, making her push that aside. "We need to climb." He pointed at a wall-mounted ladder that extended up into the darkness, seeming to go on forever. "No way to get through on this level."

"Then let's get climbing," Jess said. "Sooner the better before they sweep in here and figure out where we are."

"I'll go first." April didn't wait for comment, but got her hands on the rungs and started moving up.

"Let's hope they haven't found the carriers," Jess murmured. "Or it's going to be one hell of a long, cold swim."

Chapter Twelve

IT WAS A long climb. Jess realized after a few minutes that whatever she'd done to herself was going to make the effort extremely uncomfortable, but she sucked it up and pulled herself up after Dev.

Pain was relative. Where she'd been injured now felt like a knife had been stuck into it again, and she felt like she'd maybe broken a rib again.

But there was no med, as Kurok had pointed out, and no option, so she pushed it to the back of her mind and just kept going. So far things were going better than she'd expected. They'd gotten in, found the new tech, found out it wasn't all it was cracked up to be, found Kurok, rescued him, and were now trying to extract.

Really, could have been a whole lot worse.

Not to mention she'd gotten to see Dev go a little crazy on her behalf, the look of intense fury so out of place on her cute face that laughing at it had almost lost her a hand.

Jess glanced up, to see her moving easily and lightly up the rungs, the line of her jaw visible as she watched Mike ahead of her.

Damn she was good looking. Jess let the thought distract her, glad she had something to think about besides how much danger they were in and how much her body hurt.

She wished they were somewhere else. She wanted a few days just to hang out with Dev again, pretty sure they weren't going to get that anytime soon. Jess sighed, dredging up a memory of the taste of hopping shrimp and how it felt to have Dev kiss her.

"Pssst."

Jess only barely stopped in time, her shoulder bumping Dev's leg. The climbing had stopped and now she looked up to see Kurok slowly easing into a duct that ran along the top of the wall they'd been climbing and she was relieved to see her climbing was over for a while. She climbed up another rung and felt Dev's hand come to rest on her shoulder, a friendly bit of warmth that made her smile, if only briefly.

Far off, she could hear klaxons. "Bet they're running all over the place looking for us."

"Yes," Dev responded quietly.

They moved up a few more rungs as April disappeared into the duct, settling near the entrance to let the others get a bit farther inside. Jess glanced at Dev's face as they remained momentarily still, and saw a tension there that seemed new. "Hey."

The pale eyes tracked to hers. "Yes?"

"You okay?" Jess put a hand on her arm as she prepared to move off the ladder. "You look pissed off."

Dev paused in mid motion and looked at her, one pale eyebrow lifting.

"Never mind. We'll talk later." Jess heard a loud bang behind them and she guided Dev forward and scrambled after her, getting the hatch cover closed just as running boot steps sounded loud and echoing below, expecting and hearing the sound of hands and feet on the first set of rungs on the ladder. "Move it, people."

"Heard 'em," Mike said.

Jess waited for Dev to get a body length down the duct before she turned and sealed the hatch with her blaster, leaving a square of blackened metal. She reversed herself and rushed after them, realizing the tiny space and cramped motion was even more annoying than the climb.

Jess caught up to Dev's heels and now they progressed with silent speed, heading toward a T-junction she could just see the outline of ahead of them. She could hear sounds below and behind the duct they were in, and briefly hoped the space was important enough to prevent the enemy from just vaporizing it.

She felt air pushing against her though, and figured it was part of the ventilation system, and when you were primarily below ground, that was, in fact, important.

They hit the corner and started to the right, and the duct started to slant downward. At first the pitch was gentle, then Jess could feel gravity tugging at her, pulling her forward as the angle steepened.

It was also getting darker inside and colder, and as Jess reached out to touch the duct wall, she felt moisture on it that faintly stung her fingertips. A few body lengths farther she felt herself slipping and knew where they were headed.

Instinctively she reached out and grabbed Dev's ankle. "Turn around," she said. "Go feet first." She released her hold and braced her arms on either side of the duct as she swiveled herself around and watched Dev do the same. "Okay, go."

It was dark past her and the sounds of the others had faded a little. Dev slid a few feet more then she shot forward as the angle steepened further. Without hesitation Jess shoved herself after her. She let gravity take her, but got her gloves on and used friction to control her speed so she didn't overtake Dev.

An explosion sounded to their rear, and Jess yanked her hands in as she felt a pressure wave building behind her. She caught up with Dev just as a rumbling roar vibrated the walls of the duct and bright light erupted behind them and cast sharp shadows ahead.

They reached a sharp turn just as the blast wall hit them, and then they were falling as the duct turned straight down, just barely ahead of the fireball. Jess kept her head tucked down, and tried to ignore the heat against her neck, as they passed outside the duct and were in free fall in the air.

Everyone was eerily silent. She could smell water strongly, though, and she crossed her legs and tucked her arms around her body. "Dev, cross your ankles."

"Yes." Dev sounded nervous.

Then they heard in succession three splashes, and judging the depth by the sound, Jess reached out suddenly and caught hold of Dev's shoulder, pulling her closer and wrapping her arms around Dev just in time to get her secured before she sensed the impending impact and they hit the surface of the water.

Ice cold. The brined chill invaded their suits immediately as they plunged downward. Jess released one hand and clamped it over Dev's mouth and nose, unlocking her legs and kicking hard against the downward motion. She felt Dev start to struggle and kept a firm hold on her, as their plunge slowed.

The chill faded a little as the water got trapped in her suit, and they started upward as a cloud of bubbles exploded around them. Jess kicked harder and blinked a couple times as the water stung her eyelids. They reached the surface and their heads emerged in the air.

She released Dev's mouth but kept hold of her as she shook the hair out of her eyes, looking around in the dense gloom and spotting motion nearby. "You okay?" she asked Dev, keeping her mouth close to Dev's ear.

Dev coughed a little. "Yes," she finally said, after clearing her throat.

"Good." Jess turned on her side and started swimming, heading for the edge of the huge pool they were immersed in. Cavern walls rose around it, and there was no obvious exit, the water touched the rock on all sides. "Not sure we just didn't slide out of the frying pan and into the fire though."

Dev paddled for a moment, then memory kicked in past the thrumming shock and she remembered how Jess taught her to swim. She moved from a hesitant motion to a more confident one, as she followed Jess through the water to the far wall where the others were gathering.

In a moment they were all face-to-face. "Now what?" April asked, keeping her voice low.

"What is this place?" Mike asked. "Collecting tank?"

Doctor Dan had one hand on the wall and rubbed his eyes with the fingers of the other. "Desalinization sump." He looked around the cavern. "They're on to us. They flooded the exit." He pointed at the wall across from where they were. "That leads outside."

"How deep?" Jess asked.

Kurok studied the wall. "Fifty feet. Which, on one hand probably saved our lives, but on the other—" He cleared his throat. "And it's at least three hundred feet through the flooded tunnel to the outside."

Jess nodded. She stripped off her water kit and handed it over to him. "Put that on." She said. "Everyone else, gear up." She turned at a faint echo then ducked as overhead floodlights came on, bathing them in stark brilliance. "Move. Fast."

The first blaster fire hit the wall a second later, as everyone got their gear in place and Jess shoved them toward the far wall.

Kurok grabbed her arm. "What about you?" he asked, watching her intently. "If you think I'm leaving you back here, you've got another thing coming, Jesslyn."

Jess smiled briefly at him. "I'll be fine. I can hold my breath."

"No one can, that long."

"I can." Jess ducked a sizzling burst. "Move it or it's gonna be a moot point." She grabbed both Kurok and Dev and shoved them underwater, as she heard a power launch land in the water at the far end of the cavern. She ducked her head under and pitched downward, into the dark depths of the water.

Dev had her mask on but she was half turned in the water, watching Jess with a worried expression on her face. Jess smiled at her, aware of the tiny bubbles of air trickling from her nostrils.

They were sinking down in the water and she spotted the outline of the luminescent tag on April's blaster. Going horizontal in the water she pushed her two charges forward, and swam after them with easy kicks.

Above them, she could hear motors approaching and she angled lower, watching April and Mike watching them approach. She lifted a hand and circled her finger, pointing at the almost invisible, flooded entrance tunnel below them.

Kurok and Dev kept looking back at her, and as they all reached the tunnel level, Kurok turned and made to lift off the mask he was wearing, signaling that he would share it with her.

Jess pointed at the tunnel insistently and pushed him toward it. The pressure was building on her chest, and she let a few more bubbles slip out before she realized Dev was swimming toward her, a determined look on her face.

She grabbed Dev and tried to turn her around but Dev pointed at her mask, and looked adorably worried about her. Jess sighed, but when she looked past Dev she saw the rest of the group headed in her direction.

Jess released Dev, and held her hands up in a stopping motion. She hurriedly emptied her lungs of the rest of the air and felt her body twitch, as it sensed what was coming. She consciously contracted her chest and, as Kurok reached her and Dev grabbed for her arm, she coughed out the last free air and let her lungs expand, drawing in the icy cold water.

It was a shock, as it always had been right from the very first time she'd done it, back in the day, back when she was just a kid and had no idea what she was doing until it was too late.

It was almost pain, a rush of tingling ice as the water filled her and her lungs struggled to react, switching from their normal function to one so different. But after a moment it was done, and she felt the familiar sense of effort in drawing in liquid rather than gas, that drag on muscles not often used for this purpose.

Jess blinked again and felt the clear inner eyelid slide down over her eyes, allowing her to focus and just in time, because the sound of underwater sleds cut through them and they were out of time. Jess pointed urgently at the tunnel and started toward it, sweeping them all ahead of her as they got out of their own way with wide eyes still staring at her.

There was no time to consider the implications. Jess increased her speed, and herded them all ahead of her as they entered the tunnel and started through it.

The sleds caught them halfway through and Jess turned, pulling her blaster out and hoping the sealing held as she pointed it and fired. The energy burst lit up the tunnel, outlined their enemy and fortunately didn't cause the weapon to blow up in her hand. She locked her knees together and moved her body in a smooth motion, aiming at the nearest sled and firing.

She could hear the weird sizzle as the blaster fired through the water, the seal at the muzzle allowing the energy out. The beam hit the sled and it veered off, slamming into the wall of the tunnel as the other two sped up and came at her.

She heard the roar of the ocean coming closer. The sleds had light fins, and were mech models, not intended for surf and she sped up herself, ducking a blast that nearly hit her head and glanced off the roof of the tunnel.

Two return shots came past her from the other direction, and the two chasers dove for the tunnel floor. Jess sucked in water faster, the strain of the mechanics of breathing liquid adding to her already protesting body's discomfort.

She pointed the blaster down and got a shot off, as she kicked against the wall to avoid a return hit from the sled's gun. Another shot came past her, then a second, and as the sled aiming for her tried to avoid it, a wash of surf came in the tunnel and shoved it sideways into the third.

Jess turned in the water and got her arms flat against her sides, letting her body settle into a rhythmic motion that caught up to the rest of the team as they reached the end of the tunnel and headed for the protective grid. Just short of it the water rippled, and then a blue light burst into being, outlining the metal and pulsing its own warning.

Everyone hauled up shy of the metal and they turned, as the sound of more chasing sleds echoed loudly behind them.

Trapped. Jess ran her eye over the grid. It wasn't scan, just plain old electrified with enough current to turn them into octopus crisps. The squares were small, probably large enough for them to get through, but one current wrong would send them into the rippling blue light before any chance of avoiding it.

Mike and April looked at her, as Jess cautiously approached the glowing surface, holstering their blasters for now.

Dev settled against the floor of the tunnel, her heart thumping so fast it was shaking her. She felt overwhelmed, and programming or not, all her confidence had slipped away, leaving her scared and unsure of what to do.

So she watched Jess, moving around in the water without any gear at all on, breathing water.

Nothing in her programming had prepared her for that. Even Doctor Dan was watching her, his eyes wide, his head shaking back and forth almost unconsciously.

How was she doing that? It was like someone going out into space without a suit.

Unable to fathom it, she turned and regarded the grid. She could feel the power running through it from where she was, and realized they were trapped behind it. A motion caught her eye and she turned to see Mike and April turn and face the tunnel, drawing their guns and preparing to fire.

Light blazed down from the chamber, and she counted four, and then six big lamps approaching them. Doctor Dan floated next to her and took out the gun Dev had given him, putting himself between her and the coming lights.

He looked over at her and gave her one of his kind, sad smiles, reaching over to pat her on the shoulder.

Dev turned to look for Jess, finding her near the bottom of the tunnel, just short of the grid, examining something on the surface there. She pushed off from the wall and swam over, watching in fascination as Jess's mouth opened and she sucked in water, her shoulders and chest moving visibly.

Jess looked up as she approached and pointed at the ground. Dev settled to her knees next to her and looked at what she was looking at, which was a box welded into the tunnel surface. Jess pointed at the box, then pointed at the grid, then shrugged her shoulders in question.

Dev looked at the box. Then she turned and looked at the tunnel wall, then tipped her head back and looked up. She pointed at the ceiling, where a half round duct was visible, then followed it with her finger as it stretched back toward the inside.

Jess moved suddenly, grabbing her and throwing her down as blaster fire hit the bottom of the tunnel next to them, sending a wave of heat over their bodies as they tumbled in the water, drifting dangerously close to the grid.

Mike and April returned fire, but the inside of the tunnel lit up with counter fire, as the ten sleds barreled toward them. Jess grabbed Dev's lower leg with one hand and turned to drop onto her back, reaching up and triggering her blaster pointed at the ceiling just past Dev's ear.

Dev flinched as a rolling blast of water hit both of them, and before either could react they were shoved against the grid with an audible crunch. Instead of being blasted into a crisp, they were just bumped and bruised, and Jess managed to get her hands on the metal and pull herself through and into the open sea.

The sleds arrived a second later, and slammed into the grid.

The rest of the team opened fire as they swam rapidly toward escape, and for a long moment the entire tunnel was filled with crisscrossing blaster beams.

Then Mike, April and Doctor Dan came rolling out into the sea, Jess aimed her gun inside and fired off a pinpoint shot, and the grid reactivated and shorted explosively as it arced across the sleds jammed against its surface.

The power of the blowout scattered them and sent them tumbling through the water, bouncing off the rocks that lined the channel as they fought to regain control of their motion.

Jess was the first to do so. She quickly whirled in mid motion and headed for Dev, who had managed to get a grip on a piece of rock and was looking around in a daze. Just past her Jess spotted Mike and April, and furthest away, Dan Kurok.

As she reached Dev's side she looked back at the entrance to the tunnel, and saw it half energized, sputtering and flashing as the sleds, or what was left of them, drifted apart and bodies drifted without internal motion.

Well, that gave them a few more minutes. Jess pointed at the surface and started swimming upward slowly, taking a route parallel to the coast.

Fifteen minutes later, they were surfacing in darkness, only the sound of the surf around them. Jess had led them to a small pinnacle, and they clung there catching their breaths. Or in Jess's case, exchanging hers as she spent a moment expelling all the water in her lungs, preparing herself for the effort as she lifted her head out of water and got herself up into the air enough to lean forward and cough as hard as she could.

There was always that one moment of near asphyxiation.

So there they were, heads just above the surface, lips blue and shivering, four of them staring at Jess as she coughed and hacked and nearly ended up dry heaving as her body reluctantly resumed processing air.

"They'll be after us in a minute," April said, after a long moment of silence.

"Yes," Doctor Dan said, in a weary tone. "Everyone all right?"

Jess rested her arm on a rock, her head on her arm. "As all right as I'm gonna get," she said, her voice a hoarse rasp. "Carriers are half a mile that way, around that point." She indicated the darkness that blanketed everything. "Gonna be a bitch getting there."

"Yeah, thought that was a different direction we were going in,"

Mike said, quietly. "Guess we better start swimming before they figure out what happened in the tunnel and launch a patrol."

"Sorry about that," Kurok said. "There's a cross tunnel there that would have taken us under the rock all the way along the coast, but it was closed off. No way to get into it when it's flooded like that." He looked at Jess. "That's quite a trick."

Jess coughed again. "Yeah, I'm a hit at parties with it." She looked around. "Maybe we can get out and go overland." She examined the coast, only barely seen in the night.

"Tumbled rocks. Be a hike," April said.

"It's mined," Doctor Dan said. "Probably not a good—" He fell silent as another sound came over the waves. "Ah, they're on the way."

A boat's engine rumbled, getting louder as they listened. "Okay," Jess said. "We should go down again. We've got enough charge in those canisters to last 48 hours." She coughed again, pushing away from the rocks as she prepared to duck under the surface again. "Keep the slope on your left hand side. We'll make our way near shore."

The sound of the boat got louder and they scrambled to get gear in place and get under the water. Dev settled her mask and tried to ignore how cold she was, when suddenly, the noise triggered something in her. She reached out to Jess and grasped her arm. "Wait."

"What?" Jess moved closer. "You all right?"

"That sound is something I remember," Dev said. "It's..." She pulled her scanner out and lifted it above the waves, waiting for the water to drain before she popped the cover and booted it up. "I think I..."

A light pierced the darkness, sweeping around.

"Better think fast, Devvie," Jess said. "We've come too far to get splatted this easy."

The scan came back. "Look, Jess." Dev showed it to her. "It's the fishing boat."

"The fishing boat? What fishing boat?" Jess peered at the screen, rubbing her salt irritated eyes. "You mean...you don't mean Sigurd's boat? The one we stole?"

"And brought back," Dev said. "Yes, it is. It has the same profile."

The other agents and Kurok were clustered around, peering over Dev's shoulder along with Jess. "What does it mean?" April said. "What's it doing here?"

"Good question. Along with, who's driving it?" Jess said. "In either case, that boat's something we need, and maybe cover enough to get us back to the carriers. So we're gonna find out who's in it the hard way."

Kurok cleared his throat. "Maybe they'll pick someone up floating in the water," he said.

"Not one of us voluntarily," Jess said, briefly. "We stole the boat last time."

"Not one of you, but maybe me," Doctor Dan said. "Some old

scientist washed overboard of something. Worth a chance, isn't it?"

"What if it's already been commandeered?" Jess said, after a moment's silence.

Doctor Dan smiled. "Then I'm no worse off than I was, and I can likely distract them long enough for you all to get away."

"What makes you think we'd try?" Jess smiled back at him. "But you can distract them long enough for us to climb on board."

Kurok chuckled a little. "Deal." He took off his underwater rig and handed it to Jess. "Good luck." He slipped off the rock and started swimming toward the sound and light of the boat.

"You too," Jess said, just loud enough to be heard above the surf.

When he swam out of sight she settled the mask around her neck and regarded the rest of them. "Let's go," she said. "I'm not going to wait for them to make a decision, whoever they are."

"Right." April got her rig adjusted and disappeared under the waves. Mike was right behind her, and they both moved off in the direction Kurok had gone.

Dev and Jess regarded each other for a minute in silence. Then Jess moved forward and tilted her head, giving Dev a long, warm, passionate kiss. When she backed off, Dev's lips looked far less blue, and her expression looked far less bleak. "C'mon. When we get out of this, you and I are going to find a place and lose the world for a good long time."

She put Dev's mask in place and took her hand, putting her own mask over her face and slipping under the surface with Dev in tow, the last sounds she heard the clanging of a bell, and the sound of changing gears.

THE LIGHT BEAM penetrated the water, sending a spear of green tinged white almost far enough to hit Jess. She finned clear of it, then went still as she felt the tickle of scan on her skin.

The other agents felt it, and hands went to blasters instinctively. Jess watched the light outline Kurok's body for a long moment, then she turned in the water and headed for the far side of the boat.

As they passed under the hull the engines rumbled audibly. Jess looked up and could see a faintly circular motion starting. So they were turning toward Kurok, who was taking a big chance.

It's only life, right? Jess focused on a low rock outcrop just beyond the boat and when she reached it she turned, studying the position of the boat and sorting through her options. Only life, and it never paid to plan too far ahead because crap like this happened and you just had to go with it.

Jess pointed up at the hull, making climbing motions with her hands. The eyes watching her looked doubtful, but the heads nodded and she started upward with a quiet, sinuous motion.

Her throat hurt. It felt raw, and sucking in a breath of air sent prickles of discomfort across her chest. Jess grimaced and swallowed, knowing she'd be paying for her little party trick for a good long while. She put the pain aside and studied the hull above her, now closing in as the boat moved slowly across the surface.

Big engines churned the water, making it hard to see, but she caught sight of the side, and the flushing panels for the big tanks and headed for them.

Chancy. Right between the engines. But she knew where they led. Jess pointed to the hatches, which were in the open position allowing water into the holding tanks, and the rest of them nodded. Useless right now to tell them how tight the timing would need to be. She just made a sign for them to stick close behind her and went for it.

It was fast, and hard, and as she banged through the open hatch into a tank full of irritated fish, she had to wonder how good an idea it was to begin with.

As her hips cleared the opening she whirled in mid motion and caught the edge of the hatch, reaching back through and yanking Dev past her. Mike and April caught hold just as the engines increased power, and they swung around, slamming Jess into the tank wall.

Mike lost his grip and his body went into the prop wash, as April grabbed him by the belt and held on. Jess reached back through and added her own hold, pulling April into the tank and getting a good grip on Mike's arm.

April had the sense to get out of the way. She released her hold and swam clear, coming to rest next to Dev, holding onto the back tank wall.

Mike got hold of the edge of the hatch and pulled himself in, turning as he cleared it to make sure he still had all his body parts. He shook his head and floated free, banging against the tank wall as he checked his legs.

Jess turned her light on and sent a beam through the tank, seeing the reflection as thousands of eyes were mirrored back at her from the nearly full tank.

Damn good thing Mike hadn't gotten cut. Jess spared a grimace for the idea, then she pointed forward and started to swim toward the other end of the live fish hold.

Above her, she could hear the tackle being retracted, and hoped it meant that Kurok was on board. There was too much metal for her to hear any voices, but she heard muted tones of what might be yelling. That could be good, or bad for them.

The fish parted as they swam through. It was a mixture of catch, some larger specimens with a host of smaller ones, a lot of cod mixed with some barracuda, and a few small sharks. Jess ignored them as they moved through, nothing was close to their size and likely to want them for lunch, and the bulk of bio hid their human signatures to any average scan.

She was aware of Dev swimming gamely at her side. A sideways glance, though, showed her a very tense look on Dev's face. It occurred to her that she might be pushing Dev past her abilities, given she'd been less than a month on the job.

But Dev's jaw was clenched in a stubborn way, and now that they were in the holding tank, she was taking brief moments to look around at the fish they were swimming through with a hint of curiosity.

Then she seemed to sense the attention and her eyes met Jess's, a brief smile appearing on her face as she licked her lips.

Jess felt a flush of warmth flood her skin, and was glad the mask hid her blush. Crazy. Ridiculous for her to react that way given how long she'd been on the job, and all those years of learning control.

Dev took hold of her arm suddenly and she jerked her attention back to her partner, then realized they were about to crash into the wall. She put a hand out to stop them and waited for the rest to catch up, light from the deck filtering down through the heavy hatch cover and painting them in greenish blue stripes.

Jess slowly moved to the surface, staying flat against the wall until her head emerged into the small space between the top of the tank and the hatch. The others emerged a moment later, and they remained quiet and still, listening to the sounds now very audible through the deck of the boat.

"Bring it up!" A loud voice yelled. "Hurry!"

The hydraulics cut in and they felt the boat shift as it pulled something up.

Jess listened to the boots crossing to watch, and when they faded, she eased the service hatch up a trifle and peeked out. A moment of watching, then she pushed it all the way open and pulled herself up through it, clearing the way and rolling out of sight behind the big bait lockers.

All the men on the boat were on the far rail, watching the crane pull in something in a net. She couldn't see any faces, but a quick scan of the profiles didn't trigger her memory of any bad guys, and when the other three joined her, she stayed crouched where she was, holding her hand up for silence.

The crane was swinging over when powerful floodlights suddenly lit them from the cliff side, and then the roar of engines sounded over the waves.

"Kill your engines. Prepare for boarding," A loudspeaker pealed out. "Remain where you are or you will be shot."

Jess exhaled. "Gonna be one of those days."

"Going to be?" April asked, with a quizzical expression.

The crane came to rest with its net on the deck. It was wrapped around a man shaped figure, but the crew ignored it as they scattered to stations, yanking open the big weapons chest against the back wall and arming themselves.

"Stay still." Jess watched the action, as the crew returned to the rail, all of them with their back to her as they waited on the approach of the heavy armored cruisers.

Every crewman had a weapon. There was a surge of motion suddenly, and a familiar figure shoved his way to the rail and stood, hands planted firmly on his hips as the boats approached.

Dev smiled, recognizing the captain. "Look, Jess."

"I see." Jess managed a brief grin herself. "Old bastard. Knew he was too tough to get squashed in ice."

The first destroyer swung to, floodlights hitting the side of the fishing vessel and whitewashing it in glare. "Stand to."

"Kiss my ass," The captain yelled back. "What the hell d'you want? You're scaring off the damn fish!"

The man with the repeater stared at him in silence. "You're in restricted waters!" He finally yelled. "Prepare to be boarded."

"Like hell!" The captain yelled. "You put a foot on here I'll blow it off!" He brandished an old, scarred blaster. "Show me on what chart it says this is restricted? It's just an old shoal!"

"He's got guts," April said, mildly. "They could blow him out of the water in ten seconds."

Jess braced herself against the wall and rubbed her eyes. The tension was ratcheting up in her and her body started to twitch. It took a lot of effort to stay pressed against the side wall, behind the steel separator that was between them and the rail the crew was lined up against.

"They could, but they're not," Mike said.

"They won't." Jess peered through a rope hole in the wall. "They depend on fish loads, just like everyone else does in the big pop centers. Piss off the independents and you end up eating limpets and scraping algae."

April nodded. "They have leverage. The elders taught us about that, back home."

The destroyer motored closer, and swept the deck. "We're looking for a man overboard. Have you seen them?"

Sigurd laughed. "So now you want my help?" he said. "Get lost! There's nothing here but fish, buddy." He waved the blaster at them. "We've been here for hours. Didn't see any man overboard. Overboard of what? That rock?" He pointed at the pinnacle.

The boat came even closer, and Jess could see them sweeping the deck with scanners. She pressed back, turning her body sideways to them. "Ready."

"See them." Mike aligned himself next to her, as Jess tucked her head down a little behind the bait chamber.

"What the hell are ya doing?" Sigurd yelled. "Stop that!" He released the catch on his blaster audibly and then fired off a blast, making the other vessel erupt in angry chaos. "Keep your filthy tech to yourself!"

Someone else fired on the other side, and the next minute bolts were going everywhere, hitting the metal deck and deflecting.

"Hold!" The other ship captain bellowed. "Hold your fire!"

"Assholes!" Sigurd called out. "Consider your dock closed for us!" He waved a hand at the crew. "Pull in the nets! Let's get out of here."

The crew burst into motion, heading for the big net wheel in the back and holstering their weapons to grab tackle around the deck. The hydraulics kicked in and the crane arched over to open up the back hatch of the tank, as the net started to retract and bring its catch into the hold.

The net the crane had brought on board was forgotten, near the front of the deck and apparently empty and lifeless. The destroyer idled nearby and didn't move away, the scanners sweeping them despite Sigurd's threat. But as the net came aboard, and the shining bodies of fish started to disappear into the hold, the scans faded.

"Find other waters." The captain of the destroyer ordered. "We won't hold fire next time, hear me?"

Sigurd made a gesture at him, his arm outlined in the lights on the back of the deck with its rude symbol. The captain watched the ships slowly turn and start quartering in a searching pattern, keeping themselves between the shore and the fishing vessel.

Now powerful lights were coming on at the shoreline, and the waters were churned and illuminated, outlining anything below with piercing light. A shout went out, and a loud double thump sounded, then a low rumble that erupted into a booming roar that exploded up through the surf and sent a shock wave outbound that rocked the fishing boat violently.

But the crew took it in stride, and once the end of the net was aboard Sigurd yelled for the helm to turn around, and take them on an outbound course to the west. The crane rumbled overhead and two of the crew attached it to the big hatch, standing back as it swung the big portal closed.

The destroyers and their explosions faded off behind as they moved away from shore and into the waves. The fishing gear was lashed down and the crew gathered near where Sigurd was standing, his arm braced against the steel hull, the blaster cradled in his other elbow.

Silence fell, only the whistle of the wind, and the slosh of the sea heard over the rumble of the engines.

Jess judged the distance, then she pushed off from the wall and stepped around the bait locker, with the rest of her little gang behind her. She stopped a few body lengths from the rest of the crew, her hand resting on her blaster. "Dev," she said. "Go check out your buddy."

Dev slid out from her shadow and trotted across the deck, kneeling down next to the net.

Sigurd studied Jess. He moved away from the control station and came over to her, the blaster cradled in one arm, not quite pointed at her, but not quite not. He stopped just within reach and tilted his head to look up at her, pale eyes as cold and hard as hers were. "Know why I'm here?" he asked, after a moment of silence.

"No," Jess answered, honestly. "Last time we met you abandoned me and this tub to a trap in the ice. Didn't expect we'd be meeting again."

Sigurd nodded. "So I did." He glanced around. "So I was paid to do. Didn't expect to see you again either. Or this boat. But you brought it back."

"I did," Jess said. "Never considered otherwise. Runs in the blood."

The fisherman shifted a little, the gun easing to one side. "Well." He glanced around. "I don't like owing people." He scowled at her. "I screwed you over, and you repay me for that by leaving me a boat, with a profit, and enough god damned black diamonds to retire on. You suck, Drake."

Jess smiled, with only a little humor. "You're welcome." She caught the looks of the crew, which were far more friendly than she remembered. "Hope everyone got a cut."

The captain nodded. "You didn't ask me how I knew where you were."

Jess waited.

Sigurd chuckled. "I saw you come in." He gave her a piratical grin. "Just before dark, over the horizon. Wondered what the hell you were up to."

True? Not true? She shrugged. "Don't care how you knew." Jess pointed at the horizon. "Need to drop us off past the western turn. We'll swim in. No sense in risking this tub."

"Then we're even," Sigurd said. "I drop you, we're done."

"Yes." She turned her head. "He okay, Dev?"

Dev was helping Doctor Dan sit up. He looked more than a little battered, and there was blood on his head, but he lifted a hand in her direction and waved it.

"All right. Let me get this thing pointed right." Sigurd handed his gun off to one of the crew. "Sit down for a few minutes. I don't want those goons to catch on." He climbed up to the control bridge, leaving them to take his advice and sit down on one of the equipment lockers.

Doctor Dan came over to join them. "Well." He looked around. "Unexpected."

Jess nodded. "It's not over. We've still got to get to the carriers and get out of here." She made space next to her so Dev could sit down. "I'll feel a hell of a lot better once Dev's got her hands on the throttles."

Dev managed a smile.

One of the crew approached with a drink container and a stack of cups. He offered them the cups in silence and they took them, holding them as he poured something steaming into them. "Agent," he said to

Jess. "Sorry about the ice."

Jess lifted the cup in his direction then brought it to her lips, the half spicy scent of seaweed tea reaching her nose as she sipped it.

"We heard about the bases," the man said. "One of them from North was a cousin." He turned and left them, as the fishing vessel started a slow, almost meandering arc that took them away from the brightly lit search site, as another explosion reached their ears.

"They're going to end up blowing up something important," Doctor Dan said, his hands wrapped around the cup he'd been given. "But at least it's keeping their attention."

No one asked anything. Jess slowly drank her tea, aware of Dev's body leaning against her, glad of just these few minutes of stillness and peace.

She was tired, and she hurt. She could see that April and Mike were equally exhausted, though neither had said even a word of complaint. She knew Kurok was hurt, and she could see Dev was stressed. And now they would have the challenge of entering the water again, then finding a way ashore unseen, then finding their carriers and hoping like hell they were still hidden and their two techs were safe, and not dead.

All that to worry about, not to mention finding a way home from deep enemy territory, when she knew every soldier they had would be hunting them, and then, if they did manage all that, having no idea what she was going home to.

Ugh.

She sipped the hot tea, appreciating the warmth on her sore throat, knowing that no discussion of anything would take place before they were safely in the carriers. That was all right by her, since it gave her some time to think about what they'd done, and try to understand it.

The boat started motoring around in a searching pattern of its own, as though it was looking for fish. There was some chance they were still under surveillance, and Sigurd was taking no chances as he meandered slowly west, heading for the promontory headland their carriers were hidden behind.

At least, she hoped they were. She didn't think she could trust Sigurd to take them home. She glanced at Dev. At least if he did, they'd both get some rest. The thought of curling up in bed with Dev was so enticing, she almost wished—.

No, she didn't. Jess finished her tea and stood up, adjusting her over suit and preparing it to go into the water. "Be glad to get these off and get something dry on," she said. "We've got a med kit in the bus, Doc."

Kurok smiled wryly at her. "I think we should get as close to shore as we can," he said quietly. "If the tides out, there's a rock wall. If they can pull up against it we can stay dry."

"You know a lot about that place," April said.

"Yes," Doctor Dan said. "I was born there." He leaned back against the wall. "Grew up there, until I became part of a project that ended up with me changing sides." His lips twitched. "But that's a story for another time."

"Wow," April said, with a note of respect in her voice. "That must be quite a story."

"Mm." The pale haired man made a sound in his throat, glancing at Jess and then looking away. "It was."

The crew stayed away from them. They worked at their tasks, and got the nets ready, just going about their jobs as though there weren't five strangers sitting on their deck, and patrols watching their movements.

A few minutes later, one of the women came on deck, with a pot of something and a stack of worn plates. She put it down on the locker and offered April a spoon, then walked away, disappearing back down into the interior area of the ship.

"This safe?" April indicated the pot.

"Is anything?" Jess handed out the plates, and the utensils piled on them.

"Good point." April dumped portions of the fisherman's typical fish stew on the plates and then sat down and started in on hers. "Better than that stuff at the pole."

Jess took a mouthful and had to agree. She watched Dev from the corner of her eye, as Dev stolidly worked through the stew and gently nudged her with her elbow.

Dev looked up at her in question.

"Want more tea?" Jess asked.

"No, I'm okay with this." Dev pointed at the stew. "It's warm," she added. "But I agree I will be very glad when we can change into something dry." She seemed to perk up a little at Jess's continued attention. "I'm really glad the fisher people came out okay."

"Me too," Jess said.

"But they said they left us there on purpose." Dev frowned. "That wasn't good."

"They got paid to." Jess scraped up the last of her stew. "It happens."

"Then why are they helping us now?" Dev whispered. "It's confusing. Couldn't they be getting paid to do bad things now too?"

"Anything's possible." Jess also kept her voice very low. "But Sigurd's shackled with the same ten ton ball of honor that I am. When we were with him before, it was a handshake deal. He had no pact with us, just did it as a favor to his old uncle. Must have been a lot of cred, to get him to walk away from this thing."

Dev frowned.

"When I brought the boat back, I put him in deep debt to me," Jess went on, in a casual tone. "Both in cred, and in honor, and he's got to pay that off."

"Oh. He has to?"

"Has to."

"I see." Dev finished up her stew. "I am going to speak to him then." She put the plate down. "I want to see if he got my note." She ducked past Jess before she could react, and headed for the control center, moving past the crew and mounting the steps with stolid confidence.

Jess put her plate down and paused, not sure if she should follow or not. She glanced at Doctor Dan, who was sitting quietly, having finished his meal.

"Not what you expected, hmm?" Kurok asked.

"No," Jess said.

"Me either." Kurok sighed, shaking his head. "Me either."

Chapter Thirteen

DEV OPENED THE door to the control area, pausing when the men inside turned to look at her.

Two of them immediately headed her way, but the captain lifted his hand. "Leave her," he said. "Take off," he added, gesturing to the door. "I can handle this crate."

The men walked past Dev, making a point of staring at her as they went by. Dev merely looked back at them, waiting for the door to close and taking a moment to enjoy the lack of cold wind.

Sigurd kept his hands on the controls, but one eye on her. "So."

"Hello." Dev came over and stood next to the console. "This was a very pleasant thing to drive. I liked it."

The captain's eyebrows hiked up. "You drove it?"

"Yes," Dev said. "I had to."

Sigurd eyed her. "So. You're a jelly bag brain?"

Dev nodded. "I'm a bio alt. I don't think I have any jelly in my head, though. There's not much room with all the programming in there."

"That's freaking strange," the captain said. "I never would have pegged you for that."

Dev took that as a compliment. "Well, I didn't expect you to let us die in the ice. So I guess you really don't know about people, do you?"

Sigurd turned his head fully and looked at her. "You wrote in my log."

"I did." Dev put her hands on the console, flexing the fingers a little as the chill left them. "I wasn't sure what happened to you and your family, but I hoped you made out okay, and I wanted you to know that."

"Why?" he asked. "We screwed you over. Left you to croak. Hoped the ice crushed you and this tub. They promised me they'd replace it."

"Yes, I know. But I still hoped you made it out okay," Dev said. "A lot of people try to hurt us. I was taught to expect that."

He sighed. "Great. Enjoy that hopeful attitude while you can, cause life's gonna beat it out of you." He glanced at her again. "Anyway, those bastards double crossed me and we ended up running for our lives from 'em. My fault. Paid a kid for it." He looked out at the water. "So get out of here, okay? I gotta figure out where I can stop where they don't know I'm letting you off."

"Okay. Goodbye." Dev touched the console and turned, retreating from the control surface and heading for the door. "Good luck."

"Yeah, you too," he said, without turning around.

Dev closed the door behind her and climbed down the steps,

passing the two crew members who immediately clambered up past her. She started around the corner only to crash headlong into a tall body coming the other direction, and bounced back, trying to catch her balance. "Oh!"

"Ah." Jess grabbed and steadied her. "There you are."

"Here I am," Dev said. "That discussion was not very successful, but I'm glad I had it. I was in discomfort thinking those people had all died. I'm glad they didn't."

"Since they just saved our asses, me too." Jess leaned against the wall and stuck her hands in her pockets. "Be glad to get back in our bus though."

"Me too," Dev echoed her words. "It's been a day full of much discomfort."

"No kidding."

They both fell silent for a bit. Then Jess cleared her throat. "You did a hell of a job in there, by the way." She indicated the way they'd come. "Didn't have a chance to say anything before."

Dev leaned on the wall next to her. "It was difficult."

"Very," Jess said, giving her a sideways look. "Cold?"

Dev nodded. "There was a lot of under the water things." she said. "I was just thinking how nice a hot shower would feel."

"Mm. Yeah it would."

They were both silent again, for a moment. Then Jess draped her arm over Dev's shoulders and simply stood there, as the fishing boat made its lazy circle and started to drift toward the promontory. The waves were building and it made the vessel rock as it slowed, the lights outlining white tinged waves all around them.

April came over to stand next to them. "Storm coming in. Heard the crew talking about it. They don't want to stick around."

"We don't either," Jess said. "Another ten minutes and he'll be close enough to that wall. Let's get ready."

They gathered on the port side of the deck, staying behind the bait locker as the boat maneuvered back and forth, setting out their nets and then moving clear of the lines, slipping sideways in the water as they turned to view the set. Then, casually, Sigurd turned the bow around, and as he did the lights on the boat blinked out and five dark clad figures hopped onto the seawall.

Then the engines revved, and the lights came back on, and the boat moved around the promontory as it laid out another line of nets, rocking in the waves as from the darkness, one of the destroyers appeared, splashing them with floodlights.

Jess led the way across the seawall, broken in spots and dangerous. She got to the end of it as they heard the destroyer engines, and jumped off onto the rocky beach they'd landed on.

One turn of the lights and even the carrier's camouflage skin wouldn't help them. Jess bolted across the surface and led the way to where they'd left the craft, coming around the corner of the rocks and knowing a moment of perfect relief as she spotted the faint outline in the reflection of the destroyer's floodlights.

April and Mike split off and got to their rigs as Doctor Dan followed Jess and Dev to theirs, Jess barely leaving enough space for the hatch to open without smacking her in the face as she palmed the lock.

Battle lighting was on inside and the hatch shut behind them as they entered. Dev went to the pilot's station and strapped in, undoing the catches on her water suit and peeling it down off her shoulders and exposing the clinging under-suit beneath it. She started her preflight checks, getting ear cups settled and reflecting that she was gladder to be sitting down in her seat than she could have possibly imagined.

Jess stripped her outer suit off to the waist as well, glancing over to where Doctor Dan was fastening the restraints around him on the drop rig seat. She got into her own chair and swung her panels around, hearing the rising hum as Dev powered systems in the faintly blue lit darkness of the inside of the carrier.

The front window went from opaque to clear, and she could see searchlights moving in the darkness over the water. "Dev, give me power please."

"Yes." Dev shunted batteries to the weapons systems and got the engines online. "Tac 1 to Tac 2 and 3, status?"

"Tac 2, ack," Chester said. "Two to go."

"Tac 3, ack." Doug waited his turn. "Ready."

"Dev, get ready to lift. I think your fishy buddies could use some help out there." Jess got her targeting systems aligned and leaned back in her seat, very glad of the support and wishing for some painkillers. Now that she was sitting down, it was getting harder to push the pain aside, and she took a deep breath then released it, forcing her concentration.

"One moment." Dev got her power grid aligned and stripped her gloves off, dropping them to the carrier deck as she curled her hands around the throttles. "Ready."

"Go, go, gadget," Jess said. "Hang on," she advised Doctor Dan. "I learned that the hard way."

Doctor Dan tightened the restraints on the rig and leaned against it, giving her a brief nod in return. "Anything not water's good for me right now."

Jess studied his face. "You gonna last?"

He regarded her with a wry expression. "I have broken ribs," he said. "If one of them doesn't puncture a lung, I'll be fine. Thanks for asking." He ended that with a slight grin, seeing the grimace of sympathy on Jess's face. "I wouldn't cooperate with them and they didn't like that."

"You went with them," Jess said, not quite asking the question.

"I did," Kurok answered. "They wanted me. I wanted to see what they were up to. Neither side got anything positive out of it since they wouldn't tell me why they wanted me, aside from hinting they wanted me to teach them how to create something like her." He moved his head in Dev's direction. "And, in the black humor department, they somehow forgot what business I was in before I went upside, and ended up shocked and enraged when I killed a few of them after they spent a few hours applying electrical leads to me."

"That what we busted up?" Jess knew what that felt like, and acknowledged a moment of true sympathy for the man. Now that she had time to sit quietly and look at him, she realized he probably had more than broken ribs.

"I figured I might as well see what all the fuss was about as long as I was being beaten up for it." Doctor Dan relaxed against the drop frame, letting his hands rest on his thighs. "And yes, they'd just caught up with me when they suddenly realized I was the least of their worries."

Jess let her head rest against the padded chair. "Glad we found you."

Kurok smiled. "I'm glad too."

Dev boosted fast, up and over the ridge of rock with the other two carriers right behind her. As they headed over the water they spotted the fishing boat facing off against the destroyer, dodging a bolt of blaster fire. "Jess!"

"Yeah, I see 'em." Jess swung the targeting system around and drew a bead on the enemy vessel. "Jacktards."

"They have seen us," Dev said. "I think they're going to shoot."

"I think I'm going to shoot first." Jess locked on and fired a long burst. "Take us right at 'em."

Dev nodded, and complied, sending the carrier at almost water level past the fishing vessel right at the destroyer. She saw the energy suck a moment before Jess cut loose on the forward guns, stitching across the side of the ship in a barrage that brought a thunder of explosive eruption that lit the night sky for a brief moment.

Then the water boiled, and the destroyer was gone. Dev flew the carrier through a dark cloud of smoke that dispersed as she bent their course into a tight curve, feeling the welcome pressure of G-force against her body. She slowed the carrier as they approached the fishing vessel, and peered at it. "They seem intact."

Below them, the bell on the ship was ringing. Dev piped the sound inside, as the other two carriers lifted and joined them. They hovered briefly, until the fishing vessel started back around to pick up their nets, several figures on the rail visibly waving at them.

Jess chuckled. "Now they owe us again." She safed the weapons. "Dev, take us due west, stick to the coast, stick to the waterline. Tell the kids to follow us."

"Will do." Dev transmitted the instructions, then plotted her course and swung the carrier around to point and engaged the engines.

It felt so good to be sitting down in her space. Dev wished she'd had time to completely change, but the warmth inside the carrier was penetrating her chilled skin, and she adjusted the temp a bit upward, as the shivers had almost worked their way out of her body.

It occurred to her then that they had likely done well with this mission. Some big important thing had been destroyed, and they had Doctor Dan with them. She and Jess were both functional, and she hadn't wrecked the carrier this time. Excellent, really.

She just hoped there was someone left for them to report it to.

"Keep a tight eye out, Dev. If they pick us up this is going to be ugly." Jess got up from her position and opened a locker, pulling out a dry shirt and pulling it over her head. She got one for Dev and moved forward, putting it down on her console. "Put that on. You must be an ice cube."

Dev had just finished engaging the autonomic systems, and she lifted her hands clear and picked up the fabric gratefully. "Thank you," she said. "It was really cold in that water."

"Yeah." Jess patted her shoulder. "I'm going to heat up some tea. My throat's killing me."

Dev pulled the shirt on, the warm, dry fabric feeling wonderful against her skin. She released her restraints and stood up, pulling the water suit all the way off, storing it neatly on a hook and removing a standard jumper from her kit. She pulled that on and fastened the catches over the shirt, at once a lot warmer.

She rubbed her hands and sat back down, reviewing her course and checking the wiremap closely. The coast was rugged, full of cliffs and outcroppings, and though the autonav was programmed to avoid collision, she didn't want to take any chances.

There had been a lot of chance taking, this last while.

She heard Jess moving around and getting her drink, and wondered how Doctor Dan was doing. A glance in the mirror showed Jess's profile, but she couldn't see Doctor Dan from where she was sitting. Then something caught her eye. "Jess?"

"Hmm?" Jess turned around and came over to her, handing her a steaming cup.

"I think you did yourself damage," Dev said, gravely. "There is blood on your back."

"Yeah? Oh crap." Jess turned her back to Dev. "Fresh?"

"Yes." Dev put the cup down and got up again, touching Jess's shoulder blade. There was a spreading stain on her shirt. "May I look at it?"

"Sure." Jess rested her hands on her console, feeling the brush of cool air as Dev pulled her shirt up, the pain now becoming evident to her since she had to focus on it. "Damned knife."

"Traitor's knives are sharpest of all." Doctor Dan had half turned in the rig area and was watching.

"So true," Jess said, after a moment. "There's a kit behind the locker there, Dev. See if you can clean it off, and put something over it. "

"Yes." Dev went to the locker and retrieved the aid kit. "Doctor Dan taught us to do this." She smiled a little, and looked over at her mentor. "We would get hurt sometimes in training."

"Yes." Doctor Dan smiled back at her. "I remember it well."

Dev brought the kit back and got the cleaner and some plas bandages out. She eased the shirt up over Jess's shoulder and studied the injury. "Something has penetrated your back here," she said. "Also, it is very bruised. Right here." She touched the edge of her shoulder blade.

"Is it the same place I got hurt last time?" Jess studied the console.

Dev regarded the skin before her, touching the scar now red and visible. "Yes," she said. "It appears to have opened up?" She gently cleaned the place, aware of the sound as Doctor Dan released his belt and came around the weapons console to peer at the injury.

"Hmm," Kurok said. "Let me take over this, Dev. I've had a little more experience." He removed the pad and the cleanser from Dev's hands. "Have your tea. I think your lips are still a little blue."

Dev was glad to step back and let her teacher take over. She scanned her boards again, then sat down in her chair, picking up her cup again and sipping from it.

She didn't think her lips were blue, since she felt quite warm now. She settled her ear cups in place and started a comm scan, listening for the faint sounds of enemy radio. She caught the faint echo of the carriers behind them, and then she keyed in the sideband system. "Tac 1, Tac 2."

"Tac 2, ack."

"Standby for nav sync."

"Ack."

Dev sent their course and lock, and waited for an acknowledgement, trying not to think too much about how tired she was. "Is it okay, Doctor Dan?" she asked, noting that the wound already looked a lot better.

"Oh, I think it'll do fine," Kurok murmured. "This was a really bad puncture."

"Yeah," Jess said. "Dalknife, six inches, to the hilt."

Doctor Dan stopped moving and craned his head to look around Jess's shoulder. "Beg your pardon?"

"Dalknife," Jess said. "Must be new since your time. Carved from basalt rock. Triangular, sharp as hell, but with burrs all along the blade so it carves you up like a seaweed milkshake."

Kurok pulled his head back and looked more closely at the old wound. "That explains the triangular bifurcation," he said. "That must have—"

"Nearly killed me? Yeah." Jess didn't sound upset about it. "I lost what felt like half the blood in my body before they got me into a chill kit and back to the tank."

"Wow." Doctor Dan seemed at a loss for words

"Yeah, that's what the meds at base said." Jess sighed. "They're not really sure how I managed not to croak. Certainly Joshua meant me to."

"Joshua?"

Jess glanced back at him. "My last tech," she said. "My former partner, who went to the other side." She eyed her own shoulder. "Thought it healed."

"Mostly," Doctor Dan said, in a quiet tone. "Looks like most of the internal is healed, but this outer part split apart. Maybe in the fight." He carefully applied a plas tack and eased the edges of the opening closed, putting a layer of goo over it and putting a bandage square in place. "There you go."

"I banged it up at base when they went for you," Jess recalled.

"I remember that." Dev reached over and put a hand on Jess's arm, giving it a squeeze. "Against the door." She heard a hail on comms and turned to answer it. "Excuse me."

Jess straightened up and slid her shirt down, then she went over to her locker and got out of the water suit, trading it for a regular issue. She turned, to find Kurok watching her, with a quiet, grim expression.

She managed a brief grin, then sat down in the gunners chair and relaxed, glad, at least, she hadn't done anything newly lethal to herself. Bruises, for sure, but that didn't involve external blood loss.

Doctor Dan perched on the edge of the rig casing, just to her right. "You know, I didn't understand, truly, what the situation with your former partner was, when they asked us to participate. They didn't explain, and Alex didn't either."

Jess glanced at him. His eyes were shifted slightly off her, a hard, sea ice glint to them. Dressed as he was, with that look, most of the scientist about him had faded away leaving something more primal in its wake. "They just wanted it fixed," she said.

Kurok now focused on her. "They said it was a trust thing. I didn't get it. I couldn't imagine what a tech could have done that caused that much upheaval."

"Think I was some prima dona or something?" Jess's lips twisted into a droll wryness.

"No," he answered quietly. "I knew you weren't. I thought it was political. It wasn't." He indicated her back. "That wasn't. That was a personal betrayal on a level I can hardly comprehend." He shook his head. "Not from...not from one of us."

Jess felt something long tense relax in her, unexpectedly. She watched him faintly shake his head, one hand slowly closing and opening, so very obviously remembering a time when he had been what Joshua had been, trying to fathom doing what he'd done. "Yeah," she said. "You got it."

Dev watched them both with deep interest. This was a side of

Doctor Dan she'd never seen, and it was fascinating, because as he said those words she felt the programming in her echoing them very intensely. He was aghast at the thought of that betrayal, and she felt that in her gut, in perfect echo.

He had said, one of us. That was the first time she'd heard him refer to himself that way, but it was true. She could see that now, see how he was more like Jess than anyone she'd known in the creche. More like Jess, and April, and Doug, and even Jason, back at the citadel.

"Yes." Doctor Dan sat down in the equipment ledge. "I do get it."

Dev went to the dispenser. "Would you like some tea, Doctor Dan? I think that clothing you have is still wet."

He gave her one of his gentle smiles. "I would like that a lot, Dev. Thanks."

Jess got back up and went to the gear locker, rummaging inside it. "Here." She dug out a thickly woven over shirt and handed it to him. "That'll probably fit."

"Ah." Kurok touched the fabric. "Something from home, eh?" He glanced at Jess. "Haven't seen that pattern in a while." He took the cloth. "Drake's Bay harbor shirt."

Jess smiled in reflex. "Always keep one around for gale force conditions." She was glad to shift the conversation to something far more mundane. "It's woven to keep wind and sand out." she explained to Dev, who was looking curiously at it. "Next time we're there, I'll get you one."

"It's pretty." Dev reached over and touched the fabric. "I like the colors. It reminds me of the cloth thing in the big room there."

Doctor Dan looked up at her. "You've been to the Bay, Dev? I didn't hear about that."

Jess took a cup of hot tea back to her station. "Happened after you went hostage," She said. "My mother was in an air crash. We went to her processing."

Several conflicting emotions flashed over Kurok's face. "I see," he murmured. "Sorry to hear that."

Dev retreated back to her chair and checked the nav. Everything seemed stable, and comp showed no scans, and no targets, save the other two carriers. Nothing was following them.

She thought about the shirt, and about getting one if they went back. Maybe they would go there if the base was damaged, Jess had said, and Dev found that thought appealing. She liked the place, even if people were strange, and there seemed to be discomfort about her, and Jess there.

"Yeah, well, it was more an excuse to get out of the base, and see what I could do about coming out to find you," Jess said, with a smile. "She and I never really got along after I went."

"Ah. I see."

Dev glanced in the mirror, and saw that Doctor Dan had taken off the wet shirt so he could put on a dry one. The light inside the carrier wasn't bright, but she could plainly see patterns on his arms, faded, but visible against his pale skin. A good portion of his skin was also darkened with bruises and crossed with thin red marks and cuts.

It seemed like he was in discomfort. But he put the shirt on and picked up his tea, and smiled back at Jess, his eyes gently twinkling in the overhead battle lighting.

It seemed like things were starting to be better again. Dev sipped her tea with a sense of lightening tension in her, and she settled herself into her chair as the feelings of uncertainty and doubt faded.

Really, it seemed like they could do anything.

DAYLIGHT FOUND THEM skimming over ruffled gray waters, warily eying a dark black line off in the distance heading for them.

Dev had just settled back into her seat after a short nap and she had a ration box clamped down next to her as she studied the met report. Behind her, Doctor Dan seemed to be sleeping almost standing up, and Jess had just leaned back in her seat and closed her eyes for a while, after driving while Dev rested.

She felt okay. It would have been excellent to have slept a little longer but the irresistible urge to close her eyes was gone and she felt like she could keep going as long as she needed to now.

Her chair was still a little warm from Jess's body, and she smiled as she leaned back in it, checking their course and reviewing the results of her most recent scan. There was nothing around except the other two carriers. Even the waters they were cruising over seemed empty of most life.

They had left the land far behind. Nav was reporting they were just a few minutes shy of crossing the invisible line that divided her side and the other side, and she directed the scan downward to review the ocean bottom below.

Yes, there it was. She traced the line on the bottom that marked the intercontinental plate, remembering her lessons about the geology of the planet downside they never saw. There was a certain sense of relief as she crossed over it, even though she knew it really did not keep anyone from following them.

It meant they were that much closer to—Dev paused and considered. Was the citadel home? Had the creche been home? She tapped the word into comp and waited for it to come back, studying the results with interest. What was home, anyway?

Home was a place of refuge or residence, apparently. It was a place one belonged to, where they kept their possessions and where they did a significant part of their daily living.

Well. Dev pondered. That, for her could be either place, or, in fact, this carrier. She'd done a significant part of her daily living so far sitting right in this very seat, but she was pretty sure that wasn't really what was meant.

Ah. 'Archaic–home was often not a place but philosophical location, where one would feel at ease and at peace, a comfort of the heart.'

Hmm. Was there any place that fit that for her?

Dev heard a faint sound behind her and she glanced in the mirror, seeing Jess shift a little in her chair. Her eyes were closed, and she was using one of the thick jackets as a blanket, her head resting against the padded surface of her swiveled back chair.

The lights were dimmed inside the carrier, only the consoles emitting a low, faint blue glow but she could see Jess's even, slow breathing and she felt herself relaxing as she watched. One of the few peaceful moments she'd encountered thus far in her short sojourn at Interforce, she realized, had been curling up with Jess to sleep, and she wished they could do that now.

Even without the sex thing.

Dev sighed, and returned her attention to the console, setting up another scan with slightly different parameters and letting it start. The course Jess had given her would take them north of their base, almost to Quebec City, and then south, but first there was this storm to get past.

There were no ice caves to hide in, she noted mournfully. Perhaps they would get to the outer edge of the lonely escarpments past Quebec before the storm caught them, and shelter there. She adjusted the thrusters a little, and regarded the output of the scan, glad to see nothing on the horizon aside from the threatened met.

Her ear bud crackled slightly, and she pressed it a little more firmly into her ear. "Repeat?"

"Tac 1, Tac 3," the soft response came back. "This is Mike."

"Ack," Dev responded in a low tone. "Status?"

"Nominal," he said. "Reporting low band chatter, sea level based, northwest."

Dev checked her own comms, seeing the faint signal. "Ack," she said. "Ident?"

"Negative," Mike said. "Fishing boat, maybe."

They'd out flown the only fishing boat Dev developed a personal interest in. They were days behind them now, and she didn't think getting involved with another boat would be an excellent thing to do. What would Jess do, though? Would she want to see what was out there?

Dev frowned, shifting her attention from the comms to the reflection and back. Jess wanted to get back to the citadel, that was for sure, and diverting could get them in trouble with the weather. She wondered if she should wake Jess up to ask.

But Jess looked so tired. Dev wavered another moment, then clicked into comms. "Tac 3, Tac 2, Tac 1. Divert ten degrees northwest, long scan, report."

There was a brief silence. Then the comms came to life. "Ack,"

April said. "Ten degrees, at mark."

"Ack," Mike sounded distinctly relieved. "Signal locked, parsing. Standby."

Dev adjusted her own course and nodded, feeling a sense of relief, and also, of correctness. She picked up her dispenser of tea and sipped from it, then set it down and selected a seaweed cracker from her ration and put it in her mouth.

She wasn't sure why Jess didn't like them. They were crunchy and slightly spicy and they went well with the tea. It also provided some contrast to the fish roll, which tended to be a little bland.

Another sound made her look up again, but this time it was Doctor Dan, who came over to her and sat down on the side of the console, holding a ration kit. "Good morning, Dev."

Dev smiled. "Hello," she said. "Are you in less discomfort now, Doctor Dan? After your rest?"

"Oh, somewhat, yes." He sipped his tea. "It's been a very long time since I've had to deal with being kicked around like that, no doubt about it."

His voice was soft, and a little hoarse. Dev studied him from the corner of her eye, noting the painful looking bruise along one of his cheekbones. "Why did they hurt you?" She asked, keeping her voice very low to avoid waking Jess.

"Mm." Doctor Dan pondered the question. "Probably because I was doing my very best to make trouble for them. They don't like that, you know. I wasn't being very correct to them."

"Oh." Dev listened to the scan results, then restarted it when it came back empty. "I guess we were doing that too."

"You were," he said. "Doing a damn fine job of that, in fact. Better than I did. But that does usually end up with someone getting into a bit of discomfort."

"Like Jess's back."

"Mm." Kurok nodded slowly. "But the original hurt, Dev, that was a very wrong thing," he added, gently. "It made me very angry to see that, you know, because what you are doing, this work, involves a lot of trust."

"Yes," Dev said. "It would be like you hurting one of us."

Doctor Dan went very still, his eyes staring at the steam from his cup for a long moment before he looked back up at her. "Yes, it's that kind of trust. You have to trust that the things I do to you are not going to hurt you."

"I do," Dev responded. "We all do." She half turned to look seriously at him. "Not everyone else."

Kurok put his cup down and laced his fingers together, resting his chin on them. "Why is that? Why me, and not others, Dev?"

Oh, that was a good question. Dev shifted her eyes to the window and looked out at the choppy sea, almost a black color frothed with white as it passed under them. "I don't know," she finally said, a little unsettled. "I just feel like you wouldn't hurt me. I always did—we always did. I talked to some of the others, and to Gigi. You remember Gigi?"

"Yes." Doctor Dan smiled at her. "I do remember Gigi."

"We always thought you cared what happened to us."

Doctor Dan made a low noise in his throat. "I do care. In a way, Dev, all of you are, to me, as though you were my children, the ones I never had myself."

Dev smiled, and her eyes lit up.

"So maybe that's what you feel, when you feel that way," he said. "What happens to you all matters to me, even though I know those things can sometimes be bad, and unhappy things."

"Bad things happen to natural borns, too," Dev said, after a pause. "Like what happened to Jess." She reached out and touched his hand, where another bruise was evident. "And to you."

"That's true." He returned her smile, then it faded. "When bad things happen, it's hard for natural borns to trust other people, because it could happen again. But I think Jess does trust you."

Dev nodded. "She knows I care about what happens to her. And I do. But Doctor Dan..." She glanced at the console, and adjusted a setting. "I think that made me do something very incorrect. When I saw them hurting Jess, I—

"You hit them," Doctor Dan said. "I saw you."

Dev nodded. "Yes. I did. That was incorrect, wasn't it? I remember the programming for that."

"Ah." Doctor Dan opened his ration box and removed the fish roll inside, setting it on the console and fishing the crackers out with it.

"That's a complicated question, Dev." He leaned back a little, against the side of the control area. "When I was preparing you for this work, I did do some changes to that programming, because I knew you might end up in a situation like that one. I wanted you to be able to respond to it."

Now, that was a surprise. "You did?"

"I did." Kurok bit into his fish roll. "Because I think you realize that I used to do work very much like this."

"With Jess's father."

There was a long pause before he answered, and his face twitched a little. "Yes." He finally said. "I didn't know you knew that."

"Jess found out before we left." Dev sensed some serious discomfort on his part. "They sent her some of her father's things, and one of the things was a picture."

"Of us?" Doctor Dan said, after long breath.

"Yes."

He sat quietly and finished his roll without saying anything else for a few minutes. Dev finished hers as well, and waited, since she could see he was thinking hard about something. She checked the console, and the chron, and calculated it would be another ten minutes or so before they were close to the signal's location and could see anything.

Doctor Dan rested his elbows on his knees and nibbled on his crackers. "I didn't expect that, Dev, but yes, it's true. I was her father's partner, way back when." His face looked quiet, and thoughtful. "So you see, I knew very well what I needed to prepare you for."

"The programming is excellent, Doctor Dan. I've known everything I needed to." She indicated the carrier. "Especially about this vehicle. It's been difficult, but I could do it."

He smiled, a warm sweet smile that made her smile back. "Thank you, Dev. It's always nice to have your work recognized, isn't it? I don't get that opportunity often."

Dev knew a moment of delight, seeing his unexpected reaction to her words. Of course, she knew what that was like, to have your work praised, and yet somehow she never thought— She looked at Doctor Dan again. "Thank you," she said. "I'm really glad I got this assignment."

"Even though it's so hard?"

Dev nodded. "Yes. It's hard, but it's good work." She glanced in the mirror then looked back at him. "And I'm glad I'm getting to help Jess." Another glance in the mirror would have shown her a pair of interested blue eyes watching that had now gained a faint twinkle in them, but Dev focused her attention on her mentor. "That's been really good."

He grinned a little. "You like your partner."

"Very much. Jess has been so nice to me, and she's so excellent at this work."

"Mm. She comes from a long line of people who were very good at this," Doctor Dan said. "Sometimes natural borns have traits, like sets can have, and they inherit them from their mothers and fathers in the same way that we develop sets to have certain talents in the creche. You understand?"

"Yes. Is that how she does the fish thing?" Dev asked. "That was a very big surprise. There were some people in the citadel who said Jess was a fish, but I didn't think they meant that so literally."

Doctor Dan looked thoughtful. "That was a big surprise to me, too, Dev. I can tell you, having pulled him out of a number of underwater situations, that she did not inherit that from her father. It must be something that was being modified slowly through generations in her family. It's very interesting and I hope I get a chance to talk to her about it when we're done with this part of the mission."

"I think Jess is amazing, and I'm so glad I got to do work with her." Dev got it all out in a rush, feeling a warmth on her face and a slight feeling of confusion. "I really like her."

"Yes, I know you do." Doctor Dan's smile broadened. "I'm glad." He patted her knee. "No matter how hard this gets, Dev, remember that part. It's the really important thing. It's very important to be able to take good care of our friends, right? So that's why I changed your programming a little, so that you'd be able to do that if you had to." He hesitated. "Don't ever feel incorrect about helping people you care for."

Dev felt a true sense of relief. She didn't like thinking about being so incorrect. "So it's okay for me?"

Kurok nodded. "It is okay for you, because we're asking you to do very difficult things that most bio alts don't get to do. So don't worry about it."

Dev nodded at once. "It's like the sex thing, right?"

Doctor Dan chuckled unexpectedly, putting his box down and rubbing his face with one hand. "Ah, well, yes, I guess it is, sort of." He sighed. "In that, it's all right for you to do things that your creche mates will not get to do, because of the work you're involved in."

"Good." Dev was satisfied. "Thank you for telling me that."

He patted her shoulder and went back to his fish roll, chuckling a little to himself and shaking his head.

"Tac 2, Tac 1."

Dev touched her ear cup. "Tac 1 Go."

"Scan complete, standby to sync," Chester said. "Check tab 2."

Dev engaged the comp and retrieved the scan from the other carrier, reviewing it and matching it against her own. She was aware of Doctor Dan peering over her shoulder, and moved aside a little to give him a better view. "We heard a comm signal," she explained. "We weren't sure what it was. "

Chester's scan showed only a ghost profile. She compared it to her own, and tuned the comp a little more, warping the sine waves and resending the probe.

Doctor Dan peered at the screen and tilted his head just slightly, his eyes narrowing a little. "That looks old," he said. "Reminds me of the remote base stations they used to run on the coast, before they put the sat relays in." He looked thoughtful.

"Hmm." Jess's voice startled both of them, and they looked up to see her coming to stand behind Dev's chair, draping her long arms over the top of it. "Sorry. Couldn't sleep through people complimenting me. What's up?" She gave them both a wry grin.

Dev blushed, wrinkling her nose as she sorted through the surge of emotion. "I'm sorry, did that cause you discomfort?"

"Nope." Jess peered at the screen. "We pick something up?" She eased around the other side of the chair and leaned against it, her elbow resting on Dev's shoulder.

"A signal." Dev pointed it out. "It's just an echo on Chester's scan but I can see the sine of it." She traced the line with one fingertip. "It's not very strong."

"No." Jess shook her head. "What did you say it looked like?" she asked Doctor Dan.

"Local signal hub," he said. "Used to be a lot of them in relay, before we had topside."

Jess regarded the readout and then keyed in met and brought up the storm front, her eyes flicking from one to the other rapidly. "Okay. I don't want to leave this unseen, but we're out of time. Let's do a water level overfly of the coordinates, then take us up and to the north, Dev. Get over that line of clouds."

"Yes." Dev got her restraints in place, as Jess pushed off and went back to her seat and did the same. Doctor Dan collected the remainder of the rations and stowed them, moving back to his position in the drop rig and strapping down. "Do you think it could be another fishing boat?"

"Maybe." Jess got her targeting systems up and synced, powering the forward guns up with a light touch. "But I'm not going to take any chances. Someone paid Sigurd to skunk us."

"Seems an easy answer to that," Doctor Dan said. "We know they were looking for you for Gibraltar."

"Seems like, but I'm not sure it's them," Jess said. "We saw some funny things in the white. Found a cavern full of jacktards pretending to be Interforce who were gunned down, but not by us." She got her gloves on and settled into her chair, leaning back and letting her eyes focus past the screens.

"Rivals?" Kurok asked.

"Don't think so." Jess tightened her restraints. "There's something out there I think we've been missing. Tied into the leak we had at base, and how they've been able to penetrate us pretty much at will lately."

"Hmm."

"They got all the way into our shuttle base after you," Jess said. "A dozen security sweeps and we can't find someone who has the intel and access to allow an attack force of that size to get all the way into our pad? Really?"

Doctor Dan eyed her thoughtfully.

"And they knew you were there." Jess tuned the guns. "Dev, bring us in." She settled herself. "Let's make sure we don't leave some loose end at our backs that ends up burying a knife in it. Have had enough of that this year already."

Dev got the carrier off auto nav and brought the craft down to wave level and cleared the light layer of fog, giving them a clear view at last.

In the target zone they could see a small rocky island. As they approached, craft launched against them. "Here we go." Jess flexed her hands. "Bet they didn't expect us."

"Bet they didn't," Doctor Dan said. "And we didn't expect them either," he added. "Whoever 'they' are."

FLYING THE CARRIER into battle was very different then just

flying it from place to place. Dev tried to take in everything around her as she bent their course downward, skimming the tops of the waves as they bore down on the island.

Two blocky forms were headed right at them at equal speed and she felt the weapons systems draw power as Jess took aim, then scan blared back at her with solid green blips and comm crackled urgently. "Jess!"

"Yep, I see it." Jess lifted her fingers off the firing controls but didn't remove her hands from them. "Broadcast our ident."

Dev did so, blasting out the signal that defined their craft type and serial number across a wide band.

"Incoming, incoming."

"That's Jason." Jess keyed comms to sideband. "Tac 1, Tac 2, Tac 3, stand down. Potential friendly."

"Potential?" Doctor Dan watched the screens with interest.

"You never know." Jess keyed to main comms and selected one of the emergency short-range channels they used. "BR270006 calling BR083003, copy." She listened to the crackling. "Jason?"

Blast of static. "Holy shit! Jess!"

"Definitely Jason." Their speed slowed as they closed in with the two oncoming carriers.

"They are damaged," Dev said. "Twenty five percent power output, and very fractured external skin."

"Jason, go back and land. We'll follow you in."

"Who you got there?" Jason's voice came back at once. "Scan's nothing but scrap in this thing."

"April and Mike and their techs," Jess said. "Me and Dev, and the doc." She watched the two crafts carefully, seeing them shift off axis and try to hover on jets that were visibly sputtering. "We're just coming back from the other side."

"Op codes are correct," Dev said. "But those machines are severely non optimal." She started a calibration scan, moving away from the erratically shifting craft. "There are three persons on board. One in the closer carrier, two in the other one."

"Okay, Jess," Jason's voice crackled through. He sounded exhausted. "Fucking glad it's you."

Yeah. "Tac 2, 3, standby to land on that rock pile," Jess instructed. "Drop in on the east side."

"Ack."

"Ack."

Dev trimmed her landing jets as she followed Jason's carrier in, close enough now to see the horrible damage. One engine wasn't functioning at all, and there were rents across the back and side of it that had taken out part of the clear plas as well.

Worse than she'd done her first flight, in fact. Dev checked the register and confirmed the second craft belonged to Elaine and Tucker, and that Jason seemed to be alone in his. She wondered what that meant, and hoped it didn't mean something bad had happened to Brent. Though it seemed likely, since things right now were so difficult.

But her fears were unfounded, as she gently settled the carrier on top of a pile of rocks near the water, and spotted Brent's powerful form climbing up from the waterline to meet them.

He was dripping wet, and there was a fish in one hand, large and silvery and still twitching. He looked over at them as they settled on the uneven surface, and Dev saw a look of relief on his face.

"Now let's see what the hell's been going on." Jess released her restraints and stood up, slapping the holster with her hand blaster on it to her flight suit before she headed for the hatch. "Set up a long scan, Dev. Don't want to get caught with my ass on this rock pile."

"Yes." Dev started that up, as she heard the thump of the hatch opening. A blast of cold, wet, salty air blew in. She watched Jess and Doctor Dan emerge from around the side of the carrier and walk toward where Jason had gotten his carrier safely landed.

She finished setting up the scan and released her belts, pausing to stop and get her jacket and put it on before she headed for the outside. The ramp was only partially extended, as the rocks were preventing it from fully deploying. She carefully transferred her weight from it to the slippery stones as she got outside.

The line of dark clouds was moving ominously closer, and she fastened the jacket's catches as she made her way across the rocks. April, Mike, Doug and Chester caught up with her as they reached the others, where Elaine and Tucker had also arrived to hear Jason starting to explain what had happened to Jess.

"Fucking disaster." He sat down on a rock nearby. "Big ass fucking disaster. We started getting weird ass scan not long after you left." He rested his elbows on his knees. "Three, maybe four hours. Everyone thought it was just some strange met or something, but we kept losing long range scan, and then short range was going in and out. So Bain asked me and Lain to do a standard patrol."

Elaine also sat down, bracing her hands behind her. She had a painful looking burn on one cheek, and had been limping. "So we did," she said. "Six hours, until we saw a big storm coming in and figured we should get back inside before it got to us. On the way back to the base, all hell broke loose."

Jess was leaning on a tall boulder, her arms crossed over her chest. She remained silent however.

"We were about a quarter hour out from the pad when we started getting squirts on the emergency freq, but they didn't make sense. Power outages, things going crazy, the pad roof opening. Couldn't tell what was going on, but then we got into visual and we knew."

"We knew." Elaine echoed him. "We could see the tonks blasting at the side walls."

Jess looked grim.

"So we came in from the west and went to work," Elaine said. "Did the best we could. Figured we were making some headway when the storm came out over us and we ducked out of it, but they didn't."

"They kept attacking," Jason said "Every system we had was being blasted by met and they just kept flying." He glanced at Jess. "Someone mighta mentioned they came up with that instead of that grow shit."

"They're connected," Doctor Dan said quietly.

Both agents looked hard at him.

"It's some kind of energy transforming system," Kurok said. "Originally transferring hydro to photosynthesis, but someone found out how to use it to change EMF polarity and let it slide past instead of disrupting."

Everyone was briefly silent, watching him with intent eyes.

"Sorry," Doctor Dan said to Jess, after the silence had become uncomfortable. "What with everything else we really didn't have a chance to talk about it."

"Anyway," Jason continued. "We were trying to find a way around the storm when we heard you incoming." He looked at Jess. "Whatever the hell was going on just got crazier then. We saw Bain get out." His expression only twitched a little, but the effect expressed his feelings about that more explicitly than words would have.

"Yeah," Jess said. "So then what?"

"They got the base sealed," Elaine said. "Complete lockdown. No matter what those bastards wanted they weren't getting in. So we took off."

"Lock down," Jess murmured. "No comms?"

"Nothing. Sealed like a virgin outsider," Jason confirmed. "Wouldn't respond to emergency, to squirts, idents, nothing. We got out of there before they came back with something bigger to blow the doors open with. Headed out after your trail, but then we went headlong into all of them trying to get back."

"That was a long ass fight," Elaine said. "If they hadn't been tweaking these things we'd be vapor right now. As it was, we only got away because they got some kind of recall and took off."

"Probably was Bock, calling them in to skunk us at the pole." Jess spoke quietly into the wind-ruffled air. "He's dead. I killed him after I found out he turned us over to them." She added, watching their jaws drop. "I've seen North. If Ten looks like that, we might as well go hunt p—" She caught the frown on Dev's face and stopped. "I mean, scrounge. Maybe take over the pole again and see what we can live on."

"Bock." Elaine spoke the name slowly. "He was the hole?"

"He was a hole," Jess said. "In more ways than one. Though he didn't start to be so much of an ass until lately." Her expression turned thoughtful, and she glanced at Dev. "In fact, not until after we came back from that second run."

Jason exhaled heavily. "Anyway we just barely got to this place, and we've been hanging out here trying to fix these damn old buses enough to get back home." He paused. "Whatever home is now."

Jess regarded the incoming weather. "With that coming in to hit us, I think you should leave the damn things here and come on ours. We managed to get through our mission mostly intact." She regarded the three other carriers. "Let's lift, and find some shelter other than this rock, which is...what...Bermuda shoals?"

Jason nodded. "Sounds good." He stood up. "Glad you made it." He waved his hand. "Let's pack up and get moving. Brent, sorry we wasted your time fishing."

"S'okay." Brent regarded the fish with his usual glum expression. "No idea what to do with it anyhow. Figured we'd do it raw." He glanced at Jess. "Though I heard you can cook 'em."

"I can. Just not now." Jess sighed. "Hell. Maybe if Ten is a graveyard I'll take you all back to Drake's Bay with me. Make my family's day."

Doctor Dan snorted lightly under his breath, his lips twitching. "I see not much has changed there."

Jess produced a brief grin, then pointed to the carriers. "Let's go."

Tucker and Brent went to grab kits and everyone else headed for the three carriers, Jason letting them all go ahead as he dropped back with Jess. "Hey."

"Hey," Jess repeated.

"You sure about that space doc?"

Jess nodded. "Yeah. He's okay."

"You figure out what his background is?" Jason asked. "There's some weird stuff we heard about him, and with all this scamming bullshit going on, don't want to take a piece of it back with us. He can get lost between here and there, you know what I mean?"

"I know what you mean." She kept her voice down, watching Doctor Dan and his protégé heading for her craft. "Yeah, I found out what his deal was. We can talk later about it, but he's okay."

"He was us?"

"He was us," Jess confirmed. "Matter of fact, he was my dad's partner."

Jason almost tripped and went sprawling, saved only by Jess grabbing his arm and steadying him. "What?"

"Yeah, small fucking world, huh? We'll talk later." She gave him a slight shove toward April's carrier. "G'wan. We got enough troubles without inventing any from him."

She got back on board as Dev was spooling the engines up and she sat down with a sigh. "Dev, lift, then give me full power. I'm gonna blow up those crates." She settled into her position and keyed up the guns, pulling down the restraints and buckling them in an absent motion.

She was glad they'd found Jason and Elaine. Of all the agents at

Ten, she liked them the best, and she had the most confidence that they weren't part of the problem.

At the last minute, Brent scrambled on board and hit the hatch lock. "Hullo," he said, looking uncomfortable. "Jase said to fly with you."

Jess had to smile inwardly. Jason was one of the few who would challenge her judgment and act to protect her, even if she had no need or want of it. And he knew she wouldn't likely shoot him in the head in response. Not that Brent was an agent, but he was big, and muscular, and he'd take orders from her.

And he wasn't a bio alt, whose creator was, in Jason's mind, still suspect.

Dev turned around and smiled at him. "There's a seat up here." She indicated the jump seat next to her console. "But please hurry. We're starting to get wind alerts."

Brent looked a smidgen happier, stowing his kit in the locker and going up to join Dev in the pilot's station. "Hey."

"Hey," Dev responded. "I'm glad you aren't damaged."

He had a few scrapes on him, but he half grinned in response. "Yeah, back."

Dev got them underway, feeling better about the mission now that she knew for sure that not everyone in the citadel had become dead. She'd developed a mild liking for Brent, and thought they had gotten along pretty well before all this started.

She handed him over a set of ear cups and got the carrier to altitude, pausing and rotating as she sent power to the guns. A moment later, the carrier vibrated as Jess fired, blowing first one and then the other damaged craft and sending pieces of them flying off into the roiling ocean.

"One way to get a new bus," Brent said. "Damned piece of crap."

Dev took them into a tight curve, then headed northwest, running a long scan to determine if they were going to make the coast before the storm caught them, nudging the throttles forward and taking them to full speed.

They crackled through the sound barrier just as a thunder boomed overhead.

Chapter Fourteen

THEY MADE THE coast with a minute to spare. Dev dove at full speed toward the cliffs, already losing some control as lightning exploded around them, both Brent and Jess yelling advice at her and pointing to barely seen gaps in the stone wall through the blinding rain.

She saw the slot canyon and turned the carrier on its side, not entirely due to its narrow width. The sudden motion made her passengers yelp and grab for handholds, giving her a moment's peace to get the jets under control and fight off the violent gusts of wind.

She hoped the others were behind her as she barreled through the gap, spotting the crooked entrance to what seemed to be a cave on the left hand side wall. She aimed for it, dropping down and cutting the engines as a lightning flash blasted the top of the carrier, waiting a breathless five seconds for the charge to dissipate before she kicked in the landing jets.

Then they were inside. It was a bare crevice and there were cracks and gaps letting in torrents of water, but the wind cut out and gave her control to land near one wall, clearing space behind her as the two other carriers piled in hot on her tail.

The storm rolled in on top of them and there were so many lighting strikes it blinded scan completely, and nearly deafened all of them until she cut the sensors and shut down everything hard.

Power was crackling everywhere around them. It was worse than the first storm she'd felt outside Quebec, and Dev had all she could handle to make sure the systems were safe and the guns deactivated. Brent activated the heavy shield, that slid down by gravity alone, and the entire craft vibrated with the force of the thunder booming overhead.

"Holy crap," Brent said.

"Indeed," Doctor Dan said. "Forgot how much I don't miss weather in space."

Dev was glad the shield was down as something thumped against the carrier with enough force to make it move on its skids. "Thank you," she told Brent. "I'm not really used to all this weather either."

Brent snorted, giving her a baldly skeptical look. "I can't freaking imagine what you had to fly through up there then."

That was, she supposed, a compliment. "Mostly sims," she said. "They emulated weather, but not like this."

He studied her. "No shit, that first time out with us was your first real gig?"

She nodded, giving him a sheepish little smile.

"Fuck." Brent shook his head in bemusement.

"I'm going to make sure those other two landed okay." Jess had her jacket on. She got her hood up and sealed a moment before she hit the hatch, then jumped back and half turned as a blast of lightning outlined the opening in brilliance.

"Maybe not."

Doctor Dan dove across and slammed the hatch shut, throwing his arm over his head as another blast nearly came inside. "Bloody hell."

Jess blinked furiously, her hand shielding her eyes. "Shit."

Dev got up and went over to her, putting a hand on her arm. "Jess, are you damaged?"

"Over flash." Jess shut her eyes and dropped back into her seat. "What the hell is going on with this weather? This something else they're cooking up, Doc?"

"Not that I know of, no." Doctor Dan cautiously picked his head up, and then moved back to his makeshift seat. "One thing we learned the hard way, eh? You can't screw with mother nature." He studied Jess. "You all right, Jesslyn?"

Jess kept her eyes closed, still seeing the after flashes against the inside of her eyelids. She felt a moment of narrowly avoided massive stupidity, and the warmth of Dev's fingers on her shoulder was guiltily comforting.

After a brief moment the warmth increased, as Dev's hip pressed against her shoulder. Jess opened one eye halfway, and peeked up. To her relief, though there was still an after flash, she could make out Dev's features as Dev looked at her with that deep, intense concern. "Well you don't have two heads. I'm probably okay."

Both of Dev's eyebrows hiked up.

"And I could see that, so it seals the deal." Jess leaned back in her seat and relaxed a little, opening her other eye cautiously and very glad they had most of the internal lighting off. "That was a dumbass thing to do. Thought we had more cover in here."

"We were talking about weather before," Brent said. "Gettin' worse. You said it. Ain't nothing like this I remember from when I was a kid."

Jess considered that, thinking back to her childhood on the coast, and the days and days she'd spent outside on the water. "No, me either," she said. "Met said, back at Ten, storms were increasing. Problem is no one knew why."

"Figure this was what Syd drove through?"

Doctor Dan cleared his throat "Syd? From North?"

"Used to be." Brent glanced at him. "Oh, right. Happened after you were gone."

Kurok looked from him to Jess and back, his fair eyebrows lifting in question.

"They took out North station. Seven of them got out, two made it to Ten alive. Barely," Jess said. "Probably now it was a waste of time, and waste of Dev's heroics."

"They destroyed the base?" Doctor Dan repeated "Both of them?"

Jess heard the note in his voice, and smiled grimly to herself, knowing that ferocious urge to retaliate down to the nth degree. Kurok was one of them, all right. No matter how long he'd spent up on that station, or what he'd done up there, that loyalty was baldly evident. "Yeah. With that energy weapon, we think."

Kurok exhaled. "Stupid."

"Comms out," Brent said. "Saw the other two land safe, though."

"Thanks Brent." Jess remained where she was, closing her eyes again. "Guess we should just stay put and wait for the worst of it to pass." She ran a few things through her console, bare responses from the few systems Dev had left running. They had at least an hour to wait, she figured, before they could move out again, go west, and south, and come in to the citadel to see what was left.

If anything was. The idea of moving on to Drake's Bay was becoming more real, and now she had to consider the idea that bringing a squad of Interforce home might also make it the other side's next target.

Never let the other side have the last blood. Wasn't that the rule? Jess let out a slow breath.

The rain redoubled, its thundering roar and the booming overhead was almost continuous. They all fell silent and sat quietly, listening to the noise. Jess checked the met screen again and then shrugged, leaning back and composing herself to grab a power nap.

Funny how that was so easy now. She was in the middle of a death storm on a mission from hell, and she felt her body relax as though she was back in the citadel in her own bed. When Josh had been her driver...hell, even before, she'd have been gulping kack and taking stims the whole damn time.

There was something tremendously fucked up going on with her. But a nugget of pragmatism shrugged its shoulders since really, what else was there to do?

She heard Kurok settle himself on the shelf, apparently with the same idea. "Just get as much rest as you can," she said. "Not much else to do until this passes."

"Yup," Brent said. "Anyway bad news can always wait."

Dev set the long range scanner up to do a continual sweep, then she tilted her control chair back and let her muscles relax, her peripheral vision catching sight of Brent getting as comfortable as he could on the jump seat.

The carriers weren't really meant for comfort. The seats were functional but mostly unpadded, the other surfaces hard and unyielding. It was meant for relatively short missions, even the food stocks were generally set for no more than a week.

But if you were tired enough, you could sleep, and Dev felt that stealing over her, the thrum of the rain becoming almost hypnotic. She half turned her gimbaled chair so she could see Jess's station, and after a few minutes watching her rest, let her own eyes close.

THUNDER WAS STILL rumbling as Dev brought the carrier in a wide arc to the southwest, coming up on a line roughly close to the one she'd used the last time they'd approached the citadel. They'd received no communications from the facility and Jess was standing behind her, hand resting on her chair as she watched the craggy slope approach.

"Crap," Brent said. "Place looks dark."

"There are no emissions from the facility." Dev confirmed. "Scan shows no pattern."

Jess sighed. "Dev, go for the side entrance I told you about the last time." She was already in her battle suit. Now she went to the area near the hatch and added her long blaster to its leg holster. "I'm sure this is gonna suck. Brent, tell the other two to drop after me, and we'll meet just inside that hatchway."

Brent trimmed the comp responses and squirted them to the others. He nodded, and continued his work.

It was raining outside. There had been no response to their secure channel squirt, and no reaction to their presence. Jess had a bad feeling about all of that and steeled herself to find inside what they'd found in North base.

"Jess," Dev said. "Incoming message, single band, on base frequencies."

Jess darted back over to her and studied comms intently. "Huh."

Brent craned his neck to look. "That's base," he said. "Took 'em long enough."

"Should I make a standard contact?" Dev asked. "The signal is correct." She waited for Jess to nod, then keyed in the frequency. "BR270006 to base. Copy?"

There was a brief silence, then comms lit up. "BR270006, centops. Standby for class A scan."

Jess nodded. "That's right," she said. "Brent, tell the others what's going on."

Brent nodded.

Doctor Dan had eased up on the other side of her, his hands on the back of Dev's chair. "Hopefully finding us inside won't trigger a destruct sequence."

Jess eyed him. "Was that a joke?"

"Maybe." Kurok produced a faint, wry smile.

They felt the scan, heavy and intense, passing slowly through the craft, leaving behind a tingle that had an almost slimy consistency. Jess tried not to hold her breath, her hand flexing as the scan passed through the chips in it, causing a deep itch.

"What's that?" Dev asked Doctor Dan, in a low tone.

"Full genetiscan," he replied briefly. "They'll match that to the files, to make sure whoever on this carrier is safe."

"I see." Dev adjusted her ear cup. She could hear the faint hum of the radio sub carrier and tuned it a little, waiting for a response. "I'm glad someone's there, at least."

"BR270006, confirmed. Please have your flight approach emergency entrance twelve south, be aware there is no facility."

"That doesn't sound good," Brent said. "Bay must be trashed." He cocked his head slightly. "That sounded like Mike."

"It did," Jess said. "Dev, the south twelve is down near the base of the mountain there." She pointed at a now visible half round opening near the ground. "Hatch is open. Usually they don't use that for things this big. Just send the collecting trucks out that way."

"Okay." Dev dropped their altitude to almost ground level and started a slow approach, tuning scan as they angled around the barren rock surface and came in line with the entrance. She turned on the front floodlights and engaged the landing jets, aiming for the very center of the bare opening. "There does not seem to be much power on."

"Scan was on emergency beam," Brent said. "They must be on batts."

Jess drummed her fingers on the back of the chair. "Hold up, Dev." she said, her eyes sweeping the inside of the cavernous entry. "Tell them we see some obstruction and we're going to find an alternate entry."

Dutifully, Dev relayed the message.

"You can see inside there?" Doctor Dan asked, in a quizzical tone.

"No. Well, yes," Jess said. "I can see inside, but I don't really see any blockage. I'm bluffing."

"BR270006, there is no reported damage in the entry. Please proceed." Comms crackled overhead, as Dev piped it through, half turning to look at Jess in question. "Also, Jason wants to speak to you on side-band five."

Jess picked up a headset and put it on, tucking the ear cup into her ear. "Jase?"

"What's the deal?" he asked. "You think we won't fit?"

"Something doesn't smell right," Jess answered honestly. "Why that bay?"

"Only one clear enough?"

Maybe. Jess studied the bay, calling up in her head where it was positioned in the citadel, and what led to it. "Go on and enter. I'm going to go park on five deck." She put her hands on Dev's shoulders. "Take us to that place I showed you first," she told Dev. "Jase, if they ask, just say I didn't think we'd all fit. Keep in comm sync though."

"Ack." Jason clicked off, and then April's carrier moved slowly ahead of them, toward the indicated bay with Mike's coming in behind her.

Jess watched them approach for a minute, then squeezed Dev's shoulder. "G'wan."

Dev gently eased them across the harsh and stony ground on the back side of the citadel, the rain pattering noisily against the stone and running in rivulets down the slope. "Centops, this is BR270006. We are sending Tac 2 and Tac 3 ahead." Dev spoke quietly into her comm. "We have propulsion damage and are not certain of close in steering."

Both Doctor Dan and Jess turned and looked at her in surprise.

"Nice." Brent nodded. "Last thing they want is a bus slamming in there."

"Acknowledged, BR270006. Standing by."

Dev fired the side jets and slowly brought the nose up, running through some steering tests in apparent random that ended up with the carrier lifted up several levels and coming even with a small, half ledge midway up the slope. "Is that the one?" she said. "I didn't want us to get in trouble for refusing to do what they were saying."

Jess looked amused. "So you lied to them."

"Yes." Dev nodded. "We know how to do that," she added, after a pause. "It's not something they teach us."

Doctor Dan chuckled softly under his breath. "She's right. We don't teach that. It's part of what makes us human." He took a step back. "Are you going to go in that door?" He asked Jess.

"Yes." Jess went over and retrieved her long rifle, going to the hatch and seating the rest of her weapons more firmly. "Put me down gently, Dev. I don't want to use the drop pack. They'll pick up the plasma ejection." She flexed her hands. "If I get in, I'll open the big door and you can land."

"Want some company?" Doctor Dan asked.

"After I open the door. It's keyed to me. Seeing yours and Brent's body parts flying off into the mist isn't on my schedule at the moment." Jess could sense the wall coming closer and she put her hands on either side of the hatch, waiting. "Open when ready, Devvie."

"Ah," Doctor Dan said softly. "You're the safety officer."

Jess turned her head and looked at him, a faint smile on her face. "Senior agent. If they haven't re-keyed it. We'll find out in a minute."

The hatch opened, and a blast of cold rain smacked her, sharpening her attention before she jumped out of the carrier, landing on the nearby rock ledge with a faint skidding motion. She could feel the edge of ice in the downpour and quickly went to a small angle in the rock and stepped inside it, bumping open a scan plate and putting her hand on it.

Now, one of two things would happen. Either she'd get blasted half to hell, or the door would open. Jess was tired, despite her nap, and didn't really want to be blown out into the rain.

She felt the tickle against her left palm, the remedial scan finding the chips embedded in her and keying to them. After a long pause, she heard a soft click, then felt a vibration where her shoulder was pressed against the stone and then an opening appeared to her left, outlined in lurid blue.

Deep scan. She drew her breath and stepped inside, feeling the penetration to her very core. There was no way to fake this out, it did a walk of the entire DNA chain and she swore she could feel it do just that as it wound inside her and the bio scrape held her in stasis until it was done.

Either you passed, or you died. It was an isolated system, not hooked up to centops, and only the principal and the sec comp who keyed it knew whose codes would work and those two were never command level. An obscure and somewhat cynical check and balance.

Abruptly the scan broke off and released her, and she started breathing again. Apparently Bain's note hadn't gotten to security, nor been deemed official, and she was still a grunt.

Jess smiled grimly, as she drew her blaster and very slowly moved inside, feeling the change as her vision flattened and sounds become sharper and more clear. A small hallway doglegged to the right and she slid into it, listening hard.

It was cold, and damp, and only emergency lighting was on. She didn't hear anything other than faint mechanical, so she moved further in, getting around the dog leg and into the larger area beyond.

It was empty and silent.

The emergency bay was generally shut down and unused at the busiest of times. There were a few lockers against the wall that had gear and weapons in them, and at the far end past where a carrier could park, there was an entrance into the ops level of the station.

Everything might be on the up and up. Jess went over to the manual controls of the large external door and triggered them, opening the casing and exposing the very old fashioned and completely hand operated chains that opened the hanger bay. She unlocked them and holstered her blaster, cautiously starting the process of ratcheting the bay open.

Rain spattered in immediately, along with a powerful beam of light from the front of the carrier, waiting patiently outside. Jess got the door opened enough to let Dev land, and the landing jets flared as Dev slid inside, cutting off and dropping the carrier to its extending skids in very short order.

The hatch popped open and both Kurok and Brent hopped out. "Jase's screaming for ya," Brent said. "They tried to slam the door shut on them, that new kid got their bus halfway out and blocked it." He gave Jess an appreciative look. "You called it."

"Yeah." Jess sighed. "Sometimes I hate being right." She climbed up inside the carrier and went over to where Dev was shutting down the engines. "Hey."

"Hold on a moment," Dev said into comms. "Jess..."

"Yeah, I know." Jess picked up a headset and put it on, keying the comms to the backup board. "Finish shutting down." She pressed the ear cup to her ear. "Jase?"

"Fuckers!" He bawled in her ear. "Where the hell did you go? We're hauling ass across the rocks, fuckers were in there waiting for us with blasters. April let off a barrage and we got out while they were picking up their own heads and asses."

"Keep coming along the ridge line to the big gray rock. Check behind it." Jess sighed. "Thought this was too easy."

"So they got this place." Jason was still fuming, sounds of the storm surrounding him. "Lazy ass jacktards, let 'em take it."

"Kids with you?"

Brief silence. "What? Oh." Jason coughed a little. "Yeah everyone's here. You said that big rock? What...oh." There was another silence. "I see it. Be there in a minute. Out."

Jess put the comm set down. "Shitcakes. Well, at least the place probably isn't a smoking hole."

"Yes." Dev was just climbing out of her seat. "I told centops we had mechanical difficulties, and they advised we were no longer on scan. I suggested it might be the angle we had to hold at." She turned and regarded Jess solemnly. "They did not call after that."

Jess sighed. "I'm going to have to shoot them all to get into bed with you, aren't I?"

Dev blinked a little, then issued a hesitant half grin.

Jess grinned back and motioned to the hatch. "Sooner I start the better." She put her hand on Dev's back as they walked down the carrier ramp and back into the bay. "Let me go wave them in and shut the door."

She ducked out into the rain and shaded her eyes, spotting six jacketed figures bolting along the rough ground headed toward her. They were hidden from the oversight above by a ridge of rock, and a minute later they gained the hatch and pelted inside.

Jason rambled to a halt, his jacket shedding rain everywhere "Fuckers!"

"Uh huh." Jess closed the manual hatch and looped the chain around the mechanism. "Keep it down. I'd rather them not be sure where the hell we are for the moment."

The rest of them shed their jackets and then gathered around her. "Did you know that was going to happen?" April asked, checking the blaster seated at her side.

"Still not sure what did happen. Not sure if this place is taken over, or they think we're outlaw," Jess said, in a calm voice. "Though based on the fact the hatch let me in, it's starting to look more like we got bad guys inside." She glanced around the cavern. "Not that you can see much in any case."

"Emergency power," Doctor Dan said, as he finished a circuit of the bay. "Could just be manual ops."

"Could be." Jess went across the bay past the carrier to the inner hallway and pulled out a panel, peering inside it. "Perimeter system is active, according to this."

Dev squirmed in next to her and peered at the old tech with interest. There was a very basic representation of the citadel, faded tracings of hallways and chambers, with dimly illuminated rings here and there. "This is the central place, isn't it?"

"Yeah." Jess put her fingertip on a spot near it. "Problem with that is, if we go through any of these gates they'll know where we are."

"That's a bad thing?" Brent asked.

"If someone other than us is in charge up there? Yeah." Jess rested her hands against the outer walls of the console. "You know how centops is. They've got the big over scan that shows them where everyone in the city is." She pondered the problem. "I'm sure they're on their way here now."

"If they know where it is." Jason folded his arms across his brawny chest. "Not everyone did. If they've taken over, no guarantee anyone told them about this."

"No guarantee they didn't. Depends what jacktard was in ops." Elaine said. "Glad Sandy'd already bought it. She'd have had them waiting outside with an antipersonnel mine."

"Well." Jess left the hatch and went to the small and nondescript door that would lead further into the citadel. "No sense hanging around letting them have time to figure it out. Let's go." She cautiously palmed the lock and felt it give way under pressure from her shoulder, moving outward into a tight, enclosed space. She eased into it and cleared the way for the others, moving forward into the chute like corridor until she was at the far end.

There was a turn to the left, and then another, the walls melding at the end of that from the natural gray rock to the smooth surface of the inside of the citadel.

She drew in a breath, and the air smelled familiar. Clean and sterile, with a hint of mech on it and a faint tinge of salt air, this far down, this low in the facility. No stink of battle, or of burning, she noted.

Another ten minute's walk east, and she'd encounter the rough-hewn hallway that led to the intake cavern, and on the far side of the corridor they were about to emerge into the entrance to the lower spaces where bio alts lived.

Jess paused, and considered that, as the rest of her little gang filled up the hall behind her. She'd been down there maybe once, maybe twice, just on a fam tour years back, and remembered very little of it.

Cautiously, she approached the opening, its slanted gap blending into the walls and making it invisible when looked at from the outside. She paused just short of it and listened, but no sounds trickled in, no motion or even a far off klaxon. A gentle touch on her back nearly made her gasp, but she bit the inside of her lip and looked back over her shoulder.

Dev was there, her pale hair distinctive in the shadows. She held up her portable scan. "There are people approaching," she whispered. "They have weapons."

Jess glanced at the screen. "Yeah. That's not good news." She moved forward and slipped into the outer hall, finding it dark and empty. Not surprising since these were the very lower levels of the facility and only really frequented when something needed fixing, or you wanted to get to the cavern.

Jess had always been after the latter, and had found the entryway to the manual chamber years back, but never bothered wondering what it was for until she'd been taken there the night she'd made senior. She'd always figured it was a storage space, for the gear they used on the outside.

Everyone did. No one was encouraged to ask about it. She looked down the long, empty corridor and walked quickly along it, spotting the first distinctive outline of scan at the other end.

"Psst," Kurok hissed softly, and pointed at a dark, sealed doorway to the right.

"What?" Jess looked at it. "We go in there, they'll have us cornered. It's a storage chamber."

"It isn't." Doctor Dan went over and opened a panel. "At least, it wasn't." He amended, peering at the circuitry inside. "You used to be able to get down into bio alt living quarters from here."

Jess studied him with interest. "What does that get us?" she asked, one eye watching the scan console. "They're probably in there scared crapless."

Kurok keyed in a few codes. "That's probably true. But they're far less likely to shoot us than the people on their way here. So unless you're prepared for a very long and probably lethal firefight in the hall, let's see if we can find another way into central."

With a faint click the door opened. They slipped inside and Jess got her hand light on, shining it around a bare and apparently abandoned chamber before Kurok shut the door behind them. "Not much in here."

"No." April got her own light on and stepped to one side. "There's a portal there. Looks like it hasn't been used for a while, but that..." She stepped closer and peered at a looming piece of mech and her nose twitched a little. "What's that?"

"Processing unit," Doctor Dan said, quietly. "That's the outer wall skin there. This is where they handled bio alt dead." He fell silent, then went to another door on the far side of the chamber. "This should be a lift." He touched a palm pad and lights came on in the chamber, low and stark.

Dev eyed the big machine, feeling a chill come over her. She remembered the processing she'd witnessed and felt a desire to get as far away from the device as she could.

Elaine had been listening at the door and now she took a step back, drawing her blaster. "We're out of time. They're coming in."

"Keep trying, Doc." Jess joined her, and Jason took up a position next to the processor. "We'll keep 'em occupied."

"I'm sure," Doctor Dan muttered, as he pecked at the console. "Damn it."

Dev and Brent peered at the controls from either side of him, while the other techs plastered their backs against the wall. They'd just gotten into position when the door blasted open and then the room was filled with plasma fire.

Jess dropped to her belly, her eyes taking in the attack squad and absorbing the clothes and the stance, freeing her trigger finger to pinpoint them. She took out the first one and then blew an arm off the second, her body halfway protected by the step she was sheltered behind.

It was loud.

The attackers yelled in battle language that wasn't theirs, and they had full armor on. Jess heard April let out a yell and saw a figure flying past her, but she squirmed around and put herself between the bad guys and that door and just kept firing.

The armor took a lot of hits, but Jason kept up a crossfire in counterpoint to hers, and after a few minutes the door closed again and they were inside with six dead enemy bodies, a room full of plasma smoke and the smell of burned flesh.

"Everyone okay?" Jess asked, after a brief pause.

"Yeah." Jason came out from around the processor, going to the door and swiftly opening it to peer out. "That was ridiculous."

"Bullshit." Elaine grimaced at a long burn down her arm. "But now we know. It's them."

Jess got up and rolled a body over, examining the full armor. "Any luck, Doc?"

"Yes and no," Kurok said. "I got the door to trigger, but most of us can't go through it. It's keyed to organisms with biosynaptic control collars."

Dev reached up and touched her neck in reflex. "Like mine?"

Doctor Dan studied her somberly. "Yes." He glanced at Jess. "They locked it down from inside. Apparently someone took some care to keep them safe."

Dev went to the door, hauling up as Jess got there ahead of her. "No, she can't," Jess said, her body blocking the door. "We've got no idea what's down there. They could all be compromised."

"They could be," Kurok said in a mild tone. "Nevertheless, she's the only one of us who can go."

"They're going to come back," Jason said. "I can hear an alarm."

"Yeah." Elaine pulled her head back in. "Lot of boots heading this way."

Dev regarded her tall and irritated obstacle. "Jess." She could see her partner was in discomfort. "I think I could do good work in there."

"You do good work everywhere." Jess studied her intently. "But you've got no idea what's down there."

"That's true. But if I go, I'll find out," she responded in a mild reasonable tone. "And if I can get to the control sets, I can let you all in."

Jess was aware of Kurok's eyes on her, but he remained silent as she weighed the risks.

"Incoming!" Elaine yelled, getting back from the door as Jason and Mike grabbed the dead bodies and jammed them against the inside of it.

No real choice. "Go on," Jess said. "Be careful, huh?" She moved away from the inner door and took up a position in the angle of the alcove, taking aim at the doorframe and putting a thin bead of plasma around it.

"I will." Dev touched her on the side and moved to the door, as Doctor Dan keyed in something then gave her a nod. She went into the square space and felt scan take her, the collar on her neck twitching a little as she closed her eyes.

It seemed to get hot. She felt a moment of panic. Then the inner panel slid open and there was a step down and she moved over, and the panel shut with a bang behind her.

She was alone.

Then she turned and a second door opened, and she was facing a wall of bodies, and a bright light blinded her.

INSTINCTIVELY, DEV THREW her hand up in front of her eyes and then closed them, half turning her head. "Ow." She could see the flashes from the intensity of it on the inside of her eyelids. "Please stop!"

The light shifted, and she heard voices, whispers that resolved into her short name. Cautiously, Dev opened her eyes and looked at the crowd, seeing row after row of bio alts, all staring at her.

"NM-Dev-1." It was one of the Kaytees. "How did you get here?"

Dev blinked a few times and let her hand drop. "Hello Kaytee," she said. "We just arrived at this facility. What's the situation?"

The bio alts were very upset, she could tell. She could now see anxious faces and there were smudges of dirt and bruises on the Kaytee's face.

There were three or four Kaytees in fact, and some Beeayes, in the front. Behind them, she saw the other sets, some of them hurt, many with blood on them as well.

"Incorrect people came and did bad things," the Kaytee closest to her said. "They made a lot of natural borns dead, and some of us, too." He showed his arm, which was covered in a clumsy bandage. "We can't get to med."

"That's bad," Dev said. "Are there many of them, the bad ones?"

"Yes," a second Kaytee said. "They came in through the big bay, and the place where the shuttle comes. They made the base systems incorrect." He looked exhausted. "Nothing is working. There were some big explosions, and only batteries are up."

Dev nodded. "They have a new gun," she said. "I was at North Base. It made everything burned there."

"Yes," a Beeaye said. "That's what we heard." He winced, and held his left arm with his right, close to his body. "The natural borns made us come in here, and locked the hatches."

"The bad ones, or ours?" Dev asked.

"Ours. They were afraid more of us would be made dead. Tech Super Clint made us come in here," the Beeaye said. "We don't know what is happening upstairs. The systems are all down, but they put on the scan to keep the incorrect people out from here. They said no one could get in."

"Yes," Dev said, again. "I was upstairs, and I was the only one who could come through the door." She pointed behind her. "We came in a secret way, and now I have to make it so the people who were with me can come down here."

The Kaytee looked doubtful. "Will they hurt us? They told us to stay here and not let anyone in."

"It's some of the agents. My partner, Jess, and also, Doctor Dan. They want to fix things."

"Doctor Dan?" The name echoed back from many lips. "Doctor Dan's here?" The Kaytee asked. "They said the incorrect people took him far away and made him dead!"

"We rescued him," Dev said, knowing a moment of intense, personal pride at the reaction, and the widening eyes of these, her own kind. "He was far away on the other side. We had to do a lot of difficult things to get him back. But we did, and he's here, in the other room."

"The bad people here said they would stop doing incorrect things if the natural borns gave them the one you are with," a Beeaye said, hesitantly. "The one you called Jess? They are very angry about that one."

"I know," Dev said. "We did bad things to them. But that was because they were keeping some of the natural born from here from coming back." She glanced behind her "But we have to let them in here or I think the bad people above are going to make them dead."

"If we let them in here the bad people may make us dead," the Kaytee said. "They already made a lot of us dead. We don't want to get hurt again."

Dev straightened up, the faint lights catching on the piping and insignia she was wearing. Her collar was covered and theirs weren't, and she wondered if they viewed her as one of them, or one of the natural born. "We have to let them in. It's the correct thing."

The group hesitated, many eyes going to the Kaytees as the most advanced of the sets among them. But it wasn't a Kaytee who finally spoke up.

The Beeaye nearest Dev shook his head. "They may make us dead anyway. It doesn't matter. We should help Doctor Dan."

Now a lot of voices erupted, and heads nodded "We have to help Doctor Dan," one of the Peeares said. "He will keep them from making us dead. He'll know what to do."

Dev waited, as the discussion went around. She knew she had no way of forcing the question, so she waited to see what the result was going to be before she took things into her own hands. She had the programming for that, and it was her job.

She would help Jess and Doctor Dan, even if the others refused to do so.

Maybe the Kaytee knew that because he looked at her, and he nodded. "We should help Doctor Dan," he said. "And Beeaye is right. They might make us dead anyway."

They cleared the way to the control consoles, where three bio alts were sitting and watching screens. Dev went up onto the platform and one of them moved to make room for her, letting her sit down. "They have systems locked upstairs," he said. "We can't touch anything."

Dev pulled the pad over and examined it. Then she keyed in a routine and entered her credentials, waiting to see what would happen. One of two things was likely, either the systems would stay locked, or they wouldn't.

After a moment the screen cleared and gave her access. She nodded and started keying in other things. "They did not block access from here for someone with operations credentials," she said. "That was not optimal for their objective."

Bio alts were all gathered around watching her attentively. "They did not expect any of us to have them," the Beeaye said. "You are the first."

"I am the first," Dev said. She called up the routine for the door and studied it, mindful of the need to hurry. She didn't know what was going on in the outside room, but she didn't think it could be good based on the thumps and bangs that were transmitting through the stone and metal between her and where Jess was. "Get away from that access and be safe," she ordered. "I am going to open it."

Bio alts all scattered to the walls and crouched down, obeying her as if she was a natural born, even the Kaytees. Dev altered the programming and recompiled it, and an instant later there was chaos everywhere.

Dark clad bodies tumbled through the opening and fired back the way they came, then bigger fully armored forms came hauling through with a deflector, sending blasts back over everyone's heads.

Dev instinctively dove off the console and got behind it as the room filled with blaster fire, and falling bodies, and a lot of yelling. It smelled of burning substance and scorched stone and she tucked her head behind the panel and hoped Jess was okay.

She heard Jason, say "get down," and she closed her eyes, pressing against the wall as she heard a powerful explosion, and the vibration nearly sent her tumbling.

Screams broke out, and then, after another rattling explosion, she heard the sound of hatches sealing with a deep, ear impacting whumphing sound.

Then, abruptly, it was quiet.

Jason's voice broke it. "Fuck, that was close. I get 'em all?"

Dev got up, freezing when she saw the floor covered in bodies. "Oh." She blinked in the heavy smoke and felt her heart sink, as the impact hit her. "What did you do to them?" she asked Jason, her heart starting to race.

All bio alts, the ones she'd just been talking to, were on the ground, limp, unmoving.

Jason was half covered in blood and he stared at her, then looked across the space filled with bio alt dead. "Sorry," he said. "Didn't have time to code anything but us."

Dev took a step back and bumped into the console, feeling like she was going to be sick. She saw Doctor Dan start to move toward her, but a second later Jess was there instead, putting a hand on her shoulder. She looked up at her. "They let me open the door because I said they would be safe, and they believed me."

"They sent a bunch of them in after us," Jess said, in a quiet tone. "We were out of options, Dev." She looked around. "Check them. They might have just been coded for unco."

"Do we really have time for this?" Jason asked impatiently, falling silent when Jess's blaster came around and targeted him. "Did you just totally lose your mind?" he asked her. "They're bios."

Jess stared at him, then looked at Dev, then looked back at him. "I might have lost my mind, but not about this. Bios or not, they're ours. Check them."

"She's right," Doctor Dan said. "You're responsible for them. It's in the contract." He moved past Mike and April and went to the first of the bodies, lowering himself next to it. "They're not krill."

"It's not going to matter if they catch us in here. We'll be feeding the krill," Jason said. "We don't have time for this." He caught a motion and looked back at Jess, who had taken the safety off her blaster. "You're seriously going to shoot me?"

"Yes," Jess said. "But for insubordination under fire this time." She motioned the rest of the agents. "Check them."

She stayed by Dev's side as the agents started moving amongst bio alts, and joined Doctor Dan in kneeling by their side. "If those were our grenades, they should have had them passive coded. I helped test the damn things."

Jason shook his head and went to the group near the wall, stepping over the broken and obviously dead bodies of the enemy soldiers. Elaine had already knelt next to one of the AyeBees, touching the side of his face with relative gentleness.

Kurok looked up from a Kaytee. "They're hard down," he said. "But I think I can probably bring them back up."

Jess felt Dev's shoulders relax a little. "How long?"

Doctor Dan shook his head. "Don't know. No gear here." He stood up. "We can leave them where they are. They'll just stay down." He straightened slowly and rubbed his hands together. "Maybe this was the safest thing for them, Dev." He came up onto the platform. "Are you all right?"

Dev took a deep breath, and released it. "Yes. I think so." Her knees were shaking, but the feeling of wanting to throw up was easing, a little. "That was a terrible feeling, Doctor Dan."

"I know." He patted her on her other shoulder, since Jess had possession of the one closest to her. "So now what?" he asked Jess. "Now that we didn't get blown up, that is."

Jess sat down at the console and started accessing things. "First thing is, secure that damn door," she said. "This your login, Dev?"

"Yes." Dev sat down too, because she felt like she would fall down otherwise.

"Good work." Jess keyed through systems, mirroring the ones from centops and hoping no one up there was watching. "Surprised they didn't close—oh, okay I see what you did." She chuckled softly under her breath. "Clever, Devvie. Very clever."

When Dev didn't answer, Jess looked over at her, surprised to see a few tears sparkling on her face. She was leaning forward with her elbows on her knees and her hands were folded together, tense enough to have her knuckles show through the skin over them.

Kurok sat down next to her and patted her arm and Jess felt a surge of emotion that made her forget completely about the console. She half turned away and then saw all the rest of the agents and techs headed toward her, now that the fate of the bio alts appeared settled.

They were watching her. Jess felt briefly at a complete loss, all her instincts driving her to pay attention to the woman next to her, and the cold hard knowledge of her training that told her she better do otherwise or risk losing control of the group. Jason had already called her into question, and though he'd backed down, she knew the barb had legitimate sting.

Damn it.

With a good deal of effort, she wrenched back around just as April reached the platform, forcing her eyes to reread the screen twice before the details registered.

Jason braced his hands on the console and peered at the screen, apparently setting aside their previous disagreement. "So what's going on up there?" he said. "That centops?"

"Yeah," Jess muttered. "Just standard scan. Not sure what the hell they're doing, but they know we're here."

Mike and April sat down and started to key in screens, using general access that would be expected from bio alt area. "Maintenance is off line," Mike said. "Power's about twenty percent."

Brent came over and wedged himself on the other side of where Dev was sitting and cleared his throat self-consciously. "Thanks for getting us in," he said. "They were about to fry my ass in there."

"You're welcome," Dev answered quietly. "I'm glad everyone is safe."

Jess's hands started to twitch and she lost focus, not really caring what was on the screen in front of her. "Fuckers. I just want to get them out of here."

Jason patted her on the back. "Easy, Jesseroo. Don't lose your mind again on us. We'll get 'em out of here."

"They've got control of centops, and main ops," April said. "I can't get any parsing from there at all." She regarded the reporting stats. "Most of the systems are down. The bay is locked open, and it looks like there was a lot of boom in there."

"Yeah," Jess said. That's the one big place we're vulnerable, if that big hatch is open. But we've got scan in the corridors."

"Scan's off," Jason said. "Makes sense, or they'd be dropping like flies going through the halls."

Oh. Yeah. Right. "Well, then we can go through them, too, if they haven't figured out how to reset it to block us," Jess said. "Anyone want to guess what they want? What they're holding out for?"

"You," Jason said bluntly.

"That much for revenge?" Jess tilted her head and stared at him. "Get out of here."

Doctor Dan cleared his throat. "That's one detail I managed to ferret out. Sorry I neglected to mention it. I've been a bit distracted."

"Yeah me too." Jess turned away from the console and let her knee bump Dev's, getting a quick flash of those pale eyes and the briefest of grins in return. "So what did I do, outside blowing out half a mountain?"

"Their ruling council was meeting in it at the time," Doctor Dan said. "You wiped out half the leading scientists, and all their top politicians. Which I think explains, by the way, their interest in me," he added, in a musing tone.

The agents turned and stared at Jess.

Jess remained quiet for a short while. "I wasn't aiming at that," she finally said. "I was just trying to be a distraction so Jase could get those teams out."

"Shit, yeah," Jason said. "No way were they a target. We didn't even know they were there." He looked at Jess. "Did we? Did Bain know?"

"Not that he told me," Jess said. "That facility wasn't even a specific target." She looked at Kurok. "We wouldn't have even published it, since we knew we had a leak."

"Mm." Doctor Dan grunted. "Alex said nothing about that. Possibly on purpose, if he thought they would try to compromise me." He continued without any seeming emotion. "Certainly, the other four who went with me didn't last long."

"They tortured them?" April asked.

"No. They killed them outright," Kurok replied. "Didn't have any use for them. They had no intention of negotiating. They just wanted me and knew I would insist on coming with the others if they went."

Jason studied him intently. "Did they know that? The guys who went with you?"

"No. They weren't Interforce. Alex thought if he gave them some administrators it would pacify them." Doctor Dan patted Dev on the back. "He held you and Jesslyn in much greater esteem."

"It could have been tables turned easily. I—" Jess looked at Dev. "We could have been blown out fifty times in that. It was only Dev's flying that saved our asses." She got up. "So I've got two choices. Either turn myself over to them and hope they take me and leave, or we have to take the base back and hope it frustrates them enough to give up."

"And the reason they're interested in her," Doctor Dan concluded. "Is that Dev's been a greater success than any of us had intended. If I could replicate that success for them, it would solve a number of their problems."

Dev straightened up and wiped the back of her hand across her eyes. "I tried to do my best," she murmured. "Was that incorrect, Doctor Dan?"

"No," Jess answered before he could. "Fuck them. You just do what you do. What happened wasn't your fault."

Dev looked at her, then at Doctor Dan, who smiled and nodded. "But many people took damage." She looked around at the still, silent forms of bio alts, and the dead soldiers. "Is that really correct?"

"No time to argue about it." Jason tapped the screen. "They're doing a sweep, and if they have enough firepower they're just going to blow out that door. We're sitting ducks."

Jess absorbed all the eyes on her, and knew a moment of truth in her guts.

"Jess." Dev's voice was suddenly loud and next to her. "You weren't really considering allowing them to take you away were you?"

Jess turned her head to meet Dev's eyes. "If I thought they would just take me and fly off, and leave the rest of you alone, I would. But I think they just set this up as a trap, and once they get me, they'll blow this place with everyone in it, and if I'm going to die today, I'm not going to do it gagged and immobilized."

"So we really should have flown off back to the pole," April said. "This is an end game."

"It's always an end game," Elaine said. "Didn't they tell you that in school? We're always expected to splat for the cause." She rubbed some dried blood off her hands. "Granted, we try not to splat in huge numbers. It drives the school crazy trying to replace us."

Jess looked at her, then scanned the rest of them. "So is that what you want?" She asked bluntly. "You want me to turn myself into them and let you all get out?"

They all stared back at her.

"That's not what I meant," Elaine said. "It is what it is, Jess. Don't get all crazy about it." She leaned against the console. "Let's just figure out what to do and get it done, before they blow out that door and make this whole scene irrelevant. You got a plan?" She looked pointedly at Jess.

Jess felt her shoulders hunching defensively and she stood and paced a little, ending up next to the big screen. She studied it, her mind completely blank until she realized she was going to have to turn around and say something, because they were all waiting for her to.

She was tired. She was hurting. Her lungs were aching and she had no idea what the hell to do except just go run into central ops shooting or—

Or what?

Slowly she turned and looked at Kurok. "There any way into the security hall except the blue corridor?"

Doctor Dan exhaled a little. "Yes there is," he said. "But I'm not sure what that gets you. Operations hall is closer to central than security is."

"There's a rig being held in Security we might be able to use to get past them."

"Wait." Jason held a hand up. "You're not talking about that brain thing? The one that splatted Devon?"

Jess nodded.

"What is it?" Kurok asked.

A loud, hollow thump sounded on the other side of the wall. "Okay, we're out of time," Jess said. "Let's get to security sector. We might be able to pick up some allies there. Depends on how far they penetrated in the maze." She got off the platform and headed for the inside corridor.

Dev instantly trotted after her, carefully stepping around the silent, slumped bio alts scattered around the room. She caught up to Jess as the rest of them also started moving, and had a brief moment to catch Jess's hand and squeeze it.

Jess looked back at her.

"I don't want you to give up to them," Dev said, quietly. "Or if you do, take me with you."

The pale blue eyes watching her suddenly warmed, and softened, just before the rest of the group reached them. She winked at Dev, then waited for Doctor Dan to come up to the door. She gestured him forward. "After you."

Kurok pushed the inside door open and passed through it, and they all followed, leaving behind the room full of silent figures and scattering of dead ones.

Chapter Fifteen

IT WAS DARK, and cold, and the walls were covered in condensation. Jess stood at the end of a long, damp corridor with her hands braced on either side of a small doorway.

The rest of the group was stretched out along the hall on the other side of her, waiting in silence for the return of Dan Kurok.

"Where the hell is he?" Jason said, speaking over Dev's head to Jess. "He cross us, too?"

"No." Jess didn't wait for Dev's reaction. "He's square." She didn't even sound angry about the question. "If he's taking his time, maybe that's a good sign. He got farther."

Jason leaned back against the wall then he slowly let himself slide down it, coming to rest with his forearms on his knees. "Okay, maybe." He sighed. "Fuck, I'm tired."

Jess pushed off and thumped against the opposite wall, deciding to join him in sitting. "Park it, Devvie. We might as well take a break for a minute."

Dev sat down next to her, wrapping her arms around her knees. "It's difficult to wait," she said. "I hope Doctor Dan is okay."

Jess squirmed over a bit, until her shoulder was pressed against Dev's. "He knows where he's going," she assured Dev. "I knew Bain had some back channels, behind ops and that office he used, but they were locked down."

Everyone had settled down, and now that she was sitting, Jess hoped Kurok would take a few minutes more as it would at least give her a chance to come up with some kind of plan once he did come back.

Dev exhaled softly and the sound made Jess turn and focus on her. "Hey."

Dev returned her gaze. "Hello."

"You okay?" Jess asked, in a barely audible mutter.

Dev didn't answer for a moment, then she cleared her throat. "I think so."

"Think so?" Jess asked. "That thing in the room bug you?"

Dev's pale brows twitched.

"The mine messing up the—" Jess paused. "Everyone in there getting blasted?"

"That bothered me, yes," Dev said. "It felt very incorrect, when that happened." She leaned closer to Jess. "I feel like I hurt them."

"Why'd you open the door?" Jess asked, in a mild tone. "Back there? They were safe in there."

Dev stared at her in silence for a bit. "You were being attacked," she said finally. "You were in danger. They would have made you dead."

Jess nodded. "You put me above them. I bet you never thought for a second before you opened up that hatch."

"I didn't," Dev said. "That's incorrect, isn't it?"

"No. It's absolutely correct." Jess put her head against Dev's. "There's an us and a them, Dev. Us is you and me, and them is everyone else. Hope you don't want to change that."

Dev sat there for a few moments. "Are you saying it's correct that I would want you to be safe, even though that meant all those sets, and everyone else were made dead?"

"Yes."

"Really?" Dev stared at her in total absorption.

"Really."

"I don't think that's what they intended with my programming," Dev said.

"But?"

Dev frowned. "What but? Is this one of those ass things again?"

Jess started to shake, and she lifted one hand to cover her face.

Dev sighed after a moment of this. "It's true though." she said, a touch mournfully. "I valued your safety more than I did theirs, or even mine. So I guess whether it's correct or not is sort of a non-question."

Jess shifted a little. "I would have done the same thing, Dev. So don't sweat it. We don't really have the time or space to worry about it now anyway."

Dev thought about that, pondering if she was, in fact worried. She decided she was really too tired to be worried and just wished the whole thing was over. She could talk to Doctor Dan about it afterward. Surely he would be able to tell her what the truth of it was.

Then, between one breath and the next, the lights went off and they were plunged into total darkness.

Jess surged to her feet and the rest of them followed. She found the door opening by touch, and without pause backed a step and kicked out at it, impacting the panel with a sodden crack.

"Hope that wasn't your leg," Jason said.

Jess kicked the door again, and this time it flew inward, and she followed it, all in such pitch darkness not even a shadow showed. "Let's go," she called over her shoulder.

Dev scrambled after her, holding one hand out ahead of her to prevent her from crashing into anything. The only thing she could hear was the scuffling of their motion and the rasp of Jess's skin against the wall ahead of her. "Jess?"

"Sh." Jess ducked past something unseen and reached back to grab hold of her hand. "This is behind Bain's office," she said. "Let's get through it and go take centops."

"Sounds good," April said. "No sense hanging around in here."

"No sense worrying about scan either," Jason said. "Let's just kick the ass out of anything we find."

Dev just stayed by Jess as she started forward, unlocking a door just in front of them and swinging it open. She paused and listened, then turned on her hand light and shone it around, picking out the staid interior of the office Bain had used when he'd been in the citadel.

Empty, and dark. They moved across it and went to the door, where a lifetime ago Jess had talked to Bain about her promotion, reaching the door just as thunderous explosions rocked the walls around them.

"That's not good," Elaine said.

Jess paused at the door and waited for them to join her, then unlocked her blaster and raised her other hand, pausing, then letting it fall.

Jason moved past her in silence, bumping the front door to the office opening and passing through with April and Mike right behind him. Elaine stayed next to Jess, and the techs stuck together and brought up the rear as they all emerged into the outer hall.

There should have been security guards, but nothing living was there and they moved on through the outer chamber and then through the main hall door into the sector corridor. Far off they heard more explosions, and very faintly, shouting.

Jess and Elaine kept up a watch as they moved quickly through the hall, coming around the curve and into the main space, where the air was already getting stuffy. "Handlers off," Jess said. "Dev, run your box, see what's coming at us."

Dev and the rest of the techs already had their scanners out and going, the screens reflecting in ghostly silver and outlining their faces. "There are life forms heading in this direction." Dev said. "They are moving fast."

"Not as fast as we are." Jess urged them forward and they caught up to the rest of the agents, as they came around the circular wall that pointed them into the operations center. The big door was dark and open, and they went through and then stopped.

It smelled of blood, and burned flesh. Jess shone her light around and went still, seeing mostly destruction all around them. "Shit."

"Unsalvagable," Jason said. "Let's move on."

"Let's move on," Jess repeated, turning and leading the way out of the room. "Sounds like they're running. You figure the bay?"

"Yep."

"Let's go." Jess took the lead now and they broke into a run, heading down the hall toward the carrier bay, as the sounds of fighting grew louder.

A moment later the corridor was filled with fast moving bodies and Jess felt her senses tingling, as she swung her blaster around and targeted the first of them. "Ware!"

"Got 'em!" Jason let off the first blast, and then ducked as one came back at him, and then the hall was full of blaster fire, lighting up the shadows as they bounced off the rock walls.

"Down!" Jess yelled at the techs, before she nailed a bad guy in the jaw with her elbow and took him down, using his body as a shield as a long yellow beam nearly blew him apart.

April was hugging the corner of the wall and aiming past it, letting out long bursts and then drawing back as fire hit the wall next to her. The enemy they were firing at was wearing full armor, and their bulky, hardened figures were deflecting the blasts as they poured forward.

Jess got down behind the dead soldier and propped her gun up on his hip, ignoring the blood and burned plastic all around her. "Dev! You down!"

A hand touched her thigh and she nearly hit the roof, stifling a squeak as she only just stopped herself from whipping around and clobbering her partner. She wrenched around and fired, catching one of the enemies in mid leap about to land on her. The blast shoved him sideways and she ducked and felt the impact on her shoulders, but she shoved backwards and sent him against the wall.

"Clear!" Mike's voice rang out, and Jess grabbed Dev by the arm and hauled her up as they started down the hall again. There were three bodies on the floor and Jason and Elaine were shooting over the rest of their heads as another three of the enemy retreated before them, firing as they went.

Jess studied the pattern, then stopped and ducked behind the curve of the wall. "Hold up!"

The team flattened themselves against the wall.

Jess saw the flicker as the enemy paused and waited. Then she turned and faced Jason, who had ended up behind her. "They're drawing us." She watched him nod. "Wanna step in it?"

He shrugged. "Choices?"

"Bad, none." She let out a low whistle and shouldered her blaster. "Let's speed it up. Techs, stay down."

Dev obediently crouched and felt the warmth as Brent and Chester came up next to her. She could see Doug dimly across the hall, and then there was rapid motion as Jess led the agents across the hall and into the opening where two corridors met, lighting everything up with blaster fire.

"This sucks," Brent said, succinctly. "Want this shit to be over."

"Yes." Dev agreed. "This is definitely non-optimal." She watched anxiously as the agents disappeared from her view and then loud noises happened, bright flashes coming from around the bend of the corridor.

"Don't sound good," Chester said.

Dev had her scanner out and she watched the wiremap, shifting a little so Chester and Brent could see it. "Isn't there something we can do to help?" she asked, finding nothing readily at hand in her programming. When it came to ground battle, firefights, the agents were the ones who took the lead and the techs were supposed to keep their heads down and stay out of trouble.

"Let's go in there." Dev got up and pointed to a half open hatch. "That's the cafeteria, isn't it?"

"What's left of it." Brent moving past her and they piled into the room, Chester getting his light on and flashing it around as they took cover from the stray bolts coming down the hall.

The room, though dark, was relatively undamaged, and Brent went over to the wall panels to see what he could make of them.

"Not much we can do," Doug said, his head inched around the half open door, watching. "No guns, no guts, no glory."

Brent snorted. Tucker came over and sat down next to him, resting his elbows on his knees.

It seemed wrong. Dev kept her eyes on the wiremap, on the figure she knew was Jess moving through the halls, the outline almost obliterated by the energy flares from the blasters.

She saw Jess's outline jerk suddenly, and impact against the wall.

She felt strangely lightheaded. "Brent." She turned and offered the scanner. "Could you hold onto this please?"

"Sure." He took the instrument. "Dropped mine out on the—where ya going?"

Dev slipped through the open door and started down the hall, heading around the corner and through the next crossing, picking up speed as she approached the long series of archways that led to the shuttle bay.

She could smell smoke and burned electronics, and as she cleared the next entry she saw the battle. The enemy behind the blast doors and the agents pinned down in front of them, unable to go any farther.

Jess was curled up near an overturned cabinet, and as Dev headed for her she sensed a surge of energy coming at her and dove for the floor. "Look out!"

From behind her the hall was filling with enemy, blasters raised.

Dev rolled for the far wall as she saw the agents start to turn and she slammed into the hard surface, as a bolt hit the rock right over her head.

A hand grabbed her arm and she was pulled along the floor, blaster fire almost stinging her shoulder as she found herself hard against the wall, Jess's tall body in front of her.

Jess was yelling. The agents were firing, the enemy was firing back. Dev heard someone cough loudly, then Jess called out Jason's name.

There was no answer.

She felt everything slow down a bit, as the thought occurred to her that they were in very big danger, and it was likely that very soon they were going to be made dead.

Dev knew what that was. She hoped it would be fast, and that it wouldn't hurt, too much. She felt Jess press against her and reached out to take hold of her, very glad she'd at least made a connection with someone, and got to understand what that love thing was.

She was very glad she'd gotten to know Jess. Gotten to do good work, and be as close to a natural born as one of her kind could be.

She'd gotten her mark, after all.

A loud, crackling boom filled her consciousness and she tucked her head along Jess's side, feeling Jess shift suddenly and turn to cover her, wrapping her arms around Dev and pushing her against the wall as a flow of energy passed over and through them, a flaring edge of pain that sent her to the edge of consciousness.

Then a thumping sound, and a blast of air replaced it, and the darkness blew out, replaced with piercing haloed lights that made stark beams through the smoke now visible in the hall.

Jess released her and turned, sweeping up her blaster in a deadly motion, only to swing its muzzle up as she got up on her knees and swiveled around.

The enemy was on the ground, bodies contorted. The archways were lit with a familiar blue glow and the overhead lights had all come on along with the air handlers. "Someone got the systems back on," Jess said, rising to her feet. "Status?"

"Okay." April got up from the ground, finally looking stunned and a bit overwhelmed. "Mike?"

"Ow." Mike was sitting with his back against the wall, cradling his right arm with his left. "Broke something."

Jess headed over to where Elaine was crouched over Jason. "April, go get the techs." She circled Jason's sprawled legs and knelt down on the far side of his body. "Take one to the head?"

"Yeah." Elaine exhaled. "If med's down, he's toast." She regarded the long, dark burn that scored half his face, and the charred remains of one ear. "Stupid bastard. I told him to duck."

Jess turned and regarded the rest of the space. She went to the comms panel on the wall and keyed it, hearing a soft crackle in return, but no response. "Tac," she said into it. "Any comms, respond."

She waited, then repeated the message.

Another long silence, then rather than from the comms, they heard a response coming from the cross hallway just before the shuttle bay.

"Not much to say." Dan Kurok limped into view, his eyes flicking over them with something like relief. "Took you long enough to get them down here." He sat down on a box, looking completely exhausted. "This is the only area with any grid I could bring up. Once I'd taken everything down that is."

"That was you?" Elaine studied him.

A faint, very wry smile appeared on Doctor Dan's face.

"Thought they were leading us on." Jess looked up as the techs came into view following April. "Let's rig a carry, get Jason to med." She eyed the hall. "If this sector's got power, that one might too."

"Marginal," Kurok said. "This was the last of them, I think. They got comms as I got into the back halls and they took off, left a squadron behind to clean up." He studied the bodies on the floor. "Hope that's all of them. There's not much in the way of protection left here." His eyes lifted to Jess's. "And they will be back."

"What about people?" Elaine asked. "Anyone else from the teams here?"

Kurok just looked at her.

She shook her head. "Shit."

"Maybe Bock was right," April said. "He said it was over. We were just prolonging it."

Jess watched them rigging a sling, then she walked back over to where Dev was seated on the ground, extending a hand down to her. "He was right." She hoisted her partner to her feet. "But it doesn't matter because we don't stop just because it's a lost cause." She studied Dev. "You okay, Devvie?"

What, really could she say to that? "Yes." Dev looked around at the dissipating smoke, and the bodies on the ground, and her battered colleagues, and Doctor Dan. "Seeing as I thought they were going to make us dead."

"Not yet." Jess sighed. "Maybe soon."

"I see."

"Let's see how hard we can make it for them."

IT DID SEEM a lost cause. Dev was on her knees, her head inside a wall panel as she studied the readouts on her retrieved scanner. There was so much damage everywhere, it seemed very difficult to know where to start with fixing it.

Brent was in the next panel. "Crap. This is bullshit."

Dev construed that to mean Brent agreed with her assessment, and she made a small noise of assent. "The batteries are being drained at 10 percent per standard hour. Then there will be no power available."

"We can suck off the carriers for a few hours," Chester said. "But that's it."

Brent touched the comm set on his head. "Tuck, you there?"

Dev continued her evaluation, trying not to think of the long corridor they were next to that led eventually to her quarters, and rest. There seemed to be no end in sight to the trouble, and she'd reduced her wishing to a simple one for some water and maybe even a packet of those seaweed crackers Jess hated so much.

The power generation systems were offline, that being the crux of the issue. Without them, the citadel had to run on what power was in the batteries, and that was draining rapidly. "How were they operating before? The systems were up when we were downstairs."

"Someone had the security systems turned off," Brent said, darkly. "Whatever jacktard let them in, prob. Hope they're carbon char somewhere."

Dev pulled her head out of the cabinet and looked at him. "You mean, someone here was on their side?"

"Sure," Brent said. "Knew there was a stinker left here. Let them in the first time, when they bombed the bay." He tapped his comms again. "Tuck? What's up in med?"

Dev could see the tense lines in his face, and she knew a moment of understanding there, that despite the gruff words and attitude. There was caring there for his partner, who had looked very damaged to Dev before they'd taken him away.

Doctor Dan had gone back downstairs to bring up the downed sets, and Jess had started inspecting the facility to see what harm had been done to it, apparently having taken no damage herself in the fight.

"Okay, thanks," Brent said into comms, crouching back down and going back to studying the panel. "They got power to med."

"Damn good news," Chester said. "They can splint up Mike's arm, too."

The comm set in Dev's ear rustled and she turned her attention from her scanner. "Ack?"

"Hey, Dev." Jess's voice burbled through. "Your buddy got some help up and going and we cleared out centops. Bring the wrenchers up here. Got better access."

"Ack." Dev stood up. "Jess said we should go to the operations center. They have made it more optimal."

"And they've got chairs." Doug climbed down out of a service hatchway. "No damn connections here anyway, just service trunks. Two of the big power transfer banks got fried. This is a mess."

"Yes." Dev closed her scanner and secured the panel. "But at least no one is trying to make us dead at the moment, and we have good work to do."

"You bios talk funny," Doug said, as they headed down the hall toward centops. "You know that?"

"We talk funny?" Dev eyed him. "We don't spend most of our time talking about excrement and posterior body parts at least. I had to load a custom dictionary into my scanner just to know what all of you are saying most of the time."

Doug eyed her, trying to hold back a smile. Brent didn't bother, snickering under his breath as they moved through the central hall and past the now active scan gate into ops.

"Hey, what was that with you giving me your box and taking off before?" Brent asked, suddenly. "You looking to get fired on purpose?"

"No," Dev said as they approached central systems. "I was concerned that Jess was in danger." She glanced up as the emergency lighting overhead flickered a little. "So I wanted to see if I could help in any way."

They reached the ops door and the conversation stopped. They entered and found Jess and April inside.

The ops center had taken considerable damage. Two of the console banks were burned and dark, and there were blaster scores on the walls. But the emergency lighting was on and two more of the banks had some limited screens active, and the room was cleared of any bodies.

"Ah, the wrenchers are here." Jess looked up from a large piece of plas she had spread out on the console top. "What's the status?"

"Batts are crap," Brent said. "Got maybe three hours left."

Jess nodded. "That's what the scan said here too." She indicated one of the two working consoles. "We need to get the exchangers up. We don't get power going we might as well just get in the buses and go fishing."

"Yah." Brent sat down at one of the working stations. "Nothing's working down there."

"Want me to take Doug and see what the status of the intakes is?" April asked. "Might as well move the carrier into the big bay anyhow."

Jess nodded. "Do a fly around and get a comp scan while you're at it. We need to get at least enough cycles to get scan and met up."

April nodded and headed for the door, with Doug following her obediently.

"Lift's cycling from downstairs," Brent said. "Getting biologic readings. Looks like the Doc got things going down there." He studied the screen. "We should get scan relayed in here until we can get power up. Those buckheads could be sweeping down on us and we'd never know it."

"I have our carrier configured to relay that," Dev said. "So far there is nothing approaching and the weather seems all right." She took a seat and started connecting her portable scan to the console. "I will send it in here so everyone can see it."

"That's my driver." Jess put a hand on Dev's back and gave it a little friendly scratch with her fingertips. "There were fewer bodies in here than I thought there would be. Only two." She changed the subject. "We took them to processing, and after Elaine finishes with Jason and Mike in med, she's going to do a foray to see if there are more. There's a lot of people missing."

"Maybe they got out?" Brent said. "Could be they were trying to evac when they were getting crunched."

"Well, if we don't find bodies, and there's nothing floating ashore, that's a possibility." Jess turned as there were footsteps in the hall, and then let her hand drop to her blaster as the doorway was filled. "Ah. You."

"Ah, me," Dan Kurok said. "I've brought all bio alt sets up, and instructed them to start repair, or restoral, whatever they are capable of. They told me someone should check the carrier bay out, as they thought some might be trapped in there."

He sat down in one of the watch chairs and leaned back, his pale eyes reflecting the emergency lighting despite their bloodshot nature.

"Home sweet home, eh?"

Jess returned a wry grin to him, then keyed comms. "April, ack?"

"Ack." April's voice came back, with the sound of wind behind it. "We're moving across the external fascia."

"When you're done with recon, inspect the carrier bay. Word is people might be in there."

"Bodies might be in there too," April said. "My guess is they dropped some nasty in the top there. Big place, all you'd need is gravity."

"Find out and report," Jess said. "We'll be working on the tie lines in here."

"Ack."

"So, they were on batts the whole time?" Brent looked a touch confused. "I don't get it. When we got here it was like they had no idea we were coming, except that hatch on the north side."

"They were on batteries," Kurok confirmed. "This place has big ones. I had quite a bit of trouble getting them shut completely down." He looked at his hands, and then flexed them. "No way to get the systems they were using to watch for everyone off except for that."

"So they had scan?"

"They had, I think, very limited internal wire plots," he said. "I got the sense, when I was sneaking around trying not to get shot that whatever the plan was originally, there wasn't much left before we got here." He looked thoughtful.

"Common problem," Jess said. "All right, I'm going to go down to the intake cavern." She glanced at Dev, who immediately stood up and set her scanner down on the console. "We'll be back."

They walked out into the dimly lit corridor and Dev felt glad they were now by themselves and it was quiet. A motion flickered in and out of her peripheral vision, and she recognized one of the BeeAyes carrying a box away from the cafeteria. "I'm glad Doctor Dan made them all right."

Jess nodded, her face quiet and pensive. "Know what I feel like doing?"

The question opened up a lot of possibilities. "I'm afraid I don't," Dev finally answered.

"Wish I could go to my quarters, take a shower, eat two sets of rations, and sleep for two days," Jess said. "This is so fucked up I don't see an end to it."

"Mm." Dev nodded a little. "I would like all that, and also, to lay in bed with you."

Jess managed a smile at that. "Really?"

"Absolutely."

"Yeah, that would be nice," Jess said. "Damn, I'm tired." She draped her arm over Dev's shoulders as they walked through the unnaturally silent halls. "Y'know, I just don't get what was going on here.

They come here, supposedly to get me, but then they take off, and leave a watch squad who can't even tell when they're being infiltrated by us?"

Dev shook her head. "I don't understand most of this either."

"I mean, what the hell?" Jess went on. "You know?"

"No, I don't know. What's hell?" Dev noticed they were passing one of the dispensers in the hall. "Can we get a drink?"

"Sure." Jess detoured over to the alcove and bumped the door open, removing a container and handing it to Dev, then taking one for herself. The residual cooling in the casing had kept the temperature relatively down, and she popped open the drink and took a sip while she stood there thinking.

Jess turned, as something out of place caught her eye. She set the container down and drew her blaster. "Stay here." She started down the side hall toward a half open door that had no business being accessed.

It was an unmarked door and there was silence beyond it. Jess cautiously pushed it open with the muzzle of her blaster and waited, ears cocked, as the rough crunch of the manual opening faded. After a moment she glided around the edge of the doorway and into the room, hitting the preamp on the blaster and lighting up the room in pale blue wash.

Then she replaced that with the glare of her hand light and holstered the gun, letting out a long, aggravated sigh. "Dev!" she called out. "C'mere." She keyed her comm set as she heard Dev's light footsteps approaching, and half turned as Dev entered. "See if you can get some lighting on in here, wouldja?"

"Yes." Dev turned on her own hand light and explored the room, finding a control console across from where Jess was. "It appears this facility isn't used." She sat down and keyed in a command. "It's empty."

"That would be the problem." Jess tapped her comm set again. "Centops, Tac 1, ack?"

"Centops," Brent answered. "Go-head."

"I'm in sector blue thirty," Jess said. "Looks like they borrowed a few things."

"Ack," Brent answered. "Relay?"

"Ack," Jess responded. "We'll pick it up later. Proceeding."

"Ack. Relay and mark," Brent said, clicking off.

Dev had succeeded in getting the low level illumination on, and now she turned and regarded the empty room. "What is this space?" she asked. "I don't think you showed it to me before."

"No," Jess said. "Let's get walking and I'll tell you about it." She waited for Dev to join her and they headed down the hall again. "That room...it's a complex. There's more than one space in there. It's where all the black ops stuff ends up."

Dev nodded gravely. "It seemed quite dark."

Jess regarded her. "Was that a joke?"

Dev shrugged.

"Anyway, the biggest thing we had in there was a new weapons rig that you kind of plugged into," Jess explained as they got to the access hallway. "It's gone. Few other things are too but that one—" She shook her head. "Hard to say if it's more dangerous to us or them."

"Like that thing they made," Dev said. "That was dangerous to them, wasn't it?"

Jess thought about that as they walked down the steep passageway into the cavern. "Yeah," she said, after a bit. "But this was...well, if they figure out how to make it work, all those fights you saw us in? Us against them in the hall? It would give them an advantage."

"They wear more things than you do," Dev said, eventually. "Is that to protect them?"

Jess worked the airlock into the final cavern. "Yeah. Our plasmas are more intense than theirs, and they don't train agents like we do." She led the way into the rock pathway. "They care about living. It's what makes us crazy to them." She paused, regarding the huge space. "We're harder kills because we don't care."

Dev's brows creased. "So this thing will make them not care?"

Jess produced a brief, grim smile. "It wires your guns into your head. You fire at the speed of thought." She put her hands on the rock, her fingertips twitching. "I let them rig me into it once." She turned and looked at Dev. "You never want to stop shooting. I nearly took out the test chamber."

Dev frowned. "I don't think I understand that," she said, in an apologetic tone. "Is this a good thing, or a bad thing?"

Jess shook her head and pointed down to the board storage area. "It's not stable. Next guy who tested it fried himself. They ended up giving him a mercy kill."

The waves were thundering in from under the rock wall, and the spray coated them as they reached the platform and looked out over the fractious water. Unlike the previous time, when the intake tunnels were in work and the water was swirling in a powerful, predictable way, now the waves were smashing against everything, breaking hard against the rocks and sending explosions of water halfway up to the ceiling of the cavern.

It seemed wild and frenzied. Jess leaned back against the rock wall, and folded her arms over her chest. "What is going on here, Dev? That's the question."

"Well." Dev copied her pose, glad to be still and quiet for a bit. "I was thinking about that when we were on the carrier on the way back here, and one thing that seemed interesting to me was those people on the other side are really focused on you."

"On me," Jess repeated, in a doubtful tone. "Why me?"

"That's what I was wondering." Dev said. "They got that man

Joshua to do bad things and caused you difficulties. Then the man, Bricker tried to use me to make it less difficult, and after that, the man Bain got you not to leave. Then they paid the captain to do bad things. Then they were trying to get us on that market island, and they chased us and when we got back, we found out they took those people and Doctor Dan and wanted you in return for them."

"Hmm. Yeah," Jess said. "I thought it was because of the Gibraltar run, but you know what? It started before that." She frowned. "It started with Joshua, but turn an agent, and go through all that just to put me on ice? Why?" She unfolded her arms and paced a little. "I'm a good agent, I've got a pretty decent record, done a bunch of missions. But nothing more or less than someone like Jason, or Elaine, or hell, even Sandy had done."

"I see."

"That's why they were all pissed when they bumped me to senior, by the way." Jess produced a self-deprecating smile. "I wasn't about to turn it down, but I really hadn't earned it. Shoulda probably been Elaine." She crossed her arms again. "But I guess Bain had his reasons."

"Doctor Dan told me I could trust you, and the man Bain," Dev said, unexpectedly. "So maybe there was a reason for that. Maybe there are things we don't know." She paused. "That happened a lot with us in the creche. They would do things a lot and you never really knew why because they didn't tell you everything."

Jess looked thoughtful. "Doesn't really matter now I guess." She studied the cavern. "The raceways down there look clear. If they're all right on the outside we can try a restart after we check the transfer stations."

"What will happen then?"

"We get power." Jess started trudging back up the ramp. "We can bring systems up, and talk to home base, and figure out what the hell we're going to do when those bastards come back here." She paused, and looked back at Dev. "But they'd have done that already, right? Send word to HQ about all this?"

"The man Bock seemed to think that was a bad idea." Dev joined her. "Remember he said, that they would think bad things about us if we did that?"

"He just didn't want us to communicate. He tried to get them to kill us, remember?" Jess frowned. "Of course they'd tell the top they killed two bases. We need help."

But as she said it, she felt that pang in her gut that meant a warning. She remembered something that Bain had said, so long ago now that it felt like someone else's lifetime. "But there's no point in worrying about that right now I guess. Let's just get things up and running here so at least we can—" She paused, in thought.

"Have a meal," Dev supplied a conclusion for her. "It has been a while."

Jess chuckled, and shook her head. "How about we stop and get some of those damn awful crackers?" she said. "I hate them, but at least they're something and they never spoil."

"Excellent idea."

"CENTOPS, TAC 2."

Jess got her comms in place. "Centops, ack." She took a swallow of kack to clear the seaweed crackers from her throat. "Go ahead, April."

"External intakes look okay, no obstructions seen," April said. "But we just dropped into the bay and got shot at. Think we need some backup from inside."

"Ack." Jess got up. "Will check."

"Jess." Dev looked up from her console. "A Kaytee says the doors to the bay are secured from the inside. They just reported." She selected a cracker and put it in her mouth, munching quietly. "I have asked them to put on comm where they can."

"And a Kaytee is?" Jess sat back down.

"One of the pilots," Dev said, listening to her comms. "A PeeEff also says they have found the cut in the transmission lines and are reviewing it."

"Where is that?" Brent asked. "I'll go have a look too."

Dev turned and looked at him. "Level six, west service corridor B."

Brent got up and headed for the door, which was now properly secured and scan protected, and opened after he passed the gateway. "Let you know," he said before the hatch shut.

Jess studied the marginal wiremap. "Dev, you got any way to patch comms to the service bay? Let me talk in there?"

"I will try." Dev hunted through the systems she had access to. "There are a lot of things very suboptimal," she said. "I think whatever the disruption was on level six, also removed service for scan and comms." She tapped further. "I can possibly activate any vessel comms and relay."

"There are carriers left in there intact?" Jess asked, going over to peer over Dev's shoulder. "Oh, okay. I see. The transports are still in there."

"Yes."

"Give it a try." Jess studied the wiremap intently.

Dev patched the comms on the board through an emergency relay, and then to the service craft left in the bay. "It's done."

"Attention." Jess watched the relays trigger a faint trickle of communication. "Attention, this is centops, reg centops. Drake eleven on comm." She waited a moment. "Ntac, respond."

"Centops, Tac 2. Relaying external." Doug's voice echoed softly in Dev's ear. "Scan shows motion inside, sending vid copy."

"Ack," Dev answered, studying the vid. Doug had his carrier up on the lip of the escarpment, just barely at the edge of the opening, but she could see the destruction even from there. "Oh."

Jess leaned against her. "Oh, crap. Look the hell at that."

The entire top hatch was disrupted, the metal edges peeled back and gaping, one whole side lying over, draped down the side of the cliff. It was as though some huge force had exploded from within, forcing the hatch up and out of its seating deep in the rock.

A crackle. "Drake!" A voice came through comms. "Ntac, sendit."

"Wants validation," Jess said. "Don' blame him. I could be anyone up here saying I'm me."

"That sounded like Cliff," Dev said, in a low tone. "Should I talk to him?"

"Hang on." Jess put her hand on Dev's shoulder. "Meet in my neighbor's bunk to pick up your shells," she said quietly into the comms. All the code in the world was good, but sometimes, there were personal bits that were worth more. "Ack?"

There was a long silence. Then the sound of breathing. "Ack." Cliff's voice sounded, even on ratty comms, profoundly relieved. "Topside?"

"Friendly," Jess said.

"Tell them to come. Lot of cleanup needed here." Clint's voice now sounded exhausted. "Inside hatch's warped. Can't unseal."

"Ack," Jess said. "Standby. Tac 2, copy?"

"Tac 2 moving," April said. "Rolling vid."

Jess settled down in the chair next to Dev as the grainy vid resolved, a soft rumble of thunder in the background adding appropriate soundtrack to the view of destruction below.

DEV ADJUSTED THE landing jets on her carrier as she carefully lowered it into the carrier bay, tilting it forward and holding in pattern as she lit up the work area underneath her.

The destruction was extensive. She could see three recon craft hard against one wall, blackened and scorched, but at least in one piece. They were the ones with active comm she had tied into.

Dev shook her head. It was hard to recognize the service bay. Everything was charred and blackened, the only clear space was two landing pads on the far side of the space. April and Doug had landed on one of them, and they were examining the destruction while she stayed in the air giving them light.

At least six carriers were blown apart in blasted bits, all with the typical pattern they'd seen in the North station. Dev was glad she was still in the air, since her scanner was indicating to her lumps and chunks of what was, once, people.

People she might have known.

Her comms buzzed softly. "Centops, BR270006."

"Ack," Dev answered.

"Go ahead and land on pad twenty-four, Dev. We're about to start up the intakes."

"Ack." Dev shifted the jets sideways and moved over April's carrier, lowering the craft slowly until it landed on its skids with a soft bump. She secured the systems and put everything on standby, then released her restraints and got up. After a brief hesitation, she pulled on the jacket she'd gotten in Quebec City, then steeled herself and went to the hatch, triggering it open.

It didn't actually smell as bad as she'd expected, and she walked down the ramp to the platform and stood there for a moment, looking around.

The faint sound of light rain coming in from the ruined roof hatch pattered around her, and the soft echoes of April's speech and the dull thunk of Doug trying to get the inside hatch open.

It was incorrect, and unpleasant, and Dev sighed as she climbed down off the platform and headed over to where Clint and April were standing. She'd gotten halfway there when she felt, rather than heard, a vibration through her boots, and saw the other two look up and around.

"Man, I missed that sound." Clint looked relieved, managing a brief smile as Dev arrived next to them. "Hey, Dev."

"Hello," Dev responded. "I'm sorry there's so much unpleasantness here. But I'm glad you didn't get damaged."

Clint blushed visibly. "Glad you didn't get offed either," he said. "I figured if anyone would pull through, it'd be you guys."

"Was that the generators coming back online?" April asked. "That rumbling?"

"Not yet. They have to run the water through for a few minutes before it builds up the turbines," Clint said. "But that vibration means they got the intakes going." He looked past April. "It's not as bad as it looks."

April gave him a skeptical look.

"The bodies are mostly theirs." Clint looked her right in the eye, then turned to Dev. "You were right about those cards. We couldn't do much about it though. They came in and blew out the roof with that new thing. Focused the lighting on it someone said."

"Yes, something like that," April said. "So, did they all just leave out of here or what?"

"Got a comms, long range," Clint said. "We knew something was going on, saw all the batts go offline, but we couldn't get through to anyone." He studied April. "We didn't think any of the teams would really come back here." He sat down on the edge of a service console. "Figured they'd just tank the place."

"Thank you for making the sets safe," Dev said, after an awkward pause. "That was excellent of you."

Clint managed another slight smile. "They're all right," he said.

"Didn't want them to get snuffed."

Abruptly, the overhead lights flickered on, what was left of them, and all around them the clicks and pops of returning power was causing boards to flash and signal lamps to come on. That was followed by a sodden crack, and they all turned to see the inner hatch slowly peeling open.

"Good job, Doug." April started over to where he was just stepping back. "So what do we do to secure this place? We got anything we can do about that hole in the roof?"

Doug dusted his hands off and stood aside as they joined him, and the open hatch started to admit slightly grubby, jump-suited figures in, all with faintly illuminated collars. "C'mon in, people."

A Kaytee slipped in and spotted Clint. "Chief." He looked as relieved as he was able to. "May we help?"

"Sure." Clint waved them in. "Let's start cleaning up I guess."

The Kaytee turned to Dev. "Is it optimal?" he asked. "May we do this?"

Dev had her hands in her jacket pockets, and she straightened a bit as they all turned to look at her. She was surprised, and a little disconcerted at the question, understanding almost belatedly that they were waiting for her permission to proceed. "I think that would be excellent, Kaytee," she said after a brief pause. "We have a lot of work to get things correct."

The Kaytee looked relieved. "Yes," he said, touching the comm set in his ear, with something like pride. "A lot of good work to do." He half turned and whispered into the comms, and then started toward the service bay, as more bodies started to slip in past the half open door, pausing to look around at the destruction before moving inside.

"They put them on comms?" Cliff asked, looking at Dev. "And hey, you in charge of them now?"

"Me?" Dev blinked at him. "I don't believe I am in charge of anything," she said. "Jess had me talk to these sets. I am just familiar to them." She didn't see the point in revealing the internal status consideration of bio alts. There was already enough discomfort around and she didn't want to add to it.

"Only staff left here," April said. "Made sense to cable them up."

"Right." Cliff pushed himself to his feet. "Hope someone shunts some power to the chow hall. I'm hungry."

Doug came over, dusting his hands off. "Me too. Hey, that's a slick jacket, rocket lady."

"Thank you." Dev decided the thought of something more to eat than crackers, even if it was a cold fish roll, was excellent. "We should go see if that's ready. I'm sure the people in the central operations room could use some food as well."

"Lead on," Doug said. "Not much else we can do here until they're ready for us to lift out debris."

Dev regarded them all with a sense of bemusement. Then she merely shook her head and threaded her way across the rubble on the floor and slid through the hatch, glad to leave the discomfort of the destroyed facility behind her.

Chapter Sixteen

"OKAY, THAT'S MORE like it." Jess studied the ops board, now pulsing with restored power.

"Yes," Doctor Dan said. "Nice to have eyes and ears again." He scanned the screen. "Met isn't incredibly awful."

Jess started up the ops routines, and sent the restart sequences to comms and scan. All around her she could hear the faint, but perceptible hum of power, and though they were still deep in the crapper, it made her feel a lot better.

"Got the divert to batts in," Brent said from the next board. "Recharging."

"See if you can get some techs up to start pulling those boards." Jess indicated the two fried subsystems. "I've only got remedial weapons on this one."

"Ack." Brent went to comms, then paused and glanced at Doctor Dan.

"Right." Kurok slid into a seat next to him and put a comm set in his ear. "They'd probably listen to you, but they'll listen to me faster."

"Or, Dev," Brent said.

Doctor Dan's lips tensed into a faint smile, and he half nodded. "Attention, this is Doctor Dan," he said in the comms. "I would like a team of PeeKays and TeeBees to come to the operations center, and bring everything needed to rebuild centops stations P15, and P212, quickly."

The comms crackled immediately, soft, eager voices answering him. "Thank you," Kurok said, and clicked off comms. Then he leaned on the console and sighed. "Hasn't been the best week of my life, tell you that."

Jess was about to comment on that when the door opened. Dev and Doug entered, their arms filled with ration bags. "Ah." She found herself smiling. "Now it's perfect in here."

Dev came over to where she was seated and put down her burden. "We thought it would be a good idea to have a meal," she said. "The machines are not yet restarted, but we found these in the preparation storage area."

"Don't have to ask me twice." Brent came over and claimed a ration, then retreated back to his seat.

Dev handed over a ration to Doctor Dan, then sat down next to Jess with her own. "Clint thinks it is possible they have a mesh screen that can be attached to the bay roof to help cover it."

Jess had opened her ration and was scarfing a fish roll. She chewed, then paused and swallowed. "Hey."

"Yes?"

"Thanks." Jess lifted the roll.

"Welcome." Dev glanced at her, then grinned a little turning her fish roll around to find a place to bite into it. Now that the air handlers were back on, it was less damp and chilly, and she was starting to feel more comfortable, almost like she was ready to unfasten her jacket, in fact.

"That looks sexy on you," Jess said.

Dev paused in mid chew and looked at her in surprise.

"The jacket," Jess clarified. "I thought it did when you got it, but now I really think so." She was keeping her voice low, but not whispering.

"Um." Dev swallowed hastily. "Thanks, I like it," she added. "It's comfortable. I was cold when I got off the carrier but it's getting warmer now."

"Yeah, environ's coming back up." Jess scooted her chair closer, setting aside her worries for a short time out. "Kind of cool to just talk about stuff for a few minutes, huh?" She rested her elbow on the console and her head on her hand.

Dev put her rations down and pulled a bit of cloth from one of her pockets, standing up unexpectedly and using the cloth to clean off Jess's dusty, bruised face. "You appear to need rest."

Jess her eyes closed, and there was a faint smile on her face. "Do you know how long it's been since someone wiped my face off for me?"

"No, I don't," Dev said. "Was it a long time?"

"Very."

"Do we know what tasks we want to accomplish now?" Dev asked. "Or do we have time to take a rest?"

"Good question."

Jess felt the gentle brush of Dev's fingers against her skin and thought about how good it would feel to just do something as normal as go back to her quarters, get washed up, and take a nap in her bed. It felt like it had been months since she'd done that, though she knew it hadn't actually been all that long.

It was ridiculous, but she just wanted to do one mundane shift. Wake up and go to ops, get a met report, scan the overnight squirts. Jess opened her eyes and looked around at the half destroyed room, at fried consoles now being worked over by bio alts, and at the scorched places on the floor she'd scraped up what she assumed were colleagues' remains.

Jess reached out with her free hand and circled Dev's leg with it, just savoring the simplicity of the contact and acknowledging how good it felt when Dev rested her forearm on her shoulder and they just spent a few quiet minutes being together.

Dev moved, circling around Jess and standing behind her, putting her hands on her shoulders and starting to knead them. "I looked this up in comp," she said. "Let me know if I do it wrong."

It was nearing second watch, Jess knew. The skies would be darkening into dusk. "Brent, we get the sit report off to HQ?"

"Yup," Brent said, his mouth full of mushroom cake. "Sent it, but nothing back yet."

Jess leaned back and let her head rest against Dev's body. "Put a low band signal out, see if anyone's in hiding," she said. "Not enough wreckage here for everyone."

"Will do."

The door opened again and Elaine entered, coming around the console to take a seat next to Jess. "Med's fully synced. I got Jase in the tank, he's holding his own." She exhaled. "Nice to get systems back. How's met?"

"Quiet," Brent said. "Glad Jase's all right."

Elaine nodded. "Yeah, me too. Arias's got a formcast on his arm, he went off to work down in the pit." She glanced at Dev, who was still standing behind Jess, her hands working her neck. "Oh that's nice. Didn't know they programmed them for that."

"They don't," Dev answered, before Jess could straighten up. "I looked it up in comp." She could feel the tension suddenly wind into Jess's body. Though Jess didn't move, all the muscles in her arms and shoulders coiled under Dev's fingers and she stopped trying to squeeze them since there didn't seem to be any point to it. "It is nice."

Doctor Dan had been quietly watching. Now he stood up. "I'm going to go get a wash and a hot cup of something. Based on the last scan metrics, we're clear for a couple hours all around. Might as well take advantage of it." He gave them all a meaningful look. "Right?"

Elaine nodded. "Not sure how the hell we managed to get this all done, but here we are. You tell the west coasters?"

Jess nodded. "Brent sent a squirt. Maybe they'll send someone up from Picchu before the next front rolls in. Without met, I don't think they'll come at us."

"I'll take watch then," Elaine said. "Go on and chill, Jess. You've had a longer run than we did."

Thus held out, Jess was unable to refuse the offer. "Okay." She stood up and clapped Dev on the back. "Let's go get that shower you wanted, Devvie. Buzz me if anything shakes, E."

"You know it." Elaine took over the console, pulling over an unopened ration and settling in.

"I'll stick." Brent said. "Got scans running."

Jess lifted a hand and they left ops, walking the short distance to the entrance to Jess's quarters, while Doctor Dan went in the other direction. "Have a good rest," she said over her shoulder at him.

"You too." He gave them both one of his gentle smiles. "Dev, we should talk later, after we all get some sleep."

Dev just nodded, before they parted and went to the

entryway to their space.

Jess touched the lock pad and the door opened, the lights inside perking up as they walked inside. "Ahh. Home sweet home," she said, walking in a few steps and stopping, letting her senses scan the inside of the room.

The air handlers had been on long enough to clear the damp chill from the room, and a slow inspection allowed Jess to relax as she noted the telltales that confirmed no one had entered in her absence.

Not sure why they would—even with the enemy rampaging around the citadel her personal quarters could not have come up on the list of interesting places, given that there was nothing in them that she treasured or even probably much cared about.

Her eyes fell on the trunks that had come from her father, and she paused, reviewing that supposition.

"I'm going to go get in the shower." Dev ambled on toward the door separating their quarters.

"Mind if I join you?" Jess asked, after a pause.

Dev looked back at her. "Why would I mind that?" she asked, in a puzzled tone. "The space is somewhat small for both of us but it should be sufficient."

"Just asking." Jess sighed. "My brain's exhausted like the rest of me." She undid the catches on her jumpsuit top as she followed Dev into her space, not entirely sure why the thought of just using her own facility was making her uncomfortable. Brain crick maybe?

Maybe.

Dev's space was emptier than hers. There wasn't any clutter around, and the only thing sitting on her work desk was the square, somewhat worn shape of the book she'd left behind. "Gotta get you some knick-knacks, Devvie.'

Dev paused and turned to look at her. Then she sighed and trudged toward the comp screen, only to be pulled gently to a halt as Jess intercepted her. "I don't know what a knick is, much less a knack."

"Just things you keep, reminds you of stuff." Jess turned her and prodded her toward the shower.

"Oh. Like that little oil thing you got me at the market. Yes, I have that in my space up there." She pointed to the relaxation area.

They entered the shower and Dev was very glad to turn on the water, feeling the mist hit her face as it spattered against the rock wall. It felt good to step under it, and feel the warmth hit her skin, a relief from the persistent damp cold.

Jess eased in behind her and Dev heard her let out an almost silent sigh. She turned to face her, seeing her leaning back against the rock with her eyes closed, droplets from the shower dotting her skin. "Jess?"

"Mm?" Dark lashes fluttered and lifted, as Jess opened her eyes to peer back at her.

Dev studied her gravely. "You seem...um..."

"Damaged? Incorrect?" Jess ventured.

"Upset," Dev said. "Are you mad about something?"

Jess regarded her for a moment. "I'm here naked with you in a shower. How mad could I possibly be about that?" She smiled. "I'm not mad, or upset. I'm just freaked out about what we just went through and I don't really know where to go from here."

"Do we need to go anywhere?" Dev asked. "I think I like it here." She was enjoying the beat of the water against her back and she offered Jess some soap. "We did good work here, correct?"

"Well." Jess took the soap but instead of using it on herself, she started scrubbing Dev with it. "If you mean, is it good we're back in control of the citadel, and the bad guys have run off, sure. If you mean, is it good that they saved all the bios, and not all the carriers blew up, and we got power running again, sure."

Dev shyly took a handful of the soap and started washing Jess's skin. There were a lot of bruises under the surface of it, and one long scratch down the inside of her arm. "I see."

"I just don't know what to expect next," Jess clarified. "Are they going to come back again with the met weapon? Are they going to try to do something with the stuff they stole from here? We can prepare at some level but then—how did they get in the first time? Even with the power off, the batts would have kept them out. I just don't get it. I don't understand now what they're after."

"Besides you."

"Dev, I don't think it's me. I don't buy it. I'm not that important. I think they're using me as an excuse."

"An excuse for what?"

"That's what I don't know. I don't know how far this goes." She moved closer and lowered her voice. "I don't know what I can trust." She cradled Dev's face in her hands. "Except this. Except you."

It felt quite overwhelming. Dev understood she had no programming for this. The feeling went beyond any instruction or class, and touched a deeper and more primitive part of who she was. She took a breath. "That makes me so happy."

"Happy?" Jess's forehead touched hers.

"Yes," Dev whispered. "I want to be a part of you."

Jess's eyes opened wider, in a moment of unguarded wonder. "Really?"

"Absolutely really."

Jess circled her with both arms and pulled her close. She closed her eyes as she felt the pressure return, and as she stepped under the force of the shower it felt like it was washing her clean.

All the vague sense of failure dissipated. She was able to shift all the accomplishments they'd achieved in the recent past into perspective, having this one touchstone cement into place. It was odd. She'd never needed anything personal at all, and now she felt like this change had become important as—

"Jess," Dev said. "I think it's possible I might fall asleep right here. I cannot breathe in the water like you can, so I think we should finish before that happens."

Jess started chuckling. "Yeah. Thanks for reminding me. I need to get an antidote into me before that little stunt gets me into med." She pulled back and tilted her head, giving Dev a kiss on the lips. "I want to be a part of you, too."

It was good. Dev enjoyed the kiss and felt a jolt of happiness inside. It was very good.

And on top of it, she sensed there was sex practice in her very near future.

THERE WAS, IN fact, a lot of good things in her very near future, but not quite sex practice yet. Dev was dry, clean, in fresh sleep clothing and she had a cup of hot seaweed tea sweetened with some of the honey they'd brought back from their last mission. She watched curiously as Jess applied an inhaler to her nose and mouth, taking deep breaths from it.

She, too, was in the brief sleep clothes and as Dev watched she flexed her toes a little as she sucked in another lungful.

Somehow, she stopped thinking about what was going on elsewhere in the citadel. The world had shrunk in a way, down to the room they were in, and the two of them, alone.

"Is that a medicine?" Dev asked, after a while of silence.

Jess nodded. She pulled the mask off her face and cleared her throat. "It's an antibiotic vapor. Kills anything I might have picked up sucking in all that salt water." She paused, and regarded Dev soberly. "What do you think about that?"

"I think it's amazing," Dev said. "If you mean how you breathe water. That's the most amazing thing I have seen yet downside."

"Hmm." Jess took another few breaths, then lowered the breather again. "Part of my sordid family history." She glanced at Dev. "My mother, in one of her crazier moods, decided she'd toss the genetic dice and paid off some crackpot she found to tweak her eggs."

Dev's brows contracted. "Excuse me?"

"Kind of like what they do for you, up there." Jess examined the inhaler, finding it empty. She set it aside. "He switched a few things around and when I was born, the result was this." She indicated her chest. "They thought I had a birth defect at first. Were going to terminate me."

Dev blinked hard. "Excuse me?" she said again, a little louder.

"We've got no resources for people who can't contribute, Dev," Jess said, in a mild tone. "They don't keep defective babies." She took a sip of her own tea. "Where was I, oh yes, my internal arrangements.

Anyway, what I ended up with was a kind of feathery cups around all the air tubes in my lungs and when I put water in them, they filter out the oxygen and deliver it into my bloodstream."

This time Dev merely shook her head slightly.

"Huge breakthrough. Mom had all sorts of plans for me," Jess said. "Then of course I tested in." She indicated the citadel walls around her, and produced an ironic smile. "She never got over that. My father just laughed his ass off because she'd done it without asking him."

Dev sipped her tea in silence for a while. "I've taken some of the biologic programming," she said eventually. "That was very dangerous to attempt."

"Sure," Jess said. "She was nuts. I could have come out with two heads and ripped her apart in the process."

Dev's face scrunched.

"Anyway, it's borderline useful, as you saw. I don't do it often." Jess sighed. "Hurts like hell, and there's this to contend with after." She lifted the inhaler. "But I gotta tell ya, it was worth it seeing your face." She chuckled. "Your eyes nearly came out of your head."

"I was very surprised," Dev said. "So was Doctor Dan."

"Hard to say if I'd pass it or not." Jess examined her hand idly. "We've been adapting for a while out there." She held the hand up and spread her fingers. "Got a little bit of webbing already, and my skin repels the cold water. Common over at the Bay."

Dev put her cup down and moved closer, taking Jess's hand and examining it. There were scars along the back, and there, between each finger, a rounded bit of skin where on her own hands there was none. "Wow." She looked up at Jess. "They're so careful about making changes up in the creche, and here it's just happening."

"The ability to adapt is what kept humanity alive," Jess said. "So many species couldn't and died."

Dev curled her fingers around Jess's and looked at her. "You're amazing."

Jess grinned unexpectedly. "Nice for you to say that, instead of saying I'm a freak. In school they thought I was."

Dev looked thoughtful. "Yes, I know what that feels like," she said. "I felt like that in the creche, because I was the only instance of my set." She reflected. "It's sort of like the same thing."

Jess was about to protest, and then the words penetrated and she thought about them instead. "That's exactly what that feels like," she said. "I always felt like I was different. Even in school where everyone there was supposed to be different, I never felt like I belonged."

"Because of this?" Dev touched her hand.

"Because of everything," Jess answered. "I just always felt..." She glanced off across the room. "I never felt like I fit in. Even when I was tested, and accepted into the corps, and went through the training. There was just something there that never felt all the way right."

"Like something was missing."

"Maybe."

"I thought maybe my weird feeling would go away once I had a contract," Dev said. "And it did."

"It did?"

She nodded. "I felt like this was my place."

Jess got up and put the inhaler on her workspace, then came back and sat down next to Dev, leaning forward and letting her elbows rest on her knees. "Maybe they programmed you for that."

"Oh, they did. They gave me programming about this place, and a lot of the tech in it. But it wasn't something in my head that thought that, it was something in here." She touched her stomach. "It was a bit like..." She let out a relieved sigh. "Ah...like that."

Jess thought back to her arrival at the citadel and tried to remember what that had felt like. Had she been glad to be there? Had it been a welcome, or just another set of challenges?

Had it ever been home? Had her home ever been home? Jess shook her head and lifted her hands, wiggling her fingers. "Want to go to bed?"

"Yes." Dev set her cup down. "I would like that very much."

Jess turned and studied the latest readouts from ops. They were still very quiet, just standard entries from Elaine, and a few tech notes from Brent. Weather was stable.

With a slight grunt she stood and waited for Dev to join her, then they walked over to the bed in her quarters and settled onto it, the lights in the room dimming obediently as they sensed the pressure on the soft surface. "Damn, that feels good." Jess stretched out and felt her body relax. "Comfortable as that chair is, it ain't like sleeping."

"No." Dev curled up next to her and reached out to touch Jess's arm, fitting her fingers around it in a gentle clasp. "This is nice."

Jess rolled onto her side and smiled. "Want to do something nicer?"

"Yes, I do." Dev took Jess's hand and kissed it, feeling the skin warm under her lips. "But if we're supposed to rest, shouldn't we?"

"No." Jess leaned over and kissed her on the lips. "We should do what we want to do, cause you never know what's gonna happen next."

Dev was more than glad to defer to her partner's wisdom in that regard. Her body was already appreciating the touch, sensation growing and making her both want to touch Jess back, and for all to continue.

The lights dimmed further, and only the slight glow from the screens on Jess's workspace and the trim around the walls was visible, casting them both into shadows. Dev felt the fabric of her light shirt being pulled up and then Jess's touch was exploring her skin and the pleasant sensation increased.

She touched Jess back, and heard a soft sound come from her. That was interesting. She repeated the motion, suspecting she was pleasing her partner and also making her feel good as well.

She wanted that. Even more than she wanted to feel good herself. Jess had seemed sad to her, despite her demurral, and she wanted to see if she could make her feel happy.

So she called up all the things she'd learned about sex, and set to work applying them, touching and tasting and listening for those little noises, feeling Jess's breathing get faster as she moved closer and their bodies pressed together.

Dev was glad to discover the fact that when they were lying down it didn't matter that Jess was so much taller than she was. Jess's arms curled around her as she continued her exploration, moving down Jess's body with a sense of pleasant curiosity.

She slid her hand down and found Jess's shorts already gone, and realized her own were too. She wondered for a moment when that had happened, then forgot about it as a touch caressed her inner thigh and her breathing caught from it, a surge of desire flooding through her, making her press her head against Jess's stomach.

Her body felt warm, for the first time in days. She even felt a little sweat breaking out, as she returned the touch and then went further, trying to remember what it was that Jess liked her to do as she felt Jess's body shift and tense under her, a low growl rumbling from her throat.

Ah yes, she remembered the motion and the touch, and the position that was just like—

Jess's body started to convulse, the grip on Dev tightening as she kept up the rhythm until she could hear gasping, then she relaxed the pressure, gentling and slowing the motion as Jess slowly relaxed, rocking them both lightly in an embrace.

Dev was pleased. She thought she'd done the right things. "Was that okay?"

Jess laughed silently, her body jerking with it. "Never got programming for that, really?"

"No." Dev fitted her body against Jess's with a feeling of contentment. "Not at all."

"Fuck." Jess slid her hands along Dev's slightly sweat dampened sides. "You could get paid to do that."

Dev enjoyed the touch, especially when Jess started gently teasing motions of her own. "I can't get paid for anything, actually," she said. "But I'd rather not do it with anyone but you."

"Ah, is that so?" Jess's attentions got a little more intense.

"Yes," Dev whispered, her body starting to hum with pleasure. She welcomed the heat as Jess pressed against her, and wondered how she could have even thought getting rest would be better than this.

JESS LAY QUIETLY, on the very edge of sleep. Her body was sensitized yet sated, knowing a sense of inner peace so rare as to almost not be trusted.

Almost.

Dev was curled up next to her, pale head burrowed into Jess's shoulder, and one arm flung over her, the steady warmth of her breath tickling the bare skin.

It felt so good. So good, and so very unusual for her. She'd never experienced the feeling she had right now, not ever before when she'd shared a bed with someone. Never felt this relaxed, this at peace with herself.

Even knowing it wouldn't last, that a minute from now, or an hour, or even if she was lucky a handful of hours, she'd be back in the maelstrom and facing death, or worse, couldn't stop her from savoring this feeling of peace, and contentment, and yes, of happiness.

Didn't matter. Jess wiggled her toes and let her thoughts slip, savoring the feeling of sleep taking her over, tucked under the covers in her own bed, with her own...

What, really, was Dev? Her partner? Yes. Her lover? Jess smiled briefly. Well yes, apparently so. Her friend? She thought about that word, tasting it cautiously on the back of her tongue. Yes, maybe Dev was that, too. If they both survived, it would be interesting to discover what they ended up being.

Dev belonged to Interforce though. Jess frowned. They'd paid for her, and like all the rest of the bios in the citadel, Dev was property of the corps and had no say in her future.

Maybe they could last long enough for Jess to retire, and then— She remembered, abruptly what her brother had revealed at Drake's Bay. Jess's eyes opened and she looked up into the darkness of her quarters. If she retired, and went civ, could she pay off Dev's contract and bring her to the Bay?

She'd have all the resources of the Bay behind her now, wouldn't she?

Dev stirred in her sleep and nestled closer, the dim reflection from her collar catching Jess's eye. If she did buy her contract, could they take that off? Would Dev want to have it off, if it meant no more programming for her?

Hmm. Jess shook her head and firmly closed her eyes. Time enough to think of that once they got out of the mess they were in now. No sense in counting your shrimps before you brought the basket up, right?

Right.

At last, she let sleep take her, resolved to get as much rest as fate would let her.

HANDS GRABBED HER and she twisted, pulling against straps that kept her flat on her back, wrenching her arms to pull them free to fight.

It was dark. It was loud. She could hear screams and explosions. Nearby there was laughter, and then she felt the hot agony as a knife plunged into her and her back arched as she tried to move away from it.

An ankle came free, and she twisted more violently, lifting her knee up and kicking out against the hands holding her down. A body slammed down over her and she let out a deep growl, her eyes flickering shut and then open as the rage built, bringing clean energy to her.

A yell of alarm, and she convulsed, throwing the body off her and breaking a strap holding her wrist. Now she was half free. She slammed her fist into a moving head and grabbed hold with her fingers, feeling one sink into an eye socket. She used the body as a shield to intercept the energy beams she sensed coming at her.

The body fell over and she used the momentum to pull her up against the straps, feeling the strain and then the heavy snap as the leather parted and she was on her feet.

"She's loose!"

Jess let the rage take her. The pain in her back faded, and she slammed against the nearest body, knocking them back, revealing, for a split second the handle of a blaster that she got her fingers on and yanked from its holster.

"Look out!"

She was caught up in the dream this time, its vivid starkness playing out, but the waves of horror she'd felt before in it wasn't there. This time she felt her heart pounding, and her skin flushing, but instead of feeling terror, she understood she was the genesis of it.

It was an exhilarating sense of freedom, startling and new and in the foggy way of dreams she knew a moment of wonder as she went with the newness of it, fading back into the action and surging forward.

Hands grabbed her and she spun them off, letting her mind slide down into that space where everything went black and white and she went from captive to hunter, turning and spinning as she pulled the blaster into her body and then unlocked it, recognizing the keys as one of her own.

Josh's blaster. She brought it up and ducked a thrown arm, swiveling in the other direction as she let out a long blast of energy, cutting through bodies and consoles as people dove in all directions away from her.

Then she saw the doorway open, and fill with armored bodies and she kept on going with the blaster, getting the guards in the face in a swath before she got all the way around and saw Josh.

Just long enough to see his eyes widen before she blew his head apart in a splatter of bone and blood.

No thought, just instinct, her legs propelling her body up into the air as return fire lit the space she'd been in and she twisted and kept firing, the blaster growing hot in her hands.

Stark and clear and raw, she threw herself into the battle and lost all regard for her own safety. She was aware of a rush of energy that sent her back up into the air and into a twisting turn that had blaster fire shooting to every side of her, but somehow missing a hit, and the delicious sensation of tumbling in midair as she returned the shots with pinpoint accuracy.

Then her peripheral vision caught a motion. She turned and aimed as a black sheet of glass slid closed, giving her just one brief glimpse of a profile before it was gone, and the wall sealed with a blue tinted edge as she stared at it, frozen in a moment of time.

A voice whispered in her ear. Jess felt the dream slowly fade, with her in frozen stasis, the shock of realization moderating to a knowledge of her true surroundings as she opened her eyes to find Dev gazing at her in total, absorbed concern.

"Dev."

Dev looked around, then back at her. "Yes? Are you all right? You were moving around and I thought you were dreaming."

Jess took a few breaths, as her body came down from the battle high. "I was. I was having that same bad dream but— "

"You weren't yelling this time." Dev settled back down next to her. "It didn't seem dangerous to interrupt you."

"No." Jess paused to think. "It wasn't the same. Ended weird. Or maybe...I don't know if I...maybe it was me that was different this time. I wasn't," she paused briefly. "I wasn't scared. Something changed."

"Is that a good thing or a bad thing?"

"I think it's a good thing," Jess said. "I think I remembered something. Maybe."

She checked the chrono and then relaxed again, putting an arm around Dev and letting her eyes drift closed. "We can worry about it in the morning."

"Okay."

"Along with everything else. "

THE SOFT CHIME of first watch sounding woke her up. Jess glanced at the chrono in some startlement, then blinked the sleep out of her eyes as she propped herself up in bed.

No dreams this time. Just a long space of delicious oblivion, almost as normal as it once had been to wake up here.

A slight sound nearly made her bound out of it, then she belatedly recognized Dev's form as Dev entered from her own quarters and came over to the bed, a steaming cup in her hands. "Hello." She offered Jess the cup. "Would you like some tea?"

"Sure." Jess pulled her legs up crossed under her and took the cup. "Been up long?"

"About a half hour," Dev said. "I checked with operations, and things are still nominal, so I thought it would be all right to let you rest a while longer."

Jess sipped her seaweed tea and observed Dev over the rim of her cup. "You feel better today?"

Dev smiled. "I do," she said. "Do you?"

Jess considered that. "Yeah. My back's a little sore still. But okay aside from that." She stretched her body out a little and realized it was true. "Let me go check in." She got up and went to the workspace, carrying the tea with her. She sat down and ran her hands through her hair, then started to key up the screens.

"Jess?"

"Huh?" She glanced up to find Dev approaching, a bit of her discarded clothing in one hand. "What's that for?"

"If you're going to go on vid comms, you might consider putting a shirt on." Dev said. "I know if I was on the other end of the transmission it would be very distracting."

Jess glanced down, then grinned. "Ah, they're used to my ugly old carcass." She took the shirt Dev offered her anyway, and put it on, then triggered comms. "Ops?"

Dev went over to the other screen and tapped something into it, reviewing the results intently.

The vid cleared after a moment and Jess was looking at April. "Morning," she greeted. "How's life?"

April was in a fresh jumpsuit, and looked alert and rested. "Good morning. Elaine and Brent are off shift. Jason is stable in med, and Mike is getting the bay recommissioned."

"Thanks." Jess nodded. "How's met?"

"Line of storms is building, expected overhead plus four," April said crisply. "Mike said they got a screen up over the bay, should stand up to the rain."

"Right." Jess felt a sense of the inevitable brush over her. "Plus one, in the recon chamber. Let's put the plan down. Let everyone know."

"Ack," April responded immediately. "Plus one."

Jess closed comms and leaned her elbows on the desk, regarding Dev with a bemused expression. "I guess it's time to go be in charge, Devvie." She pushed herself to her feet. "Let's get ourselves in order and get some grub, and go do what we do."

"Jess?"

"Hmm?"

Dev came over and touched her side. "You do not have an ugly old carcass. Not if the comp dictionary gave me back the correct reference."

Jess smiled at her. "Ah, you're a sweet talker, you are." She affectionately cupped Dev's face in her hands. "C'mon, Devvie. I'm a wreck."

Dev shook her head, her eyes watching Jess's intently. "You're the most beautiful person I've ever known."

Jess felt the blush, and she blinked a little, finding herself surprisingly tongue-tied. "Um." She cleared her throat gently. "I don't think anyone ever said anything like that to me before."

"Really?" Dev straightened up as Jess tilted her head down and they kissed. "I don't know why not." She gave her a hug. "But I'm glad I got to say it."

Jess smiled, staring across her quarters as she returned the hug, rocking them both back and forth. "Me too." She finally said. "Meeee too."

THE OPS STATUS room was familiar and not, patched walls combining with the well-remembered long table shifting Jess's perceptions as she circled the latter and paused at the head of it, resting her hand on the big chair there before tugging it out and settling into it.

She motioned Dev to the monitoring console up a step on a platform at the back of the room. Dev seated herself and started tapping the tablets when the door opened and the rest of the agents and techs filed in.

Jess was in a fresh jumpsuit, with her insignia on the collar, and given what had happened, she knew that in fact, as well as in theory, she was in charge here. There simply was no one else, and even if there had been she'd have taken it.

Jess started talking once everyone had sat down. "Okay. So we have a marginally functioning base here."

Brent nodded in agreement. "Marginally. One thing we do have now is power. Batts are all topped up and we charged all the carriers while we were at it."

"Good," Jess said. "We've got a storm front coming over in three hours. Anyone want to give me odds we'll get a wave of boom with it?"

"No odds," Elaine said. She still had the look of recent sleep about her. She'd woken up and insisted on attending the meeting. "Fuckers'll be back, unless they already have what they came for."

"The weapons rig?" Tucker asked. "Good luck to 'em with it. Hope it fries them like it did the last poor asshole who put it on."

"Maybe they'll figure out how to use it. You almost did." Elaine looked over at Jess. "I heard them talking after you tried it."

"Not almost, I did." Jess shrugged "Wasn't particularly hard. You just want to kill everything in your path and it helps you do it. They were more scared of me in that thing than I was of it."

The other agents studied her thoughtfully. "So," Elaine said. "Did they want it and you separately? Did they want to prevent you from using it? Or did they figure to make you an offer you couldn't refuse?"

Instead of immediately scoffing at the idea, Jess considered it. "Good question. What do you think, Dev?"

Dev looked up from the console. "What do I think?" She repeated the question. "I don't have enough information to have an opinion."

"That never stops us, kid," Elaine said. "Here, opinions are like assholes and breasts. Everyone has at least one."

Dev blinked at her.

Jess chuckled dryly. "If I had to bet, I'd bet they just wanted to fry me for Gibraltar, and they took the rig because they found it accidentally. They sure as hell haven't made me an offer. They've been way too busy trying to shoot me for that."

Elaine exhaled. "Maybe it would have been better if they had. Maybe you could have brought us with you. This looks pretty dead end to me here, Jess. That would have at the least got us inside there."

"If they didn't kill us," Jess said. "No way they'd trust me no matter what the offer was."

Mike and April remained quiet, their eyes shifting from one to the other. Their techs were sitting quietly also, in chairs on the far side of the room near where Dev was busy again at her console.

Elaine shrugged. "Still a dead end here."

"Might be dead end," Jess said. "Based on this stuff." She indicated the plas damage reports with a thumb. "We can probably get the outer guns up, and some of the shields, but if they come full at us, that won't last long." She pondered the plas. "We'll get some of them though. I'll make sure they have some regrets before they tank us."

"Storm'll skew that too." Brent was sitting at the table with them, not with the rest of the techs. He had that faint air of slight discomfort of someone not sure of their place. "Scanners can't tell the diff between plasma fire and incoming lightning. We could end up firing at clouds."

"That's not correct."

Everyone turned to look at Dev in surprise. Dev swung around and looked back at them.

"The spectrum is different, according to this comp." Dev pointed at the console. "It's point four three five out of phase." Her voice was quiet, but confident. "That is tunable."

The room went silent for a minute.

"Lemme see." Brent got up and mounted the step up to the console, pausing behind Dev and peering at the screen.

"Dev rigged her comp to find fish schools at depth," Jess said. "So she's probably right."

Brent glanced over his shoulder. "Didn't say she wasn't."

"Anyway." Jess returned her attention to the rest of the group. "We'll operate under the assumption we'll be attacked when the storm hits. Let's get whatever defenses we've got up, and shunt power to them so we don't just let them roll over us. Then if they penetrate, and come in again, we'll draw them to a central point."

Elaine nodded. "Logical place would be centops."

"But we would have to leave a trail of broken doors to it through the heart of the citadel," Jess said. "Likely?" She watched her fellow agent lift a hand and let it drop. "We keep them as close to the perimeter as we can. If they hit the carrier bay focus them into maintenance level six, and if they get into the shuttle bay use security main."

"That makes sense," April said. "So the deal is we leave breached entries to both spots?" she said. "And booby-trap 'em?"

Jess nodded. "You and Mike take care of that," she said. "The rest of us will work on the defensive systems, unless Dev's already done that." She eyed her partner.

"Not quite yet," Dev said. Brent was now seated next to her, pouring over the data on the screens and leaning on his elbows as his eyes flicked over the readouts intently. Dev went back to working on the screen, as Mike and April and their partners stood and headed out, leaving Elaine behind at the table.

"So we make a valiant last stand, or hope HQ sends support?" Elaine asked, propping her chin on her fist. "I'm okay with that, by the way. Worse ways to go."

"Jess," Dev interrupted gently. "I am getting biologic readings in what is listed as a storage facility."

Jess got up and came over to see, Elaine circling the table to join them. "What is...oh." She leaned on the back of the seat Dev was in. "No ident?"

"Scan is not working well in that location," Dev said. "It's just showing bio." She paused. "And it's not some of us."

"Us?" Jess eyed her.

"Biological Alternatives," Dev clarified. "We have these." She touched her neck, as if reminding Jess. "They do read on scan."

"Don't forget you're more us." Jess indicated herself and Elaine. "Maybe I can talk to your buddy and see what we can do about that necklace."

Dev's eyes went a little rounder, and she tilted her head as she focused intently on Jess. "What?"

"Later." Jess glanced at Elaine. "Let's go find out what that target is," she said. "Dev, you two stay here and get as much working as you can in weapons and defense."

"Yes," Dev said. "But Jess, please take care."

Jess paused and regarded her, a faint smile crossing her face. "I will." She lifted a hand in a wave and headed out the door, Elaine ambling after her, not without giving Dev a long, considering look.

Dev stood up. "I think the systems in the operations room are more functional," she said. "Would you like to move back there to work on this task?"

Brent stood. "Sure. Why not?" He led the way down the step and out of the room. "So you and Jess hook up?" he asked her, as they walked along the corridor.

"Yes." Dev had taken care to look the term up the last time Jess had used it.

"Didn't think that was reg," Brent said. "Guess it don't matter much now, though."

"Yes, it is not correct for bio alts," Dev said. "But I was told it was all right because of the job I am assigned to." She touched the pad on the door to the operations room and it opened obediently for her. "However I think you are correct in saying at this time, it does not seem important to worry about."

"Sucks," Brent said. "But I'm glad you guys hooked up," he volunteered suddenly, surprising Dev. "Been good for Jess."

Dev sat down at one of the big consoles, and put her hands on the pads, but she didn't start keying anything. "What does that mean?" She finally asked, turning to look at Brent, who had settled across from her.

He looked back at her, looking a little startled. "Huh?"

"That thing you said about it being good for Jess?"

"Oh." Brent hunched over the inputs. "Nothin'."

Dev waited, but there seemed to be no other response forthcoming, so she shook her head and went back to the screens, calling up all the schematics of the citadel and studying them.

"Hey," Brent said. "She's hot, huh?"

Dev watched her own reflection in the display as her brows contracted over her eyes. She turned her head and peered at Brent in bewilderment. "Excuse me?"

"Jess," he said. "She's hot, huh?"

Hot. "Um." Dev was now quite distracted. "In my experience I've found her very pleasantly warm, actually," she said, slowly. "Is there a purpose to the question?"

Brent grunted and shook his head, then went back to his console, tapping into the pad with stolid deliberation. "Fuckin' A."

Dev pinched the bridge of her nose and went back to her scan, shaking her own head in silence.

JESS WAS AWARE of Elaine's eyes on her as they stalked the corridors, ignoring bio alts heading in the opposite direction. "You figure it's some of us hiding?"

"Maybe," Elaine said. "So tell me. What's that thing like in bed?"

"What?"

"You heard me."

"You mean Dev?"

"Yes. The jelly bag brain," Elaine responded. "Your little mech tech toy."

Jess glanced at her. "You trying to piss me off on purpose?" she asked, in a mild tone.

The next moment she was inside the corridor, and Elaine had her blaster pressed against her ribs. "Yes, I am. Because I don't know who this Jess Drake is, and I have to wonder if they didn't get to you after all. The Jess I know would have shot me for saying that."

Jess felt a sense of shock and belated awareness of danger. She looked intently at Elaine's face. "You want me to shoot you?" she queried. "You don't think we've got enough trouble here without you and I scrapping it out? Really?"

"They get you, Jess?" Elaine stared right back at her. "Let me end it. You don't want that on you, not with your history."

Jess felt the tension start to build in her. "They didn't get me," she replied. "Maybe I'm just tired."

"Bullshit."

"Maybe being able to trust my partner made a difference."

"Bullshit."

"Maybe I just got a thing for her."

"Really?" Elaine unlocked the blaster. "I don't think so. I think they bought you and now we're just the remnants being turned over to those bastards."

Jess's fingertips twitched. "Don't be stupid."

"I'm not. You've been acting like a space case civ since you got back. Either they got you, or you're on something. Either way, you ain't running me."

The motion surprised both of them, but Elaine more, as the weapon smacked against the far wall and Elaine was on the ground, bent over Jess's knee, fingers gripping her throat like a vise, inches from having her back broken.

"Nobody bought me." Jess's voice held a familiar rasp. "And the last thing I took was a bio pack inhaler since I had to breathe water out there saving everyone's ass."

Elaine looked up and saw the ice veneer on those pale eyes and in that moment she relaxed completely, holding her hands up in surrender, palms exposed. "Now that's more like it."

Jess relaxed her fingers. "Just because I'm not a fucking maniac all the time doesn't mean I turned," she said. "That's a bullshit thing to say."

"You're different," Elaine said. "Look what it took to get you to do this."

Was she? "I'm tired." Jess straightened up and pulled Elaine up to her feet. "And Dev's made a difference, but not what you think." From an objective view, she didn't even resent Elaine's attack. She might have done it herself if they swapped positions.

She had been acting a little weird. A little soft, maybe, distracted by the focus on these new and strange emotions she'd been experiencing. Still, no call to shove a gun up her nose.

Elaine went over and retrieved her blaster, safing it and shoving it into her side mount holster. "So you're not screwing with her? I don't believe it. You can't tell me those vibes are fake."

"C'mon." Jess led the way back through the cross-corridor and into the main, walking with long, impatient strides. "Our sleeping arrangements are really none of your fucking business."

Elaine kept up with her. "What's the big deal? I sleep with Jason, and with Tucker, and everyone knows it. We all knew you weren't bunking with Josh, but you've never been shy about that."

"Dev's different."

Elaine rolled her eyes. "No shit."

"Not like that." Jess felt suddenly uncomfortable. "She's just a nice kid."

They started down the slanted path to the storage bays, tucked at the base of the cliff where the stone held the chill all the time.

"She's technically off limits," Elaine suddenly said. "Not that I figure that would stop you."

"Didn't stop her." Jess felt a faint flush color her cheeks and was glad of the gloom of the corridor. "She's pretty close to being one of us."

"Wishful thinking?"

Jess shook her head. "You saw the comp vid. Dev's got a mind of her own."

They walked in silence for a minute. "She's not a regular bio anyway, that's true," Elaine said, finally. "Got some smarts and I think she's stuck on you."

They reached the end of the hall and Jess cycled the lock, palming the patch at the door and standing back as the stone lined steel ground open. It exposed a man lock, and they entered, waiting for the door behind them to completely close before they triggered the next one.

The sound of the hatch opening echoed loudly, and as they stepped through, they both went quiet, and still, as the panel slid shut behind them and closed with a grinding snick.

Inside the big cavern were irregularly shaped storage capsules, originally part of the rock structure but sealed off with heavy plas, and doors that were firmly shut. Jess drew her blaster and unlocked it, making no effort to muffle the sound. She let the echo of that fade too, and then moved forward into the space.

Elaine followed, moving a shoulder's width to her left, shifting her blaster to her right hand. She touched the comms set and lowered her voice. "Ops, ack."

"Ops," Brent answered.

"Target?"

"Standby."

They moved farther into the cavern and approached the first set of storage alcoves. Jess turned her head to the left, and then the right, straining her ears for any signs of life. The fact that no one had come to greet them made her now expect intruders and not refugees from the base, and she felt a sense of impatient anger rising.

Her own comms tickled her ear. "Jess?" Dev's warm, slightly burring voice whispered. "Go," Jess said.

"Comp sweep," Dev said. "Comms set to loop."

Jess stopped walking. "Repeat?"

"Comms set to loop," Dev said again. "Admin lock, top sec."

"What?" Elaine drifted over, watching her.

Jess turned and started back to the hatch. "Let's go," she said. "Dev, break it."

"Ack." Dev responded readily. "In work."

They got to the door and Jess hit the pad, turning and putting her back to the wall as she swept the area in front of them. "Seems like something got hung up in comms," she told Elaine. "Got the feeling we're being drawn here."

Elaine didn't question it. She ducked into the hatch as it opened and turned in a circle with her blaster drawn, moving in pattern with Jess as they retreated behind the closing door.

The rumbling blast sent them back against the inner door, but the outer held, and as the inner keyed open they tumbled out and started back for ops at a run.

"Day is full of suckage," Elaine remarked.

"Getting worse every minute." Jess powered up the ramp toward the main operations corridor, as alarms started to blare and lights rapidly morphed from white to red. "And it's starting to really, really piss me off."

Chapter Seventeen

DEV FOCUSED INTENTLY on the screen, her fingers tapping lightly on the input surface as she ignored the sounds and vibrations of the room around her.

A piece of debris flew by her and she ducked, pressing her hands flat against the pad and then straightening, surprised to see the screen go blank, then show a process in progress. She looked down at her hands, then quickly looked around the room, hoping whatever it was she'd done wasn't too disruptive.

The door burst open and Jess appeared, outlined in raging red light with Elaine behind her. "What's up?"

"Somethin' blew up in the cave," Brent said. "Plas based, but our sig."

Jess hauled up short. "Ours?"

Brent nodded. "Key frequency defense plus four," he added. "Like maybe they thought you were the bad guys."

"Huh." Jess circled the console Dev was at and safed her gun. "El, secure med, and get everyone under cover," she said. "Can we get comms to the cavern? Bitch if they're some of us making a last stand."

"No." Dev sorted through the requests. "Comms is cut to that whole sector, and most of scan." She indicated the boards. "This junction here appears damaged."

The door opened again and Jess's hand went to her blaster, then paused as Dan Kurok's familiar outline appeared. "Ah. You."

He had a toolkit strapped around his body and if no one had known better, he'd have been taken for any other tech in the corps. "I think we've got incoming." He slid into a seat next to Brent and pulled a pad over. "Ahead of the storm."

"Scan's clear," Brent said.

Dev pulled over a pad of her own and called up the link to her own carrier, parked on its pad in the damaged carrier bay. She accessed its systems and studied the output, keying in and starting a scan from its position. "Jess..."

Jess's shoulder bumped hers as she leaned closer and her eyes tracked to the reading Dev's finger was pointing to.

Dev heard the hitch in Jess's breathing and felt her straighten up as the door opened yet again and April bolted in, blaster in hand.

"Someone was bringing the grid down." April's voice was breathless yet crisp. "I blew out a body in a cabinet but didn't stop to pick up the pieces."

"Brent, lock everything down," Jess said. "Go to emergency code two, and seal everything you can."

"Ack." Brent went to work.

"No time to draw them elsewhere." Jess slammed a hand against the console. "Fuck I'm tired of not knowing what the hell is going on."

Dev spoke into her comms. "Yes, please move clear." She triggered beam level protections in the carrier bay, watching the power re-balance as Brent sealed the access. She paused, then switched over to a second set of comm syncs. "Kaytee, Kaytee. Ops."

"Here," the soft voice answered.

"There is danger," Dev said. "Incorrect persons are in the facility, doing damage." She looked up to find Doctor Dan regarding her from the next console. "Please make yourselves safe."

"We will take care," the Kaytee responded. "May we make the incorrectness stop if it is possible?"

Dev looked at Doctor Dan. After a very brief moment, he nodded. "Yes," Dev said, into the comms. "Doctor Dan says that is permitted."

"We understand," the Kaytee said, and the comms clicked off. Dev took a breath and released it, then shifted her attention to her carrier scan. "Jess, there are crafts coming toward this facility," she said. "Systems are now stable," she added, as she felt Jess's hand touch her shoulder, fingers warm and powerful as they squeezed gently.

"All right, let's seal everything we can, and make it—" Jess stopped speaking as the inner door to ops opened, the one that led to the technical spaces. She turned to face the door, drawing her weapon as it filled with large, armored bodies.

"Ah, ah." A tall, gaunt figure eased past them. "No shooting, Agent Drake. These fellows have no sense of humor." Alexander Bain had his own blaster firmly in his grip, though the muzzle was pointed at the ceiling.

The armored bodies had long blasters cradled in their arms, the security insignia of Interforce silver and bold on their chests. There were six of them, and they spread out to cover the agents in the room.

Jess left her free hand on Dev's shoulder but shifted slightly so her body was between the guns and Dev. "Glad we bothered to clear the shuttle bay for you." She kept Bain in view, the security agents in her peripheral vision.

"Alex." Dan Kurok stood up and faced him. "What's going on?"

"Ah, that's the question isn't it?" Bain paused behind the damaged master console at the top of the stepped rise. "As Agent Drake noted, I appreciated the effort to allow my cruiser to land. Fortunately it will also allow me to leave, once my business here is finished. Pity you interrupted that." He glanced at April.

"You were taking the power down?" April asked hesitantly. "But—"

"Yes. This facility has become...hmm...let's say a pawn in a much larger struggle. A down payment, as it were." Bain studied them. "This will make an excellent forward base."

Jess felt a sense of shock as the words penetrated, matching up with the faint, instinct driven suspicions that had started to bubble up in her. "For them."

"Certainly," Bain said, in a mild voice. "You should have listened to Mr. Bock, Drake. He was telling you the truth about it being over. It is." He checked a chrono strapped to his wrist. "In perhaps an hour, the West coast facilities will be finding that out as well."

Kurok walked forward, ignoring the gun muzzles swinging in his direction. "You sold out."

"Oh, come now, DJ." Bain waved his free hand. "You know better than anyone how fluid sides can be." He leaned against the chair behind the console. "I thought perhaps you realized what was in the wind when you volunteered to be captured. Didn't figure you'd be back so soon." He produced a chilly smile. "Didn't offer enough?"

Kurok's posture shifted, just slightly, just enough to make Jess's nape hairs prickle. "They didn't offer me a dime, Alex," he answered softly. "But then I didn't go for that."

Bain eyed him. "You went for Tagaron."

Kurok smiled faintly.

"You always were a sentimental idiot." Bain shook his head. "After all this time? I hope you left him intact."

Doctor Dan's smile broadened, but showed no real humor at all. "I'm afraid I didn't." He glanced at Jess. "I didn't mention it at the time, but that's why they were chasing me." He looked back at Bain. "So now what, Alex? They just come in and take over?"

"Yes," Bain said. "A foothold on this coast, then the rest. I'm afraid I wasn't able to get the rest of our leadership on board with my plan, but no matter. It's just a little more time."

"So that's why you've been blocking comms, and why Bock did," Jess said calmly. "You didn't want them to know."

"Of course not," Bain said. "And indeed, you proved yourself to be the one consistently inconsistent obstacle in this entire affair, Agent Drake. You never did what I expected."

"Not even when you had Josh try to take me out?" Jess said.

"Indeed." Bain tilted his head in her direction. "And you can see, I couldn't allow you to leave the force after that, Drake. You're far too dangerous." He cleared his throat. "Stephen would have shot you, of course. You never would have gotten to the harvesters, not with Drake's Bay coming into your control. Too much resistance there."

"I'm not an easy kill," Jess said, in a quiet voice.

"Certainly not," Bain said.

Dev just sat there listening. There was so much going on that was wrong. She could see how angry Doctor Dan was, and she could feel the tension in Jess's body, and the shock of the agents and techs in the room was almost palpable.

This was very, very bad.

This was betrayal, like the betrayal Jess had suffered when her partner had damaged her in that other place. She could see it in Jess's posture, and in Doctor Dan's expression, and in the look of fury in April's eyes.

"So," Bain said. "I will ask you all to go into the recreation facility, where we will seal the doors. Then I'm sure our friends will find something entertaining to do with you. Terribly sorry about it all. Nothing personal, you understand. I appreciate all of your talents, I just cannot afford them at this time. Ah, ah, none of that." He pointed his finger at April. "My dear, this suit I'm wearing will send that blast right back at you and I would hate to damage the equipment here."

April slowly let her hand fall away from her gun, glaring at Bain with seething intensity.

The security agents pointed their blasters at them. "Put your weapons on the table." The nearest one to Jess barked. "Or I'll blow your arm off."

Jess stared steadily at him, leaving her hand on her blaster, her nostrils flaring slightly as she stood quite still in the silence. "Sure you want to leave me behind?" She met Bain's eyes directly. "I might just kill them all."

Bain's ice gray eyes narrowed a trifle.

"You said yourself I was too dangerous," Jess said. "You feel safer with those six bozos or with me?" She ignored the looks of startled outrage from her erstwhile team. "Maybe I want to go with you."

Dev felt a completely different kind of shock. Was Jess really doing what it appeared?

Would she go with the man Bain?

Would she leave them all behind?

Will she leave me behind?

There was a momentary silence. Then Bain broke it. "Drake, you do interest me," he said, with a faint almost rueful smile. "Do you really expect me to believe you'd turn your back on this place, these people, your history, and change sides? Come now. I know better. I knew your father, didn't I?"

Jess remained calm, breathing easily. "So what has this ever offered to me? I was going to be mustered out until you showed up." She took a step forward, putting a bit of distance between herself and Dev. "This place? These people? My family'd be glad to see the last of me. You know what I am. You want to waste that?"

"I see." Bain looked thoughtful. "Hmm. Ah, you might have a point there, Drake. It seems to me you act more for your interests than anyone else."

Jess smiled. "I'm not my father."

"That's for sure," Kurok said.

Jess ignored him. Ignored the look she knew she was getting from Dev, who was smart enough to realize what she was saying and know her own betrayal.

It was what it was.

Dev felt a wave of unhappiness flow over her. She looked down at the console, not wanting to meet any of the other eyes in the room.

"I owe you more than I do Interforce," Jess continued. "No matter how you did it or why."

Something that might have been a faint charmed smile appeared on Bain's face. "Hmm." He checked his chrono again. "Put your weapon down, Drake, and I might consider it."

Jess pulled her blaster out and tossed it to one side without hesitation. She kept her back to the rest of the room, not daring to look at any of them.

Especially not Dev. She could almost sense the horror and confusion from her, and the steaming fury from Kurok, standing just to her right.

That, at least, she understood at a deep, gut level, and taking one very short peek at his face, Jess suddenly knew at her very core exactly what, or more specifically, who his loyalty was anchored to and finally she had a personal understanding of why.

But she was out of choices. Turn her back on those security rifles and she'd be dead.

"Well then," Bain said, after a long pause. "The rest of you, to the door. I would shorten your distress, but certain machinery in this facility is not worth risking blaster fire." He waved them forward. "It appears Agent Drake and I have something to talk about."

Jess was nearest the door. She kept her eyes shifted as the rest of them slowly started moving, walking past her as Bain came down and stood at her side. "I'm not often surprised, Drake." he said, conversationally. "Quite an interesting sensation."

"Yes, sir," Jess murmured softly.

Dev came past her, trying to catch her eye. But Jess refused to meet it, only just keeping from biting the inside of her lip as her peripheral vision caught Kurok's hand coming to rest on Dev's shoulder, and the faint, soft intake of Dev's breath.

There was a pain there she hadn't expected. Jess drew a breath in and pushed past it, focusing on what she knew she had to do.

April was the last to come past her. Now Jess lifted her head and met her fellow agent's glance for one very long moment, as April shifted her direction just slightly as she moved around a chair, her face a stolid, stony mask.

"I will have to rearrange some things. Find a place for you," Bain said. "I'm sure your new colleagues will be...hmm...even more surprised than I was."

"I'm sure they will." Jess's heart started to pound. "But I've never really been predictable, they tell me."

Bain chuckled. "Something that might well prove

to my advantage. Hmm?"

"Maybe." She felt the blood rush to her skin as her senses sharpened and she dislocated her thinking brain from her instincts as April came up even with her and she let second thoughts and regrets go. The energy flooded through her and her hand shot out, fingers closing around the knife hilt at April's hip. "Or not. Like now, for instance."

She drew and spun and slammed her hand and arm as hard as she could into Bain, feeling the grinding shock as the blade in her hand penetrated his light armored jumpsuit and cut through him, as a blast of energy hit her and filled her world with fire.

She let out a roar and yanked the knife back out, then plunged it back into his body again, the hardened blade cutting through his energy suit and sending a keening scream up into the air.

She heard Kurok shout, and Dev yell her name and a scramble behind her, but all that mattered was feeling the hot blood on her hands and the jerking of Bain's body as he gasped in her grip.

She hit the wall and took Bain's body with her, feeling something hit him as she yanked the blaster out of his hand and spun again, letting instinct drive her as she fired back toward the guards and dropped to her knees to avoid the returning fire.

She could smell blood, and she was lifting her blaster to fire again when something hit her and blew her back against the wall again, knocking her into darkness as she felt the world fade away, the sound of her own name echoing weirdly following her.

PAIN WOKE HER. Even breathing hurt. Jess felt something shift under her, relatively soft and yielding as it cradled her body. She forced one eye half open to see what was going on.

A scanner pulled back out of her view and was replaced by Dan Kurok's face, a spattering of blood staining his cheek as he gazed at her. "You were wrong," he said, glancing at the scanner. "You are most precisely and exactly your father." He shook his head. "Pair of idiots, the both of you."

Jess managed a faint smile as she tilted her head up a little, to find Dev looking back at her, since she was the owner and operator of the surface Jess was lying on. Dev looked totally and completely freaked out, and she could see from the look of her eyes that she'd been crying.

And still was, apparently, as a tear emerged and rolled down her cheek. "Sorry," Jess managed to croak at her. "I land on ya or somethin'?"

Dev answered by hugging her, which hurt, and didn't, all at once.

"Sixty minutes to arrival." Brent's voice echoed softly.

"Guns six and eight are up," April replied. "If they come in east we can maybe get one or two of them."

Jess could hear the sounds fading in and out. She tried moving a hand, then stopped immediately when a bolt of pain resulted. She thought she heard the door open, and the sound of a bio alt speaking, but all of it was being overshadowed by the thump of Dev's heartbeat under her ear.

"Bain?" she muttered.

"Extremely dead," Kurok answered her, gently pressing something against Jess's upper arm. "Don't try moving. You blew out your neural net. Don't be surprised if you smell blue and pink for a while."

"Okay." Jess was happy to comply. "They still comin'?"

"Yes," Doctor Dan replied. "Your crazed dramatics merely delayed our collective splatting by perhaps an hour." He gently lifted Jess's other eyelid and peered at the exposed pupil. "Three of them blasted you right after you hit him."

"Ugh."

"Thought we lost you early there for a minute." He released the eyelid. "But you are, in fact, a damned hard kill, Jesslyn Drake."

"Fucker." Jess managed to get out. "Died too fast. Wish I'd had time to make small pieces out of 'im."

Kurok sighed. "Damn you, Alex. I should have realized something wasn't right. Idiots upside didn't let me talk to Bricker when he came. He knew something. I never thought he'd..." He paused, and shook his head. "Now asking us makes sense."

Dev released one hand and touched his knuckles, but remained silent.

"Bricker needed someone Bain couldn't touch," Jess whispered. "Finally saw one of my nightmares out last night. Remembered to the end. Saw him there. Watching Josh try to take us out."

"Alex?"

Jess nodded. "Think he wanted to take over the cit easy." she whispered. "Just have 'em hand it over. Thought he had everyone's number."

"But he believed you wouldn't turn," Kurok said, in a quiet, serious tone. "And like an idiot I told him Dev wouldn't either, so the two of you had to go."

Jess nodded. "Somethin' like that. Harder he tried to see us croaked, better we got at escaping it." She managed a brief smile. "Didn't put it all together in time."

"No," Kurok said. "And our past together blinded me."

"He blocked comms. Dev found it." Jess closed her eyes. "Then I knew for sure."

Kurok glanced past her. "Yes," he said. "Sorry I was only half right about the trusting thing, Dev."

Dev sniffled a little. "I saw his vehicle land. I thought that was a good thing."

Doctor Dan sighed. "That was the half wrong. I told you it was okay to trust him."

"Sorry I made you think you were all wrong." Jess felt the gentle hold on her tighten. "Had to get him close." She felt exhausted by the small effort of speaking. "Least I'll croak knowing I got that bastard first."

Kurok patted her hip very gently. "Rest," he said. "Take care of her, Dev. Let me go see if there's any havoc I can help with." He stood up and hitched the scanner to his tool kit, moving over to take a seat at one of the battered consoles.

There was a quiet moment, then April got up and came over to them, crouching down next to Jess and resting her fingertips on the steel floor. "That was ace," she told Jess bluntly. "Glad you used my blade for it. Most blood honor it's ever seen."

Jess managed another small grin. "Glad you got my sig."

April shook her head a little. "Tried to make my head believe you were turning and it just wouldn't go," she said. "Not when you refused to look at any of us."

Jess was quiet for a moment. "'Specially her." She moved her head a tiny bit toward Dev.

"'Specially her." April agreed. "So now we go down in flames. But that's okay, you know? It's right." She touched Jess's hand, then stood up and went back to the console, sitting back down and getting on comms.

So now, at last, Jess shifted enough so she could look up at Dev, who was seated against the wall with both arms wrapped around her. Dev looked as though she'd been through a full speed carrier wreck, and as she looked back, what she was feeling was open and very evident on her face.

Jess felt...well, she wasn't sure what she was feeling, but it was very warm, and very powerful and it was making it hard to breathe. "Hey, Devvie. You're not too mad at me are ya?"

"No," Dev said, after a brief pause. "I though they made you dead, and I was—" She stopped and took a few breaths. "I didn't want that."

Jess was glad she was lying still. It felt good to be able to stop, and think, and say what she wanted to say. "In about sixty minutes we're probably both going to be made dead. But I'm real, real glad I got to know you."

Dev just nodded back.

"My dad once said..." Jess half smiled. "You'll know what love is because it's the only thing that hurts as much as it feels good." She nodded a little. "He was right. But it's good."

"It's good," Dev repeated softly. "I'm glad you didn't really want to go with the bad guys, Jess. I would have missed you so much."

Unexpectedly, Jess felt tears sting her own eyes, as she felt Dev hug her close, and the pressure of her head pressing against the side of her own. It unlocked something inside her that she really couldn't quantify, but whatever it was made her want to get up and move around and be a part of what was going on in the room.

She didn't want this to end. "Gimme a hand up," she told Dev. "Let's go see if we can help."

"Doctor Dan said for you to rest," Dev said, even though she helped Jess sit up anyway. She waited, watching Jess work to catch her breath, before she stood up and carefully held on to her arm as Jess rose with her.

The pain was really overwhelming. Jess just stood there breathing for a moment, holding onto Dev so she wouldn't fall right back down. Every nerve in her body felt like it was being smacked with a round head hammer, and it was all she could do to lock her knees in place to remain upright.

After a minute she looked around. There were a pile of bodies, the guards and Bain, in one corner on the lower level, and the walls and one of the working consoles had deep, angry black scores on them from the firefight. Near her the wall surface was covered in dried blood, and she could smell the copper scent now as her senses settled.

Mike Arias was seated next to April, his arm in a plas casing, and Brent next to him had a bandage on his head. Tucker and Elaine were on the second console, he with a black eye, and she with half the hair on her head burned off and a scorch mark covered in a bandage across the side of her face.

Elaine briefly looked up from her screen and gave Jess a wry smile. Then she went back to her inputs. No real need for her to say anything, apparently.

Jess managed the few steps over and took a seat at the end of the desk, resting her elbows on the steel surface as Dev sat down next to her. She looked at the screen output, her eyes focusing on the incoming scan, showing a dozen ships pretty much nearly on top of them.

Doctor Dan came over and sat down on the other side of her, just as the outer door opened and one of the Kaytees entered, looking around at them. "Over here, Kaytee." Kurok lifted a hand. "I'm going to send them back downstairs," he told Jess, as Dev headed toward them. "Maybe they'll get lucky."

Jess turned and looked at Dev, who was looking right back at her. "Don't suppose you want to go with them, huh?"

"No," Dev answered straightforwardly. "I would not."

Jess nodded, and looked back at the screen. "Then let's just go out doing what we do."

DEV STUDIED THE oncoming vessels, forcing her mind to focus on the problem at hand and not on the horrible thing she'd just been through.

Everything seemed mixed up and upside down. Jess had been right. She had no real idea now who to trust except for Jess herself, and for a moment even that had been in doubt.

She felt her eyes sting again, remembering that. An awful feeling that haunted her even when she told herself that all Jess had been doing was acting.

Doing her job. Making the man Bain believe she was joining him, to get him to let his guard down.

And yet still it hurt. Dev looked up as a warm touch covered the back of her hand, and found Jess regarding her, bloodshot eyes blinking slowly in evident discomfort. "Would you like a drink?" she asked.

"Yeah, but not the kind they have in here," Jess said, with a faint grin. "Hey, you okay? You still look freaked out."

Dev shifted her gaze briefly, then returned it. "I really thought they made you dead." She indicated the security guard. "And that really bothered me." She felt Jess's grip on her tighten. "And I thought you were going to leave me here and it made me feel so lost. I think I want to throw up."

Jess's eyes widened, apparently getting more of an answer than she'd expected. "Ah," she murmured. "I'd never have left you, Devvie." She lowered her voice. "Honest."

Dev managed a smile in return.

"Dying, on the other hand." Jess gave her a wry grimace. "I'm pretty good at that."

Dev exhaled. "Yes," she answered, briefly, then changed the subject. "Jess, the bad guys are almost here."

"I know." Jess chafed the back of her hand with the edge of her thumb. "It sucks right now."

"I wish we could just go have a snack on the ledge and watch the water," Dev whispered. "I don't want to be dead, and I really don't want you to be."

Jess leaned back in her seat and gazed around the room. The citadel was as ready as it was going to be and most of her colleagues were just quietly resting where they were, eyes focused on the displays. Kurok had his head cradled in his hands, and for a moment, for her, the world went still.

That happened, sometimes. Jess was never sure if it was a real thing, or just something her mind conjured up to give her a chance to think for a minute.

Sometimes a good idea came. Sometimes in that quiet moment, there was clarity and facts, which had been running around in the back of her head, presented themselves in the form of a solution to whatever problem she had.

But no. Jess exhaled, and the world rushed on again. There was no magic solution for this. The armored carriers would come in and attack them, they would do their best to defend the citadel for as long as they could, and then, if they penetrated it would come down to a hand-to-hand in the corridor.

"Short range scan has them," Brent said. "Standing by to bring up the guns."

"Bring them up," Jess ordered. "Wish I could help you aim 'em, but I've got the reflexes of my dead aunt right now." She stared at the comp screen, ignoring the pain. "Dev, send a broadband out, all alert, any endpoint."

"Yes." Dev settled her ear cups and exhaled. "Base Ten, Base Ten, all call. Inbound hostile, alert prime. Take cover." She put it on replay and scanned her screen again. The call beam spread out neatly from the citadel, and she could see faint echoes back, passive acks that were scattered across the landscape.

"Thanks," Jess said. "Now send out a broadcast internally. Tell all the noncoms to take cover, and seal themselves out of operational areas."

The door opened, and Doug entered, carrying spare rifles slung over his shoulders, and a sack full of mines. He set the mines on the console near April and a moment later, Chester came in similarly laden.

Dev spoke quietly into the internal comms, repeating Jess's message, and now the techs set up the long blasters near their agents, as the agents settled into the weapons rigs, fitting their hands into the ceiling mounted triggers relatively the same as the ones in the carriers.

There was a set above the seat Jess was in, but she didn't even attempt to pull them down, watching her fingertips twitching as waves of pain rippled through her body. She doubted she could lift her arms above her head, and the shot Kurok had given her was only slowly returning her nerves to a normal state.

There would be no fighting for her, not any time today anyway. "Dev?"

"Yes?"

"Listen." Jess leaned carefully over toward her. "If they end up shooting this place to pieces, I ain't going to be able to do much about it."

Dev considered this. "I see."

"Stick over there with Doug and those guys," Jess said. "They might do better."

Dev adjusted an ear cup and folded her hands on the console. "I think I would rather stay here, next to you," she said. "If that's all right."

"You want to get killed? Probably by my skull coming off my neck and breaking yours?"

Dev looked up, her expression suddenly as open as Jess had ever seen it. In an instant, unexpectedly, the woman sitting next to her was no longer a bio alt, no longer even a tech. She was just this person Jess found herself really caring for.

"Yeah," Dev said. "I want to share whatever happens to you. I don't care what that is." She spoke the words carefully, as though considering each one with great care. "No matter what the programming says."

"It says otherwise?"

Dev nodded. "We're supposed to value our lives. Since we do have value. People pay highly for us."

Jess carefully propped her chin up on her fist. "You're nuts."

"Yes. I have come to that conclusion also. I have gone far outside the programming for what I'm doing," Dev said, in a mournful tone. "That is, I suppose, nuts, if the definition I looked up about that is correct, and you are not referring to an ancient plant once consumed as a snack."

"Me too." Jess reached over and took her hand, bringing it over and placing a kiss on the back of her knuckles. "Stay here by me, Devvie. Been such a long time since anyone's given a shit if I lived or died, I might as well enjoy it."

"Six minutes, mark," Brent said. "Coming into range. Comm blackout."

"Shunting power to the guns." Doug had settled into his station and had a comm set on. "We've got plenty of juice, at least."

"Front side battery is up," Tucker reported. "Generators are tapped to full."

Jess looked up to find a full, comprehensive display in front of her. She glanced at Dev, who was busy with her own screens, and blinked her eyes a few times to get them to focus. "Unless they open up when they're in range, hold off," she said. "Let them get right in our faces."

"They'll see the power grid up," Elaine said.

"Maybe they'll figure Bain left it that way," Jess responded. "They sending out any comms?" she asked Dev, who shook her pale head. "He would have told them to come right in, soon as he landed in the shuttle bay."

"Funny we didn't pick that up on scan." Elaine shifted to look over at her. "Just how many layers does the scum go down here, Jess?"

Jess sighed, understanding the comment. "Dev caught his speeder in the bay, on our carrier's scan. I just didn't have time to investigate it before we were in the weeds." She caught sight of Kurok, settling into a tech station, and keying it on. "Hey, Doc, how'd his boat slip in behind scan?"

"Keyed reflector," Doctor Dan responded, almost absently. "He's...well, he was, top sec. The idea was, he might have to come into a facility that had been turned."

"Irony's a little crunchy," Elaine remarked.

"Yes. Well." Kurok rubbed his eyes. "What can I tell you? It's old technology. They had it when I was still active."

The rest of the agents were now listening intently. "You were a tech, huh?" Elaine asked, after a brief pause.

"Yes." Doctor Dan looked up at her, seeing the doubt. "Agent

Drake'll vouch for me. I think she probably has a picture of me in diapers, or something like that." The tiniest bit of a twinkle entered his pale eyes. "Not that we really have much time for that sort of thing, and anyway if I wanted to blow this place up or shoot someone, I would have done so already."

"Three minutes," Brent called.

"He's fine," Jess said, returning Elaine's inquisitive stare. "Just concentrate on aiming. We're not going to have much space to miss in."

Keyed reflector. Dev turned that term over in her head, feeling it tickle some programming, deep down. She nudged it back and forth, and tried to call up what it evoked, but it remained elusive, just out of her mental grasp. Keyed reflector. That meant, she reasoned, something that would...maybe..."Doctor Dan."

Kurok looked over. "Yes, Dev?"

"If they could do that for the man Bain's vehicle, making scan ignore it, couldn't the bad guys do the same thing with our guns and their vehicles? Make them reflect the beams?"

Kurok answered thoughtfully. "They could, if they had the frequencies, Dev. Those change...or at least they did, regularly." He adjusted his screen. "Here they come."

"In range," Brent said, calmly. "Freq's changed last week. They did it cause that guy said to." He pointed at Bain's body. "Weren't scheduled for another ten days...just remembered that," he added, somewhat defensively. "I'd just come on shift and heard some guys saying it in the mess. They thought it was a good idea to change 'em."

Everyone's eyes shifted to the dead body, then they all looked over at Jess, who'd straightened in her seat. "Change them now," she said, without hesitation. "Hurry."

The techs dove at their inputs and started tapping, while Jess and Elaine pulled the scan to their own stations. "Faster," Jess said, seeing the line of destroyers now on visual, close enough for the outboard cams to resolve them.

"The codes are locked, Jess," Dev said. "We can't change them."

"Fuck." Brent added a half second later as he came to the same conclusion.

Jess got up and almost ended up on the ground as she grabbed for the edge of the console when her body seized up. "Fucker!" She got over to Dev's chair and looked at her screen, seeing the admin lockout, and the request for creds that had denied Dev access. "Gimme."

Dev slid out of the way and gave her access, as she watched Jess tap painfully on the screen.

"They're spooling up," Tucker said. "We're gonna take it right in the kisser. If they've got our codes it'll cut through the shields like water."

Jess cursed and got the last few letters of her own creds in and entered them. "Let's see if we can't hoist his ugly dead ass on its own petard," she said. "He upgraded my access."

"Probably was going to lay the blame of everything on you if it went sour," Elaine said. "Your login over everything."

"Yeah, rogue agent," Jess muttered. "We'd all be dead. Who'd dispute it."

The damn screen seemed like it took an eon and longer, the pulsing white dot in the center expanding and contracting as though it were breathing. She heard the yell of alarm from Brent just as it finally, finally disappeared and obediently presented schematics to her. "Go!" She awkwardly hopped out of the way as Dev got her hands on the controls and her fingertips raced over the smooth surface.

The lights flickered, and she heard a far off rumble.

"Direct hit," Kurok said. "They're aiming for the turbine entrance."

"Dev?" Jess uttered.

Dev finished her work and lifted her head. "I don't really know what I just did, and I have no idea if it will work, but you can try it."

A humming boom sounded, and then several more, as Elaine, Mike and April let loose with the perimeter guns, then a crackling roar vibrated the rock around them and knocked loose a few bits of shale.

"Shields are responding," Brent said. "Fucking nice timing, yo."

Jess managed to sit back down without falling, and rested her elbows on the console, waiting for the flashing bolts to fade from her vision. "Just keep shooting."

She heard the repeated booms, an almost subliminal rumbling that was power being fed to the big outside guns, and released as the other agents aimed and fired. It was strange not to be joining them, but it was far easier to sit as still as she could and just watch the action on the screen.

"Jess."

"Uh?" Jess rotated her head slightly to look at Dev. "Hey, good work," she added, belatedly. "Thanks for keeping us from being vaporized. You rock."

"Yes, I'm glad it was effective," Dev said. "May I continue to work with your identity?"

"Sure. I'll discipline myself later. You can help." Jess managed a half grin.

Dev returned the grin, then went back to work.

Jess gave up watching the screen and watched Dev instead. She could see Dev's pale eyes flickering over the data, and she was inputting steadily, a look of impossibly cute determination on her face.

"Got one," Mike said. "Didn't expect the beam to take him. Could tell by how he was flying." He looked over at Jess. "Good call."

Jess lifted a hand and pointed her finger at Dev. "Rock star."

"Very well done, Dev," Doctor Dan said. "They've figured it out. Splitting apart and heading for the other side of the ridge, unfortunately."

"Want us to take the buses out and hunt them?" April asked. "We've got nothing for guns in the back."

"How many're left?" Jess asked.

"Ten," Brent said. "Two're heading for the carrier bay now."

"Tell them to take cover," Jess told Dev. "You're not going to make it to the bay in time." she said. "Arm your carriers to implode and wait on my mark."

Mike's eyes opened wide, but Elaine nodded. "You're going to blow the bay?"

"I'm going to blow them if they land in it," Jess corrected. "Got any better ideas?" She eyed her fellow senior agent, who gave a short, decisive shake of her head. "No? Okay then."

"No." Elaine swung her triggers around and let loose with a long blast, tracing an arc of fire across the front of the citadel and catching the very tail end of one of the enemy. "After that rig your buddy there did? I'm all in."

"That one just clipped the cliff and went down." Doctor Dan was busy with scan. "Nice shot."

"Thanks...uh...doc." Elaine swung the screen around and continued hunting. "Rookie, watch out there. You got the end guns."

"Got it." Mike had the tip of his tongue sticking out from between his teeth and bore down, focusing so hard on his comp he nearly bashed his forehead into it. "Bastard!

"Clipped him." April picked up the arc and leaned back as the enemy swerved and went for zenith, tracer fire chasing him up the ridge. "The rest of them are out of line, Jess."

"Yeah." Jess sighed. "Dev, you tell them to get out of the pit?"

"Yes." Dev nodded. "I spoke with Clint. He's in some discomfort, but he agreed to take himself and the others to safety."

"Carriers are rigged," Elaine said. "If we blow them, we're stuck here."

Jess nodded. "We're stuck here anyway. We have comp inside?"

Tucker sent the image he had of the carrier bay to the big screen, showing a grainy view of the inside of the huge space, wisps of off-gassing emitting from the four carriers, and machinery in its half reconstructed position. There were still a few moving figures in view, and Clint's distinctive one, waving an arm at a half dozen bio alt techs, who all had bundles and packs of tools in their grip as they bolted for the hatchway.

"They can't seal that hatch," April said, suddenly. "If they get in there and we don't blow them, they're inside."

"That's what these are for." Elaine pointed at the long guns. "Soon as we're done here, we'll get those all warmed up."

A flash caught their eye, and the temporary covering to the bay blew out in all directions, sending metal fragments raining down into the bay.

"Clear!" Dev yelped into the comms. "There is danger! Take cover!"

A moment later the bay was lit with landing lights and six destroyers came in fast, all wing and angled body in stark contrast to the stolid carriers hunched on their pads.

"Where's the other two?" Mike asked. "I don't see them on scan."

Dev scrambled to get comp on the back side, and widened her scan, pulling in the signal from her own carrier for as long as she figured she'd get it. "No sign."

Jess felt a jolt of alarm. "The back door," she said. "If they've got Bain's keys that might be one of them."

"It is." Kurok stood up. "One of you like to accompany me? I don't much care for surprises."

April stood and joined him. "Doug, stay here and help blow things up." She picked up a long blaster and energized it. "Let's go, Doc. I'm in the mood to kill people."

Doctor Dan paused and looked at Jess, one pale eyebrow lifting in question. Jess waved her hand at him, and was glad to restrict her reaction to that as she slowly put her arm back down.

"They're down," Brent said. "Light the trigger?"

Jess looked back at the screen and saw the hatches opening, judging the distances. "Blow the two nearest them," she instructed, shading her eyes just in time as Brent lit off the explosives, setting off the emergency destruct systems on the two carriers designed to keep them from ending up in enemy hands.

The screen whited out. Seconds later, the ripple of the blast transmitted through the rock followed by a scream of sound that cut off abruptly as Brent slammed a control. "Got 'em," he said.

Dev touched her ear bud and listened intently. She could hear booms and thumps, and then, high pitched screaming that was human and not mechanical. The white hot engine systems of the two carriers were scorching the interior of the bay with super thermal heat, and she hoped hard that Clint, and the other sets had gotten out.

Another signal and she tuned it. "Dev! It's April! Send h—" Dev turned. "Jess, April is in distress."

"Uh oh." Jess said. "Get those blasters ready, kids." She managed to get to her feet and headed toward the far wall, where the guns were leaning. "Check scan."

"Scan's down," Brent said. "We're dark to the wall."

"Shit." Tucker got up and went to an emergency station. "I'll see what I can get on the manuals."

Jess picked up a blaster and cradled it against her arm. "Dev, c'mon over here and take cover behind the console. There rest of you techs, too." She took a slow, deep breath, shoving the jangling pain in every nerve ending down and bracing herself against the rock surface.

"No sense blowing the others." Elaine got up and picked up one of the longer guns, coming over and putting the bulk of the main console between herself and the door, bracing the blaster against the top of the stations and un-safing it. "I can hear shots."

Jess heard them too. "Sounds like a lot of them," she said. "They must have popped that back hatch wide open."

"Probably loaded most of the troops in the ones that hit that, and only skeleton in the bay," Elaine said, regretfully. "We guessed wrong."

"Yeah." Jess looked up as the lights changed, from the standard emergency stations to stark red, and the alerts started to go off on every board she could see.

"Ops compromised." A harsh voice sounded. Bricker's, Jess realized. "Systems deact, standby for lock out."

The systems would lock themselves and then destruct. Jess got the blaster in position, sensing, and then feeling Dev slip in behind her. "Been fun, Devvie."

Dev put a hand on her hip, the touch warm and comforting all out of proportion to the motion. "We all hope we get to do good work and make our contracts happy," she said. "I did both."

Jess smiled wryly. "You sure did."

"And I got to be in love," Dev said. "I think every single set in the creche would wish they were me."

Jess turned her head and regarded Dev. "You glad you're you?"

Dev stretched up and gave her a kiss on the lips. "Yes."

And so Jess felt the discomfort fade, and her disappointment with their failure ease off and her mind steadied as she stopped trying to force the future and let her decisions fall where they might. The time for questions was over, and now, it just was what it was.

"We fought the good fight," Elaine said, peering down her blaster's spine. "Time to pay, Jesslyn."

"Time to pay, El." Jess drew in a breath and got her hands on the triggers, as she heard the thump of boots in the hall, and the crackle of power slamming the outside of the hatch. "Just keep shooting."

"We will." Tucker had a blaster. So did Brent, and Doug, and they joined the agents shoulder to shoulder as the hatch buckled and slammed inward to the floor.

The room lit white and blue with fire.

"KEEP DOWN!" JESS yelled back over her shoulder, as she aimed and took a shot at the edge of an armored shoulder she spotted outside the door.

The room was full of smoke, and the red lights made it dark and hard to see anything. The first wave had come flying in shooting, and now a half dozen armored forms were piled in the front part of the room, their legs blocking the hatch open and giving their comrades a shot into the ops center.

No way out. Jess could see shadows flickering on the far wall, and then a second later a mine flew in. "Shit!"

Tucker leaped over the console and booted the mine back out the way it came, getting just behind cover before it exploded and filled the entry with golden fire that rippled out and flowed toward them.

Jess turned and dove for the ground, taking Dev with her as the force flowed up over the console and over their heads. "Watch for them behind it!"

"On it!" Mike said. "Bastards!"

Jess looked up to make sure the plasma had dissipated, then she got back up and leveled her blaster, letting off a long burst as one of the enemy came right at them, clearly expecting them to be stunned. She trained her sights on his face plate and watched it heat to white hot, as he hauled up and tried to turn back out of the way.

Too late. His head exploded inside his armor and he dropped, reeling backwards as two more came in, skidding to a halt when they saw the body heading toward them and turning to retreat as two beams hit them from Mike and Elaine's guns.

Another mine. Another ducking, but this time the energy ripped through the bottom of the consoles and Tucker went down in jerking agony, his blaster flying from his hands and nearly hitting Dev in the head.

Brent heaved one of their own mines out the door and they ducked as the booming roar filled the space.

"We should just charge them. They'll just pick us off." Elaine got over by Jess. "If we're going to die, might as well do it fast, Jess. We can't hold out forever."

"Hang on a little longer." Jess half stood and got off a shot, hoping her knees would hold her. She felt Dev grab and steady her and got wedged into place against the console, forcing her body to behave. "Any idea how long we've been fighting? How long 'til that storm was due over?"'

"It will be soon," Dev said "We've been doing this for almost forty five minutes."

"Why?" Elaine asked "What the hell does a storm do for us? They're the ones who have the damn magic mushrooms, Jess. We don't, and even if we did, it does nothing for us here in the kill zone. "

Fifteen minutes. Jess exhaled. "Okay." She let the gun rest on the console and blinked the sweat from her eyes. "Elaine, take these guys out the back, down Bain's hallways. I'll cover you."

Elaine looked at her. "Cover us?"

Mike threw another mine out, and ducked. "Ware!"

"Look." Jess got her head down as plasma rippled through the room. "I can barely stand up. I'm not going to be able to keep up with you all," she said. "Get the hell out, and just go."

Dev crouched quietly behind her, listening. The consoles were all dead, locked out by the security systems. There was nothing else she could do except keep Jess company.

She could see Elaine's face as she looked at Jess, surprising emotion tensing the muscles there.

"Jess, we can't leave you here," Elaine finally said. "Screw it."

"You can." Jess lifted her head. "Everyone listen up." She raised her voice. "On ten, head out the back with Elaine on point. I'll cover."

There was a moment of silence, then Mike cleared his throat. "If it's all the same to you, senior, I'd rather stay."

"Ack." Brent went back to the bag of mines, arming another one and handing it over to him."

"Ack." Doug echoed, looking up and over from where he was kneeling next to Tucker. "I'll answer ack for him too."

Jess's eyes flicked around the room, and then paused on Elaine's face, before she turned and regarded Dev. "Can I at least get you to listen to me?"

Dev gazed steadily back at her. "Please don't ask me to leave you," she said, simply. "I really don't want to."

Jess sighed. "You're all insane." She turned and put her hands back on the blaster. "All right. Just take as many of them with us as we can I guess."

Her voice sounded indifferent, but Dev, who was just in the right spot, could see her eyes blink, and the faint flash of tears as they escaped and landed on the metal surface of the useless station.

She wasn't sure she understood what that meant. But she knew it was a strong feeling.

Elaine got in next to her and propped her blaster up on the edge of the console, sighting down it. "Y'know, I always figured I'd go like this." She let off a blast, as a dark figure flickered past the entrance. "Never thought I'd make it to retire, or you either."

"Yeah," Jess muttered.

Elaine leaned forward so she could see Dev. "And you..." She grinned briefly. "You're all right, NM-Dev-1."

Dev smiled back.

"'Specially if you hooked this one good." Elaine nudged Jess's arm, then returned her attention to the doorway, and six bodies inbound. "Here we go. For the corps!" The last words were a bellow and in a rush of energy the yell was picked up and carried forward, as the six enemy soldiers came right at them, dodging the blaster fire and returning it with their own.

Jess just kept firing, the blaster rifle thumping against her chest as she let off quick bursts, going from one target to another to another as the air itself started to burn, white fire and dark shadows taking the color out of everything as the red lights themselves died and the shots became a continuous thunder.

One of the enemies dodged past Doug's rolling body and leaped over the console right at Jess. She released the blaster rifle and drew her sidearm, continuing to fire as he came flying through the air and slammed into her, a hit she had no way of avoiding.

The pain ramped with unexpected ferocity and she felt her back hit the wall as he landed on her, hand already raised with the butt of his gun slamming down at her.

She couldn't budge her torso, but she got the blaster in between them and squeezed the trigger, the muzzle shoved hard against his belly as she felt him cough.

His hand swerved as he went for her hands instead of her head and then he was hit from the side by a small, fair haired figure that got a shoulder under him and heaved him off against the wall as Jess rolled clear.

The man bounced off the wall and reached out to grab Jess, but he was yanked away and slammed against the floor and then his arm was pulled behind him as that same, slight, fair figure landed on his back and removed his shoulder from its socket, surprising a startled yell of pain from him.

Jess started to get up, then something impacted her hard and sent her flying to slam against the wall. She drew a breath and got her hands up in time for her vision to clear and see the big armored figure in front of her raise its gun and the pre-aim splashed on her face.

Then it was gone because a body was blocking it, half kneeling, half sprawled across her with its arms raised in a protective spread merely meant to insure the coming blast would take the both of them.

A moment's hesitation on his part, some ancient animal brain instinct that held his finger for just a breath.

Just long enough for Jess to get one arm around her protector and one hand on her fallen blaster, and to reach around and aim herself, and force her hand to contract on the trigger, and her wrist to withstand the recoil as the blast took the weapon right out of the enemy's hands.

Her boot hooked his, and her other one slammed out and caught him in the groin and then he was being blown backwards as two other blaster beams hit his body.

And then, for a long moment, it was quiet.

White emergency lights were blinking on and off, and the room was full of smoke and the smell of burned flesh and blood. There was no sound from the outside hallway, where they could see blinking lights as well.

Then a roar of sound shuddered through the wall and they heard the crackle of comm, and the sound of battle language that wasn't theirs, and the sweet, sweet note of panic that meant maybe, somehow something had swung their way.

Motion now, and running boots, and the next thing they saw was a crowd of bodies in pursuit yelling loudly and carrying shadowy pieces of gear, their necks flashing with faintly colored tracing around their necks.

Jess blinked. "Bios!" She let her body thump back against the wall and felt Dev do the same, as her partner started shaking. "What the hell?"

A roar then came from the other side of the hall, and the next moment there was a huge pile up, blasters going everywhere, and the eerie cascade of power arcs energizing as the fight passed them by, leaving the corridor outside clear.

Somehow, Jess got to her feet, carrying Dev with her and they surged forward, past the consoles, stepping on the enemy bodies and joining the other agents and techs at the doorway as they bolted outside.

And then they stopped. The huge central corridor meet point was filled with rapidly falling enemy, with hand blaster fire coming from the hallway leading down to the caverns, and power arcs being fired from the technical gear carried by bio alts on the other.

"Holy shit," Elaine said, holding a bleeding gash on her side.

Then one jumpsuited figure dodged to the front, and yelled out in that same, unfamiliar battle language, a powerful and commanding tone that cut through all the noise as the figure swept their arm up and the arcs died down.

There were only two of the enemy left, and they dropped their guns, and lifted their hands, staggering back against the wall and slamming their backs against the rock surface.

And then it was briefly quiet again.

Jess forced herself forward, nudging her way through the crowd of bio alts, who turned their heads, then parted quickly when they saw who it was. She emerged at the front of them, and stopped next to Dan Kurok, who was battered and covered in grime.

April limped forward from across the lines, leaving a crowd of support staff in varicolored jumpsuits behind her.

"Next time," Dan Kurok finally said, spitting out a little blood. "I'm going to pretend I didn't see the memo."

"Fuck, yeah," April said, lifting a shaking hand to touch a blast on the side of her head. "They definitely didn't go over this in battle school."

Jess put a hand on both of their shoulders. "Nice timing. Thanks for saving our asses."

"Thank you, for drawing the attention of every god damned one of them to ops and leaving the halls clear for us," Doctor Dan said. "Wheres—? Ah."

Dev had followed Jess through the crowd of her fellow sets, and now was standing quietly next to her, just behind the three of them, with Elaine, Brent, and Doug after her.

Clint emerged from the group of armed workers, and walked over to join them. "Crappy day." He was holding one arm close to his body. "Now what?"

They were all silent briefly then everyone looked at Jess.

Jess looked around at the smoke filled, body filled, stale air filled space. Then she sighed and looked at Kurok. "Think you can get the systems started back up?"

Doctor Dan shrugged. "Oh, why not? At this rate I wouldn't judge anything impossible." He looked up as a loud rumble sounded, shuddering through the halls. "Let's just hope the rest of their fleet isn't in that storm."

Chapter Eighteen

THE ONE UNDAMAGED place was the mess hall. Jess was more than glad to be sprawled in one of the chairs in the back, as bio alts and citadel techs mingled and worked on temporary rigs set up on tables and counters everywhere.

"Got the batts back online at least." Clint had taken a seat next to her, looking exhausted. "Air handlers are cycling."

"I hear," Jess responded quietly. "If anyone can get the mains back, it'll be the doc."

"Who is he, Jess?" Clint asked, keeping his voice low. "I heard him talk their talk in the hall."

It was hard to even muster up the energy to respond. Kurok had given her another shot of something, and that had started the pain fading, but Jess knew she was almost at her limits. "He was my father's first partner," she said. "He was an ops tech. One of us."

"Oh." Clint looked surprised. "Really?"

Jess nodded. "My dad could talk their battle talk too," she added, not really sure if that was true, but not really caring.

"Right yeah," the mech senior nodded. "And hey, he made Dev, right?"

"He made Dev," Jess said. "And he sure did a bang up job there." She looked up as her partner came over, putting down a cup of water next to her hand and taking the seat next to her with one of her own. "How ya doing, Devvie?"

"I'm really tired," Dev replied in a soft, husky voice.

"Well, seeing as you were beating up guys five times your size, and throwing me around like a rag doll, I'm not surprised." Jess rested her chin on her hand. "Can we talk sometime about how techs aren't supposed to step in front of a blaster pointed at their agent?"

Dev took a sip from her cup and swallowed it.

"You did that, Dev?" Clint asked. "Wow."

"She did that."

The outer door slid open and April and Mike entered, steering their way through the busy crowd back to where Jess was seated.

"I'll go finish trying to work on the security systems." Dev got up and eased past them as they came over. "Excuse me."

The two agents sat down. "We got all the trash taken out," Mike said. "Had the bios bring up those donkey carts they use and hauled the bodies out and dumped 'em."

"Got the prisoners locked up in the storage facilities," April reported. "So Kurok says now he might be able to get the comp out of unlock since we have only friendly chips inside."

"How's the weather outside?"

"Sucks," Mike said. "Raining like crazy. Flooding in the carrier bay, what's left of it." His jumpsuit was wet. "I got into my carrier though, and ran scan. Nothing in range."

"Good."

"Your rig's in one piece too," Mike added. "I think if they get comp back up, Dev had it tied in."

"She did," Jess said. "But without comp we don't know how much scan and comm got sent back to the other side, and I..." She paused, as the lights flickered overhead, morphing from white, to red, then back to a blue tinged daylight that meant normal, whatever that really meant anymore. "Ah."

Clint got up. "Mains are back." He looked relieved. "Let me start getting things ramped."

"Thanks, Clint," Jess said, blinking a little in the new illumination. Behind her, she heard the mech in the mess systems start a low buzzing, and the working teams looked around, visibly brightening at the returning power.

"Sure, Jess." Clint blushed a little, then hurried off.

April inspected the bandage on her arm. "Seems like ten years since we showed up here," she said. "Glad to see the doc got systems back. He's pretty wicked good. I was watching him on that comp."

"Well. I guess that's where Dev gets it from," Jess said, after a moment. "Figure he used his genotype."

"That's kinda weird," Mike said, after a bit of an awkward pause.

Jess shrugged. "Is what it is." She looked past them to the door that had opened, and admitted Elaine. "What's up?"

"Comp came up, ten seconds after that comms did and there's a full sec broadcast coming in to your sig," Elaine said. "Urgent repeat."

With a sigh, Jess pushed herself to her feet, glad, at least, that standing no longer felt like she was having knives poked into her from all angles. "Could be good, could be bad," she said. "Let's go find out."

They walked back to central ops, and as she entered, Jess spotted Dev working at one of the consoles. Dev looked up as she came in, and as their eyes met Jess almost forgot what she'd come for. She angled her steps to the side and went to Dev's workbench instead of the main comms board. "Hey."

"They have a message for you," Dev said.

"I have a message for you." Jess ignored the rest of the room, and put her hand up against Dev's cheek. "That is, you look really stressed. What's up?"

"Jess," Elaine called over.

"Hang on." Jess lifted a hand in her direction without turning around. "Devvie?"

Dev's expression altered, and she smiled faintly. "I'm okay. Just a bit overwhelmed by all the stuff that happened, I guess."

"Hang in there, Dev." Jess stroked her cheek with the edge of her thumb. "Just hang in there, and maybe we'll get to sit down and talk about it soon. Okay?"

"Yes." Dev's smile broadened a little. "Now you should take your call, Jess. I think it's important."

"Not as important to me as you are." Jess knew the whole room was listening, and found herself not caring at all. "Try and chill." Now, finally she turned and walked over to the big comms station and sat down next to Elaine, tucking a set of ear cups in her ears and extending her hand to the scan pad.

"That's fucked up," Elaine said. "But you know, at this point I don't care."

"Yeah, me either." Jess smiled briefly and put her hand flat on the pad, feeling the tickle as it validated her, and the embedded chips beneath her skin. She looked up as the screen lit and tried not to blink, as the scan beam hit her eyes for a brief instant.

Then the screen cleared, and she heard the static and phasing of the looped message.

"HQ, HQ, HQ." The metallic, male voice echoed softly in her ears. "Drake J, standby."

"Ack," Jess answered quietly. "Drake, J on comm."

Then the line switched, and she heard the rumble of carrier engines and the screen lit to reveal a male face looking back at her, older and scarred, with thick, wavy gray hair. "Drake."

"Yes," Jess responded. "Jesslyn Drake, senior agent, Base Ten."

He nodded. "We got a high density squirt detailing an attack by force. Validate," he ordered. "Benson Alters on comm."

Jess remembered him, from school. "Yes, sir, I remember you from in-flight tactics class," she said. "The squirt was valid. Details in person."

The man relaxed just a trifle. "Ack," he said, to both her spoken and unspoken words. "Due local approx two. Clear entrance?"

Jess shook her head visibly so he could see it.

"Ack," he responded. "Please keep this channel open. Report as needed."

"Ack." Jess, at last, felt a sense of relief. "Will do."

The visible image disappeared, but the waveform remained, and she keyed it to overhead comms sending the soft sound of the open carrier into the room. "Open sig." She announced. "We've got fleet inbound."

The sounds of utter relief around her matched her internal feelings exactly. "Apparently a message from here finally got through," she said. "So whoever made that happen, I love you."

After a brief pause, everyone looked at Dev, who looked up in surprise, a visible blush appearing on her face. "Um." She cleared her throat. "With everything else that happened I am not sure I did that."

"Did I say you did?" Jess's brows arched slightly.

Dev blushed more deeply.

"Now, if I was a betting woman..." Elaine drawled. "And I checked the logs, I bet we'd find someone's creds on that message in here."

Doctor Dan looked up from a console he had his head completely inserted into. "Please don't make Dev pass out," he said. "She's had a tough day." He got up from the floor and sat down. "And I think that was the best news we could have hoped for."

"Got that right." Jess sighed. "Maybe this is closer to over."

"Let me make sure everyone's on PTT." Elaine was busy with her board. "Full power's back, and the noncoms are getting the rest of daily operations up."

"Yes," Doctor Dan said. "My advice now is, we all get some rest before the cavalry gets here, and starts asking questions. They'll be on scan and keep off any other funny business here." He glanced at Jess. "You might want to take a trip down to med."

Questions. Yes. Jess recalled all the things they'd been through, and how that was all going to look to HQ. "Let's hope they believe us." She stood up. "Let's go, Dev."

Obediently Dev left her work and joined Jess at the door, dusting her hands off as they left ops, and walked together down the hall. "Are we going to med?"

"Yeah," Jess said. "I need another shot, and you've got a bump on your head."

"I do. It hurts," Dev said. "Is it over now, Jess? Did we win?"

Jess walked along in silence for a few moments, then she nodded. "For now, I think it is. And I think we survived more than we won. But I'll take it."

Dev reached out and took her hand, closing her fingers around Jess's. "Me too."

JESS PAUSED TO dust a bit of debris off her sleeve before she presented herself to the intelligence room. She held her hand to the plate and felt the tickle of scan as it read her.

The cavalry had, in fact, arrived. A dozen carriers and six destroyers, carrying enough troops to handle an invasion force, which is what they'd apparently been expecting. Hard to say, really, who was more surprised when the most they had to do was post patrols and find places to park, since the carrier bay was half in pieces.

The door opened, and she entered, giving the three men at the end of the table a nod before she settled herself in the end chair facing them.

"Agent Drake." Bensen Alters leaned on his elbows. "Thanks for coming to talk with us. I know it's been a long couple of days for you."

"It has," Jess said, resting her own elbows on the table. Her nerves had finally returned to normal and she'd gotten enough med to function, at least until this part was over. She was tired, and wanted her bed, and she suspected that showed.

"You doing all right, Drake? I saw you logged into med earlier."

Jess nodded. "Got caught by three deflected blasters," she said. "Rang my brain out."

She'd been the first they'd called, as she'd figured. She was the senior agent in charge, after all, regardless even of the other position Bain had dangled in front of her. Now, having to face these men, she was glad she hadn't officially accepted it.

Alters cleared his throat. "This is John Bezette, and Jason Elk." He introduced the other two. "Fleet captains."

"Agent." Elk nodded at her. "Your father and I went to the academy together."

Jess nodded back. "Pretty much everyone in the corps has gone to something or other with some part of my family," she said wryly. "I have yet to meet a long termer who doesn't have—no shit I was there—stories about one or the other of us."

Elk smiled briefly, lifting a hand in acknowledgment.

"When we got your message, there were many who found it very hard to believe," Alters said. "In fact, quite a few people thought it was a trick, aimed at luring us into a trap."

"I can imagine that," Jess said. "Especially if that was the first you were hearing of problems out here."

Alters nodded. "Exactly."

Elk looked around. "Based on what we can see here, that message got out just in time."

Jess nodded again. "Not really sure where to start," she said. "But I guess I should begin with advising you that Alexander Bain is dead."

The three men exchanged glances.

"I killed him," Jess said, after a brief pause. "When he informed us that he intended to turn over this facility into enemy hands, and that he was working on their behalf to overturn not only this organization, but all of Atlantia." She folded her hands. "There were five witnesses to that, aside from myself, including Doctor Kurok, from LifeForce."

Elk sighed. "Well, that's news." He glanced at Alters. "Carlsen was right. He's going to be insufferable."

Alters stood up. "What I am about to say is probably going to surprise you, Drake," he said. "But you've done us a great service. Aside from responding to your SOS, my task here was to find Alex." He looked profoundly relieved. "I'm damn glad he's dead. I wouldn't have known where to start asking him questions."

Jess was, in fact, quite surprised to hear that. "You knew about his game?" she asked, cautiously.

Alters glanced at the two captains. "Just before your note came in we finished beating off an attack on the west coast facilities," he said, quietly. "Now I understand what part that had to play in it. They draw us there, by the time we recover, they have a firm beachhead here."

"Except they don't," Jess said. "Somehow, we stopped them."

"Somehow." Elk smiled grimly.

"He killed Bricker," she said. "Bain, I mean."

They stared at Jess. "John Bricker's dead?" Elk asked, after a startled pause.

Jess nodded. "First day Bain got here. Said he..." She shrugged. "Who the hell would question the old man? We all just took it for granted that he was trusted. Ops was sending notifies back to base, had no idea comm was looped and locked."

Alters nodded. "Bricker was his nephew." Jess nodded. "He told you that?" She nodded again. "We knew there was a leak here. He said he knew who it was."

"Apparently he did. Intimately," Jess replied dryly. "Bricker knew something too. He wanted to bring in techs from what he knew was an untainted source."

"Bio alts," Alters said. "That must have spooked Alex. According to the shuttle's records, he arrived on the same transport the test case did."

"He certainly did." Jess considered what a personal mixed blessing that had turned out to be. "Surprised the hell out of everyone, but I was glad to see him."

"Were you? Oh yes." Alters looked at a bit of plas in his hands. "He reinstated you. Promoted you, several times." He looked up at Jess. "Definitely favored you."

"Until I knifed him." She smiled grimly. "He wasn't too happy with that, probably."

Elk studied her. "If it all went bad, he was going to make you the leak," he said. "You had top creds here. His way out if it fell through."

"Occurred to me," Jess said quietly. "But we didn't much care about consequences at that point. Just dying right."

Alters regarded the plas. "What was his game, really? What could they offer him that he didn't have on our side? He was the old man."

"Mm" Jess nodded.

"He had power, status, his place in Picchu...unlimited resources. Unlimited access to contraband if he wanted it. I don't get it." Alters shook his head. "Why this? Why now?"

"Wish I knew," Jess said. "What Bock told me was that we'd already lost. That I was just postponing the inevitable. Last couple times I was over there, they had more resources, seemed like they were doing better."

"But how much of that was because he was undermining this side of our territory?" Elk countered.

"Hmph. True," Alters said. "We'll have to dig in and find out what the deal is."

"Lot of people were lost here." Bezette spoke up for the first time, in a soft, slightly husky tone.

"Too many," Jess said. "Far too damn many."

"But it would have been far more if you hadn't come back, Agent," Alters said. "Tell you what. Let us review the centops security monitor feed, and then we can talk about what happens next."

Jess nodded, and stood. "Fine. I'll be in my quarters if you want me." She headed for the door.

"Drake," Alters called out.

Jess stopped, and paused at the door, her hand on the sill.

"What do you think now, about that whole bio alt thing?" Alters asked. "Seems like a crazy idea to us."

Finally, Jess smiled a real smile back at them. "Best thing that ever happened to me," she said bluntly. "Bricker was right. You won't ever get something like me from that, but I wouldn't trade my tech for any other on the planet." She hit the door latch and went through, leaving the three men behind.

"Huh," Elk said. "Didn't expect that answer." He glanced at Alters. "Want to have a talk with this thing while the comp is spooling?"

"I do," Alters said, in a musing tone. "I really do."

DEV ENTERED THE room with Doctor Dan at her heels, his hand planted firmly on her shoulder. She paused on seeing the three men sitting there, then she went to the table and sat down.

"I think we just intended to see Tech NM-Dev-1," Alters said, mildly.

"I never paid attention to anyone else's intentions before. I'm not aiming to start now." Doctor Dan took a seat next to Dev and folded his hands. "Dev can speak for herself, but if you think you're going to throw an interrogation at her, you've got me to deal with."

"Oh we do?" Alters stared at him in fascination. "And you are...?"

"Ah." Doctor Dan leaned back and hiked one knee up, circling it with his hands. "Currently? Daniel J. Kurok, Chief geneticist and senior administrator of LifeForce, Bio station 2."

"Ah." Alters nodded and sat down, as though that explained Kurok's presence. "You made her."

"I did," Kurok said. "But more to the point, I'm legally responsible for Dev."

"I'm sure you have all your legalities in place, Doctor, but this is really an Interforce matter," Elk said, politely.

"Ah." Kurok mimicked Alters' earlier grunt. "Well in that case, consider me DJ Kurok, senior tech, Field class 32." He smiled at them. "Alex was kind enough to recommission me, to make traveling the halls easier. I didn't think he expected the eventual outcome of that." He pointed at his collar. "So these aren't fake. I earned them the hard way."

The three officers stared at him for a moment in silence. "Well,"

Alters finally said. "I guess you can stay then, since it's likely we're not going to make you leave."

Doctor Dan smiled his gentle smile at them. "Brilliant answer. Carry on."

Dev had been sitting quietly, listening to it all. She was extremely glad to have her mentor at her side, and it was very interesting to hear him speak about both of his identities. "Thanks, Doctor Dan."

He patted her hand. "Now, go on. Ask away," he said to Alters. "I assume you haven't seen the sec vid yet or we probably would not be bothering with this session."

"It's spooling," Elk said. "We really just wanted to talk to her about her experience here."

Dev folded her hands. "I have had an excellent experience here," she said. "I've gotten to do a great deal of work, and I think my participation has been a positive one." She cleared her throat. "Where would you like me to start?"

The three officers exchanged looks again. "Well." Alters cleared his own throat. "How about at the beginning?"

"HOLY SHIT." ELK turned and looked at Alters as the door closed behind their erstwhile interviewees. "Is she for real?"

"Can't wait to see those vids." Alters had his chin resting on his fist. "She's a lot smarter than I thought she'd be. That's a serious brain in there."

"No kidding," Bezette mused. "I saw the original vids from the Gibraltar run. I thought it was a joke, you know? Someone screwed around with the recorder, but then we got the intel from the other side on the blowout. That kid can fly."

"So Drake pegged it." Alters chuckled. "Bricker was right. But can they duplicate that? She's a developmental, that doc said. A one off."

"Guessing he can," Elk said. "He knows what it takes better than anyone does. Better than any of us, anyway." He shook his head. "DJ Kurok. Who'd have guessed? Never did know what happened to him after he mustered out."

"You knew him back then?" Alters asked, curiously.

Elk shook his head. "Not so much. He was Justin Drake's tech. Justy raved about him. Never had another partner like him, from what he said, before he retired. Always thought there was a story there. Justy wasn't emotional about much but he always was about DJ."

"He came from the other side," Bezette said. "That was the big deal about him. He got swiped as a juv in a capture in the dev station over there. They brought him over. Someone had the big idea to see if he could be turned, put him in psych, they figured he might do for field school."

"What?" Alters said. "From the other side? Were they nuts?"

"Nope, that's why they paired him with Justin." Elk nodded. "Family bleeds Interforce colors, you know? Someone in psych told me there was no such thing as un-turnable but Drakes were the closest thing to it. Solid as granite to the point of pigheaded blind devotion to the cause."

"Drake." Bezette sighed. "Family full of wildcats and wide-eyed insanity. Glad they kill on our side though, tell you what."

"So did Kurok turn out to be trustworthy?" Alters asked.

"Hmm." Elk drummed his thumbs on the table. "Now that I'm remembering all this...I think they weren't ever sure if he totally bought into the force, but what he did buy into was Justin Drake. So maybe it all worked out that way. He was a damn good tech, from what I heard."

"Justin left a lot of enemies on that side," Bezette said. "He knew he had limited time out. Never cared, though. Too bad they got him. Heard his shooter got a medal for it."

"Based on these..." Alters held up the plas. "His kid paid them back for it in typical double Drake fashion."

JESS WAS LYING on her back in her bed, hands folded over her stomach and eyes closed when she heard Dev enter her own quarters next door.

It felt impossibly good to just be relaxing, having someone else be in charge of the chaos for a while. She was mildly curious as to what would end up happening to her, but where once that would have given her a gut ball of anxiety, now she felt almost nothing about it.

Would they muster her? Jess doubted it. No matter what the ins and outs of what they'd been through, she knew she'd done what she could and the bottom line was, the base was still intact, and still theirs.

So it would be, what it would be. Jess turned her head as the door between their quarters opened, and Dev entered. She came over and sat down on the edge of Jess's bed, and returned her smile. "Hello."

"Hello, Devvie. You're a sight for sore eyes."

Dev leaned closer. "Are your eyes sore, too?" She asked in a concerned tone. "What does med do for that?"

Jess chuckled. "That's just one of those stupid archaic sayings, Dev. It means I'm glad to see you." She reached out a hand and touched Dev's leg. "They grill ya?"

Dev eyed her. "You don't really mean cook, right? They asked me some questions. But Doctor Dan was there to keep it all straight. He told them they weren't allowed to be mean to me."

"I like him more and more every day," Jess said. "They weren't mean to you, were they?"

Dev shook her head. "No. They asked me a lot about things here, and how I did tech, but they were all right." She studied Jess's face. "I hope they let me stay."

Anxiety from a completely different direction smacked Jess in the kisser. She jerked up, propping her weight on her elbows. "What makes you think they won't?"

Dev blinked in some surprise. "Well, they said this was something that the man Bain had approved, and now..." She let the words trail off, seeing the alarm in Jess's face. "I think they thought I did good work, Jess."

"Fuck." Jess was now sitting bolt upright in bed. "They asked me how I felt about the project before I walked out of there and I told them it was the best thing that ever happened to me." She ran her hands through her hair. "I didn't think those guys were that dense. Let me go talk to..." She paused and looked at Dev, who had captured her fingers and was holding them. "What?"

"Really the best thing?"

Jess took a breath, then paused, caught by that husky whisper. "Um." She felt a blush heat her cheeks unexpectedly. "Yeah."

Dev exhaled slowly.

"So let me go talk to them." Jess rolled out of bed and headed for the door, pausing when her comms lit. "Damn it." She swerved to the desk and hit the relay. "Drake."

"Agent Drake?" Alters's voice filtered through. "We're done reviewing the vid. Can you come to the debrief room, please."

Jess exhaled. "Sure" she clicked off. "C'mon. You come with me. We might as well find out our fates together."

Dev scrambled to stand up and came over to join her. "Will they get upset?"

"Don't care." Jess took her hand and led her out the door, glad, in a sense that soon she'd know the worst, one way or the other. Dev leaving? Screw that. She'd go with her. Jess was pretty sure she could talk Kurok into taking her to station, if she had to.

It was only a minute's walk and they were at the debrief, and she scanned them in. Alters was alone in the room, and he looked up as they entered. "Ah," he said. "Agent Drake, I didn't expect—"

"This is my partner," Jess said, taking a seat and motioning Dev to do the same. "Deal with it."

Alters studied both of them. Dev was wearing her tech's jumpsuit, with her insignia on the collar, and with the suit fastened all the way up, her collar was covered and invisible and as such, she and Jess looked like any other agent and tech pair he'd ever seen. "Okay," he said. "This won't take long anyhow."

Jess folded her hands and waited.

"The vids conclusively back up what you told us," Alters said. "In fact, they over told the story. You left out a few things. I have packaged them up, and squirted them back to HQ for their records and review." He cleared his throat. "They'll have to make the overall decisions on what happens to this base, and North base, in terms of personnel. I think you realize we can't let Alex's administrative appointments stand."

Jess nodded. "I expected that."

"On the other hand, my rank does allow me to make field appointments and so, with the concurrence of central HQ, I will confirm you in your senior ranking," Alters said. "Whether they will eventually appoint you further is out of my hands at this time."

"I don't want any further appointment."

Alters looked up from the plas in his hands at her. "At this time, I understand that."

"At any time," Jess stated clearly. "I don't want to be advanced in rank. I want to remain a field ops agent."

"You could change your mind in the future, Drake," Alters said. "Some of us did y'know."

"I could," Jess admitted. "But I probably won't."

"Probably not, if you're bred as true as these records indicate." He smiled faintly. "But in any case, I have officially updated your records fleet wide to include your senior rank. So, I guess congratulations are in order."

"Thanks." Jess nodded, and stopped, waiting. Since he didn't speak again, she turned her head and regarded Dev, then looked back at him, eyebrows lifting in question.

For a moment he paused, a puzzled expression on his face. Then it cleared. "Ah." He shuffled the plas. "Doctor Kurok has agreed to pursue the continuance of the biological alternative technical program." He looked up at Dev. "Though it surprised the hell out of HQ, and no doubt will continue to confound many in the corps, I agree with you in that this is a very valuable project that should be continued."

Dev sat up a touch straighter, and her eyes brightened, but she remained silent.

Alters leaned forward. "There is a matter of your legal contract," he said to Dev directly. "We have to sort that out. We can't have you beholden to an outside organization, no matter how helpful they are. You understand?"

"Not really," Dev said. "But as long as I get to stay with Jess, I don't care."

Alters blinked. "Ah."

"I've got some ideas," Jess said. "I'll talk to Kurok."

"Ah." Alters repeated. "We'll be leaving ten carriers and two destroyers behind." He said. "HQ is sending cargo planes out with resupply and re-provisioning until you can get things sorted here." He glanced at the plas again. "So the final thing I have to discuss, Drake, is a legal matter."

Jess managed to stop internally bouncing with her own happiness long enough to focus on him. "Legal matter? You going to charge me with something?"

"No." Alters bit off a grin of his own. "I wouldn't know where to start with that, given claims from various foreign agencies, so we're going to ignore all that as we usually do. Our legal team in HQ will deal with damage quotes and the rest."

Jess nodded. "Fine."

"No, the legal issue is property allotment." He folded his hands and looked at Jess. "You're not supposed to have any."

She shrugged. "I don't."

"You do." Alters said. "It registered at HQ just prior to all this. You attained majority stake in Drake's Bay homestead."

Jess blinked. "No I..." She paused. "Oh shit." The exclamation issued from her as she realized. "My father coded his shares to me, but that was only in the event I went civ."

Alters nodded. "And for 36 minutes, Drake, you did. You processed final exit, until Bain had you rescind your resignation and you were reinstated back in. You were civ."

Jess sat back, honestly dumbfounded. "Oh hell," she finally said. "No way."

"In fact, if Stephen Bock had, as Bain stated, killed you on exit, it would have been an illegal act and we'd have been liable for it," Alters said. "Would have been damn messy, if your estate made a claim."

Dev merely watched both of them, looking from Alters to Jess, unsure of what was going on.

"So what do I have to do?" Jess asked, after a long moment of silence. "My father did that, apparently, to keep the Bay out of the hands of my family. Or really, my mother. She's dead now."

"We heard that," Alters said. "I'm not really sure what you do with this. I assume you didn't know it was going to happen?"

Jess shook her head. "Didn't find out it was even in the cards until I was at my mother's out-processing. Explains why my brother freaked out though. He must have gotten a notify." She paused in sudden realization. "And why he called me at base night after I came back in."

And why she'd gotten that call, to attend her mother's out-processing. "Probably were waiting for me to say something. Make a claim." She shook her head. "I had no fucking clue."

"Huh." He frowned. "I'll have to ask legal. But until then, you are the controlling shareholder of record." He eyed her. "You might want to record a will in that case. Until it's sorted."

"Yeah, okay," she said. "What a mess."

Alters's face twitched. "Pardon me if I don't sympathize." He held up the stack of plas. "We're going to be sorting this mess out for months." He stood up. "Well, Drake, good luck. Good work. I'm sure commendations and rewards will be coming down the pipe after this is all processed."

Jess dared a glance at Dev. "Got what I wanted," she said, quietly. "Everything else is gravy."

Dev grinned. "Me too."

Alters shook his head and rolled his eyes. "Field ops." He waved the stack of plas. "Dismissed, people. Go get a beer and a rest. You earned it."

And finally, Jess felt that sensation of impending disaster ease, as she stood up and thought about just an ordinary night after what seemed like an eternity of standing on the edge of an abyss. "Sounds good. C'mon, Dev. Where'd we leave off? Me teaching you to surf, right?"

"Right," Dev said, as they left the debrief chamber and moved back out into the hall. "And you said you could do something with fish."

"Ah, yes. My cooking skills that I bragged about. Right."

"And maybe we can take another shower."

"Sure."

"And practice that sex thing again."

Jess laughed, putting her arm around Dev's shoulders as they eased into the slowly growing traffic in the halls, as normal life started coming back around them.

IT WAS UNDERSTANDABLY quiet in the lounge. Everyone was busy getting things back together, and time to relax and drink would be found later, after the biggest portion of the tasks had been completed. So that left the big room silent and mostly darkened, save a few tables in the back that were dimly lit and occupied.

After a moment, the door to the lounge opened, and Jess entered. She paused and looked around, spotting Kurok in the back and heading over toward him.

He had to smile. The tall, lanky frame was so like Justin's, save the differences of sex. Jess had the same way of walking, and the same way of holding her shoulders. He watched her until she came right up next to him then gestured to a seat. "Hello there."

"Hi." Jess sat down. "Scan said you were in here. Thought I'd stop by to see how you were."

Even the vocal timbre was Justin's. "Oh, just fine thanks. Can I buy you a beer?" He leaned back, feeling a sense of relaxation at her presence. "Getting things back together?"

"As they can be." Jess said, looking up and catching the eye of the bio alt server, and nodding at him. "Gonna take a while."

"Mm."

Jess held out the package she'd been carrying. "Thought you might like this," she said. "Sea jacket, and some stuff of my dad's they sent me."

Startled, he reached out and took it without thinking, putting it down on the table. "Thanks," he said, after a brief pause. "You didn't have to do that."

"No," Jess said, smiling as the server came over and handed her a mug of beer. "Dev likes this, y'know." She indicated the beverage. "She's a hoot."

That brought a smile to Doctor Dan's face and distracted him from the package. "I would accuse you of trying to corrupt her, but I started that process the night we left the station. I wanted to make sure she was exposed to a little vice before she got here."

Jess chuckled. "She's done okay. I took her to Jonton's in Quebec City and introduced her to hopping shrimp."

"Ahh." Kurok's eyes lit up a bit. "Now that, I miss. Even given all the product we have on station, I remember those shrimp." He licked his lips in memory. "And Jonton. Quite a character."

Jess leaned back in her chair and hiked one boot up over onto her knee. "I hear you're going to make more of her."

Kurok studied his glass for a moment, then he looked up and met Jess's eyes. "I'm going to design a production set, for operations technical," he said. "But there'll never be another one of her."

Jess nodded. "Too much of you in there?" she ventured, seeing a sharpening of those pale eyes. "C'mon, Doc, look in the mirror."

A moment of delicate balance, then Kurok smiled, and his expression softened. "For a minute I almost forgot who I was talking to," he said. "Yes, I contributed a few spirals to Dev. But she's turned out to be her own construct. She's grown so much in the short time she's been here I hardly recognize her anymore. Her integration went so much further than I had reason to anticipate."

"Uh huh."

"So yes, I will create techs for Interforce," Doctor Dan said. "Who knows? Maybe I'll figure out how to make some of your type, too." His eyes twinkled at her. "I have some Drake DNA up there somewhere I'm sure, and now that I know about those gills of yours I want to have a closer look at it."

Jess's expressions sobered. "Oh, Doc." She leaned forward and rested her elbows on her knees. "You don't want to do that." She exhaled. "After all, what would they do with us then? Give us a shot of trank and out-process us at age six?" She saw his face go still. "We all know what the battery is."

"Jess."

"We know." She shrugged a little. "We know it finds the misfits. The psychos." Her voice took on a slight huskiness. "The serial killers. The twisted loners. Finds the kids with no conscience and prone to violence." She looked up and met his eyes. "Finds them and separates them out and gives them to Interforce."

Kurok looked into those calm, resigned blue eyes.

"Hey, it gives us structure and discipline." Jess's tone turned a bit mocking. "Make us feel special, and trusted and noble right up to the point they put a gun to your head at grad and you either go in, or go down." She glanced off into the distance. "When you find out what kind of monster you really are."

Doctor Dan had put his cup down, and leaned toward her, resting his elbows on his knees so his hands were very close to Jess's. "Except they're wrong."

Her lips twitched. "You know better than that."

"I do," he said. "I know better. I'm a geneticist now, Jess. I study humanity for a living." He reached out and touched Jess's fingers. "More to the point, I was able to study someone like you at very close quarters for quite some time. Trust me. Your father was no monster, and neither are you."

Jess reluctantly met his gaze.

"You have too much heart." He smiled gently. "You care too much, Jess, and you love too easily." He saw the blush, and closed his hand around hers. "That's the only reason I agreed to leave Dev here. I trust her with you."

They were both quiet for a bit. "Push comes to shove, they don't want you to have hooks in her," Jess said, in a serious tone.

"Reasonable," Doctor Dan said. "But I won't transfer her legal status to Interforce. I trust you. Not necessarily them."

"No, you wouldn't, and shouldn't." Jess's eyes took on a glint. "But you might consider transferring her contract to the controlling stakeholder of a long established settlement."

He studied her warily. "What settlement?" he asked, in a puzzled tone.

"Drake's Bay."

Doctor Dan leaned forward and stared intently at her. "And the other half of this story is? I know how they feel about bio alts at the Bay, Jesslyn. I was surprised you took her there."

"She's my partner."

Kurok shrugged one shoulder. "Yes, of course," he said. "That would matter but I still don't understand."

Jess signaled the server. "That'll take another round," she said. "It's a quirky string of circumstances." She cleared her throat. "And a delicate piece of timing."

Kurok laughed gently. "Now I know I'm talking to a Drake." He shook his head, and set his glass down, folding his arms and waiting. "Quirky is the only kind of circumstance they have."

DEV WIGGLED HER toes in contentment, turning a page of her book as she lay comfortably on the couch in her quarters. She had a cup of hot tea by her elbow, and a pad nearby showing the ops consoles. It felt very good to just relax for a while.

She had one of her off duty jumpsuits on, and she'd had another shower. She'd actually gotten a chance to order some resupply on top of it, though she didn't expect that to happen until they got all the rest of the citadel sorted out.

The agents and officers who had come from HQ were standing watches, and at the moment she thought the man Alters was the one who was in charge.

Everyone still seemed to be looking to Jess for answers though, and Dev thought that was good, and right, and that Jess was enjoying it. After all, she managed to fend off the whole bunch of bad guys by herself, and as April had said, it was a trust thing.

So funny, really, since she'd been brought here specifically to address a trust thing, hadn't she?

Dev read a few pages, then put the book down and folded her hands on her stomach, gazing quietly at the ceiling of her relaxation area. So much had happened since then.

Doctor Dan had spoken to her. Dev still felt a warm sensation thinking about it, he'd praised her so much she hadn't even known what to say after a bit. She felt like she'd really just tried to do her best with everything, but he seemed to think she'd overrun even the highest expectations he'd had for her programming.

So awesome.

Dev stretched luxuriously and settled back onto her couch, then glanced up at her door as it opened and Jess entered. "Hello, up here."

"Devvvieeeee!" Jess surprisingly gamboled up the steps and pounced on the couch, nearly bowling both of them off it and onto the floor. "What are you up to?"

Dev goggled wide-eyed at her. "Um." She looked around. "Up to my relaxation space?"

Jess rolled off onto the floor and stretched out on the padded surface, extending her long legs out and crossing them at the ankles. "Just visited Jason. He's gonna be all right."

"Oh. I'm really glad to hear that." Dev sat up and regarded her supine partner. "Brent was worried."

"Yeah, me too," Jess said. "Looks like most of the support staff's checked in and most of the bios too. Things are coming back into normal trim."

"The sets really liked being on comms," Dev said. "And also, helping defend this place. They're really excited about what they did."

"They and the mechs saved our asses," Jess said. "Maybe we can..." She paused. "I talked to Alters. We'll see what happens."

"Excellent." Dev sat cross legged and rested her elbows on her knees, looking down at Jess. "Maybe you could speak to them? They think you're amazing."

Jess pointed her thumb at her own chest. "Me?"

Dev looked around the space. "Yes," she said. "Did you think there was someone else I was referring to?" She watched Jess twiddle her thumbs. "You seem in good spirits."

"It's been a good day, in the end." Jess's eyes twinkled gently. "I got what I wanted."

Dev smiled at her. "Me, too."

The comm crackled overhead. "Ops to Drake."

"Ah, work is never done." Jess rolled over and punched the commset on Dev's console, tapping in the keys for ops. "Drake here."

It was April's voice. "There's an assembly in the mess, requesting your presence."

Jess pondered that. "All right. Be over shortly."

"Ack."

Comms clicked off. Jess and Dev regarded each other. "Wonder what that's all about?" Jess sat up. "You better come with me. I might need some asses kicked."

"Jess." Dev sounded adorably exasperated. "I would never do that to the people here."

"Hey, they all saw you tossing those janks around," Jess said. "Maybe we should see if we can build one of those grav gyms here. Ya think?"

"I think you will not like it at all," Dev said as they went down the steps and toward the door. "It's difficult."

"Bet they put up with it if they end up being able to seriously kick ass like that."

It was comforting to see the halls full of people, and the lights at normal levels. Dev kept up with Jess's long strides as they angled through the central corridors heading for the mess. She realized that she not only saw more bio alts than she had before, they now seemed to be going out of their way to make eye contact with her.

She straightened up a little and reached up to make sure her insignia were adjusted correctly, just as they got to the door to the mess and passed inside.

There were a bunch of people inside. April and Mike, Doug and Chester, wearing a plas bandage and an arm sling, Brent and Tucker, Elaine, all the ops personnel who had been with them on the rescue and the return.

"Hi," Elaine said, as soon as the door closed, and the low hum of conversation died. "So, Jess, I got bushwhacked and asked about burns." She got straight to the point. "As in, when can we get them."

"Ah." Jess understood now what was up. "I see." She perched on one of the tables, regarding the small crowd. "So what's the question?"

April cleared her throat. "We'd like to get our first." She indicated Mike and herself. "And our partners wanted them too."

"I explained techs don't get them," Elaine said. "It's not reg."

"Well." Jess folded her arms. "It used to be reg," she said, in a mild tone. "Back in my dad's day, apparently."

"His ghost come back and tell you that?" Elaine replied, in an equally mild tone.

Jess chuckled. "No. We saw the doc with his shirt off. He's got them. And matter of fact, Dev's got one, too." She regarded her partner, who had quietly taken a seat at one of the tables. "I think if it's going to be a tradition, it should be one for everyone who thinks it means something, not just agents. Techs do scary things and get hurt too."

Doug positively beamed at her. Chester pointed at his arm in silence.

"That your call?" Elaine asked. "You're senior."

They all turned to Jess and waited.

Jess kicked the floor a bit with her boot. "You know," she said, not looking at anyone, really. "We all took a big hit in the trust department here lately. For a little while, I wasn't sure of anyone. That's a really crappy feeling."

"Was crappy for us, too," Brent said from the corner. "What Josh did colored all of us." He indicated himself and Tucker. "Everyone looking cross at us, wasn't fair."

"No, it wasn't," Elaine said. "We knew that."

"Probably got some people killed," Tucker said, quietly. "Sure got Sandy killed. I did the recon on her comp spool. She took the stick from Nappy. Didn't trust him flying and it bit them."

Jess nodded. "I think some of what was really going on was an attack from within." She felt her way with a slight hesitation, the ideas forming unexpectedly. "Separating techs and agents. Making the culture different. Stopping that." She touched her arm. "Making agents compete."

"Huh," Elaine murmured. "Fractured."

Jess nodded.

"I felt isolated," Elaine said, suddenly. "Especially after what happened with Josh. But you're right, Jess. It started before that."

"Right. So." Jess straightened up. "Well, what we just went through, when we were in there, anyone think about trusting?"

April and Mike looked at each other, then at their techs. "We trusted you," April answered. "And I don't really have an explanation for that, because we barely knew you, and everything was going to crap."

"Sometimes, I guess, maybe, you just trust the gut check," Jess acknowledged. "Like I did with Dev. I had no real reason to believe. It was ridiculous. A tech given the knowledge in a week that you all get in years in field school." She looked at her partner. "But something in me said, yeah, okay. This is all right." She reached over and ruffled Dev's hair. "And Dev went all in."

Dev cleared her throat, slightly embarrassed by the intense attention.

"So anyway," Jess said. "If you want a mark, get one. For that last one, we should all get the same." She unfastened her jumpsuit at the neck and peeled it down off one arm, exposing the marks there. "I'll go first."

Elaine stood up. "I'm in," she said. "And I know Jase will want one."

Jess looked at Dev.

"Absolutely," Dev responded, with a smile. "That was amazing work."

"I want one." Brent leaned on the table with both hands. "I always did," he added, with a slight flush. "And y'know, maybe people like Clint might want in, too."

Jess smiled, as the group closed in on her. "Get on comm then, and ask him." She glanced at Dev. "Give your buddy a buzz. Long as we're all being crazy, he might want in for old time's sake."

"Better go to med and grab a tub of cream then," Tucker said. "Gonna need it."

IT WAS COLD and raining outside. Dan Kurok stood quietly watching through the blast proof glass portal as the shuttle very slowly settled itself into position on the pad ramp. The rockets fluttered closed, and the locks fastened, off-gassing filling the space around the shuttle as a team of bio alt mechs started forward with ground umbilicals.

He sighed. It was hard to quantify really how he felt. In one sense, it was good to know that things had stabilized and he felt satisfied to go back to station and get on with things.

In another sense, though, he had grown, again, unexpected roots in this place and there was a part of him that really didn't want to go.

Dev was part of that, of course. But the truth was, he now admitted privately, that as long as he'd spent on station, and how rewarding that career was, it had never developed any sense of family in him anywhere near what the feeling was he'd experienced in the last few weeks here.

A sound behind him made him turn, seeing the inner security hatch open and a crowd of bodies appear. Jess was in the lead, her arm draped over Dev's shoulders, but around and behind her were all the techs and all the agents, and behind them, the sets and mechs he'd led in his small part in the battle.

Dev slipped free of Jess's grip and ran to him, throwing her arms around him and giving him a ferocious hug. "Oh, Doctor Dan! I wish you weren't leaving. I'll miss you."

He returned the hug, his eyes meeting Jess's over Dev's shoulder. "I'll miss you too, Dev." He released her, but kept an arm around her as she turned and the rest arrived. "And I'll miss the rest of you, too. It's been quite an experience we shared."

Jess had her hands in her pockets, her black duty suit outlining her tall frame. "You should come visit again soon," she said, a smile shaping her lips. "Or maybe we'll come visit you."

"I think that would be an excellent idea," he said. "Especially when we start developing the advanced programming for Dev's successors." He glanced fondly at her. "Though we're going to have to really work at matching you."

Dev smiled in obvious delight. "Please say hello to everyone at the creche for me." she said. "Especially Gigi."

"I will." He promised.

The outer hatch unsealed and opened, and a blast of cold, wet, salty air tinged with rocket fuel gusted against them. A man in the bright blue oversuit of the interspace crew entered, looking around. "Kurok, Daniel J?"

Doctor Dan waved at him. "That's me."

"Please board," the man said. "We are off schedule."

"Ah. I see the customer service is as spectacular as always." Doctor Dan released Dev and started forward, only to be intercepted by the gang of Interforce personnel, each of whom offered a hand shake, or a pat on the arm, or from the anxiously waiting sets, a timid embrace.

It was almost overwhelming, and it ended with a swirl of motion and then Jess was closing her arms around him in a rush of energy new, and strange, and yet echoing with remembered familiarity. "Both of you take care," he said softly. "You hear me, Jesslyn?"

"You too," Jess answered, as she released him and stepped back. "C'mon. We'll walk you onboard."

The interspace loader scrambled out of the way as the gang of them filed through the hatch, out into the icy rain falling around the shuttle, escorting his passenger until they reached the ramp, and he went up alone, pausing at the top to turn and wave goodbye before he disappeared inside.

Dev sighed, her eyelashes blinking to shed the raindrops. "Bye, Doctor Dan."

Jess gave her a one armed hug, then turned and motioned the crowd to go back inside. "We'll see him again," she said confidently. "Maybe sooner than you think."

The hatch closed behind them, and the rest of the crowd dispersed, but Dev and Jess went to the window and stood there, watching until the shuttle's engines fired, and it rumbled back off the ground into the sky.

IT WAS STILL raining, though the darkness kept it to just a sound on the edges of the dome overhead as the assembly space filled with bodies.

The ramp doors were open, and everyone was wandering in, a mixture of ranks and specialties in a swarm of colored uniforms.

The mess had been restored to the point where it could offer crocks and basins of the basics, and just to one side of the food line was a cluster of black and dark green clad bodies, sprawled on the multi-level stone platforms that led up to the dais.

The newcomers sent from HQ mixed with what was left of Base Ten's ops teams, personalities already emerging and polite conversation devolving into mild trash talk that even so, barely had a sting.

Jess and Dev, along with April and Doug, Mike and Chester, Elaine and Tucker, and a carefully wrapped up, and still pale, Jason and Brent were in a crowd of newcomers.

A stir got their attention, and across the room Bensen Alters was walking up to the podium as the lights brightened a little to focus the attention on it.

Jess sat up and swung her legs off the platform, bracing her hands on the edge of it as Dev scooted over a little. "So now let's see what we're in for."

Alters had been acting commander for the week, and proved himself to be a calm and laid back presence, who focused on returning the citadel to functionality and handled the logistics of the repair teams and materials that had been flown in.

Jess found herself hoping they made his a permanent assignment. She didn't know who the other candidates might be though. HQ and Alters had left her pretty much alone the whole week, as though hoping it would all fade into the past and let normality take over again.

It was almost a bit of a letdown kind of feeling. She'd at least expected to get a request to submit a report, or something.

But no, nothing.

Maybe they'd reviewed everything again, and decided she was a cock up after all. That she should have seen through Bain earlier, or something.

Alters cleared his throat and the sound in the room died down as everyone turned to listen to him. "Good evening, people," he said. "I'll make this brief since this is a time to relax and celebrate for a few hours."

That didn't sound so bad. Jess picked up her mug and took a drink from it. Maybe they hadn't decided about anything yet.

"I've just got a few announcements," Alters said. "First off, a final assignment of command has not yet been made here. So you'll be stuck with me for a while longer."

Jess chuckled. "Bet they want to see how he does."

"Secondly, it has been decided that North base will not be revitalized at this time." He went on. "At least until we have more personnel available. The recent past has left us a little shy of that."

"So until any of that changes, this facility will be the eastern vanguard, and as such, the decision has been made to do a refresh of the battlements, and add some new weapons systems now under development."

"Ah. Good." Jess nodded. "I like that."

Alters cleared his throat again. "HQ has informed me commendations and citations are in transmit. Likely those of you affected will have something in queue by tomorrow morning.

"However, I would like to announce just one of them now."

The ops group all turned and looked at Jess. "If this isn't for you, I'm limping out." Jason said. "Dripping blood all the way back to my quarters. I swear it."

Jess shrugged. "I don't need any useless commendations."

"That's not the point. Take the respect," Elaine said. "Don't be an ass."

Jess didn't particularly think she was being an ass. So many people had pitched in, she didn't feel her own role had been that important. But she waited in silence as an officer brought a box up to Alters, and put it on the podium in front of him.

"Oh ho, bet I know what that is," Jason joked weakly. "Definitely for you, Jessie."

"Crap." Jess sighed, as she realized what he was talking about. "Shoot me now."

"In the long tradition of Interforce," Alters said, "we only have a few physical citations. We mostly like to give you all comforts and bonuses, as you all well know."

Now everyone was looking back at Jess, as she covered her eyes with one hand, a faint hum of chuckles rising in the room.

"Two of our physical citations are posthumous." Alters looked across the platforms with the start of a smile. "The third is the oldest, and can only be given to an active member. Its purpose is to acknowledge not number of enemies destroyed, or successful missions, but instead to celebrate the ideals of gallantry, of nobility and the old fashioned notion of heroism."

"Please tell me this isn't happening," Jess muttered under her breath. "Someone call an alert."

Dev looked profoundly confused. "Is something wrong?"

"Oh, Jessie. You poor thing." Jason was leaning against the wall, holding his arm to his side, but grinning at her.

Alters cleared his throat again. "This citation is remembered best for its first recipient, and though it hasn't been given in at least four generations, we'll award it to that recipient's direct blood descendant. Jesslyn Drake, please c'mon up here and get this thing."

Jess wasn't really sure how to react. She could hear the thunderous applause, and feel the hands patting her back and pushing her forward. She got control of her body and shook off the hands, but kept her own grip on Dev. "C'mon. You're coming up there with me if I have to go get it."

Dev had absolutely no idea what was going on, but she obediently stayed at Jess's side as they climbed up to the top platform amidst the cheering crowd.

Alters opened up the box and took something out of it. "I know you probably want to kill me," he muttered.

"No one wants to have to live up to this," Jess muttered back. "It's a millstone."

"Maybe." Alters carefully sorted out the bright metal chain and stepped forward. "But I didn't argue with them when they said to give it to ya."

With a silent sigh, Jess ducked her head and felt the links settle over her neck, as Alters gently laid the medal on her chest. She could see the delicate lattice of the background, and the stolid five pointed star, and the ring of letters around the edges of it.

She felt Dev shift and looked over at her, finding her inspecting her new decoration.

"It's pretty," Dev said after a moment. "Why do you think it's incorrect?"

"Tell ya later," Jess muttered.

"Try to bear up under the horror of it all, Drake," Alters whispered. "Say thanks, and go and get drunk." He patted her on the shoulder, then faced the crowd. "People, I give you our history's sixth recipient, and the fourth of the same name, of the Star of Valor."

With a long exhale, Jess turned and faced the room, accepting the applause and the whistles, and trying not to think about how red her face had to be. She clasped her hands behind her back and waited for the noise to die down, then cleared her throat self-consciously.

All those eyes looking back at her. "So I guess the first round's on me, huh?" Jess said, before she could really think of what she wanted to say. She let the resulting laughter relax her though, and then felt a touch on her arm that was Dev and that made her relax even more. "I don't think I did anything for this that everyone else here didn't do," she said. "I was just the unlucky one whose name was on the reports. So thanks." She considered. "Let's go party."

Another roar of applause, and then she was free to leave and she did, tugging Dev along with her as she escaped back to the platform and a big mug being held out to her, hands slapping her back, and a big crowd gathering to admire her star.

She would spend the night in self-deprecation and hopefully get drunk enough to forget about it. Jess accepted the clink of mugs against hers. Maybe later, though, there'd be a moment for her to look at herself in the mirror with the damn thing on and not feel like such a dork about it.

Maybe.

IT WAS LATE. Dev leaned on her folded arms as she looked out over the sea, feeling the wind ruffle her hair. It had stopped raining, at least for the moment, and the seas were calm and only lightly white capped.

She drew in a deep breath of the salt air and enjoyed the faint spray as it hit her face, leaving a coating of salt on her lips that she tasted. "It's so pretty."

Jess came over and handed her a glass, already full of the rich, golden honey mead. "So are you."

"It's very nice of you to say that." Dev held up her glass, and Jess touched it with her own. She'd learned about this curious habit and felt it was a little strange, though harmless. "And it's true I find you a lot more attractive than the water."

They both took a sip of the liquor.

"So here we are." Jess leaned on the rock shelf next to her. "Here's to hoping your second month in service is less insane than your first was."

"I think the best part of it was meeting you," Dev said. "Flying the carrier was good too." She paused again. "And those shrimps we had."

Jess started laughing. "Glad you've got your priorities straight."

"And it was awesome rescuing Doctor Dan," Dev said. "But you were still the best thing."

"I feel the same about you." Jess leaned against the wall, facing her. "Ready for some fish?" She indicated the portable griller behind her. "I know it's late, but it smells good, doesn't it?"

They settled together on the bench with a small tray between them and Dev had to agree that the thing Jess had made smelled very good indeed.

Jess held up a forkful of it and Dev took it into her mouth, chewing it thoughtfully. It had a slightly spicy and slightly sweet taste, and she licked her lips after she swallowed it. "That's very good."

Jess smiled and took a mouthful for herself. "That makes me a lot happier to hear than getting that damn medal."

"Why don't you like it?" Dev asked, after a moment of silence. "Everyone seemed to think it was an excellent thing to get."

Jess offered her more fish. "It sets an expectation," she said. "Then you always have to live up to it. You always have to be a noble selfless nitwad, throwing yourself into a pit on everyone else's behalf all the time." She swirled her mead in its glass and took a swallow. "It reduces your options."

"But Jess," Dev said. "You do that anyway. Put yourself in danger for everyone."

Jess stared at the fish. "Yeah, I know," she finally said, in a soft voice. "It's just uncomfortable thinking it's expected of me."

"I see." Dev bit down on the fork she was using. "I think."

Jess shook her head. "Never mind, Dev. You're right. It doesn't really matter, I guess."

Dev reached out and touched her hand. "If it makes you feel more comfortable, I will try to remember to jump into the pit first, all right?"

One dark eyebrow quirked. "That doesn't make me feel any more comfortable."

"It doesn't?"

"No!"

"I'm not sure letting you jump into a pit would be correct then, Jess. Can't we jump together?"

"No!"

"No?"

"Dev!"

"Yes?"

"How about you finish that fish and we both go jump together into my bed."

"That would be excellent."

"Thought you'd think so. C'mon partner. Let's go home."

OTHER MELISSA GOOD TITLES

Tropical Storm

From bestselling author Melissa Good comes a tale of heartache, longing, family strife, lust for love, and redemption. *Tropical Storm* took the lesbian reading world by storm when it was first written...now read this exciting revised "author's cut" edition.

Dar Roberts, corporate raider for a multi-national tech company is cold, practical, and merciless. She does her job with a razor-sharp accuracy. Friends are a luxury she cannot allow herself, and love is something she knows she'll never attain.

Kerry Stuart left Michigan for Florida in an attempt to get away from her domineering politician father and the constraints of the overly conservative life her family forced upon her. After college she worked her way into supervision at a small tech company, only to have it taken over by Dar Roberts' organization. Her association with Dar begins in disbelief, hatred, and disappointment, but when Dar unexpectedly hires Kerry as her work assistant, the dynamics of their relationship change. Over time, a bond begins to form.

But can Dar overcome years of habit and conditioning to open herself up to the uncertainty of love? And will Kerry escape from the clutches of her powerful father in order to live a better life?

ISBN 978-1-932300-60-4
eISBN 978-1-935053-75-0

Hurricane Watch

In this sequel to *Tropical Storm,* Dar and Kerry are back and making their relationship permanent. But an ambitious new colleague threatens to divide them—and out them. He wants Dar's head and her job, and he's willing to use Kerry to do it. Can their home life survive the office power play?

Dar and Kerry are redefining themselves and their priorities to build a life and a family together. But with the scheming colleagues and old flames trying to drive them apart and bring them down, the two women must overcome fear, prejudice, and their own pasts to protect the company and each other. Does their relationship have enough trust to survive the storm?

ISBN 978-1-935053-00
eISBN 978-1-935053-76-7

Eye of the Storm

Eye of the Storm picks up the story of Dar Roberts and Kerry Stuart a few months after *Hurricane Watch* ends. At first it looks like they are settling into their lives together but, as readers of this series have learned, life is never simple around Dar and Kerry. Surrounded by endless corporate intrigue, Dar experiences personal discoveries that force her to deal with issues that she had buried long ago and Kerry finally faces the consequences of her own actions. As always, they help each other through these personal challenges that, in the end, strengthen them as individuals and as a couple.

ISBN 978-1-932300-13-0
eISBN 978-1-935053-77-4

Red Sky At Morning

A connection others don't understand...

A love that won't be denied...

Danger they can sense but cannot see...

Dar Roberts was always ruthless and single-minded...until she met Kerry Stuart.

Kerry was oppressed by her family's wealth and politics. But Dar saved her from that.

Now new dangers confront them from all sides. While traveling to Chicago, Kerry's plane is struck by lightning. Dar, in New York for a stockholders' meeting, senses Kerry is in trouble. They simultaneously experience feelings that are new, sensations that both are reluctant to admit when they are finally back together. Back in Miami, a cover-up of the worst kind, problems with the military, and unexpected betrayals will cause more danger. Can Kerry help as Dar has to examine her life and loyalties and call into question all she's believed in since childhood? Will their relationship deepen through it all? Or will it be destroyed?

ISBN 978-1-932300-80-2
eISBN 978-1-935053-71-2

Thicker Than Water

This fifth entry in the continuing saga of Dar Roberts and Kerry Stuart starts off with Kerry involved in mentoring a church group of girls. Kerry is forced to acknowledge her own feelings toward and experiences with her parents as she and Dar assist a teenager from the group who gets jailed because her parents tossed her out onto the streets when they found out she is gay. While trying to help the teenagers adjust to real world situations, Kerry gets a call concerning her father's health. Kerry flies to her family's side as her father dies, putting the family in crisis. Caught up in an international problem, Dar abandons the issue to go to Michigan, determined to support Kerry in the face of grief and hatred. Dar and Kerry face down Kerry's extended family with a little help from their own, and return home, where they decide to leave work and the world behind for a while for some time to themselves.

ISBN 978-1-932300-24-6
eISBN 978-1-935053-72-9

Terrors of the High Seas

After the stress of a long Navy project and Kerry's father's death, Dar and Kerry decide to take their first long vacation together. A cruise in the eastern Caribbean is just the nice, peaceful time they need—until they get involved in a family feud, an old murder, and come face to face with pirates as their vacation turns into a race to find the key to a decades old puzzle.

ISBN 978-1-932300-45-1
eISBN 978-1-935053-73-6

Tropical Convergence

There's trouble on the horizon for ILS when a rival challenges them head on, and their best weapons, Dar and Kerry, are distracted by life instead of focusing on the business. Add to that an old flame, and an aggressive entreprenaur throwing down the gauntlet and Dar at least is ready to throw in the towel. Is Kerry ready to follow suit, or will she decide to step out from behind Dar's shadow and step up to the challenges they both face?

ISBN 978-1-935053-18-7
eISBN 978-1-935053-74-3

Stormy Waters

As Kerry begins work on the cruise ship project, Dar is attempting to produce a program to stop the hackers she has been chasing through cyberspace. When it appears that one of their cruise ship project rivals is behind the attempts to gain access to their system, things get more stressful than ever. Add in an unrelenting reporter who stalks them for her own agenda, an employee who is being paid to steal data for a competitor, and Army intelligence becoming involved and Dar and Kerry feel more off balance than ever. As the situation heats up, they consider again whether they want to stay with ILS or strike out on their own, but they know they must first finish the ship project.

ISBN 978-1-61929-082-2
eISBN 978-1-61929-083-9

Storm Surge

It's fall. Dar and Kerry are traveling—Dar overseas to clinch a deal with their new ship owner partners in England, and Kerry on a reluctant visit home for her high school reunion. In the midst of corporate deals and personal conflict, their world goes unexpectedly out of control when an early morning spurt of unusual alarms turns out to be the beginning of a shocking nightmare neither expected. Can they win the race against time to save their company and themselves?

Book One: ISBN 978-1-935053-28-6
eISBN 978-1-61929-000-6

Book Two: ISBN 978-1-935053-39-2
eISBN 978-1-61929-000-6

Other Silver Dragon titles you might enjoy:

Fractured Futures
by S.Y. Thompson

Detective Ronan Lee has just solved the crime of the century, or has she? The case of the copycat killer plunges her into an ancient mystery, but solving the murders raises questions about the world government's true objectives. An unexpected invention gives her the chance to travel to the past. Her target is the 21st century and her mission is to save the woman at the heart of issue. This same woman, Sidney Weaver, is a warm, personable and accomplished actress that Ronan would give her life to protect.

Unaware of what fate has in store, Sidney's life is boringly predictable until a mysterious stranger comes out of the darkness of night to protect her. She knows there's something unusual about Ronan, but despite her misgivings, she can't deny the mutual attraction. All of this takes a backseat when she's plunged into a harrowing game of cat and mouse that could destroy everything she holds dear.

ISBN: 978-1-61929-122-5
eISBN 978-1-61929-123-2

To Sleep
by Paula Offutt

To Sleep is told through the journal of Karen Miller, a nurse and student from Philadelphia. The journal begins the night three alien ships appear above Earth. When Karen awakens, she is told Earth was destroyed by a space phenomenon called the Rift and she is to be the leader of a small group of women tasked with assisting their alien rescuers in awakening the four billion or so surviving humans who are in cryogenic suspension.

Each time Karen goes to sleep, she doesn't know exactly what it will be like when she awakens. The line between what is real and what is not real becomes so blurred that Karen and the other women can only trust each other. When reality is finally defined, the six of them learn truths that will forever change not just themselves, but every genetic homosexual on Earth.

ISBN 978-1-61929-128-7
eISBN 978-1-61929-129-4

Return Of An Impetuous Pilot

by Kate McLachlan

When Jill's latest time-travel experiment goes awry, no one but Jill is surprised. But when Amelia Earhart suddenly pops out of RIP, everyone is stunned—and delighted! Everyone except Jill, that is, especially when Amelia decides she likes the future too much to return to her own time. History without Amelia Earhart? Unthinkable! But how do you return an impetuous pilot who doesn't want to go home?

It's Bennie and Van to the rescue! Together with Kendra and Jill, they try to return Amelia to the right side of history. Their motives might be mixed, but their hearts are in the right place...or are they?

Reunite with the RIP gang in *Return of an Impetuous Pilot,* the third book in the RIP Van Dyke Time Travel series, and find out where their hearts are leading them now

ISBN 978-1-61929-152-2
eISBN 978-1-61929-153-9

Destination Alara

by S.Y. Thompson

In the 24th Century technology has evolved but greed and war are constant. A rookie starship captain but a veteran of the recent Gothoan War, Vanessa Swann searches the outer rim of the galaxy for any sign of rebel activity. Her favorite pastimes are kicking enemy butt and making time with the ladies. The last thing Van wants is to team up with the Andromeda System's heir apparent and leader of the Coalition flagship, Princess/Admiral Cade Meryan.

Coal black hair, piercing grey eyes and skin the color of fresh cream threaten Vanessa's professional boundaries, but focus she must when faced with repeated attempts on Cade's life. The fate of millions and the threat of galactic war rest on Van's shoulders. Whatever the outcome, their lives will never be the same.

ISBN: 978-1-61929-166-9
eISBN 978-1-61929-167-6

OTHER REGAL CREST PUBLICATIONS

Brenda Adcock	Pipeline	978-1-932300-64-2
Brenda Adcock	Redress of Grievances	978-1-932300-86-4
Brenda Adcock	Tunnel Vision	978-1-935053-19-4
Brenda Adcock	The Chameleon	978-1-61929-102-7
Sharon G. Clark	Into the Mist	978-1-935053-34-7
Michele Coffman	Universal Guardians	987-1-61929-074-7
Michele Coffman	Veiled Conspiracy	978-1-935053-38-5
Cleo Dare	Cognate	978-1-935053-25-5
Cleo Dare	Faultless	978-1-61929-064-8
Cleo Dare	Hanging Offense	978-1-935053-11-8
Melissa Good	Partners: Book One	978-1-61929-118-8
Melissa Good	Partners: Book Two	978-1-61929-190-4
Helen M. Macpherson	Colder Than Ice	1-932300-29-5
Kate McLachlan	Hearts, Dead and Alive	978-1-61929-017-4
Kate McLachlan	Murder and the Hurdy Gurdy Girl	978-1-61929-125-6
Kate McLachlan	Rescue At Inspiration Point	978-1-61929-005-1
Kate McLachlan	Return Of An Impetuous Pilot	978-1-61929-152-2
Kate McLachlan	Rip Van Dyke	978-1-935053-29-3
Paula Offutt	To Sleep	978-1-61929-128-7
S. Y. Thompson	Destination Alara	978-1-61929-166-9
S. Y. Thompson	Fractured Futures	978-1-61929-122-5
S. Y. Thompson	Now You See Me	978-1-61929-112-6
S. Y. Thompson	Under the Midnight Cloak	978-1-61929-094-5
Mary Vermillion	Death By Discount	978-1-61929-047-1
Mary Vermillion	Murder By Mascot	978-1-61929-048-8
Mary Vermillion	Seminal Murder	978-1-61929-049-5

About the author

Melissa Good is an IT professional and network engineer who works and lives in South Florida with a skillion lizards and Mocha the dog.

VISIT US ONLINE AT
www.regalcrest.biz

At the Regal Crest Website You'll Find

- The latest news about forthcoming titles and new releases
- Our complete backlist of romance, mystery, thriller and adventure titles
- Information about your favorite authors
- Current bestsellers
- Media tearsheets to print and take with you when you shop
- Which books are also available as eBooks.

Regal Crest print titles are available from all progressive booksellers including numerous sources online. Our distributors are Bella Distribution and Ingram.

CPSIA information can be obtained at www.ICGtesting.com
Printed in the USA
BVOW07s1255280914

368573BV00001B/27/P

9 781619 291904